Legacy Letters

**Wisdom
from Screen
to Soul**

R.L. ZIMMERMAN

For my daughter Sarah,
whose encouragement inspired me
to put these stories into words.

Contents

Preface

The Legacy Letters series is about the life of Luke Cruz, the grandson of a man named Gustaf Kipling. Gus was an average man who had an exceptional idea for the benefit of his grandson. Book 1 begins when Luke is 16 years old, and the series concludes several books, and years, later when Gus gives Luke his final digital farewell. Gus, as he was known by everyone, had been diagnosed with cancer and needed to make sure that after his death, Luke would have wise and Christ-centered counsel and guidance as he grew into manhood. Gus's greatest concern in making sure Luke received this guidance was finding the right man to be that spiritual guide. But the longer Gus searched for such a man, the more he failed and the more he was disappointed in the quantity and quality of Christ-following adult men who could be approached about taking on this lifelong challenge. He mourned in his spirit, not knowing if he would ever find a man who would love Luke as much as he did. Who would be willing to pour his life into mentoring this young man the way Gus would?

All that changed when Gus happened to hear a radio commercial advertising a service that would allow him to record himself digitally in personalized letters. These letters would be safely and securely stored by the Legacy Letter Corporation and then delivered to the predetermined email address on the exact date chosen by the sender (in this case, Gus), even if that date was decades after the sender's death. All Gus had to do now was figure out what he would say in each of the letters he was planning to send to Luke.

I hope you gain as much pleasure in reading this story as I had in writing it.

—R.L. Zimmermann

Prologue

Dan stood by the locked gate, rubbing his eyes and face, trying to do anything to wake up. This eye rubbing was followed by another long yawn in a series of uncontrollable yawns that morning. Dan had once again been asked to unlock the fenced-in lumber yard of his employer. He was still spitting mad about having to be at work this morning, especially so early. After swinging the gates wide open and letting the other truck drivers in, Dan began walking to his loaded lumber delivery truck while calling his supervisor. He waited for him to answer his call, fully intending to give him an earful, and even quit if it came to that.

"Good morning, Dan. What's up, and why are you calling so early?"

Having heard that voice, and not caring how early it was, and with no introduction, Danny lit into Jim, screaming at the top of his lungs while the other drivers listened in. He wanted to know why he had to work another 12-hour shift on yet another Saturday starting at five in the morning. Now Dan was completely aware that he could have called his supervisor the day before, during regular working hours, to voice his concerns and complaints, but he thought calling his supervisor at five o'clock on a Saturday morning would be more dramatic and would help make his point more forcefully.

"Yeah, it's not so fun getting up this early, is it? Me and the other drivers want to know when it's going to stop. It's getting dangerous for us out there on the roads. I don't think you realize how hard it is for all of us to keep our eyes open. We're all tired, Jim. We're tired all day long, and I'm not the only one tired of all the work!"

Jim didn't exactly like this brash employee, but his brother owned Middlefield homes, so he had to think on his feet. If Danny or any of these other lumber truck drivers didn't keep up their current delivery pace, they would lose several contracts with some of the largest home builders in the state, with Middlefield Homes being the largest and most demanding.

"Come on, Danny," he started in a placating tone, "the busy season will be over in another month, and then things will get back to normal. Surely you can make it another four weeks, can't you? And by the way, have you looked at your time and a half and double-time pay checks recently? We're paying you and all the other drivers pretty good for working all those extra hours, wouldn't you agree?"

Danny was quiet for a long minute, and then finally said, "Yeah, I guess you do, Jim. The lumber yard does pay us pretty well. But not enough to work us to death. We're getting tired, dude, and I mean *really* tired. And I'm telling you again, if we don't get back to a normal workweek soon, it's only going to be a matter of time before there's an accident."

Jim hesitated for another long minute while lying on his bed considering his options. "Well, we can't have that, can we? I'll tell you what, take more short breaks throughout the day, stretch your legs, and drink more caffeine. You got that, Danny?"

"Yeah . . . sure, boss. I got it. And I'll let the other drivers know what you said."

Two hours later, Danny was pulling into the lumber yard to pick up another load. And in a home not too far away, two people were woken in their bed by their excited six-year-old son who was saying quite loudly, "Come on, Dad! Come on, Mom! Grandpa and Grandma are waiting for us! We gotta go or we'll be late!" Opening their eyes, they were both surprised to see their son fully dressed and ready to go spend the day with his grandpa.

"Oh my goodness, Luke," said his mother, "how long have you been dressed?"

This young lad, showing a bit of pride in his self-grooming accomplishment, proudly answered her and said, "Since last night, Mom! After you tucked me in and left my room, I got up and got dressed. I didn't want to be late to Grandpa and Grandma's house."

His father looked at him with absolute love in his face and said, "Luke, you're our little buddy. We would never do that to you."

Another two hours later, Danny was at the lumber yard again, drinking his second soda of the morning while picking up his third load of the day.

Like the gentleman he was, Joshua had opened his mother-in-law's car door and then closed it when she was comfortably inside. A moment later they started backing down the driveway as Luke waved and shouted, "Bye, Dad! Bye, Grandma! Love you, and don't worry about us. Mom said she'll make Grandpa some coffee, and I'm going to show him how to play catch with the baseball, just like you showed me."

It was almost noon, and Danny was getting tired as he continued to fight the unending need to yawn. He couldn't even remember getting there, but he was back at the lumber yard picking up his fourth load of the morning. It was then that he decided to take his lunch—three cans of caffeinated soda will only keep you awake for so long. He needed some food.

Joshua and his mother-in-law, Claire, had a wonderful morning of shopping for her birthday present, and they had enjoyed a wonderful lunch together. They were on their way home and couldn't wait to show everyone what she had chosen for her gift from her handsome and generous son-in-law.

It was one o'clock in the afternoon by the time Danny got back on the road after finishing his lunch. He had already made three deliveries and was on his way to his fourth; the day was almost over, and he couldn't wait to get home and climb back into his bed and close his eyes. What he hadn't counted on was the lunch he ate earlier digesting in his stomach and making him even more tired. He had been driving on a busy street when everything changed: his head snapped up and his eyes opened just in time to watch his truck drive straight into a nightmare. He had fallen asleep. It was only for a moment, but a moment is all it took for several lives to be changed forever.

Danny saw what he needed to do: he jumped on his brakes and tried to turn his truck toward safety. But it was too late. He woke up to the sounds of dozens of cars blaring their horns at him just in time to see the engine of his truck roll on top of and over the front half of a small four-door sedan. The weight of his overloaded trailer of lumber was pushing his truck forward and he couldn't stop it. Danny could do nothing but hang on to his steering wheel and watch as his truck pushed the car more than 30 feet to the other side of the intersection, the tires of his truck squealing and smoking the whole way. The last thing he felt was his truck rising into the air, and when it could rise no further, it came back down on top of this outmatched car. Gravity was now playing its part in this horrific accident as the truck came to rest on top of this car's small engine. The car's windows and front tires exploded under the weight of the truck, and the trailer was jackknifing. Eventually the truck came to a rest, but not before hitting several other cars whose only hope was to avoid that sweeping trailer of lumber.

Jumping out of the cab of the truck, he looked up at the lights in the intersection to see that he had run a red light. When he got to the man and woman trapped in the car, it was only in time to hear their final words. He stood up, looked around at the intersection, and began screaming for help, but no one was coming forward to give him any. Most everyone was too busy running away from the accident. Those who hadn't run still didn't come to help but instead opted to pull out their cell phones and record the aftermath of this horrific scene.

Chapter 1

The Radio Commercial

Ten years later

Finally, Gus was pulling into a parking space at the high school, exactly where he wanted to be *over an hour ago*. A smile grew on this grandfather's tender face, knowing he was onlwy minutes away from watching his grandson's last ball game of the season. He had no sooner turned his engine off and begun reaching for his door handle, when he heard what would soon become a familiar but irritating noise. *That* noise was the most obnoxious sound he had ever heard, and he couldn't believe it was purposely installed on his new phone. Yep, there it was, his new cell phone rattling in the cup holder, playing that repetitive jingle, indicating yet another person that was trying to get ahold of him.

"Will this thing ever stop ringing?" said Gus quite loudly. He had placed it there in frustration 20 minutes earlier because he couldn't get it to work and had hoped it would stop its incessant ringing on its own. But if it was his daughter trying to get ahold of him, it wasn't likely. While holding the phone in one hand and trying to answer it, the phone continued to make that obnoxious noise. Calling it "stupid" several more times, he touched the green button on this miniature device, finally silencing it, and then patiently lifted it to his ear and politely said, "Hello." He fully expected to hear the voice of someone he might know, but how they would have found his new number he wasn't sure. Perhaps there was some new kind of electronic phone book he didn't know about that listed new cell numbers without asking the owner's permission, kind of like the old White Pages phone books would do. Gus waited for what he considered to be a very long minute for someone to reply to his salutation, yet there was no answer. He looked toward the ball field, getting nervous and upset that he was missing his grandson's ball game because of this little thin box with numbers on it.

Hearing no response and coming to the end of his patience, he politely said "Hello" for a second time, and then a third. Still, he heard no response to his gracious and polite greeting. *I don't have a smart phone,* thought Gus to himself as he continued to blankly look at his phone. "I got one of the stupid ones." He was on the verge of throwing it out the window while fumbling to turn the pesky thing off, and then it happened. He wasn't sure how or what he pushed, but the screen went black. Gus smiled at his good luck as he slid out of the front seat of his pickup and onto the parking lot. The best place for that phone was in his truck, but he promised his daughter to always carry it with him, so he left it in his pocket and out of sight.

Who knows, thought Gus to himself, *maybe I'll get lucky and it'll fall out of my pocket when I sit down on the bleachers.* He then shut the door to his not-so-complicated 25-year-old Chevy pickup. Comparing its ease of operation to the phone in his pocket, he thought to himself, *I love this old truck. It's old enough to not have all that new-fangled electronic equipment, but new enough to be as reliable as the day Claire and I bought it. I bet that phone won't be working in 25 years like this old truck will be.*

Now that he had a free hand, he reached back into his low-tech transportation and grabbed his rosewood dragon head cane from the passenger seat. He had originally purchased this cane decades ago while on a business trip to China. He took one look at it and fell in love with its unique wood and beauty. However, in the last several years it had become more practical than beautiful. As a result of getting old, and in order to get around with more stability, he rarely went anywhere without it. Rosewood is a heavy, dense, and naturally auburn-colored wood, and when carved, shaved, and sanded properly, it can be extremely smooth to the touch. And in Gus's case, it was not only pleasing to walk with, but it also turned out that this cane was just the right length and weight and fit in his old and soft hand, like no other cane he had used before. Now Gus wouldn't admit it, but he rather enjoyed the swinging of the cane forward and backward as he strutted to every destination Rosey accompanied him to. Gus also enjoyed the added ritz, thinking it gave him a look of sophistication.

Coming back to the present, he set aside thoughts of all other concerns. The only thought he had in his mind at that moment was wanting to watch Luke's game. Yet, with the appointment he was scheduled to attend this morning, and the phone fiasco, his arrival had been slowed. But now, to get to the game, he had to pick up his pace. With help from "Old Rosie," he was on his way to his seat in the bleachers.

It was a Friday afternoon, a beautiful day for a ball game. A ball game he was close to missing. After a short and a quick-paced walk (at least in Gus's mind), he was reminded of how late he was in getting to the game when he heard the small crowd of onlookers cheering their home team to victory. Gus reached the bottom of the bleachers where he would once again begin a climb that would end with the gift of watching his grandson's ball game. He knew he still had a ways to go before he could sit down, and after scanning the rusty old wooden bleachers, he mapped out the most efficient route to his desired destination. Then, with a determination that even Sir Edmond Hillary would have been proud of, he began to ascend this man-made mountain of seats to get to his chosen perch.

After much huffing and puffing, Gus finally made it to his desired location where he arranged the cushion he had carried with him. Taking one last look to verify his bottom side was squarely lined up over the cushion, he allowed himself to drop onto the awaiting cushion with an audible *oomph*. He finally relaxed and began to watch his grandson's team. He did take a moment to scan the crowd, and he observed the same loyal fans that had attended most of the previous games throughout the season. Most of the fans were other grandfathers watching their grandsons. There were also a few girlfriends attending today's game, as well as some younger, hope-filled ball players dreaming of what could be in their future. And, of course, there was also that one well-dressed man, sitting alone, out of earshot of everyone else at the game. He was live-streaming the athletic achievements of one particular boy; the boy's father, who was this man's boss, was apparently too busy to attend his son's game.

"One day," said Gus as his blood pressure began to rise, with disdain for the man receiving that live-stream, "I'm going to tell Luke and his mother what this man's boss did to our family."

Gus decided to ignore that man and go back to watching the game, focusing intently on one particularly good ball player. After all, that was the reason he was there. Now it may have just been the sophomores and freshmen playing that day, but in light of their excitement, you would have thought it was the varsity team playing for the conference championship. This slender, well-mannered man, who was a natural born leader, was also his grandson and the captain of the team, just like his father was years before him. Gus watched Luke's team for one short inning before looking into the first base dugout and catching Luke's eye. Gus gave him a secret touch on the side of his nose. This signal had been agreed upon between the two of them years earlier. It was a silent encouragement to Luke, and it stood in contrast to the yelling of the rest of the players and fans. But those weren't the only hand signals they had crafted: what came next was the kind of signal-making that an MLB third base coach would be proud of.

Wanting to know what he missed, Gus reached out his arm with Rosie in his hand and tapped the shoulder of a young boy who was sitting about two rows in front of him along with several other boys. When he asked about the inning and the score, the young lad smiled at this white-haired fan and told him that it was the bottom of the third and their team was down 3–1. That's all Gus needed to know before signing to Luke with his hands about what Luke could do to lead his teammates to victory. Luke was grateful that no one in the bleachers or the ball field or the dugouts saw what his grandpa was doing. It might have been difficult to explain to them why he was instructing Luke how to play the game, especially to the coach. Luke's grandpa went on for almost a solid minute with these unexplainable signs until he was finished. Then he simply stopped.

After seeing, and most importantly, understanding them, Luke began to talk quietly to everyone in the dugout. Whether it was advice on their forms or certain plays to make, he mostly wanted to get across the message that, win or lose, it was only a game and that they were there to have fun.

After dispersing all these thoughts, he looked back at his grandpa and just gave him a smile. It was a way of saying, "Thanks for making it to my game, Grandpa."

After Gus had returned that smile with one of his own, he gave Luke another sign language suggestion and then sat back and watched as another inning came and went.

Luke's team was once again taking its turn running off the field and into the dugout with the hope of adding more runs to their side of the scorecard.

For some reason, it was becoming harder and harder to concentrate on Luke's game. Gus continued watching and giving Luke more suggestions via sign language. But it didn't take long for his mind to go into memory mode. Gus may have been physically sitting and watching Luke's game that day, but in his mind he was visiting another game. He first thought about, and even saw, the games he himself had played as a teenager more than 60 years ago; a pleasant memory he held to tightly in his heart. Next came a memory from 33 years ago that would also never leave his heart. Gus was watching Luke's father, Joshua, play baseball on this same field while sitting next to his youngest daughter, Rebecca. She was a pretty, blonde-haired, blue-eyed girl with a rather precocious personality. They had a wonderful father-daughter relationship, and she chose that day for her father to meet the 17-year-old man she was going to marry. In the middle of this memory, Gus pulled a handkerchief from the back pocket of his pants; the tears created by this old memory began rolling down his cheeks as he sat alone in his thoughts. He was wiping his eyes dry of those tears as fast as they were being formed. Gus was remembering what he had said to Becca when he learned the reason for that particular father-daughter date.

"Rebecca, does Josh know about your plans?"

"Oh, Dad, you worry too much. And by the way, from what Mom has told me, if she hadn't cast her eyes on a lonely young man who had just recently started to attend the church she was a member of, you'd still be single, and I wouldn't be sitting here with you right now."

Gus had nothing to say, thinking to himself, *Poor Josh. He doesn't stand a chance. Then again*, Gus concluded with a slight look of embarrassment, *it appears I didn't have much of a chance either.*

In that moment, Gus recalled the words to an old song, something to the effect of, "I chased her till she caught me." Yup, sounds just about right.

It only took a heartbeat for Gus to go from that wonderful old memory to the memory of that terrible knock on the front door of his house ten years ago. It was the local police department with the difficult and sad news they had to deliver: Joshua, Luke's dad, and Claire, Gus's wife, had been killed in a traffic accident by an overly tired truck driver just one hour earlier. The dominos of the events that led to this tragedy began two weeks earlier when Joshua told his mother-in-law that he wanted to take her out shopping for her 65th birthday. He didn't want to make any mistakes in purchasing the wrong gift that year, so he had asked if she would like to go with him on a date one Saturday morning a few weeks before her birthday. How could she refuse such a delightful invitation? Claire loved the idea so much that she had spent the entire morning getting all gussied up for her shopping date with her handsome son-in-law.

Another thought came to Gus's mind during this deep dive into his private memories. *Thank you, dear God, for giving me such a beautiful final memory of my Claire and her girlish excitement.*

And still, all these years later, the gift that Josh had purchased for her that day was stored in a secret and safe place along with a copy of the actual accident report from the police. The EMT who had unsuccessfully attempted to resuscitate her at the site of the accident found it when Claire was removed from her car. It was in a small white velvet jewelry box still gripped in her left hand after she had passed away. It was a silver necklace with a flat silver cross that had a stamped-out silhouette of Jesus on it. Gus knew what that meant to Claire. That silhouette was a constant reminder that her Jesus was no longer on the cross but was in heaven waiting for her. Gus knew where Claire and Joshua were, and who they were with. That was ten years ago. Time sure does disappear quickly, while some memories never do.

The game was over now, and Gus had climbed down off the bleachers to wait for Luke to run by. After running into William, another grandfather he usually sat with, he said hello, shook hands, and talked for a few minutes. The topic of this conversation was the Middlefield minion that William had also seen sitting by himself and watching the game in place of his employer. Neither man had time for Matthew Middlefield, and they had to work hard not to say what they really thought of this minion's employer. But one day they would reveal everything to everybody. Moving past this long-time irritation, and seeing the boys coming their way, Gus concluded their short conversation and said, "See you next season, Will, and say hi to Kate for me," as he turned to greet Luke. Then, William, also seeing all the young ball players coming their way, asked him if he would like to pose for a picture with Luke and Luke's best friend. This picture would be placed in William's growing baseball photo album. And with one more last-minute request, he asked if it would be okay if he could get in a picture with everyone as well.

"Sure," said Gus. After all, he knew who this photo album was being created for. After the photo had been taken, and before leaving the ballpark, William turned and congratulated Luke and some of his teammates on their victory.

"Grandpa, your advice worked again. The guys listened to what I had to say, and they followed my lead. When I told them to just relax and have fun, win or lose, we started to play better. I know you're pretty smart, Grandpa, but how'd you know what they needed to hear anyway?"

Gus's eyes softened as he smiled humbly at his grandson's inquiry. "It has taken years of living, Luke, many, many years of living, along with listening to the wise counsel of men that were older than me. It's not hard to listen, buddy. What's hard is taking the right action after hearing the right counsel. And I'm talking about actions that bring you toward what you know is the right thing to do in your heart."

Not having a clue as to exactly what his grandpa was trying to say to him, he simply responded, "Cool, Grandpa. Thanks again! I have to go real quick and get my street clothes from the locker room. I'll see you in the parking lot in just a couple of minutes."

"Hey, Luke! . . . Luke!" yelled Gus, making him stop in his tracks and turn back to his grandpa. "Before you leave, can you send your mom a text message for me? She sent me one . . . at least I think it was a text message . . . when I was pulling into the school parking lot, and I haven't gotten back to her yet."

Luke was back at his grandpa's side just about the time Gus was about to explain his need for help. Over the last couple of years, Luke had developed an ear for his grandpa's requests for help, which included a sad look of confusion. Luke knew the requested help would be technology related.

"Sure, Grandpa, no problem," Luke quickly replied.

After Gus had handed Luke his phone, he opened the message center and looked at his messages. "Grandpa! Mom didn't send you just one message—she sent you four of them! Didn't you hear it dinging?"

It only took Luke a moment to answer his own question. He saw his grandfather's blank face and knew the answer. His grandpa simply didn't appreciate, or even care to embrace, these modern technologies. "Okay, okay, Grandpa. I get it. So, what do you want me to tell Mom?"

"Tell her I was at your game. Tell her you guys won the game, and then tell her we'll be home in about half an hour. Thanks, buddy."

After sending the text and handing the phone back to his grandpa, Luke ran off, following the last of his teammates to the locker room. Gus put that pesky cell phone into his pocket and began walking toward his truck. He was reflecting on what Luke had said about the advice he had received just one hour earlier. And knowing what was ahead for Luke and his mother, Gus thought, *Who's going to look after this wonderful grandson of mine when I'm gone?* He asked this question of himself with visible concern showing on his face. *Every young man or woman needs a counselor . . . a type of shepherd . . . someone who will lovingly guide them through life, especially in their late teens and through most of their twenties.*

Luke would be needing such a guide very soon, for it wouldn't be long before high school was over and important life choices would have to be made.

Gus was leaning against the front driver-side fender of his powder blue truck, still pondering this question when Luke came running back from the locker room. His backpack, bulging with clothing and books, was slung over his shoulders. Two of his friends were also running next to him when they all came to a stop in front of Gus.

"Hi, Mr. Kipling," said both boys in unison.

"Grandpa, can we give Markus and Juan a ride home?"

Gus didn't answer his question right away, for he knew whose father one of the boys was and he was deciding how he should handle this situation. But since he knew full well that Markus had nothing to do with his father's past actions, he took that thought out of his mind as quickly as it had entered. Gus decided not to punish the son for the sins of the father. "My goodness, I just realized how tall the three of you are getting. And Markus, it looks like you're going to be the tallest."

"That's the plan, Mr. Kipling. My dad is six feet four inches, and I plan to be at least that tall too. But Luke and Juan are shooting a little lower. They're hoping to be six feet tall by graduation day. We'll find out in two years who made it to the six-foot club and who didn't."

"Hey, at least I can grow a mustache!" blurted out Juan. "Unlike you two baby-faced little boys!"

And that's all it took for the three of them to get started picking on each other. They were acting just like brothers, which, sadly, none of them had. Gus smiled at Luke and his adopted brothers as they bantered back and forth laughing the whole time. It's nice to have such good friends. Markus was white with blonde hair and blue eyes, and he had a rather stocky build. Juan, on the other hand, was slim with an athlete's build, and he was Mexican. He had jet black hair, which included the mustache he was so proud of, and brown eyes. Luke was, well, a melting pot of both of his friends, having a white mother and an Hispanic father. Gus came out of his private thoughts and interrupted their bantering: "What was that question you asked me when you first walked up to me, Luke?"

"I asked you if we could give Markus and Juan a ride home?"

"Oh yeah, that's what it was," said Gus, having truly forgotten what Luke had asked him only a few minutes earlier. "Sure we can, but only on one condition." Markus and Juan both had an immediate look of concern flash across their face at hearing that there would be a condition attached to getting a ride home. They all knew Grandpa Gus was a bit of a teaser, but that didn't stop that look from flashing over all their faces, especially Luke's, because he had been the one who had offered them a ride home before asking his grandfather—and there were no conditions attached to his offer. Gus saw that look and felt bad for just a moment, but with a growing grin he asked Luke, "Do you have your driver's permit with you?"

"No way!" said Luke with a huge smile. "You're going to let me drive your truck?"

"Only if you have your driver's permit with you, buddy."

"That's like asking me if I have the best grandpa in the world. Absolutely—of course I have my permit. I never leave home without it!"

As they drove to each friend's house, they talked and laughed non-stop about the game and all its excitement. First praising each other for a well-executed play, and then ribbing one another for an error that could have given them a loss rather than a win.

The first to be dropped off was Juan. As he got out of the truck, he turned around and asked, "Hey guys, since we are now officially juniors in high school, do you want to come over to my house for a pool party? It's going to be tomorrow with the other guys on the team. We can celebrate our victory and the start of our junior year at the same time. I asked my parents, and they said it was okay to invite some girls from our class to come over too. What do you say?" Juan asked both Markus and Luke before addressing Gus.

"My dad and mom said it was okay, Mr. Kipling. They'll also be there all day to chaperone. My parents also said the party had to be over by 11:00 p.m., so no one will be out too late."

After hearing about girls coming to the pool party, Luke glanced at his grandpa before responding to Juan's question. Gus simply smiled, not believing how many words Juan could speak without taking a breath, and then he remembered those days in his own life when he first became aware of the female half of the human race. He looked towards Luke and gave a yes nod to his nonverbal request to go to the party.

"Sure! Send both of us a text with the information and we'll be there! Right, Markus?"

Markus, not able to ask his father if it was okay if he went to the pool party, looked at Luke and then back at Juan. "Sure, Juan, count me in!"

A few minutes later, carefully making his way to Markus's home, Luke changed the conversation from baseball to Markus's father. "I don't get it, Markus. Why doesn't your dad ever come to our games? From what I hear, your dad was quite an athlete in high school and college. Why wouldn't he want to watch you playing a sport? And you're one of the best players on the team."

"Luke," said Gus rather quickly, noticing that Markus said nothing in response to Luke's personal question, "I think that may be a topic for you and Markus to talk about between yourselves and not in front of your old grandpa . . . wouldn't you agree?"

Now it was Markus's turn to join in the conversation. "Don't worry about it, Mr. Kipling. This isn't a new topic for us to talk about, so it's not a big deal."

"Well, then," said Gus, "if you're going to talk about family matters in front of me, I'm going to require you to refer to me as Grandpa. If that's acceptable to you, of course."

"Awesome! Sure thing, *Grandpa* Gus," said Markus. "Juan and I have actually been calling you Grandpa for years now—you just didn't know it."

Being a little surprised by that revelation, Gus could only say, "Well . . . ahh . . . ahh . . . thank you."

"To answer your question, Luke, I don't know why he doesn't come and watch. I used to ask him to come to our games all the time, but he always said, 'Sorry, Markus, not this time.' He always had a reason for not being able to make it, of course, so I just kind of stopped asking. But I'm glad to have you watching, Grandpa Gus. It's always more fun playing a ball game with someone you know watching."

Luke was pulling into Markus's driveway as they finished their talk. As Markus walked toward his front door, Gus could only think about that man sitting by himself, recording the games for his employer to watch later. And then there was William. He wasn't allowed to talk to the boys, or tell them who he was, but he continued to watch their games in silence and support them from a distance.

Luke had no sooner backed out of the driveway and started driving home when Gus said, "What do you say we listen to the radio and relax for the rest of the trip home?"

"Sure, Grandpa. You're the co-pilot. Pick your station."

"The oldies it is!" said Gus, reaching for the radio dial.

After quietly singing along with a couple songs from the 50s and reminiscing about Claire, a commercial came on that caught Gus's attention.

"Hi, this is Bob from Legacy Letters. I'm here to tell you about a brand new service to everyone listening today. This service will allow you to impact the future of those you love through a personal digital recording of someone you know. We are the first and only electronic letter recording, storage, and distribution center available. Unlike the postal services around the world, which are required to deliver a paper letter within days after receiving them, we want to offer just the opposite service. We will deliver your in-person, digitally-recorded letters via email when you want them delivered, even if that means years or decades later. With our system of electronic storage and delivery, you can choose a standard keyboard-typed letters, scanned handwritten letters, voicemails, or digitally recorded letters of yourself to send to friends or family members. If you want to talk to your loved ones years or decades after you have departed from this world, then Legacy Letters can help that dream come true. Just look up legacyletters.com on your phone or computer and see how easy it is to speak into the future."

Gus was considering what he had just heard, thinking that this electronic age might not be so bad after all, when Luke, assuming his grandpa was still listening to the oldies, told him they were home but received no response.

"Grandpa. Hey, Grandpa, wake up! We're home. Boy, those old songs must have really taken you back this time. You were thinking of Grandma again, weren't you?" Not waiting for an answer, Luke continued talking, reminding his forgetful grandfather what else he needed to do when he walked in the house. "And Grandpa, don't forget to talk to Mom when you get inside. She texted me twice while we were driving home asking when we would be back. What's up with Mom anyway? What's so important?"

Gus heard each of Luke's questions, but in the moments between heartbeats, he was once again sifting through the life-changing memories of the last ten years. Yes, he was thinking of his wife, Claire. Even ten years later, he missed the sound of her voice, the touch of her hand, the fragrance of her favorite perfume, and the looks only a wife can give her husband. But what he had just heard on the radio would give him an opportunity that was never available before. Ten years ago, he had to put his own grieving aside for the sake of his remaining family. He had to be the strong one for the first few years. The family had not only lost a wife and son-in-law, but for his daughter and grandson, they had lost a husband and a father, a mother and a grandmother.

It had taken years for Rebecca to move past her loss, but those difficult years turned out to be the best therapy she could have received. The old saying was true: time does heal all wounds. Luke, on the other hand, had the gift of youth on his side and was therefore more resilient.

He was able to recover more quickly from the loss of his father. A portion of this resiliency was owing to his young age, but mostly it was because Gus was able to step in and take over that father-figure role in his life. But what was now barreling down the track of life directly toward them would be an emotional and spiritual challenge.

After setting aside these private thoughts, Gus answered Luke by saying, "She just wants to know about my doctor's visit I had this afternoon before your ball game."

Luke had carefully parked his grandpa's truck in the garage and was now walking through the back door and into the kitchen with his grandpa. The two of them were greeted with a loving but irritated verbal assault.

"Dad!" exclaimed Becca, standing in the kitchen with her hands firmly planted on her hips. Her cell phone on the island in front of her had an emotional paragraph of text ready to be sent. Not hearing back from her dad concerning the results of his tests, she could do nothing but prepare herself for the worst. Before the two of them walked in, Becca had almost sent yet another text message, wanting desperately to know what the doctor said. "Why didn't you call me back? You know I'm worried about what the doctor may have found during this last examination."

"Mom," said Luke as he walked by on his way up the stairs to his bedroom, "I'll be back down to tell you about the game after I take a shower."

"Okay, Luke. That'll give me time to squeeze some information out of your grandfather."

Walking into this old house of his while carrying the information that his daughter so desperately did not want to hear, Gus gained a whole new appreciation for where he had lived his life for so many years, and with whom he had lived it. Looking around the house, he didn't just see well-loved old furniture, but a house filled with warm memories. The patio in the back yard where so many family meals took place, the living room where his favorite mission-style chair sat, and the front porch with those squeaky but reliable wooden rocking chairs. Every place his eyes landed, he no longer saw the room or the furniture it held, but only the faces of those who held a special place in his heart.

"Well," said Gus as he cracked open a can of Fresca he had just pulled out of the refrigerator, "I know you're worried, Becca, but I'm 75 years old now, and worrying won't give me more time in this world. So whether you worry or not, I'm getting to the age that the doctor will find something wrong with me at some point."

"He found something? Is that what you're saying?"

"Yes, honey," said Gus with a long pause, looking at his daughter, choking up just a bit before quietly saying, "it's back. I know that's not what any of us wanted to hear, but he found some areas of cancer again. It's back, and there's no stopping it this time. No radiation, no chemo, and no drugs."

Becca went to her father and wrapped her arms around him and started to cry. He rested his chin on top of her head as he took comfort in her hug. There is something special and unique about the hugs a father can receive from his daughter. After a few minutes, she released her embrace and stepped back while drying the tears from her face. She softly asked him, "How much time are they giving you? How much time do we have before you're gone?"

"Either side of two years. They're not certain, but this does give us time to prepare."

Saying nothing after hearing that answer, and knowing how fast this time would go by, Becca asked, "Have you told Luke?"

"No, Becca, I haven't. I wanted to talk to you first . . . face to face and not on one of those pesky cell phones. That's why I didn't call you back after you texted me."

Thinking about what her dad had just said, she knew he was right. If he had told her this kind of news over the phone, she would have been really upset with him for being so insensitive.

"Okay, Rebecca. Now that you know what's going on, I have a thought about how to tell Luke about the cancer. Until then, what do you say we wait for him to finish his shower and get changed. While he's doing that, we can finish making something to eat. Now, when he does come down those stairs in a few minutes, let him eat his dinner and tell you about his ball game. Let's not ruin his appetite or his excitement about winning today's game. When the time is right, we'll talk with him about what the doctors said. I'll also call your two sisters tomorrow and let them know what's happening. But tonight is just for you, me, and Luke."

It was a long night for the three of them, and there was plenty of crying, and even some laughing. But knowing it was getting late, and being talked out by this time, they all hugged each other, said good night, and went to their bedrooms. Gus was the first one up the next morning. He was waiting in his chair, deep in meditative thought as a result of a very vivid dream he had that night. It was then that Becca walked into the living room carrying a bright red ceramic coffee mug.

"Good morning, Dad. Thanks for making the coffee." And without taking a breath, she continued speaking and asked, "So, Dad, how did you sleep last night?"

Becca was sipping cream-filled coffee from her favorite mug and wearing a light green terry cloth bathrobe as she spoke. She walked to the couch opposite from where he sat most mornings. Gus looked forward, not immediately making eye contact with Rebecca; he had a melancholy look on his face as he sat motionless in his favorite mission-style, "old man" chair. He was wearing a well-worn burgundy robe Claire had given him more than 20 years earlier. It may have been a little ratty, and it had a small hole or two, but he had no intention of replacing it with one that was not purchased by his Claire. The cushions on the chair were covered fabric, while the arm rests were made of sturdy, flat oak; they were wide enough for Gus to set his mug on. His hands had just the slightest shake to them, and those flat and wide pieces of oak helped relax his arms in between sips of coffee. The chair was easy enough to slide into, but it was even easier to get out of after waking from an impromptu nap. That's why it had always been his favorite recliner.

"No," said Gus, still distracted by his private thoughts, being more worried about his grandson than himself, "I didn't sleep very well. My mind wouldn't turn off. Becca, this may sound a little strange to you, but I'm not worried about the cancer or dying. I know where I'm going and who is waiting to welcome me to his home. It's you and Luke I'm concerned about." Gus paused again, considering the weight of the words he knew he needed to speak. "I know these worries are sinful, because I know who is ultimately in control of all things. It is he, and not me, who will take care of you when I'm gone—the same one who has been taking care of us for all the years we have been in this world that he so powerfully created. But I feel there is something I am being prompted in my spirit to do in his name, and I believe I know what it is."

"Wow, Dad, it does sound like your mind was keeping you awake all night. Okay, you've piqued my curiosity. Tell me what it is that you feel you need to do."

Taking the last sip from his sweetened coffee, Gus leaned forward, set his empty mug on the coffee table, and took in a long, slow breath. Then, letting it out just as slowly, Gus said, "First of all, Rebecca, you need to know this thing I want to do for you and Luke has a small cost to it, but it is not something to be concerned about. Now, that brings me to what I want to do with the time I have left."

By this time Rebecca was sitting on the front edge of the couch. She was curious and had a few of her own thoughts.

"You're not making any sense, Dad. First you tell me about an amazing dream you had, and how it has given you purpose in your remaining time in this world. Then you start talking about money and say it's not about the money, but you haven't even said what *it* is yet. I don't care about the money, Dad. I care about you and Luke and what our lives will be like without you."

Gus knew what was coming next, and no matter how much a man prepares himself, there is no good way to prepare for a woman's tears, especially one who takes up such a large portion of your heart.

"Can't you see," said Rebecca, choking on her words as she tried to speak, "that I'm having a hard time accepting the fact that there is a real time limit on your life, yet here you are talking about money."

And with that her eyes began to glisten.

"This conversation isn't making sense to me! All I can think about is that it won't be long before I won't be able to hear your calm and comforting voice of reason anymore. It's going to be hard on us, Dad, *really* hard. Especially since it's going to be just the two of us in the house. It's going to be like it was when Joshua and Mom died, only this time you're the one leaving us! Except we don't have anyone like you to take us in. Where do Luke and I go this time? I'll be there for Luke, but who will be there for me?" Becca's last words faded into a whisper as tears gathered in her eyes at the thought of not having her father to emotionally lean on in those difficult days and months that always follow a death in one's family.

That last statement she made about him leaving them alone struck Gus squarely in the heart. She hadn't come to the point in her own heart where she had simply accepted the fact that she had no control of this cancer in his body. He wasn't going to die because he wanted to. It was just his time.

Tears began to run down her cheeks from the corners of her eyes, as the day of his death, which had long since been set in stone, had now become a reality. There had already been so much death and loss for the family. And that's when Gus began to explain his plan.

"That's it exactly, Becca. I think I have found a way to make my death less painful. We know my time is coming, and we can prepare our goodbyes, unlike with Claire and Joshua's deaths, which were unexpected and final. This plan of mine will also give me the opportunity to talk with both of you, though they will be one-sided conversations. After I have died, I can share my love with Luke by drawing on the years of wisdom I have accumulated."

"Oh, Dad, why are you talking like that? Please, whatever you're planning to do, don't say anything about this to Luke. I don't want him to get his hopes up over something that might not work," Rebecca pleaded. She didn't pause to think, because she was too overcome by her grief. "After last night, he's already heartbroken over this news. He's lost his dad, and now he's going to lose his granddad."

"Calm down, Becca, and do me a favor. Wipe the tears from your eyes and get out that laptop of yours and look up a website for me. It's called legacyletters.com."

An hour later, still sitting side-by-side on the couch, Rebecca and Gus continued checking out the website he had heard about on the radio the day before.

Beginning to see the benefits this web service had to offer, Rebecca said, "This is an amazing service, Dad! I'm beginning to see why you quickly got so excited about it, but the big question now is, exactly what part of it did you want to use? Or, should I say, which part are you *willing to learn* how to use?"

"Becca, can't you see it? It's right there in front of your face. I'm going to use this service to do exactly what the radio commercial said—to speak into the future, and in this case, Luke's future. Becca, think about it for a minute: Joshua is gone. Luke's other grandparents are no longer alive, and Claire is no longer with us either. Besides you and your sisters, who live miles away with their own families, I'm the only immediate family member left. This is my chance to continue being an influence in his life long after I'm dead. I can talk to him about how to treat any girls he may date. I can talk to him about being a husband, a father, a son. I can give him insights into being a good employee or employer; how to treat others; what it means to be a true friend; finances, morals, ethics, values, and, of course, Jesus. And let's not forget about all the family stories I can tell him: stories from when I was young, stories about his grandma, stories about when you and Josh were first married, and maybe even a story about that baseball game date we went on when you were about Luke's age. He'll love it. Whether he listens to his old grandpa's advice through a video letter is, of course, up to him, but what I will be able to do is to give him something to look forward to and to think about through the years."

They both sat silently on the couch, considering what all this might mean. Gus was already mentally far away in his memories, planning the stories he would tell Luke. Rebecca, having a thought that could derail her father's dreams about counseling Luke in the future, had another question about his idea. "Dad, I have a question for you."

Not catching the verbal cue in her voice, he said with halfhearted interest, "And I've got an answer. What's your question, Becca?"

"It seems to me that what you're planning is pretty ambitious. Have you even thought about how many of these letters you want to record for Luke? How long it will take you to get them ready and then record them? Not to mention your biggest hurdle: learning how to use the technology on this website to make those recordings." Waiting for the gravity of those questions to sink in, she asked again, "How many of these letters are you planning to send him?"

"Well, I'm planning to use the digitally-recorded-letter part of this service so that he can see and hear his old grandpa again. It'll be almost as though I were still alive. And as for the technology, Luke can teach me how to do it, because I'm doing all this for him."

"I'm glad you have that part figured out, Dad, but you still haven't answered my question: How many of these letters are you planning to record?"

"That's a good question, Rebecca, and the reason it's a good question is because I'm not sure how long it will take me to record each letter. After all, we are talking about me being willing to learn technology. I can't believe I'm willing to embrace it, but for Luke, I'll do it. I've been doing a little calculating in my head this morning, and I thought 50 letters would be a good number." Gus paused for a second to think about that number. "Yup, 50 is a nice number. And I'd like each one to be delivered on Luke's birthday. What do you think?"

Rebecca pointedly answered his question by gently asking, "So, Dad, you want to send him a *single* letter once a year?"

Gus considered her question and then said, "You're right, Becca. Once a year isn't often enough." He thought some more and said, "And twice a year isn't often enough either. Once every three months for ten years would be perfect. So, it looks like I'll be sending him a total of 40 letters. I like that number, Becca. Thanks for the help."

"For you, Dad, I'm always happy to help out," she said with a soft smile. "I know you told me not to worry about the money, but just out of curiosity, how much are those letters going to cost?"

"Compared to what we'll get in return, Becca, nothing, literally nothing. It really doesn't matter anyway because absolutely every penny I spend for my grandson will be worth the price."

"Dad, hearing what you are going to do for Luke might make what I'm about to ask seem a little selfish, and I'm not trying to take any time away from what you will need to say to Luke, but I was just wondering if you think there might be some time, and a little money left over in the next two years, for you to record and then send me one or two of those letters as well?"

With that question, Gus lifted his arm, leaned toward Rebecca, and wrapped it around his beautiful daughter. While kissing her on the forehead and giving her a hug, he told her, "Oh, Becca. Don't worry your precious heart. I have several in mind for you already. And quit crying so much—it's getting contagious."

After their emotions had settled down, they sat and talked over the next couple of hours about all kinds of things. No topic seemed to be off the table.

It was about 11 a.m. when Luke finally made his way down the steps to the kitchen for some coffee and then out to the living room where he joined his mom and grandpa. Seeing them sitting together on the couch, he made a beeline for his grandpa's chair.

"Good morning, buddy." His grandpa greeted him with a little smile. "I know it may be a stupid question, but are you doing okay?"

Luke pictured the two of them sitting on the couch together, attempting to sear that image into his long-term memory, and then said, "I think so, Grandpa. I couldn't fall asleep at first, but it looks like I made up for it this morning."

"I'm just glad you got some rest, but I think I'm the one who didn't get much sleep last night. A radio commercial I heard when we were driving home from your game yesterday was stuck in my head. I couldn't stop thinking about it and had a hard time falling asleep."

Luke was looking at his grandpa when he referred to the radio commercial. "Was it the one from the cremation society?"

"The *what*?" spluttered his grandpa, being caught off guard.

"Luke," snapped his mother, "How could you say such a thing at a time like this!" She could not believe the words she heard come out of Luke's mouth.

In response to this unnecessary defense of his feelings, Gus decisively stated to his emotional daughter, "Oh, let it go, Becca. Those commercials are on the radio all the time, and for a reason—to talk about what to do when a loved one dies, whether it's expectedly or unexpectedly. Now I know you didn't know this, Luke, but there is a spot right next to your Grandma Claire at the military cemetery waiting for me. We won't be needing any cremation services."

"Sorry, Grandpa, I didn't know."

"Don't worry, buddy. There are a lot of things in life you don't know about yet, and that's a perfect segue into what I wanted to talk with you about this morning. I've already spoken with your mom and she's on board with what I want to do."

Luke leaned further back into his grandpa's chair and waited for him to continue.

Seeing Luke get more comfortable, Gus started speaking again. "There's a service I want to start using as soon as possible, and it will be especially valuable after I go home to be with Jesus."

Luke stared blankly at his grandpa before saying, "I don't get it, Grandpa. What good would renting anything do for you after you're dead?"

"Luke!" said his mother directly. "Here we go again. Please drink more coffee and think a little more before you fire off those kinds of questions. You should at least allow your grandfather the courtesy of explaining this service before you shoot it down."

At that moment, Gus realized that the energy level of everyone in the house was pretty low and that more verbal snapping might escalate if something wasn't done. The best remedy he knew about was always a good meal.

"You know what, guys?" said Gus with just the right amount of perkiness in his voice. "The morning is almost gone, and those three cups of coffee I drank are beginning to grind away at my stomach. I don't know about you two, but I'm getting hungry, and apparently this cancer doesn't seem to have affected my appetite yet. What do you say we make breakfast for lunch? And I can explain more about this service to you, Luke, while we're eating."

"That's a great idea, Dad," said Rebecca as she walked toward the upstairs hallway. "Why don't you get all the cooking utensils out and all the ingredients ready while I run to my bedroom. I'll be back in a couple of minutes after I get changed."

Gus looked at Rebecca, somewhat confused at her statement and what she was going to her bedroom to do. "I thought this was going to be a slow and lazy day for all of us to spend together. Why do you need to get dressed? Are you going somewhere?"

"Dad! It's getting late enough now in the morning when people might be stopping by, and I don't want to get caught wearing my pajamas if I need to answer the door."

It wasn't more than a few minutes and Rebecca was back in the kitchen. She was wearing her favorite light green blouse and dark blue jeans. And —surprise, surprise—her hair was even nicely combed. Gus and Luke looked at each other as Rebecca descended the stairwell and walked back into the kitchen. They said nothing about this quick and pleasant transformation, but they did wonder what all that primping really meant. Rebecca was just as quick in making pancake batter as she was in getting dressed, for it didn't take more than two shakes of a lamb's tail to whip up that first batch of batter. After ladling some of this creamy mixture onto the hot griddle, she waited for just the right amount of batter bubbles to appear on the bottom of the pancakes and then flipped them. Once the other side of the pancakes had served their time on the griddle, they were then flipped onto everyone's plate. After adding some pure maple syrup, Gus could see the energy level in everyone begin to rise.

"These pancakes are wonderful, Becca. Did you use Mom's recipe?"

"I sure did, Dad, apple sauce and all."

Gus was the first one to finish his breakfast, and after putting his plate into the dishwasher, he turned toward Luke and said, "You just keep eating your pancakes and sausage links and drinking your orange juice while I do the talking. And I'll start that talk right after I eat two more of those sausage links."

After finishing off the first of the two links, Gus started explaining to Luke about the service he wanted to rent, while gingerly holding that second sausage link between his thumb and index finger, like a pointer, waiting for the right moment to finish it off.

"Now then, let's get to what I want to talk about. First of all, Luke, you need to understand that the service I want to rent isn't for me. It's for you and your mom and your two aunts. Now, do you remember hearing a commercial on the way home from your game yesterday talking about a service called Legacy Letters?"

"Nope, I was busy focusing on driving your truck and making it home safely. I barely remember you singing those old songs off-key."

Gus hesitated for a moment and smiled at Luke, delighted to hear him joking while talking about such a difficult subject. Gus then spent the next ten minutes explaining the service and how he intended to use it.

"Don't you see, Luke? I can record letters to you today that will be delivered years, or even decades, from now."

"That's pretty cool, Grandpa. Do you already know what you are going to say to me?" Luke had finished up his breakfast during his grandpa's speech, and he was sitting on a stool at the kitchen island with his elbows on the countertop and his chin resting on his palms.

"Now that's the big question. I was thinking . . ."

Just then, right in the middle of Gus's sentence, Luke's cell phone rang. After Luke saw who was calling, he asked if he could answer it.

"Sure, go ahead," said Rebecca, "but make it quick. This is an important conversation we're having."

"Thanks, Mom. I'll be quick!"

Luke left the kitchen, walked toward the living room for more privacy, and then answered the phone.

"Hi, Maggy! What's up?"

Gus and Becca looked blankly at each other and said at the same time, "Maggy? Who's Maggy?"

It was only then that Rebecca saw Luke for who he had become, and he had done it right in front of her. Without her even knowing it, he had become a young man who was now interested in dating and would one day get married and move out of the house. She turned to her father with a look of empty-nest fear and desperation on her face that said, "You're leaving me soon, and Luke won't be far behind you."

"Dad, where'd my little boy go? When did he grow up? Since when has he been interested in girls?"

Again, Gus smiled and said, "Oh, how I love life! Turnabout is such fair play. I suppose you don't remember doing the same thing to me and your mom almost 30 years ago."

"Knock it off, Dad. It's not the same and you know it. You had Mom who was still at home with you when I moved out. But who will I have when Luke moves out? No one, that's who. I'll be all alone!"

"Speaking of your mother, I wish she was here to be part of this conversation. She would be loving it. But that's okay, Rebecca, because I can see her beautiful smile in my mind, and that's good enough for me."

Rebecca gave her father a more-than-loving backhanded slap on his arm as she continued cleaning the breakfast dishes. "Come on, Dad. Cut me some slack. You're not going to be here much longer, and then I'll have to tread these parenting waters all alone. And then he'll be gone—gone to the next stage in his life. And this time it will be without me!"

"First of all, Rebecca, Luke would never just walk away from you. He loves his mom way too much to do that. And secondly, I know how you can fix that problem."

"Dad! We've had this conversation before, and I'll say it again: you didn't remarry after Mom died, and you were fine with that decision. The same goes for me too. I'm fine with not remarrying either," she declared with a huff.

"I'm sorry, Becca, but it's not quite the same. I had 35 more years of marriage under my belt than you had. And, sweetie, I can't help noticing how you light up when you talk with Ricardo Sanchez after every church service. I just want you to be happy, and not alone, in the future. And from what I've seen, Ricardo drifts in your direction pretty quickly after every service, and he apparently doesn't mind spending time with you either."

Rebecca heard Luke's voice getting closer to the kitchen door as he was saying goodbye to the girl on the other end of the phone. "Can we talk about this later? Luke is almost back."

"We sure can, but do I see a hint of a blush on that pretty little face of yours?" said Gus while waiting to see her reaction.

Gus promptly received a second backhanded slap on his arm as he continued speaking, undaunted by this lackluster attempt at silencing him.

"What has happened to my little girl, my strong-willed and free-spirited daughter?"

"Dad! Not now!" Rebecca scolded, not wanting Luke to hear and join in on the teasing.

Rebecca composed herself, preparing to ask a "mom" question. It was one she knew she would be asking one day but was still not ready to ask—and definitely not prepared to hear the answer to.

Luke walked into the kitchen while turning off his phone and said nothing about the call he had just received. His mom, on the other hand, not willing to let this moment go without more inquiry, though showing great motherly restraint, casually asked, "Luke, we couldn't help overhearing . . . who's Maggy?"

"She's Markus's sister. She wanted to know if I was going to Juan's pool party today and if I needed a ride. She got her license a month ago and her parents gave her a car when she passed her driver's test."

"That's pretty generous of her parents. What's her last name? I know a lot of the families at the school. Maybe I know her dad and mom."

"It's Middlefield, just like Markus's last name. Come on, Mom, quit messing with me. You know who they are. I've been hanging out with them since elementary school."

"Middlefield, Middlefield," said Rebecca coyly. "She wouldn't be related to the Middlefield Custom Homes building family, would she?"

"Yes, Mom. Her dad owns it, and you know that. Now can we talk about her later? I want to hear about Grandpa's letters before I have to get ready for Juan's party."

Until that moment, Gus had been silent, simply enjoying the moment of lighthearted banter. But when he heard that statement, he jumped in.

"Everything is later with you two," he said with a tone that indicated there were a couple things he was putting off till later himself. "Well, unlike you two, I don't have much *later* left, so let's talk about this Legacy Letter service."

Both Rebecca and Luke seemed to be very happy in turning the topic of conversation off of themselves and onto Gus.

Unfortunately for Gus, he would have to wait to finish his introduction of this new web service one more time. Just as he opened his mouth to speak, they all heard another phone ring, but this time it was Rebecca's phone doing the ringing. She looked to see who was calling and then said, "I'm sorry, Dad, but I have to take this call. I'll be back in a minute."

It seemed odd to Gus and Luke that Rebecca let her phone ring three more times while she walked to the other room for what they could only assume was more privacy. After answering the phone, they heard her say softly, "Good morning, Ricardo." And then it made all the sense in the world. Luke and Gus looked at each other and smiled.

Her conversation lasted for two or three short minutes and then she was back in the kitchen. Seeing two huge smiles greeting her, she abruptly said, wagging her pointer finger in the air toward them, "Not a single word! I don't want to hear one single word from either one of you," before crossing her arms.

Luke had the biggest smile on his face that Gus had ever seen, and not about to miss out on the opportunity of a lifetime, he coyly asked, "Okay, Mom, it's no big deal. All I want to know is his name. I know a lot of families at church, and I might just know who he is."

Rebecca couldn't help herself as she began to laugh, and Gus and Luke joined in. After they had all calmed down, Gus asked, "Now that that's over, can I start again?"

"Yes, Dad, we can finish our talk now."

"Okay, first of all, I didn't mention it last night, but I have a follow-up appointment with Dr. Emmitt next Wednesday. He is going to talk to me about what to expect, from a health deterioration per-spective, over the next two years. He also asked if you could be at that appointment with me, Becca. He wants you to know what to expect since you will be the main caregiver until I need hospice."

The gravity of this conversation came rushing back into Rebecca's heart.

"Dad, talking about deteriorating health and hospice seems so fi-nal, so matter of fact. It makes me wonder how anyone in the medical field can do their job day after day and not have their heart broken, because I'm being torn up inside just thinking of you at that stage in your life."

"Rebecca, now it's my turn to be surprised. What do you think I dealt with all those years in my job? I saw people dying every week. It was heart-wrenching, especially when the drugs failed during patient trials. But our company produced drugs that did work for thousands of others. And for those who were helped, along with those that could not be helped, I had the opportunity to tell the life-saving story of Jesus. Those were not sad times for the ones who believed but rather times of excited anticipation for what they would soon experience. Now, it's just my turn. I'm going home. Soon it will be your turn and then Luke's turn. It's the way this broken world works."

"I know you're right, Dad, but you have no idea how much we're going to miss you."

"And here we are, full circle, back to the Legacy Letters conversa-tion. The way I see it, I should get all my letters recorded this coming year, because I don't know how well I will be physically or cognitively after that point. If I'm still doing well enough, maybe I'll be able to sneak in a couple more, if I'm not too tired. Now why don't we take a break from this conversation about me and instead talk about Maggy or Ricardo."

"Yes, of course, Ricardo," exclaimed Luke, sensing another opening to retaliate and mess with his mom. Luke walked around the kitchen, his chin resting on his hand and his head tilted up as if in thought, and said slowly, "Now let me think . . . Ricardo . . . Ricardo . . . now just who is this Ricardo guy? Oh yeah, now I remember—he's the one you're always talking with after church, right? You know what I think, Grandpa? I think he looks a little like Dad, although my six-year-old memory is a little fuzzy."

"No, Luke, I believe you're right. I was just thinking the same thing. You probably didn't know this, but your mom has a thing for good-looking Latino men."

"Okay, Dad, you just stop right there. Luke doesn't need to hear things like that about his mom."

"Who was talking about you? I was describing to Luke what his father looked like!"

"I don't know what you're getting so worked up about, Mom. We're just talking about a guy you like, and based on that call you got a few minutes ago, he seems to like you too. Unless, all of a sudden, you've gotten bashful about that topic. So what if you have a type. And the fact that you may be interested in another man other than Dad is okay with me. I guess it's up to you, Mom. You figured it out when you were 16, so I'm sure you can figure it out as a 49-year-old."

"Luke! One, I don't have a 'type,' as you call it. Second, have you been talking to your grandfather again? That's some pretty insightful advice for a guy your age. Tell me about Maggy, since we are being so open today. I was pretty up front with my dad about a certain boy that caught my eye when I was your age, so tell your mom about the girl who has caught yours."

It wasn't more than an hour later when a knock on the front door indicated that Markus and Maggy had arrived.

"Don't worry about the door, Mom," said Luke as he yelled to her from the living room. "I'll get it."

Rebecca wasn't about to miss an opportunity to meet the mysterious Miss Maggy. It had been several years since she had last seen her. Rebecca was standing at the front door with Luke when he opened it to greet his friends. Maggy and Markus were side by side, both with friendly smiles. Maggy was pretty, a curly, blonde-haired and blue-eyed girl. *Yes,* thought Rebecca silently, *they're definitely brother and sister, and most definitely twins.*

"Mom, I said I would get the door. You didn't have to come down here and take time away from getting ready for your date. And just out of curiosity, when will Mr. Sanchez be here to pick you up? Maybe

I can stay and meet him. It only seems fair since you put out such an effort to meet Maggy."

This boy of mine is way too smart for his age, thought Rebecca to herself. She then said to these three young adults, "You all have a nice time today. It was good to meet you, Maggy, and it's nice to see you again, Markus." A moment later they were all alone at the front door.

"Your mom seems nice, Luke. But who's Mr. Sanchez?"

"Just a friend of the family, but let's not worry about him. Let's get to Juan's house before the pool gets too crowded."

Luke began walking to the car with his towel around his neck. He was wearing a dull blue muscle shirt and knee-length bright orange swim trunks. "So which one of you is driving?" he asked.

Markus piped in rather quickly: "The family over-achiever will be driving today, that's who! For some reason, Maggy sees everything as a competition with me, and that includes getting a driver's license, but I'm not going to play that game with her!"

As they all got into Maggy's car, Markus kept on talking. "Just so you know, Luke, I'm taking my driver's test next week because my dad said that if I got my driver's license, we could both work as laborers for the carpentry crews this summer. He also said if the crew foreman liked our work, he would give permission to teach us basic carpentry skills."

Luke was visibly excited about having a summer job to make some extra spending money. "Markus, I don't have a way to get to work. Do you think your dad would let you pick me up in the mornings and drop me off after work with the car he's going to give you?"

"That won't be a problem, Luke, but I won't be driving a car. My dad told me that when I passed my driver's test, he would give me a company truck to drive. So I can pick you up and drop you off. No problem, man."

Could this summer have started out any better, thought Luke, because he had some news of his own to share about the quest to drive.

"Just so you know, Markus, I'm also taking my driver's test in a month, so I can help drive if you need me to. If I pass, that is."

While the boys were talking about how easy it was going to be to pass the driver's test, and about a job they hadn't even started, Maggy had pulled into a local grocery store just a few miles from Luke's house. Being a new driver meant she chose a parking spot far away from all the other cars.

Maggy was out of the car now. She said to Luke and Markus, neither of whom had made a move to open their door and get out, "Come on, you two. We have to buy some snacks for the party. It's not polite to show up to a party empty-handed."

———————————————

It was a quick, 15-minute stop, but that's all they needed to purchase three bags of chips, a large tub of chip dip, and a 12-pack of soda for their contribution to the party. By the time they had arrived at Juan's home, cars filled the driveway, along with both sides of the street around his house. After making their way around the side of the garage and through the security gate into the backyard, they saw the pool full of their classmates. Juan was standing by the diving board with what appeared to be a bottle of beer in his hand.

"Hey, Juan!" said Luke after making his way to where he was talking to a couple of other beer-drinking partiers. "I didn't know there was going to be beer at this party. It's illegal for us to have it, isn't it?"

Juan turned toward Luke and gave a loud laugh before responding with a slight slur: "Lukey, Marky, and Maggy Moo, you finally made it! Let the fun begin! Go ahead. Jump in and get wet. The water's great!"

In that moment, before Luke could respond to Juan's alcohol-inspired greeting, Juan looked through the large picture window of his house and into the living room where his parents were visibly yelling at each other. Until these last couple of years, they had all been so happy. Juan couldn't figure out what had happened that was causing all this anger, and he knew it wouldn't be long before his dad would walk out of the house and disappear for a few days. Without fail, he always returned home, giving his mother a hug and an apology, but he never gave her an explanation as to where he went, what he did, or who he spent his time with.

After taking another chug of beer, Juan turned toward Luke and handed him his half-empty bottle. "Have a drink, Luke. It tastes great. And after I perform the greatest of all belly flops, I'll be back for my beer."

Watching Juan step onto the diving board at the deep end of the pool, Maggy grabbed Luke's arm and swung him around so that he was facing her. With visible irritation on her face, she said, "Luke, Juan just called me Maggy Moo. I'm not sure what he meant by that, but if he just called me a cow, I'm outta here."

Not sure what was really happening, but knowing in his heart that it was more than just alcohol-related, Luke turned back toward the swimming pool and faced Juan. In his inebriated state of mind, Juan determined that he wasn't going to allow his dad to ruin his party. He walked out to the end of the diving board while yelling out to all his guests: "I challenge anyone here to do a better belly flop than the one you're about to see."

Everyone there—those in the water and those standing around the pool—cheered and clapped. "Bel-ly Flop! Bel-ly Flop! Bel-ly Flop!" they chanted. This continued as Juan backed up to the rear of the diving board. Then, with a big smile, Juan took off running, stopped short of the diving board, jumped into the air, and then, landing at the very end of the springboard, catapulted high into the air. His arms and legs were spread out in an iron cross fashion, and he hung in the air for a moment before falling straight down. Juan landed perfectly flat on top of the water. The cracking sound his body made was so loud and harsh that it silenced everyone. That is, until he jerked up his head and arms with his fists clenched in a victory stance. Everyone was screaming, laughing, and clapping. As Juan walked around the pool, receiving congratulations from everyone at the party for such a memorable dive, a different conversation was taking place on the other side of the pool.

After seeing Juan almost hurt himself because of his altered state of mind, Luke looked at Maggy and then at Markus, who had just walked over to where they were standing. "I know we just arrived," Luke said, "but do either of you have any desire to stay here any longer?"

Markus looked sheepishly at Luke, and after swallowing the food in his mouth, he replied, "I could be persuaded to make a second stop at the buffet table before we leave."

Gus's quest to create a legacy of letters for his grandson began. He started writing down what he wanted to say with excitement and energy. However, by the end of the third day, and certainly by the end of the first week, his excitement and energy was all but tapped out. Gus had arrived at a moment of realization: he didn't really know what he should say or how he should say it. And if that wasn't enough stress to deal with, determining the specific date Luke should receive each letter was also becoming a daunting task. Gus began to wonder if Rebecca had been right all along. Had he indeed promised more than he could deliver? It was that thought that made him realize these recordings were going to be more exhausting than he had anticipated. But he had made a promise to send these letters to Luke and his three girls, and a promise made should be a promise kept. That would mean that a lot of hard work was ahead of him.

Gus had awakened to the fact that he had erred in his estimation of the amount of effort and preparation this project would take, not only in terms of the time commitment but also in terms of the difficulty of creating each letter's unique content. It was a bit overwhelming. He knew in his heart that it was time to do what had always helped him through difficulties in life. He was again in need of spiritual guidance.

Of course, he should have done this to begin with. He needed to spend time in prayer with God and read his Spirit-inspired Bible. What was he thinking? Especially after that dream God had given him concerning Luke's future. Even at the ripe old age of 75, he was still making mistakes. He should have gone to his knees in prayer first. In order to leave Luke a legacy of this magnitude, he must first receive some spiritual guidance of his own. After taking the time to pray for wisdom, he felt compelled to start reading some psalms. Over the course of the next month, he also made his way through Proverbs, the book of Romans, and several other books in the New Testament. Halfway through his reading, it came to him.

I didn't realize it until this minute, but my life's experiences and counsel will be wrapped up in these words of divine inspiration. I'm going to take a verse, a Proverb, or a Psalm and speak to Luke about my life's experiences. And I can do this through the lens of these Spirit-inspired books that are packed with wisdom, knowledge, and encouragement.

As Gus began to read through these books a second, third, and even a fourth time, truth, knowledge, and wisdom began to pour out onto the paper as he recorded the memories of his life. The words of the Bible were revealing patterns in his life he had not noticed before. Gus could clearly see now that in his final months in this life, he was being further refined into the kind of man God wanted in his kingdom. He was also being called to perform God's final requests of him. He reflected to himself: *I may have wasted portions of my life when I was younger, but I'm not going to waste the rest of it.* Gus knew this last act of obedience would prepare him for the day of his final calling, the day of his departure, the day he would meet the One whom he had faithfully followed for the majority of his life.

The words were coming easier now, almost as if he was taking dictation, and the recordings seemed to be filled with a greater meaning than even Gus had intended. He began to see clearly now how Jesus had been watching over him all these years and was now using his life to prepare Luke for his. Gus stopped in the middle of one of these sentences and started to pray again.

"Dear Lord Jesus, I just realized something. You have given me notice that my life is coming to an end. You have given me two years to complete this task. What is it that you want Luke to learn about you through me? Lead me in your path and show me whatever you want him to learn."

Gus's prayers were answered. Starting that very night, and over the next year and a half, in the form of dreams, dreams that Christ gave to Gus, he received the teaching and counseling that would make up the heart of these letters. It had been two years since Gus started recording his Legacy Letters, and one month since his funeral. He had missed Luke's high school graduation by only two weeks. As a result of Gus's departure, the house had become overwhelmingly quiet, a very sad kind of quiet. Luke and his mom were having trouble breaking out of a melancholy mood that had fallen on them since the funeral. They passed each other in the kitchen, the living room, or a hallway without saying much more than a word. Meals were silently eaten. Phone calls offering condolences, encouragement, or offers of help had all but disappeared. What was even more heartbreaking were the times when Rebecca, out of habit, would call out to Gus, "Hey Dad, what do you want to eat for dinner?" Immediately she would catch herself, and then Luke would hear muffled sounds of his mother crying. Each time, Luke would go to his mother and console her with a gentle hug.

Now, on the brighter side, and to Rebecca's relief, these memory blunders were becoming more and more infrequent. And there was one reason, one *person*, who was making the difference. He was stopping by all the time, even as far back as six months before Gus had passed away. That person was Ricardo Sanchez.

Though slow in coming, and thanks to Ricardo's persistence, there was a hint, yes, a slight whiff, of fragrant normalcy that was beginning to bud in all of their lives. And what that new normal would look like they couldn't even imagine.

Each day Luke passed by his grandpa's open bedroom door, and each time he would stop and look in as a great sadness gripped his heart. Gus had actually been able to stay home until the last couple weeks of his life. His slippers were still by his dresser where he always left them, and his pesky cell phone was on top of the dresser next to the cologne he always wore. Sometimes Luke would walk in and take a deep breath of the lingering fragrance, and he was able to recount even more memories of his grandpa. Gus had made his bed, with Luke's help, that last morning before leaving for the hospital. Gus had learned this appreciation for starting out each day with a sense of order through the simple act of having a properly made bed. He had acquired this lifelong habit as a young man during his military days. His rosewood cane was still lying across the bed where he had tossed it before his final trip to the hospital. "Wait for me right there, Rosey. I'll be back in a day or two and we'll go for a walk." But that walk never came.

Luke remembered the events of the last two years of high school as being slow, uneventful, and sad. Unknown to him at the time, there were more events and changes to come before his grandpa's death would arrive. One of the most significant changes, which was taking place amid Luke's undulating emotions, involved his mother.

As though it were a prearranged opportunity for her heart to heal, Rebecca began spending more and more time with Ricardo Sanchez. Everyone who knew them could see where this courtship was heading. Gus liked him, and so did Luke, who had made this plain to his mother. Yet, even though Luke was happy for his mom and had nothing against Mr. Sanchez, there was no replacing his grandpa.

And so the events of life continued to unfold with little concern for time or heartbreak. This couldn't have been more obvious than when Ricardo helped Rebecca plan Luke's high school graduation party. He tried as hard as he could to create a festive atmosphere, but he fell short in his attempts; Luke just wasn't ready to accept this gift of a new father figure in his life.

This party had taken place only a few weeks after Gus's funeral, and everyone's energy and spirits had been low. Ricardo mingled with those who had come to support Luke, trying to be a calming presence during a difficult time. He smiled, shook hands, told jokes, and laughed with those who had come to show support for Luke. But he saw only limited success. It was so hard for Luke to keep smiling and having (what seemed to him) meaningless conversations; he couldn't see the effort Ricardo was exerting on his behalf. It just wasn't the same without his grandpa.

Then, out of nowhere, a feeling of sad familiarity came over Luke in an odd way. Without notice, his mind went back 12 years, and he began recalling memories when he was six years old and his dad and grandma had died in that traffic accident. It felt almost exactly the same. The same feelings of sorrow, despair, and loneliness were relentlessly washing over him.

I was too young to understand what that accident really meant, but this is what Grandpa and Mom must have gone through 12 years ago. and now Mom is going through it again. I don't know how I made it through those days, thought Luke to himself. *I'm just glad I was a kid and didn't know what was really going on.*

A few days after the graduation party, Luke was impatiently sitting in his softly lit bedroom. Tomorrow was the first day of June, his birthday. He was waiting up till midnight to see if there would really be a letter from his grandpa, just as he promised Luke from his hospital bed. Luke had his computer on with his mailbox open, unable to sleep.

Luke almost screamed for his mom when the clock turned from 11:59 p.m. to 12:00 a.m. His computer monitor blinked once before an email popped into his inbox. It was from Legacy Letters. The subject line read, "Happy Birthday, Buddy."

Luke didn't know where these emotions came from, but he instantly broke into several minutes of uncontrollable sobbing. After gaining control of himself, and before being allowed to open his letter, he had to answer some questions. Questions like, "Are you the intended recipient of this letter? Will this email address be changing in the next three months? If yes, please type in the new address below. Would you like to download this message to a personal hard drive?"

There were a couple more personal questions Luke got through quickly before arriving at the last instruction: "Please click on the LL (Legacy Letter) button at the bottom of this page to gain access to your letter."

As soon as Luke clicked the button, he saw his grandfather's soft blue eyes, his white head of hair with a flat-top haircut, and those familiar and well-earned wrinkles scattered around his face. A moment later he could hear his grandpa's voice saying, "Hi, buddy! How's everything going?"

To which Luke quietly answered, with a quivering voice, "Not so good, Grandpa, not so good. I miss you." But Gus just continued speaking, unable to hear or reply to anything Luke said.

"Luke, let me start by saying that a little more than two years ago, I took a calculated guess and picked this birthday to have the first letter delivered to you. So I'm either down the hall from you, in hospice care, or no longer alive. Either way, I'm probably in pretty bad shape. I have to tell you that I'm sorry for not being with you any longer, but our Jesus has called me home, so home I will go. You may be listening to this letter in your bedroom, but I'm singing to my Jesus in his throne room, and I'm doing it at the top of my lungs with my hands in the air stretched out toward him.

You know something, I was always a reserved man and never praised our Jesus with my hands in the air, stretched out to him, but as I sit here today, I can't see worshiping him in any other way. Also, I'll never need old Rosey again, so she's yours now. She'll take good care of you until it's time for you to come home too. And if I remember, I'll tell you the story in one of these letters of how I came to obtain Rosey. And as for your father and grandmother, I think I'll sing to our Jesus for the first 10,000 years, then I'll ask if I can sing to Jesus with them for a few thousand more." Luke hit the pause button as he began to cry again. A few minutes later, having wiped the tears away, he started playing his grandpa's letter a second time, this time telling himself to keep his emotions under control.

"Luke, I have to start out by saying that I know exactly how you're feeling in light of my death. I felt the same way when Grandma and your dad died. You need to do what I did in order to get through that time, and that is to go to our Jesus in prayer. It's hard to explain how an unseen Spirit of the one and only God can bring a feeling of joy and a sense of understanding back into your heart and life. But it's real, Luke. It's real. Just keep on believing!" Luke hit the pause button again as he wiped his eyes with the sleeve of his t-shirt, thinking about what his grandpa had just said. After hitting the pause button again, Gus continued talking.

"I didn't tell you much about when or how often you would receive one of these Legacy Letters, or what would be in them, so I'll take the time now to explain what you can expect. I'll have to admit that when I sat down to compose this first letter, I had no idea what I would be saying to you. You must understand one very important reason for these letters: I am going to be praying intensely to Jesus before I begin each letter so that he might speak through me to you. Please consider this as you receive and listen to every letter. These are not just words from your old grandpa. These are words of counsel from your Jesus *through* me *to* you.

"Now, keep in mind this is my first letter, and I'm sure the letters will change a little in format over the next year. At first, I was thinking that 50 would be a good number—a letter a year for 50 years. But with your mother's help, I soon realized that once a year would not be timely counsel. Then I considered sending you two letters a year—one on your birthday and one six months later—for the next 25 years. But again, I realized that once every six months was not going to work either, so I landed on one letter every three months for ten years. If I can sneak in a few more, I will. I'll also be sending a couple to your mom and your two aunts over these same years.

"Luke, I've determined that the best way for me to be a guide in your life, even though I will not physically be with you, is to take Bible verses that spoke to me at one time in my life and share them with you. These verses will encourage and guide you through life-changing situations and decisions you will eventually face. My hope is that you will not face them alone. I will be taking the wisdom given to all of us in the words of the Bible, but I will wrap it around my own personal life experiences. Included will be the decisions I made, which created the stories you will hear.

"My hope is that you will learn from the good *and* bad choices I have made in my life, avoiding the bad ones and embracing the good ones. You're going to be encouraged by some of my stories, and you will be disappointed with your old grandpa in others. But to learn life's lessons, you will need to hear the good with the bad and how my Jesus held my hand through all of it, even when I wasn't aware of it. If you allow him, he will also hold yours."

Luke had never thought of his grandpa as anything but good, so he wondered for just a moment if he really wanted to receive these Legacy Letters after all.

"I will attempt to send you letters and stories that will intersect with your age, and possibly your life circumstances. These letters may come too early, too late, or just in time. I promise to do my best for you, buddy. Right now, I would like to read a few verses from the book of Proverbs that speak to what I am trying to tell you in this first digital letter.

> Hear, O sons, a father's instruction,
>   and be attentive, that you may gain insight,
> for I give you good precepts;
>   do not forsake my teaching. (Proverbs 4:1–2)

> Keep hold of instruction; do not let go;
>   guard her, for she is your life. (Proverbs 4:13)

> My son, if you receive my words
>   and treasure up my commandments with you,
> making your ear attentive to wisdom
>   and inclining your heart to understanding;
> yes, if you call out for insight
>   and raise your voice for understanding,
> if you seek it like silver
>   and search for it as for hidden treasures,
> then you will understand the fear of the LORD
>   and find the knowledge of God.
> For the LORD gives wisdom;

from his mouth come knowledge and understanding;
he stores up sound wisdom for the upright;
    he is a shield to those who walk in integrity,
guarding the paths of justice
    and watching over the way of his saints. (Proverbs 2:1–8)

"These verses from Proverbs speak with love and directness about why I decided to, well, actually, why I was called by God to, send you these letters. Take my future counsel to heart, Luke. Read God's words and pray to God's Spirit for his most precious counsel and wisdom. My hope is that I may help you navigate some difficult waters in the years to come, but the true counsel will always come from the Creator of all there is—our Jesus."

Luke paused the recording again and took some time to think about what his grandpa had just told him. "Wow, Grandpa. That's a lot of stuff you just said, but I wish you could advise me on something I'm dealing with right now." Luke hit the start button again.

"One last thing before this letter is finished. I think your mom really likes Ricardo. Let her have this man in her life, Luke. He's a good man; he's a follower of Christ; he loves your mom; and I can see that he likes you too. It's been a long time since she's let a man this deep into her heart. I believe God has given them to each other. Perhaps I'll see a marriage before I go home. I'll see you in three months and then we can talk about Maggy."

"Grandpa," said Luke rather loudly, "that's not fair to make me wait three months!"

The same day Luke received the first Legacy Letter that Gus recorded, Rebecca was receiving his final one. But unlike Luke, who was consumed by the expectation of receiving that first letter, as well as all those to follow, Rebecca had none. She had only received a verbal promise from her father to send a few letters through the years, but she didn't know exactly when, how often, or how many that might be. Having no expectation of receiving a letter so soon after her father's death, this one came as a most pleasant surprise.

Rebecca had been attempting to create a new normal for their lives, which was a big part of why she was getting up so early on this particular morning. She had to make sure no preparations were forgotten for

Luke's 18th birthday party, for she had determined that today would be the first day of the rest of their new *normal* lives. While checking her email subject lines to see if she had received notice that Luke's birthday cake was ready to be picked up, a bolt of electric excitement surged through her body. She couldn't believe it, but there it was: a Legacy Letter subject line that read, "Hi, Sweetie! It's Your Pops!"

Dad, you sent me a letter already? she thought to herself while opening his letter with hands that were trembling with excitement.

After going through the same checkboxes that Luke had, Becca pushed the LL button and her father's gentle and loving face appeared on the screen.

"Hi, Becca. Let me start by saying, I'm so sorry you have to go through this heartbreak again. Luke was only six years old when Joshua and Mom went home, so all he knew was that Daddy and Grandma were not coming back from their trip but would be living with Jesus. He is older and more mature now and I have absolutely no doubt that he will be there for you to lean on just as I was there for you 12 years ago. I also know for a fact that Ricardo will be right next to you while you grieve for me. Remember the times you asked him to sit with me while you went out to pick up some groceries and other household items? Well, in your absence, we had several heart-to-heart talks, and you, my dear, were the topic of those conversations."

Rebecca was now sitting in her dad's favorite chair, curious as to what he and Ricardo might have talked about, with her cell phone in one hand and a cup of French vanilla coffee in the other. She was listening to every word he spoke, her chin trembling and her eyes beginning to glisten. She was watching the recorded letter while once again looking into her father's gentle blue eyes and listening intently to his words. She was still in a little shock from seeing him and hearing his voice.

"I've been recording these letters for a year and a half now, Becca, and it's getting hard for me to concentrate and keep up this pace. It makes me thankful that I was able to get those extra letters recorded last year—Luke will love them. But I'm getting tired more quickly and I can tell my days are getting shorter. This may be one of the last letters I record, and I need to share something very special that our Jesus has done *for* me and *through* me in creating each letter. You probably noticed that, toward the end, I spent a lot more time with you and Luke and less time making these letters. It was spending that time with you that made me think that one of the last letters I record should be one of the first ones I send out. It makes sense: I can talk about the last memories we had together, and they would be more meaningful to you if you received the letter shortly after my body gives up its spirit to our Jesus."

Rebecca touched the pause button on her phone and turned it face down on the chair's flat oak arm rest when she heard Luke running down the staircase a hundred miles an hour and talking just as fast. He was rambling on about the Legacy Letter he had received from his grandpa earlier that morning as he ran into the living room where his mother was sitting.

"Sorry I didn't wake you up and tell you, but it was midnight and you were asleep. Wow, I loved it, Mom! I listened and watched that recording three times. I could hardly fall asleep after I turned the computer off. I guess it was good that I didn't wake you up or you might have lost some sleep too."

"That's okay, honey," said his mom as she turned off her phone and stealthily wiped her eyes. "Those are personal letters from your grandfather to *you*, not me."

"But don't you want to hear what he had to say? Don't you want to see and hear him talking again?"

"Of course I do, Luke. But to start out, with the first few letters, why don't you just tell me what he said and then listen to that letter as many times as you want to. Then, if you still want, we can listen to it together."

"Okay, Mom, but you're the one missing out. It was incredible! I got a shiver up and down my spine when I saw the letter in my mailbox. It was great!"

"I think I know what you mean, Luke, but I'll still wait a little while before watching them. Like I said, these are personal letters for you from your grandpa, so let's leave it that way for now. In the meantime, I have a couple of things to talk with you about before your birthday party this afternoon. So can we sit down and talk for a few minutes?"

"Sure, Mom. Let me get a cup of sweetened Java juice first and then we can talk."

Rebecca watched as an energized Luke turned and almost skipped into the kitchen, slapping the door casing as he floated by and then drumming on the kitchen island with his hands before pouring himself some coffee. It was truly amazing to see his demeanor change so quickly after hearing the first of many of his grandpa's letters. "You were right, Dad," said Rebecca to herself, "you are already making a difference in Luke's life, even though you are no longer with us. And it's only been one letter."

As Luke walked back into the living room, with a little more pep in his step and his eyes brighter and more alive than they had been for the last two months, Rebecca jumped right into what she wanted to talk about.

"I know these last two years have been tough on you, especially in preparing for your own future. But everyone was asking me at your graduation party what your plans were after high school, and honestly, Luke, I didn't know what to tell them. As a guidance counselor, I helped high schoolers figure out their futures, yet here I am, completely unaware of what my own son wants to do for school and a future job. I'm sorry, Luke. I got so wrapped up in caring for your grandfather that I neglected you. I feel like I have let you down as a mom. So, I'm asking, what can I say when I get that question today at your party?"

Luke took a slow sip of coffee as he listened to his mother's question, then he set his cup on the arm rest. He then calmly said, "Don't worry about it, Mom. My grades dropped a little because of everything happening this past year, so you can tell everyone that I won't be going to college. It wouldn't have been very easy for me anyway. I think I'm a 'work with your hands' kind of a guy. So, as of next week, I'm going out into the workforce for at least a year or two while I figure out exactly what I want to do with my life."

"You mean . . . you're not going to college?"

"No, Mom, I'm not. At least not this year. You have to realize that college may have been for you and Dad, but I'm not sure if it's for me."

"Luke! I have always considered myself to be a pretty good reader of young people's potential, and I can clearly see that you have greatness written into your DNA. And that's not a prejudiced mom being overly prideful of her son. I really mean that, Luke. There's something special waiting for you in your future, and we'll talk about that later, okay? But for now, can you tell me what you are going to do for work? It's not a good idea to just sit around the house and do nothing constructive."

"Mom," said Luke as he leaned forward in his chair, as if he was about to make a proclamation to his mother, "I know you've seen me leave for work, so I'll just assume that it didn't register because you spent so much time taking care of Grandpa. But honestly, Mom, where have you been these last two years? Don't you remember that I've been working for Mr. Middlefield the past two summers as a laborer? And starting next week, I'm going to work for him full-time as a carpenter. I'll be learning how to build new homes and remodel old ones."

"A carpenter? My son is going to be a carpenter?" Rebecca said this with a completely blank look on her face. "Wow, I didn't see that one coming. And what about your girlfriend, Maggy? She's a straight-A student and she finished at the top of your class. Will she be going off to college somewhere while you stay here?"

"Nope. She told me right after we graduated that she had sat down with her dad to talk about her future, and her dad told her that she was a natural with her understanding of business. Her dad's company has been growing these last two years while she was working part-time in his office, so they decided it would be best for her to work full-time for the next year. I guess he wants to train her in his way of doing business before letting her go off to college. Apparently he doesn't want her to be influenced by any college professors about how to conduct business other than the Middlefield way."

"Wow! Have I been distracted and disconnected for so long that I missed all these changes taking place right in front of me?"

"Don't worry about the little things in my life you didn't know about. Think about it, Mom. You had your hands pretty full taking care of Grandpa the last two years. You couldn't be aware of everything happening in my life too. But the one thing I hope you *do* keep track of is Mr. Sanchez. He's a pretty nice guy, Mom, and I don't think he's going anywhere!"

"Mr. Sanchez . . . Ricardo! Oh my goodness!" said Rebecca as she bolted to her feet and broke out of her blank stare, still looking straight ahead. She had literally lost track of time after hearing Ricardo's name.

"Mom, where are you? Wake up, Mom! You're acting just like Grandpa!"

"Ricardo! I was supposed to call Ricardo this morning, Luke, to let him know when to pick up your birthday cake. I can't believe I zoned out like that. But I think I know what made me forget to call Ricardo."

"And what would that have been?" asked Luke.

"I think it all started when I received that Legacy Letter from your grandfather this morning."

At hearing that his grandpa had already sent a second letter, his eyes lit up even more brilliantly than they had just a moment before. He immediately smiled and asked, "You got a letter from Grandpa too? And you didn't tell me about it? What did he say? What did he say, Mom?"

"I didn't listen to the whole letter. You were coming down the stairs right when I started, so I turned it off to talk with you about yours."

"Aw, come on, Mom! You can't just ignore his letter. You need to listen to it. There must have been a reason for him sending it to you today. Aren't you even a little curious to hear what he wants to tell you?"

"Yes, I am, and yes, I will, but not right now. I have to call the bakery about your cake and then call Ricardo. Oh, and I need to finish cleaning the house and setting up decorations. I feel like such a scatterbrain today!"

"Don't feel bad, Mom. Everyone zones out once in a while. And, hey, don't forget that Maggy is coming over early to help you get ready for the party."

Rebecca sat still a second time and then asked, "What about Maggy's house? Shouldn't she be helping her mother clean their own home and get ready for her graduation party?"

Luke smiled again, knowing she wouldn't be able to grasp what he was about to say.

"Nope, she doesn't have to help at her home. That's why they hired a full-time maid and a cook. Pretty cool, isn't it?"

Luke was right about his mother's reaction. He continued to ask another question: "And just so we're on the same page, it's a small party, right? Just immediate family and some close friends?"

"Yes, Luke. I haven't forgotten *everything* we've talked about. Just family and friends are coming over."

Luke's graduation and birthday party couldn't have been more op-posite. The graduation party had literally no energy, as Luke was still mourning his grandfather's death. But the Legacy Letter he re-ceived that morning ignited a spark in his heart that he hadn't felt for months. Luke had a completely new outlook on life, and tonight's event was flying by. Looking at the clock on the wall and seeing that the party was half over now, Rebecca and Maggy disappeared into the kitchen and then reappeared two minutes later back in the living room. They were carrying a chocolate volcano birthday cake with 18 palm tree-shaped candles burning on top.

"Make a wish," said Maggy, clasping her hands together and hold-ing them under her chin with a huge smile on her face. "Then blow out your candles."

After considering his wish for a brief minute, Luke took in one very deep breath and then blew them all out. All except for one, that is. "My wish came true! I wanted to leave one candle burning for my one and only girlfriend. And there it is! And here *she* is!"

The room erupted with laughter and applause while Maggy was left blushing and grinning at Luke. As Rebecca and Maggy carried the cake to the kitchen to cut it into serving-size pieces, Ricardo asked Luke to step onto the front porch where he could speak with him privately. After a few minutes, they came back in because of all the guests clamoring for Luke to open his gifts. After about half an hour of steady unwrapping, Luke had opened them all.

"You guys are wonderful. I never expected all this great stuff, and I can use most of it every day at work."

Rebecca once again felt out of touch, because she hadn't known her own son was learning carpentry. Apparently, based on the gifts Luke received, everyone else did. While Luke was thanking everyone, he noticed Markus standing very close to Maggy. Both of them had their ears pressed as close as possible to her cell phone. It was quite ob-vious to Luke that another rather large smile was growing on her face as her eyes began to twinkle. Luke had learned through the years that a smile like this from Maggy meant something was about to happen. Just then, there was an unexpected knock at the front door. The guests continued talking among themselves as Luke went over to see who it was. Looking through the screen and seeing Maggy's parents standing there, he excitedly said, "Mr. and Mrs. Middlefield! What a great surprise! Come on in. Maggy, Markus, your dad and mom are here."

Leaning down close to his daughter's ear, Mr. Middlefield said, "I'm guessing by the way he reacted that he doesn't know what's coming?"

"Not a clue, Dad," whispered Maggy.

"And that's why I like this young man of yours. He has never expected any special treatment from me because of you," he whispered before straightening himself. "Before we step inside, Luke, would you mind coming out on the front porch? There's something I'd like to loan to you for as long as you are working for Middlefield Custom Homes."

Luke and the rest of the curious partygoers, who had now stopped their talking to listen to what was happening at the front door, all stood up in unison and walked out of the house and onto the front porch. In disbelief, they all saw a brand new half-ton, extended-cab pickup truck with the company name on the door.

"No way! I get to drive this truck?"

"Yes, you do, Luke. All I ask is that you keep it clean on the inside and washed on the outside. You'll be driving a mobile billboard, so make sure you represent us well out on the streets and highways."

As soon as Luke had calmed down from his initial excitement, a look of concern grew on his face. "But what will the other guys on the jobsites say when they see me driving this truck?"

"You just leave those guys to me, Luke," said Mr. Middlefield as he tossed him the keys to the truck and then handed him a company gas card.

"Your perfect Spanish skills have more than paid for this truck in dealing with our Latino subcontractors these past two summers. You've saved me all kinds of money, Luke, and I am grateful to you for that. You have gifts and talents that I can already see, and with my guidance, you're going to learn the home-building industry real fast!"

Luke didn't know what to do except shake Matthew's hand and repeatedly tell him thank you, and then give Maggy a big hug.

Once everyone was back in the house and only Matthew and Elizabeth were on the front porch, Elizabeth grabbed Matthew's arm, stopping him from going back in the house, and asked, "Matty, do you really like this young boy, or were you just playing with his ego? Because we barely know him."

Matthew smiled and said, "Of course I was playing with him. You're right, we don't know him. But that small voice I have heard talking to me my whole life told me to keep an eye on this one. He may be an insignificant boy today, but it won't be long before he becomes a man. I have a feeling he may end up being a painful rival in the future, so I'm going to keep a close eye on him."

"Well, that's a relief. And what about Maggy? She's been spending a lot of time with this boy these last two years. She can find a man much better than that boy."

"It's simple, Liz. When he is no longer useful or a danger to us, we'll find an excuse to ditch him. Then we'll find Maggy a young man more suited to her social standing."

Elizabeth responded, "The voice told you all that, Matthew? Aren't you concerned about anything that voice said?"

"No, Liz, I'm not. I've trusted him too long to start questioning him now."

Everyone was back in the house now, and Ricardo caught Luke's eye. Luke immediately knew what he had to do next.

"Hey, everyone, can I have your attention?" The room quieted down as Luke went on to announce, "An hour ago Ricardo asked me if he could have a few minutes to say something tonight. After hearing what his request was about, I said 'absolutely.' So go ahead, Ricardo, the floor is all yours."

"Thank you, Luke. And especially thank you for letting me take a few minutes of your birthday. First of all, I would like to acknowledge all the lifelong friends and family here tonight. I've only been hanging out with you all for about three years, more in this past year than in the first two, and I feel blessed to have gotten to know you all much better in that time. One particular member of this family I wish I had gotten to know better is, sadly, no longer with us. Gus was quite a man. Wouldn't you all agree?"

Immediately, somber and warm words of love and agreement were heard from everyone in the room.

"I had an opportunity about three months ago to spend some private time with Gus—what a guy, and what a storyteller! I also took that time to ask him a very important question. It was the same question I asked Luke on the front porch of this house less than an hour ago. The answer I received from both these men was the same."

Ricardo turned and looked directly at Rebecca. "Rebecca, I know it took you almost ten years to heal from the loss of Joshua, and another two years to allow me into that special place in your heart."

While Ricardo was speaking, Rebecca's hands had slowly risen together and were now covering her mouth as her eyes began to moisten; she had been totally caught off guard by what she now knew in her heart was coming. The room was dead silent, and everyone was looking at Ricardo and Rebecca. They were just as sure about what they were about to hear as Rebecca was.

"Rebecca, I know all too well the lonely path you have traveled these last 12 years without Joshua, because I walked alone on a similar path for 15 years since my Angelica died from breast cancer. So, I have a question I would like to ask you."

By this time, Ricardo had made his way over to where Rebecca was standing. "Rebecca, rather than each of us walking down our own paths separately, I propose that we no longer walk these paths alone . . . but that we hold each other's hand and walk down a new path together. I need to ask you the same question I was given permission to ask by Gus and Luke. Rebecca, would you do me the greatest of honor by becoming my wife? Would you marry me?"

He drew a ring out of his right pocket as he made his proposal to her. Ricardo had barely finished the proposal when he received a very enthusiastic hug and several kisses from Rebecca.

"I'm guessing that's a yes," Ricardo replied with a little chuckle.

Rebecca could only nod her head as she held onto Ricardo, tears streaming down both their cheeks as the ring was slipped onto her finger.

"Wow," exclaimed Luke amid clapping, cheering, and crying from the guests. "My mother is speechless. I hope somebody is recording this!"

It was almost two hours later, and all the guests had left except Ricardo and Maggy. Rebecca and Ricardo were sitting on the living room couch talking about what kind of wedding would suit them best, while Luke and Maggy were sitting in the kitchen finishing off one more piece of cake.

"Luke, I should probably start heading home. It's getting late," said Maggy just before sneaking in a quick goodbye kiss. As they walked into the living room and past the newly engaged couple, Maggy stopped so she could give them both a good night hug.

"Good night, Mr. Sanchez. Good night, Mrs. Sanchez. That has a nice ring to it, don't you think?"

Ricardo took Rebecca's hand and said, "I think it has a beautiful sound to it. But all good things must come to an end, and it's about time for me to head home as well. I'll come by and pick you up for church tomorrow morning at about 9:30, if that works for you."

Rebecca stepped closer to Ricardo and lovingly looked into his dark brown eyes. "Make it 9:00 so we can have some coffee before we leave."

"Okay, it's a date." They kissed good night before he stepped out the door.

"Mom," said Luke, "I'm going to walk Maggy to her car. I'll be right back after I pull my new truck off the front lawn and park it next to the garage."

"Okay, honey. While you're doing that, I'll be getting ready for bed. Lock the doors and turn off all the lights. Good night, Maggy." With a little nod to the two of them, she headed up the stairs ready to unwind and relax after an eventful evening.

By the time Rebecca was changed and in bed, she could hear Luke walking down the hall just before he gave her door a quick double-knock.

"Good night, Mom. Thanks again for the great party, and congrats on your engagement. It's not every day a son gets to see his mom receive a marriage proposal."

"Good night again, Luke. And yes, it was a wonderful birthday party. It's not every day that a son gets to watch his mom *accept* a marriage proposal," she replied with a smile.

At the sound of Luke's steps disappearing down the hall, Rebecca turned her cell phone on and opened her dad's Legacy Letter again.

"Okay, Dad. Let's see what else you have for me to hear." Rebecca began listening again from the beginning of the letter, not wanting to forget how it had started. She wasn't quite sure how to take what she heard next.

"Rebecca, of my three daughters, you are walking the closest to the Creator of this world, and I feel that it is required of me to share with you the true inspiration behind each and every one of these Legacy Letters I have recorded. You see, it turns out that I am not going to influence Luke through these letters. Rather, it will be *Jesus* revealing his desire for Luke's future *through* me in these letters. The following Bible verses mean more to me than a flawed legacy I might leave for my flawed grandson.

> . . . the time of my departure has come. I have fought the good fight, I have finished the race, I have kept the faith. Henceforth there is laid up for me the crown of righteousness, which the Lord, the righteous judge, will award to me on that day, and not only to me but also to all who have loved his appearing. (2 Timothy 4:6–8)

"You may have a hard time believing what I am about to tell you, but it's all true. When I first began to prepare the text for each one of the letters I was going to send Luke, I hit a wall—a very thick, high, and wide wall. I couldn't even connect two sentences that I felt would encourage Luke in any way. So, I did what had always helped me in the past. I began to pray and to read our God-inspired Bible.

That very same evening, after falling asleep, I had the most vivid dream in which Christ spoke to me, telling me that he would instruct me in what I should say to Luke in these letters. These dreams came to me twice a week. They were wonderful! I didn't want them to ever stop. I have read in the Bible of Jesus coming to his followers through dreams, but I never thought it would happen to me. He told me that he has a very special job for Luke to perform in this world. And receiving these letters would be crucial to Luke's development and preparation toward this mission.

But do not tell him about these dreams. I will do that myself when the time is right. Also, do not tell him how much money is in the bank for him. He is not ready to know that information yet. And finally, I have left Luke the house because, based on a conversation I recently had with Ricardo, you won't be needing it. For Luke's sake, keep your eyes on Maggy and her family. They appear to be nice people, but they do not follow Jesus. They follow the world. If she does not become a follower of Jesus, she could pull Luke in a direction Christ does not want him to go. So spend time talking with her as opportunities come along."

Gus went on to play a one-sided "remember when" game with Rebecca for five more minutes before ending his personal time with her.

"I'm all talked out for this letter, Sweetie. I love you, Rebecca, but I now have firsthand knowledge that Christ loves you much, much more than I ever could."

Chapter 2

Your Guiding Star

During the summer of Luke's rookie year in his trade, he had learned what it meant to be a professional carpenter, as well as what it meant to work a full-time, manual labor job. Over this first summer, he experienced wood slivers, blood blisters, sore muscles, long workweeks, and the need for more sleep every night. He considered these minor afflictions to be a kind of "purple heart" for carpenters rather than a discouragement to his chosen occupation. He saw it as a sign of maturing. He loved his job, but it was nothing like being the one who actually built the house.

Pulling into their driveway and coming to a stop in front of the overhead garage door where his grandpa's truck was stored, Luke saw Ricardo's Jeep Grand Cherokee parked off to the side. It was only then that Luke remembered Ricardo was supposed to be coming over tonight for dinner.

"Hi, Mom! Hi, Ricardo!" Luke said as he walked through the side entrance of the house and into the kitchen. "Ricardo, you're cooking too?" Luke asked, surprised after seeing Ricardo standing in front of the island cabinet with his sleeves rolled up to his elbows and his hands deep in a mixing bowl full of something that looked somewhat edible.

"I sure am! Single dads have to prepare meals for their children and eat too, you know. I hope you like my recipe for hot tamales, because that's half the meal."

Luke heard the words come out of Ricardo's mouth about cooking for his girls, but actually seeing him do it was, well, inspiring. It made him want to do more cooking himself.

"I love tamales, Ricardo! So if you're preparing half the meal, what's Mom making for the other half?"

"How does bratwursts on the grill, homemade cornbread, and coleslaw sound?" asked Rebecca.

"It sounds great, and boy am I hungry! Working ten-hour days really builds up an appetite."

Rebecca tried to ask a quick question as Luke bolted past her and up the stairs. "Luke, honey, how long will you be working all these ten-hour days?"

"I can't hear you, Mom," Luke shouted as he disappeared into his bedroom, "but I'll be down in a few minutes after I take a shower and clean up." His voice trailed off as he got further away.

"At least he has good personal hygiene," said Rebecca with a girlish grin as she turned toward Ricardo.

An hour later, sitting on the back patio under the picnic table umbrella, Luke was finishing off his third tamale. "Ricardo, these are amazing. They're the best tamales I've ever eaten! Is this your own recipe, or did someone give it to you and teach you how to make them?"

Ricardo took a minute to ponder that question as he leaned back on his patio chair and considered how he would answer it. In what was becoming typical Ricardo fashion, he ran his fingers through his full head of well-groomed, jet black hair while thinking before responding.

"All I can say is that behind every good cook is a wonderful and patient mother. I hope you will agree with me and say the same about your own mom someday. But in my case, Luke, I had a loving step-grandma who loved me as if I were her own blood. Now, my mother was certainly a good cook, but it was my grandmother who refined my cooking skills."

In between bites, Luke asked Ricardo, "Is that where you also got your patience? From your grandma, that is? You're always so calm. Nothing seems to rattle you. And is that why you also became a mental health therapist?"

Ricardo was amazed at the inquisitive questions Luke was coming up with. *He must really want to get to know his future stepdad*, he thought to himself.

"No, it's not. Although I'm sure it helps me with my clients. I actually believe God gave it to me, and then he helped me to refine this gift through the years so I might be able to help others."

"Ricardo," said Rebecca, loving to watch the two most important men in her life getting along so well, "now that the topic has been brought up, why don't you tell Luke why you decided to become a marriage and family therapist."

Ricardo hesitated, rubbing his chin before looking at Luke. "It's totally up to you, Luke. Do you feel like hearing a short personal story?"

"Sure, I'd love to hear more about your life, and the stories that go with it sound fun too. You have to remember, Ricardo, I need some stories to tell my friends. A guy has to have something to brag about to his buddies when it comes to his dad. The more stories you tell me, the more I can brag!"

"What a nice thing to say, Luke. Thank you, although I don't know how much bragging you can do about me helping someone overcome a bi-polar or multi-personality disorder."

At hearing that description of what Ricardo did for a living, Luke had a look of absolute bewilderment on his face. Riccardo was right: Luke wouldn't be doing much bragging about his future dad's job. Riccardo continued, "Anyway, moving on to my childhood story." He leaned back into his chair again, considering all the possible starting points of his story, before mumbling to himself and trailing off into his own personal thoughts. He was trying to decide how to begin telling his life's adventure without overwhelming Luke. He needed to decide how much he should share at the moment and how much he should reveal as they got to know each other better. "I can't remember how much I've told you, Luke, so you'll have to remind me. Did I ever tell you that my heritage is Colombian and that I was adopted?"

"Yeah, I knew those things, but that's all I know about your childhood. I mean, I know what kind of man you are today, and that's what matters most to me. So your past didn't really come to mind when I gave my blessing for you to marry my mom."

"Well, thank you, Luke. But to know why I went into family therapy, we will have to go back to my youth and my own personal family history . . . and family tragedy."

This time it was Luke's turn to lean back in his deck chair while finishing off a rather spicy brat covered with spicy mustard. He said, in between bites, "Okay, I'm ready to hear the story, if you're ready to tell it."

"Alright, Luke, you asked for it," said Ricardo, pausing to glance over at Rebecca, who gave him an encouraging smile.

"First of all, I only have one blood-related sibling. An older sister by 13 years who was already married before I was brought to the orphanage that took care of me during that time in my life. And after almost 50 years, I found out—this was three years ago—that this sister of mine still lives in the same town where I was born in Colombia. But how we found each other is a story for another day. So let's get back to my early life and how I got to America."

Rebecca smiled as she watched Ricardo tell Luke the story of his early life. She couldn't think of a better way for her two men to begin to bond as father and son.

"One day when I was five, and without any notice, my parents woke me early one morning and told me I would be spending a few days with my sister and her family. I remember being confused but excited, and it wasn't until later that I realized it was a complete lie. I was quite young, only five years old, so I don't remember too many details. One thing I do remember was wondering why my mom was crying. Everything was sort of rushed, and I just remember being excited to be sleeping over at my sister's house.

"I thought it was going to be a fun adventure, so I got changed into my visiting clothes while my mom packed all my other clothes into a paper bag. At that time, I didn't realize that she was packing everything I had into that bag and that I was actually going to be moving. I didn't have many belongings, so the bag wasn't full or heavy at all. I happily followed my parents through the streets while swinging that paper bag I was holding in my hand. I was off in my own little world while we walked, totally unaware of how my dad brutally dragged my mom as we walked through those streets, forcing her to follow him. I remember my dad banged on my sister's front door, yelling for her to hurry up. When she opened the door, all my dad did was yell at her and everybody there: 'Your brother is staying with you from now on.' He didn't even wait for a response from my sister. He just walked away, dragging my mother by the wrist down the street behind him. He didn't even hug me or say goodbye. He didn't even allow me to say goodbye to my mom. My mom didn't want to leave me, and I tried to run after them. My dad got so angry he slapped me—it was the first time he had ever done that. Of course, by then I was crying, so I can't remember if anything else was said. By his actions that morning, it was pretty obvious that he didn't care one bit about what she wanted or what she was saying, or what anyone thought about what he was doing. He just turned away again and started walking down the street while forcing my mother to leave with him. I never saw my mother again, and honestly, Luke, I don't even want to imagine what may have happened to her."

"Ricardo, that's horrible. *Really* horrible," said Luke as he put his food back on his plate, unable to eat after hearing this part of the story. "So what happened to you after your dad deserted you? How did you get to America?"

At this point in the story, eating food was the last thing on his mind. He was listening to a 50-year-old traumatic event in from Ricardo's past. Luke was completely entranced with what he was hearing. He was leaning forward onto the front edge of his deck chair, desperately wanting to know what happened next while also feeling upset at how Ricardo had been treated as a child.

"Well, I spent the next year being shuffled from one extended family member to another, but no one had the room or money that was needed to feed and clothe me. I eventually ended up in an orphanage not too far from my sister's house, which allowed her to see me once a week. That happened when I was six years old. A year later, I was adopted by a wonderful family from Dallas. My adopted mother was also Colombian, and my dad was Caucasian. By this time in their marriage, they were desperately hoping for a son and loved the idea of adoption in order to make their hopes a 100% reality. It turned out that my adopted parents already had four daughters, and they wanted to make sure their next child was a boy. So after a year in this new home of mine, where I had begun to make friends with the staff at the orphanage and with the other kids, I was shocked by more life-changing news. The workers at the orphanage told me that I was being adopted by the nice man and woman who had been spending time with me over the last two weeks."

Ricardo stopped his story for a minute, quietly considering his thoughts as a six-year-old and trying to decide how best to describe what happened next. "Luke, it may be hard to put yourself in my place, because there are times I'm amazed at my younger self and how I was able to handle everything that was happening. I remember being confused and asking what the word "adoption" meant. Not only did I not know what it meant to be adopted, I didn't even know I was an orphan, or what an orphan was. The workers had to explain what was about to happen to me. They told me there was a family that wanted me to live with them forever. Only this time, my new family would love me and never hit me or tell me to leave. There would be no more moving for me. Best of all, they told me I would have a bedroom all to myself."

Luke was still sitting quietly when Ricardo took a breath and stopped talking. Seeing that Luke was deep in thought and had nothing to say or ask, he continued his story.

"My adoptive father turned out to be a therapist, so I happily followed in his footsteps. Also, as a young man, I emotionally needed to understand why my father would abandon me and why my mother didn't fight harder to save me and get away from my abusive father. What better way than studying the human psyche to find the answers to my questions. During my years at Dallas State University, I majored in psychology and became a therapist, just like my dad. An added blessing to this quest of mine was finding my extended birth family. There's a lot more to the story, including the gift of having a Christ-following family to grow up in, but that's the short version. You'll have plenty of time to meet some of my extended family and learn more about this story, because we're flying several of them up from Colombia for the wedding."

Luke just sat there in amazement at what Ricardo had to endure at such an early age; he couldn't believe what Ricardo had turned out to be in light of the circumstances. Luke then asked a somewhat related question.

"I have a question for the both of you. If you have shared this story with my mom, you must have shared lots of others as well. And my mom must have told you lots of stories about her life too. So, just out of curiosity, why are you and Mom going to premarital counseling classes? You guys have both been married before. You're a therapist, Ricardo, and Mom used to be a guidance counselor at the high school. Neither of you seem to have any problems that you need to talk about, so aren't you good to go?"

Luke was being just a little sly in asking that question, because he was actually thinking about Maggy and himself and whether they would need to go to premarital counseling classes—something he really didn't want to do when that time came.

The eyes of Ricardo and Rebecca met for only an instant, but that was enough to let both of them know that they were thinking the same thing. *He may be mature for his age, but he still has so much to learn and to experience for himself.* Breaking the silence, Rebecca looked at Ricardo and said, "I'll take this one, honey," as she turned in her chair towards Luke. "Before I answer that question, Luke, I have several questions of my own I'd like to ask you. And by the time you answer my questions, you'll have the answer to your question."

Luke smiled at this challenge and then conceded. "Okay, Mom, go ahead. Ask away."

Rebecca, seeing a look of youthful bravado on her son's face, began asking questions that might humble this recent high school graduate. "First of all, and to the best of your knowledge, have Ricardo and I been married to each other before?"

"No, of course not."

"So, then, what you're saying is that we really only know each other as two single people."

"Yeah, I guess that's true," Luke admitted, not sure where his mom was going with this.

"Have we both been married to another person, and has that person died?"

"Well, yeah, of course."

"So, it's safe to say that we both have some personal baggage, trauma, and heartbreak we're going to carry into this marriage."

"I . . . I guess so. I never thought of that before, Mom."

"And do we both have children of our own that the other will have to get to know?"

"Sure, I suppose."

"Come on, Luke," said his mom. "Don't you think it's worth the time to really know what has made a person who they are before you marry them? Don't you think it's a good idea to know as much as possible about the person you're going to promise to spend the rest of your life with before saying 'I do?'"

"Yeah, okay, you guys are right. It's probably good to have some premarital counseling sessions before getting married." After listening to his mom's words, Luke thought the premarital counseling idea wasn't too bad after all.

"Now that you've brought up the subject of knowing the person you are dating, and might want to marry," said Rebecca, "can we take a few minutes and talk about you and Maggy? You know, that girl you have been dating for two and a half years."

Luke's eyes lit up at the mention of Maggy. "Sure, I love talking about Maggy! She's great, isn't she, Mom?" Rebecca could see in Luke's face that he was truly smitten with her, but her father's warning concerning Maggy and her family was ringing in her ears.

Before she could ask a question about Maggy, Luke piped in and said, "Do you mind if I go back to eating my brat while we talk? I'm hungry again now that Ricardo is finished telling his story, and the best part is that everything ended happily ever after. Also, Mom, how many brats are left? I'd like to take a couple to work with me tomorrow for lunch, if that's okay."

"You're working on Saturday again? What about Sunday? Will you be missing church?"

"Mom, it's just this time of year. Mr. Middlefield says that it's the busy season and that we have to work while the work is here." Luke said this with a shrug of his shoulders, not overly concerned with working weekends at this point in his life. "It'll slow down soon, Mom. I don't think it's something to worry about."

Rebecca hesitated a moment before saying, "I'm not sure if I like the kind of influence that Matthew Middlefield is having on you, Luke. And what does Maggy say about working all these extra hours?"

"She grew up with her dad and mom working the weekends. They all say it makes the vacations that much more enjoyable."

Rebecca could see that Luke was being gently persuaded and conditioned to put work and money first in his life. She needed to encourage him not to neglect his calling as a follower of Jesus, which needed to come first in his life.

"Luke, going to church is partly about creating friendships with other believers who attend the church, but it's *mostly* about spending time worshiping our God together with those friends. It is this Creator-God who helps us through the days of our lives in this world.

Please don't minimize the greatness of our Creator for the sake of the creation of a few homes and a fancy vacation!"

"Mom, I know all that stuff! Grandpa and I were always talking about God and heaven, and I don't think God will be upset with me just because I miss a couple of Sundays."

Just then they heard a car pull into the driveway and a car door shut. Then came the sound of the screen door in the kitchen creaking open and then slamming shut. This familiar sound was followed by the sweet-sounding voice of Miss Maggy Middlefield calling out, "Hey, where is everybody?"

"We're on the back patio, Maggy, eating dinner," said Luke.

"Hi everyone," said Maggy as she bounced out the patio door, her curly blonde hair flowing in the air behind her, and her stunning blue eyes focused directly on Luke. "Luke, you didn't tell me we were eating here tonight or else I would have had our cook make a dessert for us."

"I forgot about it myself, Mags. It's okay, isn't it? We'll still make the movie on time, won't we?"

Luke just got the look, and he knew what that look was saying: *Come on, Luke. What happened to our "make a plan, work a plan" agreement. Now we have to make changes to our plans, and you know how I don't like remaking plans.* But out loud she said, "Don't worry, Luke, I'll call Markus right now and let him know that the plans have changed. I'll tell him that he and his date can meet us at the theater instead of the chicken hut."

As Maggy wandered around the back yard talking to her twin brother, Markus, on the phone, with her arms gesturing and her voice rising and falling, Rebecca looked at Luke. Leaning just a little closer to him, she said, "Luke, we wanted to talk with you tonight about something very important related to our wedding. It's only a month away now, and we're running out of time. Why didn't you tell us you were going out tonight?"

"I'm sorry, Mom. I forgot. Can we talk about it tomorrow after I get home? I should have a short day at work. Will that be okay?"

"Sure, honey. That'll be fine."

Maggy had finished her talk with Markus and was sitting at the table now, eating a tamale Rebecca had served up for her while she was on the phone.

"Oh my goodness, Mrs. Cruz! Where did you learn to make these tamales? They're fantastic! I really mean it. You could sell these at the grocery store and I'd buy them! And I'd tell my friends to buy them too."

There was a moment of silence, and then everyone burst out laughing—everyone except for Maggy.

"What's so funny? Really, what's so funny? What did I say? Don't tell me: the tamales are already store-bought, right?"

That last statement brought on another round of laughter, after which Luke explained to Maggy where the tamales came from and who had prepared them.

The next day, at about two in the afternoon, Rebecca heard Luke's truck pulling into the driveway, and a minute later the door slammed shut.

"Hey, Mom!" said Luke as he walked into the kitchen through the rear entrance. "I'm home, and I didn't forget about the wedding conversation you wanted to have with me." He was wearing a pair of old work jeans that had stains and holes in them. He was carrying his lunchbox, and after emptying it, he set it on the floor by the door and made his way through the kitchen. He was trying to decide if he should get changed or talk with his mom first.

Rebecca had plenty of details to go over for the wedding as she waited in the living room for Luke to return home. The most important of these tasks was the talk she needed to have with him.

"Luke Cruz! If this is a half-day at work, I'd like you to tell me what a full day looks like!"

As soon as Rebecca said those words, she realized how unfair they were. Luke was beginning his working career and was at the bottom of the seniority ladder. He had to work when he was told to work.

"On second thought, Luke, forget what I just said. I'm glad to see you home. We can now have that talk."

Rebecca had been talking to Luke this whole time from the living room, but unknown to her, he had returned to the kitchen to get a leftover tamale out of the refrigerator. He hadn't heard a single word of complaint she had uttered. When he walked into the living room, chewing and swallowing, he said through a mouthful of food, "These tamales are great, even when they're cold. Ricardo's grandma must have been a great cook." With food still in his mouth, Luke asked, "Did you say something to me when I was in the kitchen digging through the refrigerator? If you did, I didn't hear a word you said."

"No, Luke, I didn't say anything important."

Looking at Luke as he came into the living room, her first thought was how glad she was that he wasn't upset at what he didn't hear her say. Then she was about to tell him not to talk with his mouth full, but she stopped mid-breath when she saw how clean he was. "How come you're not sweaty and dirty, Luke? Did you get changed somewhere else on the way home, or did you not even go into work?" She asked this question half joking and half serious, still wanting to know what he had done that day for work.

"I was just as surprised as you are right now at what I did for work today, but it was great!" said Luke as he sat down on his grandpa's chair.

"Well, tell me then. What did you do all day that kept you so clean? And don't spill any food on your grandfather's chair while you're eating."

"It was the strangest thing, Mom. When I showed up at the jobsite this morning, Markus was waiting for me and told me to hop into his truck after I had parked and locked mine. We drove to another basement homesite that had just been backfilled around the foundation. Mr. Middlefield was there walking around the foundation waiting for me with blueprints to the house in hand. Markus simply said, 'He's all yours, Dad,' and then he drove away."

"Mr. Middlefield told me that there would be a change in my responsibilities starting this morning and that this would be a different kind of workday. He told me I would learn that some people worked with their hands, some worked with their minds, but very few worked with both. Then he told me that in the year to come, he would find out which one I was. There was also a load of lumber sitting next to the foundation we had walked around. We spent the rest of the morning and afternoon driving from jobsite to jobsite, each of them being at different stages of completion. He showed me how to read those blueprints, how to set a construction schedule, and why it's important to understand the whole building process and not just one aspect of it. And after picking up my truck, I followed him to the office where we finished the day talking with one of his architects. They both told me to be aware of the basics of design and beauty, and we talked about how the design needs to be buildable. Every house also needs to be a comfortable space to live in while still meeting the needs of the family living in it. He also told me that I could practice designing new homes or remodels on their software whenever I wanted."

"It sounds like you had a wonderful morning, Luke. And it also seems as though you have found not just a job, but a vocation you really like." Rebecca was a little melancholy, realizing that she had missed her opportunity to help her son find his way to this exciting start to his life.

"Yeah, Mom, I really do like what I'm doing and learning. And when Mr. Middlefield asked me what kind of house I liked to work on most, he was surprised when I told him that I enjoyed working on a remodel much more than a new home. When he asked me why, I told him there was something special about watching a worn-down house come back to life again. The owners of those homes always seem to be more excited at seeing their home transformed from an old look to a new one as compared to the people building a new one. Up to that point, they could only dream of what their old home could become, but we have the privilege of making their dream come true for them. Mr. Middlefield thought for a minute and then said, 'That's a good way to look at that kind of construction, Luke. I like it.' It was a great day, Mom. I really love building, and Matthew told me that he sees great potential in me."

"First of all, I agree with Matthew Middlefield. I have always told you that you have great potential, and I'm glad that he has seen that aspect of your godly giftedness as well."

Luke sat quietly thinking about what his mother had just said. He was trying to determine whether he should share what seemed to be the intermingling of Matthew's opinion of his potential with the story of Matthew's own potential as a young man, including how he got his start in the home-building business.

"Hey, Mom, have you ever heard how Matthew Middlefield got his start?"

Looking at Luke, a little perplexed at why he would ask her such an off-the-cuff question, she answered, "No, Luke, I have no idea."

"Honestly, Mom, I'm not sure why he told me the story about how he got his start . . . unless, like you said, he sees potential in me and wants to keep me around. He asked me into his office, and here's what he told me. After college, he got his start working for a home builder who he claims taught him more about building and business than college ever did, and I'm guessing he plans to do the same for me, except that I'm not going to spend any time in college. Then he told me how much he liked this man and the people he was working with, just like my situation. Apparently, after working for this builder for three years, he quit and went out on his own. I think he was trying to subtly warn me not to do that to him.

"Then he told me about the events that brought him to the point of self-employment. The work that gave him his start actually came to him as a complete surprise. Up to that point in his life, he wasn't even looking to go out on his own. He told me it all started when he received a cold call from a friend of a friend of a friend. This friend asked if he was interested in building three new homes, one for himself and two more for two of his business associates, and that's all it took for him to get his start. Matthew said he was simply in the right place at the right time, and he had the right skills to say yes to the opportunity to go out on his own. He also told me that through this experience, he learned how to make difficult decisions, and this was the first of many choices of this type that he would make over the years. He talked more about this first decision to leave his current employer. He learned that once a decision was made, there was no looking back, no matter how difficult or hurtful the decision was for everyone involved. Matthew told me that this builder saw him as a son and not just an employee, and no matter what Matthew said to him, this builder took his leaving very personally. This apparent betrayal was the first of many difficult decisions Matthew had to make in his life.

Luke took a moment to sip his coffee and allow this information to sink in. His mom had been pretty quiet since he started talking, only occasionally sipping her coffee while seemingly deep in thought about something.

"He looked me square in the eyes and said, 'Your life will be filled with many such difficult decisions and betrayals,' and he said I should be prepared to make those decisions, no matter how difficult they might be or who may be against me. He said I should have no regrets. I guess he always wondered how things would have worked out for him if he had been given that builder's blessing. Of course, he finished this story by telling me to listen to his advice and to stay and work for him, no matter what I might want to do in the future."

Meanwhile, unknown to Luke, Matthew was having a rather frank conversation with the in-house architect, the one Matthew and Luke had met with an hour earlier.

"Matthew, why are you spending so much time with a kid who doesn't know anything about the building business? It seems like a waste of your time and my time."

Matthew just put on the smile that said, "Don't worry, everything is under control." Then he said, "Art, you know that friend of mine I told you about years ago? You know, the one I go to for counsel once in a while?"

Without thinking about this friend a second time, Art said, "Yeah, I remember. I never met him, but I know you talk with him all the time. What about him?"

"Well, it turns out that my friend has a friend who is familiar with Mr. Luke Cruz, and he feels that this young man will either implode under the pressure of learning this trade and the business, or one day he will be such a force in this town that it may be to our advantage to have him on our side. Pretty amazing, isn't it?"

Art stood there, taken aback. "What else do you have planned for this young carpenter?"

"Well, Art, to determine his potential, I'm going to send him and my son, Markus, to our local Project Management School. It's the same one I went to 25 years ago. Once we see how he performs there, we'll take the next step."

"And what will that next step be?" asked Art curiously.

"Come on, Art," said Matthew with another of his classic smiles, "you know me better than that. I can't tell you everything. It wouldn't be as much fun, now would it?"

Wow, it sounds like you've had quite a morning already, but I think we need to talk about what Matthew Middlefield taught you today, because I'm not sure if I agree with it completely. But Luke, on a different note, I have to admit that I'm a little embarrassed at what I want to talk with you about. Compared to the conversation you already had today, it makes what I want to ask you seem kind of small in comparison."

"What is it, Mom? Just tell me what you want to talk about, because whatever is on your mind is way more important than anything Matthew Middlefield has to say."

"I did want Ricardo here with me when I asked you this, but he is with one of his girls and her family this weekend. And, of course, your grandpa, my dear old dad, is no longer here to take on this responsibility."

A sudden feeling of fear came over Luke as he considered what his mom might be talking about.

"You're it, Luke. You're the only man in my life I would ask this question of, so here it is."

By this time in their conversation, Luke's emotions were all over the board. He was unable to guess if something good or something bad was about to be revealed to him, so he just sat there and listened.

Rebecca drew in a deep breath, looked Luke directly in his eyes, and asked, "I'd like to know if you would be willing to walk me down the aisle and give me away to Ricardo at our wedding?"

Luke froze for several moments as he processed this request, this honor his mother had just bestowed on him. Rebecca, seeing Luke's physical response, quietly thought about these last few years. She had watched her little boy grow into a young man, and she had experienced all the emotions that went along with those changes. She had only seen her son cry twice as an adult. The first time was at his grandpa's bedside when he saw him breathe in one last time, his chest rising and then falling as he audibly exhaled his last breath. The second time was at his grandpa's funeral when the military honor guard gave him an 18-gun salute; the crack of those six rifles firing three times each was simply overwhelming. Upon hearing his mother's request, and knowing this honor was usually given to the father of the bride,

Luke got up out of that old chair, and while crossing the room, cried unashamedly in front of her for the third time as a grown man. Luke gave his mother a hug and, through a cracking voice, said, "Of course I will, Mom. Just let anyone try and stop me."

A few minutes later, after they had both dried the tears from their faces, Rebecca changed the topic of conversation. "You know, Luke, for as long as I can remember, this room has always been the coffee-and-conversation center of this house."

She made this observation since they had, once again, both settled into their respective chairs, each holding a hot cup of coffee, ready for more conversation.

"I've had thousands of conversations in this room, conversations with everyone who has held a special place in my heart, and that includes your dad. This is also where we told Grandma and Grandpa that we were pregnant with you. And now I can add this conversation to that list. But Luke, there's one person that I haven't really had a heart-to-heart conversation with in this room, and that's Maggy. Why is that, Luke? I'm getting the feeling you don't want me to get to know her."

"Don't say that, Mom. You know that's not true. But to answer your question, I don't know if there's one particular reason why you haven't spent much time with Maggy. I've been pretty busy these last two years, just like you. So don't forget all the time you spent with Ricardo, which was okay with me. Now, as for how I spent my time, it was school, then working the summers with Middlefield Homes; then it was Grandpa getting sick and the funeral, followed by both of us getting used to Grandpa not being here; and now it's work and your wedding. I guess we're all pretty busy. Sit-down conversations aren't high on our priority list."

"I suppose you're right, Luke." Thinking quickly, she said, "We have time right now, sweetie, so why don't you tell me something about her that I don't know."

"Okay, *um*, did you know she was president of our student body our senior year, and also president of the Young Entrepreneur Club our junior and senior years? Is that the kind of stuff you're talking about?"

"Sure, Luke, that's part of getting to know her. But what I really want to know is if she is a true follower of Jesus?"

"Mom, isn't that a bit of a judgmental question for you to ask?"

"Luke, that's no more of a judgmental request than if I asked if you were a Ford, Chevy, or Dodge man. Or if I asked whether you're a Republican, Democrat, or an Independent. Or is it only judgmental if it has to do with Christianity? And where did that kind of reaction come from anyway?"

Luke was feeling verbally cornered, so he tried to give his mother a non-answer: "She's a Christian, okay. She says she's a Christian."

"Luke, honey, you know that's not what I asked you. I asked if she is a follower of Jesus."

"She says she's a Christian, but I don't think she is a true follower. *There*—are you happy that I said it?"

Rebecca looked at Luke's saddened face, knowing that she had just made him acknowledge that his girlfriend may not have Jesus in her heart.

"Why would I be happy about that answer? It actually makes me sad. I want her and her whole family to be true followers of Jesus, for their eternal sake more than anything."

"I'm sorry, Mom. That wasn't fair to say to you. It's just that I'm pretty sure that Maggy is the girl I want to marry, and I want her and me to agree on everything in our lives, especially when it comes to Jesus."

Rebecca perked up at hearing what had just come out of Luke's mouth. "Well, Luke, that's the first time I've heard the "marriage" word spoken out loud by you. And if she's going to be the lifelong partner that Jesus has set aside for you, then both of you believing in the Creator of all will be a pretty important part of your marriage."

"No offense, Mom, but I wish Grandpa was here to talk with. He always had a way of making complicated things easier to understand, and talking about whether Maggy is a Christian is kind of complicated."

"No offense taken, Luke. But I do need to tell you something he told me in that first letter he sent me."

"And what would that be, Mom?" Luke asked with a little apprehension.

"First of all, he feels you will need him more than you realize when it comes to Maggy and her faith, or lack of faith, in Jesus. Then your grandpa told me that God has something very important to prepare you for. I'm assuming he will tell you more on the first day of September, when you get your next letter."

"That's fantastic news, Mom! That's only two and a half weeks from now. I can't wait to tell Maggy."

The next two weeks went by painfully slow as Luke waited for his second Legacy Letter to arrive. Because of this self-induced pain, Luke almost asked his mom not to tell him any more secrets or exciting news that involved him or his grandpa; ultimately, though, he decided not to take away any joy she might gain from sharing such news. The two things that made the wait more tolerable were spending the non-working hours with Maggy and the extra attention he was receiving from Matthew Middlefield. Luke wasn't sure why, but it seemed Mr. Middlefield was preparing him for something; considering the talk they had several weeks back, he assumed Matthew wanted to give him every reason he could to never leave Middlefield Homes. This left Luke wondering why that would be. He was even having his architects spend time during regular office hours training him to use the CAD software, and Maggy was teaching him about how the office side of the business worked. Still, if it had anything to do with construction, Luke was in.

The busier he got at work, the faster the days went by, and it was now Monday evening, August 31. Luke was trying to decide if he would stay up until midnight and watch for his grandpa's letter or wait until the next morning when he woke up. He decided to go to bed early that night and set his alarm for the morning an hour earlier than normal. And if he woke up after falling asleep and it was after midnight, he would listen to the letter at that time.

It turned out that Luke was more tired than he realized, for he had woken up to the sound of wind chimes in his ears. It was his cell phone alarm that was calling to him. He knew that Monday had been a tiring day at work, but he didn't think setting trusses all day would make him tired enough to sleep through the night. He really didn't care. It was time to see if Grandpa had sent him another letter.

When Luke first opened his email, there was no Legacy Letter in his inbox. Confused, he tapped the refresh button. The screen flickered and up popped a letter from Grandpa. *Yes!* After answering those same questions, Luke clicked on the LL button.

"Hi, buddy. I hope you and your mom are getting used to not having me around the house, and I hope these letters are helping. Speaking of these letters, I suppose your mom told you about my dreams and that our Jesus has something special planned for your life; I can only assume that you won't be surprised by what I'm going to tell you in all the letters to come. That girl of mine has never been able to keep a secret, especially a happy one. So, how are you doing, Luke?"

Luke paused the letter and said, "I'm doing okay, Grandpa. I miss you, but I'm doing okay. And, yes, Mom told me."

Luke started the letter again.

"I've got a lot to talk about, so I had better get going. I have to admit, it is somewhat difficult having these one-way conversations, but I pray to our Jesus for help in what I should say before I begin to talk to you, as well as what I should say all the way through each letter."

Just then, his cell phone rang. "Well, I'll be. I thought I turned that pesky thing off."

Gus dug into his pocket while his Legacy Letter continued recording everything in this scene between him and this mystery caller. After finally retrieving his cell phone, he said, "Huh, looks like it's your mom calling. It must be important for her to interrupt my recording time. At least, I think she knows I'm recording. Excuse me, Luke, while I answer it, if I can."

Luke couldn't help but smile and chuckle to himself. This was so typical of his grandpa, stopping what he was doing to help take care of another person's problem. It was so him. What a wonderful reminder of who his grandpa was.

"Hi, Rebecca. I can't talk right now. I'm right in the middle of recording a letter for Luke.'"

Rebecca thought her father was just confused, especially when he asked her what she needed even after telling her what he was doing—and all this while apparently recording their entire conversation.

"What do you need?" asked Gus a second time. He then respond-ed to Rebecca's follow-up question: "No, I'm not kidding. I'm record-ing right now. What do you need?'"

There was about a ten-second pause, and then Gus said, "'Sure, I know exactly where it is. It's in my bedroom. I'll get it for you when I'm finished with this letter. Bye, honey." Women, you can't live with-out them. Actually, now that I think about it again, us guys really *can't* live without them, huh. That's actually a nice transition into what I have on my mind today. What do you say we talk about Maggy?"

Just then, Gus had another thought: "Oh, but just one more thing, Luke."

Luke grunted out loud at having to wait again to hear what his grandpa thought about Maggy. He looked at his watch to see how late it was getting.

"In case I forget that your mom called, I want to tell you what she needed. It's not a big deal. I might forget to get back to her about her request. All she wanted was to know where I keep the necklace your dad bought your grandma the day they died. If you go to my dresser and open the middle drawer of the middle row and take the socks out of it, you will find that it has a false bottom. Of course, it's not an *obvious* false bottom. So, what you will have to do is put your fin-gers against the inside front of the drawer, and then slide them to the bottom front left-side corner. After that, you will need to firmly push your fingers down and to the right of the center of the drawer, moving a skinny piece of wood that acts as a key latch. Like magic, the bottom of the drawer will swing up and you'll find Grandma's necklace there, along with some other keepsakes and important paperwork.

"Now that I think of it, I should see what's in that false-bottom drawer again, in case there's something important you need to know about. My memory is not what it used to be, Luke, so maybe we should look at those things together so I can tell you what they mean. I guess I never told anyone about that old dresser. Grandma and I just used it as a secret safe and never thought much of it. We purchased it with our other pieces of bedroom furniture at an estate sale five years be-fore she died. We never really checked for other compartments after we accidently found that one. It always made me wonder what other secrets that old furniture might be hiding. Maybe that's something you can look into for me, Luke," his grandpa said with a twinkle in his eyes.

His grandpa sat there, motionless, considering the possibilities, when Luke hit the pause button and thought to himself, *I guess I can wait to hear about Maggy for a couple more minutes.* He jumped out of his chair and bolted to his grandpa's bedroom and did exactly what he was told to do with the drawer. The bottom swung up, and there it was—Grandma's necklace. He held the box in his hand for a brief moment before opening it. As he took it out of the box, he looked at it, sadly remembering that terrible day. When he was done, he carefully put it back while whispering, "I love you, Dad. I love you, Grandma. And I love you, Grandpa." Along with the necklace were several items Luke had never seen before. It was mostly jewelry, a silver dollar dated 1921, and some envelopes with some documents in them. He looked at all the other neat things in the hidden compartment for several minutes before closing the false-bottom, putting the socks back, and returning to his letter.

Luke said to himself, *I'll show Mom the drawer when I get home tonight. I wonder what other surprises you're going to have for me, Grandpa?* Then he started the letter again.

"Now, about your Maggy. I've seen the way both of you look at each other, and I've watched the way you talk to and treat each other. I'm guessing just thinking about her makes your toes curl up in your shoes."

Luke took a quick breath as he listened to his grandpa talking about Maggy, and he realized his toes were even now curled up just thinking about her. He had never noticed that before.

"Don't worry about your toes, Luke. Mine did the same thing the first time I saw your grandma. I still remember her sandy brown hair and beautiful blue eyes, and she had quite a nice figure. She was wearing a butter cream yellow dress with white ribbons in her hair the first time I saw her. I'll never forget that image. You know something, now that I think about it, I never did ask if the same thing happened to her when she first saw me. That might be a fun topic of conversation for you and Maggy.

"Before I go on with more of my thoughts, I'd like to read to you some verses from the Bible about the type of woman God wants for you in your life as a wife. That is, if indeed your friendship with Maggy is headed where I think it is heading.

> Likewise, wives, be subject to your own husbands, so that even if some do not obey the word, they may be won without a word by the conduct of their wives, when they see your respectful and pure conduct. Do not let your adorning be external—the braiding of hair and the putting on of gold jewelry, or the clothing you wear—but let your adorning be the hidden person of the heart with the imperishable beauty of a gentle and quiet spirit, which in God's sight is very precious. (1 Peter 3:1-4)

> "Then, when it comes to husbands, Luke, God says, . . . live with your wives in an understanding way, showing honor to the woman as the weaker vessel, since they are heirs with you of the grace of life, so that your prayers may not be hindered. (1 Peter 3:7)

"There is so much more to write to you, Luke, concerning dating, courting, engagement, and marriage. Where do I start, and where do I stop? Many things can't be told to you because, quite simply, they need to be learned through living. And that's a perfect place to start. God made women and gave them to us men as a gift, the most precious gift ever, except for his Son, of course. Wives are such a precious gift that we desire to spend our entire lives with them, and believe it or not, they are willing to spend their lives with us guys. Now *that's* truly amazing! Jesus will have to explain that one to me some time.

"Be cautious and be careful, Luke, in choosing your wife. And absolutely do not make that choice based on external beauty alone. Here are two Proverbs and one line from a 20th century comedian. Consider them for the next few months:

> It is better to live in a corner of the housetop
> than in a house shared with a quarrelsome wife.

> It is better to live in a desert land
> than with a quarrelsome and fretful woman. (Proverbs
> 21:9, 19)

"Finally, last but not least, getting right to the point: 'Beauty may be skin deep, but ugly goes right to the bone!'

"If Maggy is the girl for you, then treat her better than you treat yourself. Ask for her opinion and consider her thoughts in all things. But the most critical area in a marriage is that you are both followers of Jesus Christ. If he is not the guiding star in your marriage, it could still work for you, but not to the level of his desire. It won't be aligned with what he has planned for the both of you. There's one very simple way to know more about who Maggy is, and that's by spending time at the Middlefield home and watching how her parents interact with and treat each other.

"Keep a watchful eye on Mr. Middlefield in particular. Christian or not, he is still the leader of his household, so you will learn much by simply watching him. Watch how he treats his family, his employees, his subcontractors, and his clients. You see where I'm leading you, right? Be ready to act graciously toward Maggy in case she begins to act in ways similar to her father and mother. She can't help but be influenced by her parents. We are all influenced by our parents in some way. Some grow up wanting to be just like their parents, and others grow up trying to be nothing like them at all."

Luke pushed the pause button when his cell phone chirped at him. It was Mr. Middlefield calling. After getting his morning instructions, he hung up the phone and started the letter again.

"That's about it for now, Luke. We'll talk more on this topic in some of my future letters, but for now, treat Maggy with the utmost respect. Let your mom spend some one-on-one time with her; talk about your faith with her; and bring her to church and introduce her to people there. One more thing I'd like you to do is to start spending time with Ricardo. I know this is only the second letter you have received from me, but I know you, Luke. You're already looking forward to the next letter and all those to come, but you need a flesh-and-blood godly man in your life. Someone that you can have good, meaningful, and deep conversations with, conversations that are God-centered. Talk to you in three months, buddy. Oh yeah, I can't forget that necklace."

"Sorry, Grandpa," said Luke with a loving smile on his face as he watched him lean forward to turn off the connection between his laptop and the Legacy Letter website. "But you did forget. Don't worry about it—I got your back on this one. I love you, Grandpa."

Chapter 3

Course Corrections

The Texas side of Ricardo's family that was able to attend the wedding stayed in a nice hotel, and they had been in and out of the house for two days. The Colombian side of the family had been staying at Ricardo's home for six days now, and Ricardo couldn't have been happier. To have had them stay for less time at a hotel would have been a terrible decision. Ricardo and Rebecca had talked over the idea of having them stay at his home rather than a hotel several months earlier, and both agreed they didn't want to waste all that time having to drive back and forth each day between the hotel and their house.

Ricardo wasn't the only one enjoying this reunion before the big day. His family was just as excited to finally meet this long-lost family member. None of them could believe that they had found each other after being separated for 50 years. However, as a result of the decision to have them stay at his home before the wedding, Ricardo found that his offer to sleep on the living room couch—as he had done as a boy—wasn't giving him the amount of sleep he needed. For the fifth night in a row, he was the last one in bed and the first to rise the next morning. As with the previous mornings, Ricardo had gotten up early; after the coffee had finished perking, he poured himself a cup and was quietly sipping it while waiting for his sister, Rita, or her husband, Salvador, or any of their three adult children and their spouses to come down from their bedrooms.

Several miles away, Rebecca had gotten up even earlier that morning to get changed and then drive back to Ricardo's house. The plan was to help clean up from the previous evening's activities. Then they would prepare breakfast for their Colombian wedding guests. Luke, on the other hand, had left Ricardo's home early the previous evening because he had to be at work early the next morning, which meant he couldn't make it for the breakfast event. Ricardo wasn't sure how many of his own kids would be bowing out of this next extended family gathering, but truth be told, he secretly hoped for a small breakfast with only the Colombians in attendance. His thoughts were interrupted when he heard a knock on the front door. *Oh boy*, thought Ricardo, *if that's Rebecca, she's locked out and I'm in trouble.*

After opening the door and letting her in, Rebecca looked around the living room and kitchen and said, "I'm going to forgive you for locking me out of our home this morning, and that's because of what I was expecting to see this morning. It's clean, Ricardo! It's all clean! I don't believe it. How late did you all stay up last night anyway? I left at eleven o'clock and everyone was still here, along with piles of dishes, pots, pans, and silverware that needed washing. I was expecting to spend a full two hours cleaning the kitchen with you before starting breakfast. What a pleasant surprise to walk into such a clean house."

Rebecca stopped walking around the main floor of the house, turned to look directly at Ricardo, realizing at that moment how special he was and how special his extended family was, and said, "You know something, Ricardo, I'm really getting to like this extended family of yours. They are some of the sweetest and most considerate people I have ever met. You all have that same trait in your DNA, and that DNA didn't come from your father." She hesitated for a moment, swallowing the lump that had grown in her throat before going on: "Ricardo, I feel as if I have just met your mother without realizing it. You all have been separated for 50 years, but look how similar you all grew up to be. Don't you see it, honey? Your mother must have been one sweet woman to have her DNA outmuscle your father's when you all were growing in her womb."

As Rebecca was standing and admiring the clean room, Ricardo walked into the kitchen while taking the last sip of coffee from his "Best Dad Ever" coffee mug. He gave her a morning kiss and then said, "I see it now, Rebecca, and even though I can't remember much about my mother, I do feel as though she's here with us all. Thank you for seeing something so clearly that I would have missed. You're the best, Rebecca, the absolute best. I am truly blessed to have you in my life."

They gave each other a tender hug, and then Ricardo added one more insight about that morning related to his age.

"I must be getting old, Rebecca. My kids left around 12:30 a.m., and my sister and my nieces and nephews finally made it to their rooms a half hour later. I was ready to go to bed when you and Luke left, but they all insisted on cleaning up the kitchen, the dining room, and the living room. I was barely able to keep my eyes open, let alone stop them from cleaning up the house. Anyway, they were all in my bedroom, so I couldn't very well go to bed on the couch while they worked around me! So, what do you say, would you mind pouring a tired old man another cup of morning energy to help him stay awake?"

Rebecca was more than happy to pour her soon-to-be husband a cup of coffee. She gave him a return morning kiss while gently placing his mug into his hands. She was feeling guilty now as she continued to walk around the house, amazed at the effort it must have taken to clean these rooms so late at night without her help. Her only excuse was having to drive 20 minutes home and then 20 minutes back again this morning. *Oh well*, thought Rebecca to herself, *what's done is done, and all the cleaning is definitely done.*

The blessing of a clean house meant that she had an hour to talk quietly with Ricardo, and she wanted to share with him a new memory that was created with Rita earlier in the week. So Rebecca took his hand and led him to the couch.

"Ricardo, before everyone gets up this morning, I wanted to tell you a little more about the shopping trip we all took to the Monster Mall on Tuesday. It's about something Rita told me, and I've been waiting for the right time to tell you."

Ricardo's curiosity was immediately piqued. After all, he too was at the mall that day, and he thought he had been privy to every conversation that had taken place. "Sure," he said, "I'd love to hear what I missed out on."

Rebecca hesitated, looking back toward the stairwell that led to the bedrooms while listening for anyone who might be coming down the stairs. Hearing nothing, she turned back toward Ricardo and began to speak quietly, wanting to make sure no other ears would hear what she was about to share with him.

"Well, it happened after we bought everyone new suits and dresses and shoes for the wedding. I know you didn't realize it, but there was a point when you were giving the others a guided tour of the mall and speaking in Spanish so fast that I couldn't keep up. I figured you were caught up in all the fun and excitement, so I didn't want to say anything. I walked away for a little bit and did some window shopping, and Rita must have noticed me looking through the window of the toy store. She came over and asked if we could step away from the group for a while because she wanted to speak to me about something important.

"It seemed to me that there was something on her heart she wanted to share, so without a second thought, I accepted her invitation. It turned out that she wanted to talk with me privately about the day your dad deserted you at her house. It must have been difficult for her. She was quiet at first, and then she simply stopped walking and said, 'I need to tell someone about how our father abused our mother and forced her to leave with him.'"

Ricardo was amazed at this revelation. He had been gently trying to get Rita to share her memories of that day for almost three years now, but he had never succeeded in getting her to open up. Yet, in just a few short days, Rita felt comfortable enough with Rebecca to tell her the story he had wanted to hear his entire life. *What a wonderful woman I'm going to marry*, thought Ricardo as he took a moment to simply admire her, *and what a blessed man I am. Thank you, Jesus, for allowing us to fall in love.* Then Ricardo continued to listen to the story and sip his coffee.

"The two of us had to break away from the larger group for more privacy and a little quiet. Ricardo, I'm sure you didn't even know you were doing it," said Rebecca while softly rubbing his arm with her hand, "but when you get excited about something, it's noticeable. Your hands and arms begin to fly everywhere, and your voice gets, well, you get loud, Ricardo."

Ricardo gave her a look after hearing his fiancé call him a big mouth, and he was about to defend himself. But Rebecca jumped in and said, "Come on, Ricardo, you have to admit that you were a little animated and boisterous that day. It would have made any conversation other than yours difficult to hear. Anyway, as we began to walk away from the group, Rita reached over toward me and gently slipped her hand around my arm; she was holding on pretty firmly. At first, I didn't know why, but the more I thought about it, the more I realized how Rita was always holding Salvador's arm or the arm of one of her children when they walked anywhere. It appears to me, Ricardo, that a conversation with your sister about her personal health might be worth having before she returns home to Colombia. Perhaps you could have your general practitioner take a look at her before she leaves, but you would have to get on that right away this morning."

In a moment of selfishness, Ricardo gave her a look. He didn't want to ignore his sister's needs. Rather, he was simply asking Rebecca, in a nonverbal way, to get back to the original story.

"Don't be giving me that look, Ricardo. You have to admit that Rita is almost as tall as I am but much more thin and frail. Promise me you'll talk with her about her health before they leave," said Rebecca, more as a statement than a question.

After being around Rebecca for the last three years, Ricardo knew that it was easier to just do as she had requested. "Yes, of course I will. Don't worry, Rebecca, I'll talk with her and with Salvador about her health. Now, can you finish your story?"

Rebecca looked toward the stairwell and, still hearing no movement from any of the bedrooms, continued her story. "Well, as we were walking, the thought that Rita trusted me enough to talk with me privately about such a personal family tragedy made our time together even more special. Rita told me she knew they would be leaving in a couple of days, and she felt it was time to share those events with someone. It was an honor that she chose me."

Now Ricardo's curiosity really piqued as he leaned closer and asked almost impatiently, "Come on, Rebecca, what did she say? Can't you speed up the story and just tell me what she said? You know how much I've been trying to get her to tell me everything about that day, and the whole year that followed. But she never comes out and tells me much of anything. She just changes the subject on me."

"Oh, Ricardo, you sound just like Luke when he talks about his grandpa and the Legacy Letters he hasn't received yet. But now it's you talking about your sister. It's kind of cute."

Ricardo sat quietly in his chair holding his coffee mug and warming his fingers at the same time. He opted not to respond to the "cute" statement while waiting for Rebecca to continue. After taking another sip of her coffee, Rebecca lovingly looked into Ricardo's eyes and said, "It's been 50 years, Ricardo, and she hasn't been able to talk to anyone about that day until she received your surprise phone call three years ago. Think about it, honey. Until that moment when she heard your voice, and your introduction to her as her little baby brother, she had resigned herself to the fact that you were probably deceased and that she would never see you again. You probably shocked her more than you could have imagined."

Ricardo's response to that reminder was quiet and soft: "Yeah, now that you remind me, she did sound shocked. I'm sorry for being impatient, Rebecca. Go ahead and finish your story."

"Well, while we were walking, Rita began to tear up as she shared with me that she had also been traumatized by the events of that day. She had tried to forget what happened and had been somewhat successful in blocking it from her memory. That is, until you contacted her. She absolutely loved that you contacted her, but it also reminded her of that day. She told me some of the vulgar and hurtful words your dad was yelling at all of you; how he hit your mother and dragged her away; and how you guys didn't even get to say goodbye to her. She told me that she still has nightmares about that day, and that she felt a lot of guilt for having to leave you in that orphanage. Ricardo, just imagine what she must have gone through."

Ricardo sat there thinking about what Rebecca had said. In all these years, he had never taken the time to consider what his sister must have been going through on that awful day. He wasn't the only one carrying around emotional scars because of their father.

Rebecca could see that Ricardo was processing what she had just told him. She waited for a minute and then started telling him more of her conversation with Rita. "After knowing me for only a few days, Rita trusted me enough to share these painful memories. So while you were with the others getting to know them better, she was opening up to me. Rita told me that after all these years—and now seeing you alive, healthy, loved, and with a family of your own—she no longer feels guilt about any of the choices she was forced to make for you at that time. You may have been too young to realize it, but apparently your father had been abusing your mom for quite a while. It was one of the reasons your sister didn't want to share some of these details with you. When she came to visit, she noticed your mother had several bruises on her arms and face. And when she asked about them, your mother simply brushed it off, so your sister hadn't given it much thought. On the day your parents dropped you off at your sister's house, your father had hit your mother when she refused to leave you. Your sister had never actually seen your dad abuse your mom, so she was shocked when it happened right in front of her."

"What?" Ricardo choked up, not realizing how much he never noticed as a kid. Rebecca paused for a few minutes, allowing Ricardo to come to terms with what she had just revealed.

"What you didn't know at that time was that she not only had a two-year-old child of her own, but she was pregnant with a second and was only 18 years old. She was so young and was given so much responsibility. Rita explained that she could barely take care of her own child, let alone the one that was coming. She was struggling to keep everything together. She wanted to give you an opportunity to grow up in a less stressed and healthier environment. Between the orphanage providing the food and clothes and her weekly visits, you managed to become a somewhat healthy six-year-old. All she wanted was to get back on her feet before trying to take care of you again. She had no idea you would be adopted so soon. When she was told you were adopted by an American family, she was shocked. She tried searching for you, but she couldn't afford an in-depth search. Her parents had disappeared, and shortly after that, you disappeared from her life. After years of wondering what happened to you, she was shocked when you contacted her. She honestly thought she would never see you again."

Ricardo sat there in absolute shock and silence with tears in his eyes. There was so much that he had never heard or realized. Rebecca moved closer and put her arms around him in a comforting manner before softly reassuring him, "She loves you, and she is happy with how your life has turned out, you know. She told me she is so proud of the man you have grown up to be. She's just relieved to see you so happy and well."

Rebecca's story was about finished, and it was a good thing, because they heard noises coming from the bedrooms. It appeared breakfast needed to be prepared. She looked one last time at Ricardo, who was now wiping his eyes dry, before walking to the refrigerator. "There's one more thing, Riccardo. Rita has something she has been holding onto for the last 50 years, hoping that one day she would be able to give it to you. She didn't tell me what it was, but when she comes down this morning, take her into the coffee-and-conversation room and let her tell you the story herself. Maybe ask her what was so special that she held onto it for all these years."

By this time, Ricardo was on the cusp of emotional distress, and Rebecca didn't know how to feel about his reaction to hearing the truth about what had happened that day and how it had changed the direction of his life. While waiting for his sister to come down the stairs, he found that one minute he was a 55-year-old father of three, and the next he was that same five-year-old boy—afraid, confused, and on the verge of tears. It was only a few minutes later that she came down the steps and headed for the kitchen to pour herself a cup of coffee. Not hesitating, he walked over to her and asked if they might talk privately in the other room. She looked at Rebecca and knew that this was the time to share her story with her little brother. She excused herself and went to her bedroom to retrieve something before entering the room where she would answer and ask a lifetime of questions.

Rebecca needed to leave soon. She had to get home where Luke would be waiting for her. He was working a half-day so that he could drive her to some places she needed to go before the wedding. The last stop would be at her sister's house where Luke would drop her off. She had planned to spend that night and the following morning with her two sisters getting ready for the wedding.

Although Ricardo was still recovering from yet another evening of staying up late, talking and telling stories with his recently discovered extended family, he wouldn't change one thing about this past week they had spent together. He had not been part of their lives for 50 years, and he loved every minute of these past six days. This morning and afternoon would be the last uninterrupted opportunity to get to know them before they had to catch their flight back home to Colombia on Sunday morning.

Throughout the week, there were many moments for catching up and sharing stories that brought out much laughter, along with many tears. His sister was almost 70 years old now, and somewhat frail. He couldn't believe how blessed he was to have this opportunity to get to know her and her family while she was still alive. Ricardo's stepmom was instrumental in helping him contact the orphanage he lived at before being adopted. Ricardo may be all grown up now, but she still saw him as her little boy, given to her from God, and she wanted to give him this gift of family and reconciliation. It had been only a few years since they first started talking, but they hadn't wasted any time in getting to know each other. It turns out that even the poorest people from the poorest of countries use cell phones, just like the rest of the world. Ricardo and Rita had been talking on the phone and over Skype for the past several years. When Ricardo told her about his upcoming marriage, he also told her he wanted to fly her, her husband, and their three adult children and spouses to the States and have them stay at his home for a week so that everyone could meet each other. This week had been a wonderful time of catching up and creating new family ties, but it would have to end later tonight. Ricardo had a special meeting he was unwilling to miss.

It was the end of another week of work for Luke, and it could not have been a more pleasant morning to be working outside. The temperature was hovering in the mid-60s and there was a slight breeze making its way across the open fields, carrying the sounds of happy carpenters performing their trade. Luke was loading his tools into his truck while the rest of the crew continued working. When the other guys in the crew saw what he was doing, they started giving him a hard time for trying to sneak out of work early. They would be left to finish installing the rest of the windows on this massive home without Luke.

"Come on, guys," said Luke, "you all know exactly why I'm leaving early today and why I won't be in tomorrow. My mom is getting married this weekend. I won't have to look at any of you clowns until Monday morning."

The guys all started laughing as they walked over to Luke's truck. "Man, you have got to relax. We know why you're leaving early—it's all you've been talking about this whole week."

After receiving congratulations and handshakes from the guys, Luke made his way over to the house he had been working on. Markus was waiting for him, and he helped Luke pick up the rest of his equipment to take to the truck. As soon as everything was stored in the bed of his truck, Markus leaned on the driver's side bed panel, looked Luke directly in the eye, and said, "Hey man, since marriage talk is in the air, I gotta know what's up with you and my sister? You guys have been dating for almost three years now, and there's still no wedding plans.

And you have her going to your mom's wedding with you tomorrow. Heck, even my dad and mom are going to the wedding. They're happy for your mom, but it's not Maggy's wedding. We just want to know what's up between you and Maggy? What's the holdup, dude?"

Luke had just finished locking his truck topper when he turned toward his best friend with a slightly irritated look on his face. "Cut me some slack, Markus. I just turned 18. Don't worry, I got my timing figured out for me and Maggy. And why are you three so impatient anyway?

"It's my dad and mom more than me, dude. I guess I just got caught up in the idea of you being my brother. I know this isn't a very smooth transition, dude, but I've overheard them talking about you, and what they were saying wasn't very nice. I think it's only fair that you know that they're not the perfect couple everyone thinks they are. And you certainly don't want to get on the wrong side of them. I know you think my dad is on your side because of everything he is doing for you, Luke, but not with this Maggy issue. Don't ever forget, Luke, that everything with my dad is conditional—it will always have a string attached to it. And the condition will always favor him, not the person he's dealing with. Also, be warned: he's the only one allowed to pull the strings that he has personally set in place."

"Speaking of talking," said Luke as he was beginning to show a little anxiousness because of this delay in leaving, "we'll have to do that later. Right now, I gotta go. My mom is waiting for me. She has a lot of last-minute errands for the wedding she wants me to help her with."

As Luke reached for the handle to the door on his truck, Markus said, "Later is okay, Luke, because I know you're strapped for time. But you're going to want to hear what I have to tell you about my parents, considering you may be calling them 'dad' and 'mom' one day. See you tomorrow."

Luke opened the driver's door and slid in as Markus slapped the fender of his truck and walked away. He took a moment before starting the engine and thought about the strange statement he heard Markus make about his parents. Shaking it off, he pulled out his phone and gave his mom a call.

"Hi, Luke," said his mom, "are you on your way home now?"

"Almost. I just sat down in my truck, and I was calling to let you know I'm on my way. Do I need to stop anywhere to pick something up for you, or can I come straight home?"

"Just get back here and get cleaned up. There's a special place that I need to go, and I'd like you to go there with me. See you in a little bit, honey."

Over the next hour, Luke had made it home, showered, and changed into clean clothes. He was now sitting in the passenger side of his mom's car, and the two of them were driving to a destination in a part of town unfamiliar to Luke. The ride was quiet for the first ten minutes, with neither of them saying much, that is, until Luke broke this silence by saying, "So, Mom, where are we going?"

She was silent for a long moment and then said, without answering his question, "We're almost there. It'll be just a couple more minutes." Sure enough, his mom slowed down two minutes later and turned left into The Whispering Pines Cemetery.

"I don't get it, Mom. What are we doing at a cemetery?"

Again, Rebecca didn't answer right away but continued quietly driving before speaking with a melancholy voice: "This is where your dad is buried, Luke." After more silence, she continued, "You may not understand why, but I need to visit with him before the wedding."

"Oh yeah, that's right," Luke said quietly. "It's been so long. I forgot this is where Dad was buried."

There was another moment of silence before Rebecca spoke again: "This has always been a hard place for me to visit, Luke, and I didn't want to come here alone, especially today. And it didn't feel right for me to ask Ricardo, although that sweet man wouldn't have hesitated for even a moment to come here and support me."

Rebecca had parked her car, and the two of them were quietly walking. She was carrying a small clutch in her hand, and Luke was carrying a lightweight lawn chair in his. Rebecca was leading Luke past other headstones on a flat stone walking path to a place very familiar to her. It was still the same: there were never any changes in this place. Perhaps that was intentional; it may have been for the purpose of giving those left behind a feeling of comfort and stability, knowing their loved ones were well taken care of. There were always songbirds quietly singing in the background, and Rebecca hear them. Occasionally one would even fly by.

"I know you probably don't remember coming here, Luke, seeing that it's been almost ten years since we visited your dad's grave together. I know your dad isn't here, but I just need to look at his name on that headstone and talk to him one more time before I get married. It's really hard to explain to most people how I can have a place in my heart for two men and not feel that it's wrong. It's actually just the opposite. It seems perfectly right. I need to voice my thoughts out loud to my Joshua and let him know what I'm doing. Even though I know he's not here and that he's in heaven with our Jesus, I need to know that something of him is close enough to hear my words. I guess I need a type of final approval, a blessing from your dad and a feeling in my heart that he understands. You have to know, Luke, that I had no intention of falling in love with Ricardo. It just snuck up on me. I didn't even see it happening. Love is funny that way—you don't see it coming, and then, all of a sudden, you're in it."

Luke remained silent, unsure about how he might respond to the statement his mother just made. After a few more minutes of silent walking, a strange thought came to him: he realized that he had spent more of his life *without* a dad than *with* one. It had been so long since he called anyone "Dad" that he started wondering what it would be like to say that word again.

They kept walking, each immersed in their own quiet thoughts, before Rebecca began to speak again.

"What may be difficult for some people to understand is that Joshua was taken away from me. He didn't leave me and you. He didn't abandon us, and he wasn't abusive to us. He was just taken away. There was no goodbye, no last hug or kiss, not even a final word. He was just gone. In my heart, I know marrying Ricardo is right for me, but there's just something in me that is giving me the feeling that I'm the one walking away, that I'm the one doing the abandoning." Rebecca sighed and then remained quiet for a second before saying, "It's hard to explain, but that's why I need to spend some time with him."

As they came to Joshua's headstone, Luke said to his mom, "I think this one-way conversation is going to be good for you, and I think it's okay for you to have it. And if you talk to Dad like you just spoke to me, I think you'll be just fine."

The tears were beginning to flow as Rebecca dug into her clutch for tissues as she turned and answered Luke. "Oh, thank you, honey, for saying that. You have no idea how much you remind me of your dad when you talk like that. You truly are your father's son."

She gave Luke a loving hug, after which she attempted to dry her tears. She then asked him, "Luke, can you set the lawn chair off to the side of your dad's grave and put it close to his headstone for me?"

It only took a minute to set the lawn chair up where his mom wanted it, and then Rebecca, now sitting at the side of Joshua's headstone, began reading his name and the dates of his birth and death out loud.

She started speaking to him, saying, "Hi, Josh." Her voice began to crack and falter now. "It's me—your one and only. Remember, that's what you always called me, your one and only. And that's why I have something I need to tell you."

She went on talking out loud among the trees and neatly trimmed bushes and grass, telling Joshua all about Ricardo and what he means to her. She went on like this for a long time; such emotion, such loving and longing words spoken by a voice filled with tears for her deceased husband and best friend. Luke had never heard his mom express these feelings before today. It was beautiful.

Luke thought to himself, *This must be what absolute and pure love feels like.* Luke was now standing behind her while she sat on the lawn chair. He then put his hands on his mom's shoulders as a sign of support, tearing up himself as he listened to her words. All this was done while he tenderly held her as she continued speaking to his dad. Luke thought to himself one more time, *I can only hope that Maggy and I will have this kind of love for each other through all the years of our marriage.*

Rebecca sat there for a long time playing the "remember when" game with a silent Joshua. Luke was desperately trying to remember even the smallest details from these memories his mother so effortlessly spoke back into existence.

It wasn't much longer before they left that silent home of Luke's father and headed toward another new beginning in Rebecca's life. Luke was driving now, his mom still drying off an occasional tear from her eyes.

"Thanks, Luke, for taking off work to be there with me. I hope I wasn't a bad example of how to handle these types of events."

"Just the opposite, Mom. You've been a wonderful example to me. I'm glad you brought me along to be a part of this moment. And if your love for Ricardo is even a portion of the kind of love you had for Dad, Ricardo is truly a blessed man."

"Again, Luke, you are speaking with such wisdom. Thank you, honey."

Luke drove his mom's car to all her last-minute appointments the rest of the day. Sometimes he went inside and other times he opted to sit in the car and wait. The time at his dad's gravesite had reminded Luke that there was still one task he needed to complete himself. It had been a few months since he made this promise, but a promise made should be a promise kept. He would bring his grandmother and his father to his mother's wedding. They may not be there in body, but Luke knew what would bring them there in spirit.

The last stop of the day was at his Aunt Anna's house. Rebecca was going to spend the night with her two sisters and three nieces before the wedding. The next morning, before the big event, they were going to give her a facial, fix her hair, do her nails, and help her into her wedding dress. It was an afternoon wedding, so they would have plenty of time to finish all this primping and still get her to the church with time to spare.

As Luke was driving home, an odd thought crossed his mind: *I'm not just going to be alone tonight. I'm going to be home alone until I get married. I hope it doesn't get spooky being in a house that's totally empty and quiet.*

Turning onto the street where his grandpa's house was, and slowing down as he came closer, he noticed the lights in the kitchen and living room were on.

If that's a burglar, thought Luke, *he's not very good at his trade.*

Turning into the driveway, he sighed in relief as he noticed Ricardo's jeep parked in its usual place.

"Now this is a nice surprise. My future stepfather is here for an impromptu visit. I wonder what he has planned?" Luke mumbled to himself quietly before turning into his driveway.

After pulling his mom's car into her regular parking spot, he made his way to the back door and into the kitchen, where he saw Ricardo pouring a second cup of coffee. Ricardo, seeing Luke come through the screen door, quickly asked, "I hope you didn't call 9-1-1 on me, Luke. And I also hope it's okay that I stopped by unannounced. And by the way, this one's for you, Luke. When I heard you pulling into the driveway, I took a chance that you would be up for a cup of coffee. I was also hoping you'd be up for a conversation."

"Nope, no police will be showing up tonight. But I have to admit that this is a nice surprise. And thanks for the coffee—that sounds great." Luke said this while making his way out of the kitchen and into the living room, holding the warm ceramic mug of coffee in his hands.

"So, what brings you over here the night before you get married to my wonderful mother? Shouldn't you be hanging with your family at your house?"

"Yes, she is wonderful, Luke. I still can't believe she said yes. And I can hang with my Colombian family for the next ten days. Remember, we're going to Colombia for our honeymoon. I'm here for you tonight because I wanted you to know that I am very aware of how your life is going to change because of this marriage. Five months ago, your life changed dramatically when your grandpa died, and tomorrow it's going to change dramatically once again. I thought we should take tonight to talk, as the two most important men in your mom's life. Seriously, Luke, thank you for sharing her with me. I never would have asked her to marry me without your approval. And I never would have imagined that I could give my heart to another woman. But your mom is certainly one special lady."

"Well, you got that one right, Ricardo," said Luke. A huge sense of pride in his mom was evident in his voice. "And since you're going to be the dad, what do you want to talk about?"

Ricardo didn't hesitate, because he did have an important topic to talk about. He began sharing his thoughts as the two of them walked into the coffee-and-conversation room, with Luke sitting in his chair and Ricardo, unknowingly, sitting in the chair of Luke's grandpa.

"The first big thing I'd like to talk about is this: have you spoken with your mom at all about how you are going to take care of yourself living on your own? Your meals, your laundry, cleaning the house, maintaining the yard and the outside of the house, paying monthly bills on time . . . is your job stable? You're not even 20 years old, Luke. Are you sure you're ready for this big change in your life? You can always live with us for a year or two, or three or four. That's an option."

The longer Ricardo spoke, listing all the things he would have to be responsible for, the less coffee Luke was drinking and the more thinking he was doing. He was thinking about things he hadn't considered until that very moment.

"Are you trying to scare me, Ricardo? Because if you are, it's working. At least a little bit."

They both had a short laugh before Ricardo began talking again. "No, really, Luke. I'm not trying to scare you. I just want your eyes to be fully opened so that you're aware of what's coming your way and the options you have in dealing with the challenges ahead."

"I've talked a little with Mom about the things you just mentioned, and I told her I'd like to try the independent route for at least six months before I throw in the towel. There are several guys I work with that are my age or just a little older who are on their own, and they seem to be making it just fine. If they can make it, why can't I?"

"I knew you would feel that way, Luke. That's why your mom and I agreed that she is going to come over to the house three times a week—probably Monday, Wednesday, and Friday. She'll make some meals, do some minor cleaning, and be available to just talk with. At least until you feel you are ready to be more on your own. I work late several days a week, so it's not a big deal to either of us. Also, we are only 20 minutes away, so if you ever need anything, you can just call and I'll come right over."

Luke thought about this offer for a quick second and then said, "You know what, Ricardo? I'm good with accepting that offer, because the most difficult hardship I would have to endure would be not seeing my mom, except on Sunday mornings. Yep, that would be hard to get used to."

At that moment, Luke's cell phone buzzed on the wooden arm rest of the chair he was sitting in. After glancing down to see who was calling, he looked up again at Ricardo and said, "It's Maggy. Do you mind if I answer it?"

"No, not at all, Luke. You go ahead and take some time with her. And while you're talking, I'll get a fresh cup of coffee for the both of us. French vanilla creamer, right?"

Luke looked at Ricardo, amazed at his memory, and said with a large smile on his face, "Every time, Ricardo. Every time!"

After that he quickly said, "Hi, Maggy! What's up?" There was a short pause, and then Luke said, "Yes, I picked up my suit this afternoon and it fits fine." After another pause, Luke said, "Yes, I won't forget. I'll have it in my pocket." Then another pause. "Yes, I'll be ready at noon for you to pick me up. Hey, Maggy, is it okay if I let you go now? Ricardo surprised me by coming over tonight to have our first father-son conversation and to spend some time talking about life after marriage. And just so you know, he's not talking about *his* life after marriage: we're talking about *my* life and how it is going to change after my mom moves out of my grandpa's house and into Ricardo's. I need to get back to him."

Another pause. "No, I haven't had him on hold this whole time. Like I said, he's here with me at the house." Then there was a final, longer pause: "Because you never asked me," Luke said, followed by a quick, "Okay, see you tomorrow."

Looking up at Ricardo and taking the cup of coffee being handed to him, Luke set his phone back down on the wide wooden arm rest and said, "I think I'm in trouble, Ricardo. She's embarrassed for talking so long and asking so many questions while making you wait for her to get off the phone. And apparently it's *my* fault?"

"Luke, may I give you my first bit of fatherly advice?"

"Sure, go for it. What do you have for me?"

Ricardo smiled, for he had never had a son to advise before now, only girls. He hoped his advice would be well received, both by Luke and by Maggy.

"When she comes over to pick you up tomorrow, apologize. Just get it over with and apologize. You'll have a much better day if you do that."

Ricardo visibly froze for a moment, apparently thinking very deeply about the advice he had just given. He changed his mind and his advice: "You know what, Luke, on second thought, forget what I just said. Call her back as soon as I leave. Don't let her stew on it all night. That would be even worse."

"Okay, I'll trust you on this one. And I'll also do it for Mom, so that tomorrow is better for everyone."

"And speaking of your mom, Luke, I know I have said this to you several times already, but I want to thank you again for sharing her with me. I can't begin to tell you how much happiness she brings to my life. It also seems pretty obvious to me, especially in light of that last phone call, that there is a second special woman in your life who apparently loves to care for you as much as your mom."

They sat and talked for a couple more hours before Ricardo called it a night. He knew he needed a good night's sleep before the wedding, and he was also hoping his sister might still be up for a few more minutes of conversation before he climbed onto his bed-couch for the last time.

Shortly after Ricardo had left to go home, Luke called Maggy and apologized for not letting her know sooner that he had company at the house when they first started talking. All was well between the two of them after the apology had been given and accepted. Ricardo's first bit of advice as a father had worked out as predicted. The two of them went on talking together for a long while until Luke had to finally say good night so that he could get some sleep for the big day tomorrow.

Ten minutes after saying good night to Maggy, the most unexpected feeling washed over Luke after climbing into bed. He laid his head on his soft, familiar pillow and covered himself with blankets that were old and worn out but still comforting. While lying on his all too familiar mattress alone in the house he had grown up in, Luke realized he had not anticipated being unable to fall asleep that first evening. He wasn't sure if he was thinking too much about the wedding, or if it was everything he had talked about with Maggy. Perhaps he had had too many cups of coffee in his system, or maybe it was hearing every last creak and groan the house had to offer. Whatever it was, Luke just laid there with his eyes wide open, unable to find sleep. The longer he stayed awake, the more he tried to remember if he had locked all the doors; he went back and forth on whether he should get up and check them again. Then, all of a sudden, he was startled awake. His wind chime alarm was singing in his ears. It was time to rise and shine! He had fallen asleep and not even known it—as if anyone knows when they fall asleep.

It was strange getting up on this particular morning. It wasn't like the previous evening at all, because as he quietly laid on his bed in the dark last night, he heard every last creak, groan, and whisper this familiar house had to offer. This morning he was just as awake as he was last night, but now he wasn't hearing any of those unsettling noises. As Luke walked from his bed to his closet to his dresser and back to his bed again, he heard nothing, that is, except for the creaking of the hardwood flooring under his feet as he walked. The only advice he could give to himself was to patiently wait for evening to come; he would again listen for the same noises to talk to him tonight that he heard last night. Putting this personal conversation off to the side for now, he walked down the stairwell and into the kitchen.

I wonder what I should make for my first breakfast as a bachelor this morning, Luke thought to himself as he walked down a set of steps that never creaked until that very morning. After checking out the refrigerator and then the pantry, he decided on a bowl of Frosted Mini Wheats.

I'll get something good to eat at the reception, he thought as he quietly ate his soggy breakfast.

Between cleaning up the kitchen, cleaning himself up, and putting on his new suit, the entire morning disappeared. Before he knew it, Maggy was knocking on the back door and then walking inside.

"Luke, are you ready to go? It's a little past noon already!"

She then heard Luke calling to her from the second floor: "Maggy, come on up here. I need to show you my grandpa's secret safe in his old dresser."

Maggy made her way to the top of the stairwell and then asked, "Which room are you in?"

"I'm in the first one on the right."

Upon entering this very spartan and clean room, Maggy saw Luke standing in front of an old dresser. He was wearing his new suit and looking quite handsome.

"This is it, Mags. Come on over and I'll show you how it works," Luke said with an excited smile.

"Okay, show me the secret safe. Although it's hard to focus when there's such a handsome man in the room," she teased with a flirtatious wink.

"*Aw,* come on. Knock it off, Maggy. Here, let me show you how this safe works before we have to leave. Okay, here we go. All you have to do is empty the drawer, slide your fingers to the front bottom, and then slide them again to the left. Then the bottom pops up. See? Pretty neat, isn't it?"

"Yeah, that's really cool! So which one of these hidden treasures is your grandma's necklace?"

Luke took out the small white box, opened it, and showed Maggy the necklace. "It's beautiful! Simple, but beautiful," said Maggy before looking at what else was in the drawer. "What's in these envelopes, Luke?"

Luke had looked at two of them briefly after his grandpa died. "One of them is a copy of the accident report of the collision that killed my dad and grandma, and the others are some investments. But, like I said, I'll have to show them to my mom and Ricardo to really know what they are."

After putting the necklace back into the box and then into his suit pocket, Luke closed the secret safe and said, "We'd better get going. I can't be late for my own mom's wedding."

When Matthew Middlefield walked out of his dressing room and into the bedroom, Elizabeth turned around to see what he had chosen to wear to the wedding. She had been completely satisfied with her choice of clothing and jewelry, but that was now changing after looking at what her husband was wearing.

She abruptly said, "Matthew! You can't wear that kind of suit to this wedding! You have to wear one of those old thousand-dollar, off-the-rack suits. Remember where we're going. It's just a small religious service, so we have to dress accordingly. We can't be overdressed."

Matthew had a look of real irritation at the thought of having to get changed out of one of his favorite suits and into one that was much cheaper. There were 47 suits in his changing room closet to dig through, and he wasn't looking forward to that task.

"It's just a church, Liz," said Matthew as he dropped his trousers to the floor right in front of her. He left them where they landed, knowing the maid would hang them up after they left for the wedding. "Don't people wear the best clothing they own out of respect to the pastor?"

Elizabeth turned away from Matthew with a look of disgust. "These people wouldn't understand or even begin to appreciate our kind of style, even if they wanted to. So why should we put ourselves in a position of having to explain why we are wearing designer clothes for gatherings like this? Plus, we don't want to be considered tacky by outshining the bride and groom."

Matthew didn't respond to Elizabeth's retort like he wanted to, because he couldn't disagree with it. He simply turned around and headed back into his changing room, thinking to himself, *She may know how to dress for social events, but I'm the one who can work the crowd at any event we attend.* After considering his thoughts again, he said to himself, *But I guess I do need help in clothing choices, especially with the changes that are coming in our lives. After all, people do judge you by how you look and what you wear. In that respect, we do make a good team, a force to be reckoned with in this city.*

"Hey, Liz," said Matthew as he walked out of his changing room, cinching up his burgundy tie. "I just had a thought as to how we can use this wedding to our advantage."

Elizabeth stopped her primping and said, "It sounds like you've been talking with your friend again, but since you've got my attention, what are you two thinking?"

"Well, here's my thought. After the wedding is over and people are milling around making small talk, you should hang close to Maggy and simply listen to everything these church folks are saying to her. And I'll do the same thing with Luke. After we leave the church, we can compare notes to see what kind of indoctrination Maggy is being subjected to. We have to protect our family from anyone that may

compromise our new plans. And since our future is way more important than one young man, I have no problem checking up on him as
often as it takes to find out who he really is. So if we are okay with
what we find out about him, he can continue to date Maggy. But if
we don't like what we hear, we can encourage her to date other young
men, those who see the world more like we see it. Maggy will trust my
advice, Liz. She always has and she always will. What do you think?"

"I think I love the way your mind, and your friend's mind, works,
and that's why I married you."

"Liz, there is one more thing we need to keep in mind while we're
at this church today."

"And what would that be, Matty?"

We can't let anyone know who we are, especially Luke and his
mother. As time moves along, people will believe I hired Luke as another way for us to give back to his family. And it's better if no one
connects the dots between my brother, Danny boy, and the Cruz family. The only one who knew all this information is dead, so that's a
bonus for us. And when we see how everything shakes out, if we need
to let Maggy marry Luke, we'll do it. But if we don't need to, then we'll
break them up. That's all I wanted to say, Liz. So what do you say we
get going and get this event over with?"

———

After greeting everyone in the wedding party who was standing in the
foyer, Luke saw the pastor walk to the front center of the church and
take his place behind the podium. Facing the attendees, the pastor
said, "I hope everyone is ready, because two people we all know and
love are about to get married."

And with that, he signaled for the music to begin. There would
be no best man or maid of honor in this wedding. Ricardo and Rebecca had decided from the beginning that they had both done the
traditional wedding before. They just wanted a simple ceremony for
themselves, their family, and a few friends. There were about 50 people in total attending their wedding, and this included Mr. and Mrs.
Middlefield. Rebecca felt that since they had been present for the proposal, they should be present for the wedding.

After the pastor, Ricardo was the next to walk to the altar. He reached the front of the church, and as he began to turn and face the direction of his coming bride, he saw Luke holding out his hand and giving his mother a small white jewelry box. "Thank you, my gracious Jesus, for giving your Rebecca such a gift on our wedding day."

Ricardo had heard the story of the white jewelry box many times, but until that moment, it was only a story. He had never seen the box or its contents.

At the back of the church, as Ricardo and the pastor looked on with the rest of those attending the wedding, an emotional conversation was taking place between mother and son.

"Luke, you have it! You really have it! It's not lost? Where did you find it?" Rebecca said, barely able to speak. She was desperately trying to stop the tears from running down her face and ruining her makeup before she even got down the aisle.

"We'll talk later," said Luke as he put the necklace on her. "Right now, you just wipe off those tears, and let's go get you married."

Luke proudly walked his mom down the aisle and lovingly placed her hand into Ricardo's before sitting down next to Maggy. As the bride and groom slowly turned to face the pastor, Rebecca leaned in toward Ricardo. With her left index finger she touched the silver cross, the one with the silhouette of Jesus on it, and said, "Everyone is here now, Ricardo. Everyone is here, and that includes your Angelica."

He looked at her, his eyes slightly moistened, and said, "There's one more family member at our wedding today that neither one of us thought would be here."

He gently pulled an old photograph from his suit pocket and showed it to her. "Rebecca, it's a picture of me when I was four years old sitting on my mother's lap. That's what Rita had been saving for me all these years."

The pastor, seeing what was taking place, allowed them time to talk while everyone in attendance wondered if there was a problem. But in the next minute, Ricardo had returned the picture to his pocket, and the pastor saw both sets of eyes looking at him.

"Friends and family, we are gathered here today to . . . "

While the newlyweds were on their honeymoon in Colombia—where Ricardo was able to introduce Rebecca to the rest of his extended family—Luke got over being alone in the house pretty quickly. Of course, it didn't hurt that Maggy was over on the nights she wasn't studying for her classes.

At first, Luke didn't know how to take this new educational venture. He had been under the impression that Maggy was going to wait a year before entering college. However, the more he talked to her about it, the more he realized that her dad's suggestion for her to get a business degree would help them for all the years to follow. It would seem to be a waste to use such a gifted mind on simple office work. Her dad never said it out loud but he had made many cryptic statements over the last couple of years about Maggy having more business tenacity than Markus.

These comments by her father weren't a slam on Markus at all; they were simply a recognition of the different gifts each sibling possessed. Maggy was business savvy and able to keep her personal emotions out of business decisions. Markus, on the other hand, was soft-hearted and social. And because of their dad's ability to see people's gifts, Maggy had learned through the years to completely trust her father concerning her most important life decisions. This was something Markus would have to learn to accept if he wanted to take on any type of leadership role at Middlefield Homes.

These days spent with Maggy at Luke's house were wonderful, neither one of them wanting them to end. They would make dinner together and then spend time talking about anything and everything the rest of the evening before she went home. That week was so pleasant and natural that it made Luke think of more serious and permanent matters. He was hoping for one more timely letter from his grandpa on the first day of December before having that most important conversation with Maggy's father. That conversation would stop all the questions about this young couple at the Middlefield home.

After Ricardo and Rebecca got back, the routine changed just a little, with his mom stopping in on Mondays, Wednesdays, and Fridays. Maggy would stop by on Tuesdays, Thursdays, and Saturdays, unless studying needed to be finished, which seemed to be happening more and more often over the last several weeks. On Sundays, Luke was in charge of all activities that came after the church service. Occasionally, both his mom and Maggy were over at the house at the same time, and Luke took his grandpa's advice and just let the two of them talk while he worked in the yard. Luke didn't mind tending to the upkeep of the yard, especially the rose bushes his grandpa had planted for his grandma before Luke had even been born. He loved those red and white roses and the memories they brought to his mind.

It was nearing December now and Luke was becoming his nervous self as he waited for the day the next letter would arrive. It was the same decision again: *Should I stay up late and wait for the letter? Or should I get up early the next morning? Or should I shake it up a little and watch it when I get home from work?*

Luke decided to shake it up a bit and watch the letter with a cup of hot, cream-filled coffee when he got home from work. He called his mom and explained what he was going to do, and then he asked if she would mind skipping their Wednesday evening dinner the next day.

"Of course, that's fine with me, Luke. You spend the evening with your grandpa and listen to every word he says. Say hi for me, and tell him that I love him."

"You got it, Mom. Thanks!"

The hardest part of the next morning for Luke was walking out the door of the house, knowing his grandpa's letter was waiting in his inbox. Before Luke knew it, the lead carpenter had called out that the workday was over. They had gotten a lot done and had come to a good stopping point. It must have been that oversized wrap-around deck they were working on that made the day disappear so quickly. While driving home, Luke began considering doing the same thing if another letter arrived on a workday. However, upon arriving home, he discovered that thinking about doing something and then doing it were two completely different things. After walking into the kitchen, Luke discovered that he was so excited to read the waiting Legacy Letter that he found himself in front of the coffee maker thinking, *It's going to take ten minutes to perk a fresh pot of coffee, and only one minute to microwave a cup.* It was then he realized that if he wasn't willing to wait for a fresh pot of coffee to brew before looking at the letter, he may not want to wait all day to see his grandpa again. So he opted to pour a cup from the morning pot and then place it in the microwave for a minute. Yes, he could wait one more minute. After retrieving his coffee, he headed to Grandpa's chair and pulled up the Legacy Letters website on his phone. It only took a minute to answer those all-too-familiar questions, and Luke was now touching the LL button.

"Hey, buddy! How's it going? This is my third letter to you, so it must be almost a year since I left you all. I'm going to take a shot in the dark and say that there has to have been some pretty big changes in your life since I left. With this much time passing, I feel compelled to return to my counsel about your relationship with Maggy—and my hope is that it is timely advice."

"It couldn't be more perfect, Grandpa," said Luke.

"Based on our family history, the time window for my counsel is growing short. In case you haven't noticed, the young adults in our family have a habit of marrying at an earlier age than most other couples, and I don't see you changing that tradition. Keeping that in mind, I'd like to start out this letter with two Proverbs that speak to a man finding a good wife, and one that talks about wisdom more generally.

> He who finds a wife finds a good thing
>   and obtains favor from the LORD. (Proverbs 18:22)

> House and wealth are inherited from fathers,
>   but a prudent wife is from the LORD. (Proverbs 19:14)

> Trust in the LORD with all your heart,
>   and do not lean on your own understanding.
> In all your ways acknowledge him,
>   and he will make straight your paths.
> Be not wise in your own eyes;
>   Fear the LORD, and turn away from evil. (Proverbs 3:5–7)

"Let me start by sharing with you what could be a real problem for you and Maggy. Then I'll describe the path you are on and how you got there. First, you must understand that I will not be speaking words of judgment concerning Maggy; rather, these are words of warning. From what I saw of Maggy, she is a lovely young woman, but she is not a true follower of Jesus, unless that has changed since I left you all. That's a serious problem in this potential marriage: one person believes in Jesus as the divine Son of God, while the other person believes that Jesus was just a good man. You two seriously need to talk about this issue. And Luke, you are the leader in this relationship, so you need to act like it and start talking about this topic. Because if you're not willing to be a leader in the years *prior* to your marriage, why would you think you will lead her in these matters *after* you are married?"

Luke pressed the pause button and said, "I know you just said that this letter wasn't going to be a judgment on Maggy, but that last statement you made sure sounds pretty judgmental, Grandpa. And a little pushy too."

He pressed the play button a second time.

"Now, let me see if I can describe how you got to where you are today with Miss Maggy Middlefield. First, about the time you became a teenager, you began to notice how pretty girls were. But you wouldn't admit that to any of your friends. Next, about the time you turned 15 or 16, you didn't care what the other guys were saying; you had your eye on one special girl. You liked the way she looked, the way she talked, and the way she smiled and laughed. You started spending time with her; you didn't know it then, but that is called dating. You soon found out that you really liked her. You asked yourself a secret question: 'Could I marry this girl?' You didn't realize it, but by asking your heart that question, you had just transitioned from dating to courting in order to get to know Maggy more deeply.

"You see, Luke, we date someone to see if we have the desire to court them, and we court them to see if we have the desire and emotional strength to enter into a promise of marital engagement. This engagement leads directly to a public announcement of lifelong commitment we call marriage. And that is exactly where I believe you are. You are at the end of the courtship stage, and you are ready to step into the engagement period. You can only enter this stage by asking her directly to marry you, or by asking for permission from her father to take his little girl away from him through marriage. Both you and Maggy have to have the same religious beliefs, the same ethical standards, the same family values, and the same moral foundation on which to make decisions and build your marriage and raise your children. If not, you will always have struggles.

"Luke, these are the pure and simple facts for a true follower of Jesus Christ. Please listen and follow my counsel. I truly hope this letter has been delivered at the right time, that is, in time to make any course corrections needed in your relationship with Maggy. I love you, Luke. See you in a couple months."

Wow! thought Luke. *Now that's a lot to take in. Why would you do that to me, Grandpa? You've met Maggy, and you told me you liked her. What's with this big push to know everything about what she believes before we're even married? Don't we find all those things out through the years of being married? No marriage is perfect. Just ask Ricardo, he'll tell you. Well, he'd tell you if you were alive. He deals with people's marriage issues every day.*

Chapter 4

Contentment

Luke and Markus, along with 12 other eager students of the new-home construction trade, had just handed in their final tests for their last class. The first semester of the two-year Construction Management course was officially completed.

All the students were milling around the classroom, chatting and talking with each other about some of the questions on the test, when the course instructor, Mr. Hank Arlyn, walked up to Luke and Markus and said, "Mr. Cruz, when you're finished talking with Mr. Middle-field, would you mind coming to the front of the classroom? There's something I would like to discuss with you in private." Luke was a little taken off guard by this request, but he told Mr. Arlyn he would be there in a minute.

Hearing Mr. Arlyn's request, and while looking in the other direction so as not to draw attention, Markus said to Luke, "You go ahead, dude. Spend some time with Mr. Arlyn and see what he wants. And while you're doing that, I'll be spending some time with Cindy Wellington."

And with a quick glance toward Mr. Arlyn and then back at Cindy, Markus unapologetically said, "I have to admit to you, Luke, that when I agreed with my dad to take this course, I said yes just to get him off my back. I never realized there would be such pretty builders taking this course. I can't explain it, but there's just something attractive about a girl who is five foot eight inches tall with a long brown ponytail coming out the back of her baseball cap who can drive a 16-penny nail through a two-by-six wooden stud with five swings of a 20-ounce framing hammer. Wouldn't you agree, Luke?"

"Yeah, sure, Markus, you're a real swell guy to share that thought with me. And what would your dad say about you spending so much time with the soon-to-be construction manager of one of his biggest competitors?"

Markus just smiled, not caring what his father thought about this girl, and said, "He wouldn't like it at all, and that's exactly why I haven't told him about her yet."

Luke looked at Markus with a shocked expression on his face. "Did you just say what I thought you just said? Have you and Cindy already been dating?"

"Yep, that's exactly what I'm saying."

"Oh man, Markus, buddy, I know you want to show your dad that you're not like him, but I think you're walking a fine line with him on this one. Tell you what: let's meet in the parking lot after I finish talking with Mr. Arlyn, and then you can tell me what's going on with you and Cindy."

Not waiting for an answer, Luke turned and walked to the front of the classroom with his backpack slung over his shoulder.

Mr. Arlyn had just finished speaking with another student when he saw Luke making his way to where he was standing.

"Is everything okay, Mr. Arlyn? Did I mess up somewhere in the course?"

Mr. Arlyn just smiled at Luke. He couldn't remember teaching such a gifted yet refreshingly humble student in all his years as an instructor. *What a nice change of pace*, he thought to himself. Most men and women coming through his class with Luke's level of talent know they have it. They always seem to have a certain amount of hubris, a self-confidence that isn't very appealing; there's a lot of personal bravado and a felt need to prove something to the world. More often than not, they're very arrogant and not afraid to show it. Mr. Arlyn was glad to have a student like Luke that he could pay special attention to without that attention becoming a waste of time. But there were a few very important topics he wanted to talk about with Luke before pouring more time and energy into this gifted young man.

"Not at all, Mr. Cruz. You did nothing wrong. Actually, it's quite the opposite. What I'm curious about are the grades from your high school courses. When I compared them with this course, keeping in mind the difference in subject matter, of course, I'm wondering why you're here and not at a university studying something other than Construction Management. Perhaps something like structural engineering. I saw in your high school transcripts that you were a solid B student. Did you find your class load a little demanding for you? Is that why you were never able to rise above a B average? Because from what I have seen of your test results in this course, you shouldn't be here. You're actually too gifted a student to be spending your time in this class."

Luke was caught a little off guard by these questions and by the accolades being given by Mr. Arlyn. He wasn't sure why what he did academically in high school would have anything to do with this class. After all, they were already a quarter of the way through this course. It was a little late to take back the acceptance offer they gave him back in July. He decided patience was the best course of action in this conversation. So to find out what Mr. Arlyn wanted to tell him, he thought it best to go along with him and just listen to see where this impromptu meeting was going.

"No, not at all." Luke looked around the room, stepped just a little closer to Mr. Arlyn, and began to speak in a more hushed tone. "I didn't have time to study because of personal health problems."

"Well, it certainly seems that you've recovered well."

"No, no, Mr. Arlyn, it wasn't *my* health I'm talking about. It was my grandfather's health. He had cancer and was slowly dying throughout my junior and senior years in high school. It was an especially hard time for my mom and me; we had moved into my grandfather's house 12 years earlier after my dad and grandmother died in a car accident. But in spite of losing another family member, it worked out pretty good for all of us. It's pretty simple, Mr. Arlyn: I guess I was spending too much of my spare time helping around the house those last two years, and I didn't do as much studying as I should have. And watching my grandpa slowly die during that time did make it hard to concentrate on my schoolwork. I guess my grades suffered as a result."

"I'm so sorry to hear that about your grandfather," said Mr. Arlyn with a look of understanding on his face. "One last question, if you don't mind me asking, Mr. Cruz: in spite of your personal difficulties, you still had above average grades. So, just out of curiosity, would you describe to me your study methods and habits at that time?"

Luke was beginning to show a slight look of sadness as he had to relive, if only briefly, that extremely emotional time in his life. He was quiet for a second and then explained, "Well, I would get up about an hour early every day; get dressed and cleaned up; then, while eating breakfast, I would skim the subject matter from the textbooks for the classes and tests for that coming day. I always tried to be quiet and not wake my mom so she could sleep. But no matter how hard I tried, I could see that she was still pretty tired most days, even though she denied it. Seeing her dad dying like that was pretty hard on her, and I didn't want her to worry about me as well."

Seeing the look on Luke's face, Mr. Arlyn shifted the conversation from inquiry to accolades. "Well, Mr. Cruz, she still has nothing to worry about when it comes to you. You are an extremely gifted student. To receive the kind of grades you were getting after only skimming the subject matter for one hour the morning of each class is impressive. I'm surprised none of your high school teachers recognized this fact. Your grasp and understanding of engineering is absolutely astonishing. I don't think you got even one question wrong on any of your tests. You have also picked up a basic understanding of all the mechanical trades faster than any student I have ever taught. And I've been teaching this course for 25 years, so that's a lot of students. It would be fair to say that I have taught the majority of the contractors who are currently building homes in this city. And you, Mr. Cruz, have great potential. It would be safe for me to say that you have the talent to do more than just manage the building of single-family homes. But let's keep that observation between the two of us for now."

Luke just stood there, not knowing what to say or what Mr. Arlyn meant by not telling anyone what they were talking about. Regardless, no one in Luke's life, except for his mother, had ever encouraged him like this about his potential. He was getting a little self-conscious.

"Now, Luke, if you continue to impress me over the next three semesters, and I believe you will, I will have no choice but to mention your name to some very influential people as opportunities arise."

"I don't know what to say, Mr. Arlyn, except thank you! And don't worry, I can keep this between the two of us. But I must admit to you something about building—it just makes sense to me. Everything you were teaching us made perfect sense. There was no confusion in my mind in connecting what each trade was required to do with respect to their portion of the construction of a house or a building. And the way a house is required to be designed and engineered so that it is structurally sound, as well as functional and pleasant to live in for the life of the house, again, just made sense to me. I'm really looking forward to the start of next semester's classes."

"As am I, Mr. Cruz. As am I."

Luke looked around the room to make sure that Markus was out of earshot before asking Mr. Arlyn one last question. "Just out of curiosity, Mr. Arlyn, if I'm not out of line here, how is Markus doing in the class?"

"Well, first of all, I can see that you and Markus are very good friends, and by asking about his ability in this area of study, I will assume you only have the best intentions for him. So, I'll give you my professional opinion of Mr. Middlefield Jr. No sharing of any grades, of course. What I will say is that it's a good thing his father owns the company he's working for. Otherwise, he might be in a bit of occupational trouble. He has the intelligence to pass this course and obtain a builder's license, but it is my opinion that he doesn't have the desire to be a builder. This is only my opinion, but I believe Markus is meant to do something much different with his life—and whatever it is, it's not construction. As you can see, he seems to be more interested in Miss Wellington than in this course. But again," said Mr. Arlyn with an almost imperceivable smile, "that's just between the two of us, Mr. Cruz."

About the time Luke had made his way out to the parking lot, Markus reached the point where he couldn't wait any longer. He came walking up to Luke and asked, "So, what did Mr. Arlyn want?"

"Not much. He just wanted to tell me to keep up the good work. How about Cindy Wellington? What did she have to say today?" Luke asked with a slight, teasing smile.

Markus didn't answer right away. He just smiled and looked up into the sky, thinking about Cindy and those beautiful green eyes.

Luke, remembering something his grandpa had told him recently about dating, said to Markus, "Dude, are you thinking about Cindy right now?"

"As a matter of fact, I am. What about it?"

"I didn't mean to interrupt your thoughts, but I'm curious: when you started thinking about Cindy, did your toes happen to curl up in your shoes?"

Markus quipped rather quickly, and with a little irritation in his voice, "What a dumb question, Luke! Why would you ask me something like that anyway?"

Luke, not willing to give up quite so easily on his quest to find out just how perceptive his grandpa was, asked a second time. "I'll tell you in a minute, but for now, just answer the question."

Markus didn't answer right away, mostly because he didn't want to admit to Luke the answer. Then, with a defeated sound in his voice, he said, "Okay, fine, *yes*! They were curled up, but not anymore. Now, why did you ask such a stupid question? And how did you even know about my toes curling up?"

"Because my grandpa told me that's what happens to some of us when we think about someone we really like. I guess he was right."

Looking at Luke with some amazement on his face, Markus said, "I knew your grandpa knew a lot of stuff, but that's impressive. I'll have to ask Cindy the same question and see what she says."

Wanting to hear what Markus was telling him about Cindy, Luke gently pushed his friend for more details. "Sorry for getting you off track. Tell me more about Cindy. Go ahead, what else did you two talk about?"

He smiled, thinking about their next date. "She told me that tomorrow for dinner sounded great and, to my surprise, she wanted to prepare it herself at her parents' house. So not only is she learning how to build multi-million-dollar homes, she can also prepare a three-course meal!"

"Markus!" Luke paused and lightly slapped his friend's shoulder as a type of wake-up call. "Did you just say what I think you just said? You're going to her parents' house to eat a meal that Cindy and her mother are going to prepare for you to eat with her father?"

Markus just stood there, only then realizing what he had agreed to. He was now contemplating the possible ramifications of what Luke had just laid out. Markus couldn't utter even one word, while the light bulb in his brain flickered on and off. In reality, that light bulb was more off than on.

———————————————

At the end of that same week, just before the Middlefield Custom Homes office was going to close for the Christmas and New Year's holidays, Luke was nervously calling Mr. Middlefield to ask him a very important question, a question about permission concerning his daughter. The phone rang twice, and then Luke heard, "Hello, Luke, how can I help you?"

"Hi, Mr. Middlefield. Do you have a minute to talk?"

"A minute is about all I have. I almost didn't answer the phone, but I saw your name. As Maggy or Markus probably told you, I'm taking the family to the Rockies for a two-week ski trip this Christmas. So if there's something, you need to make it quick. I was just about to leave the office and turn my phone off for the entire vacation. What can I help you with?"

Luke was feeling the pressure to put off this conversation, but he knew that there was never going to be a good time to ask Mr. Middlefield the question he wanted to ask him. He struggled past his fear and said, "I know it's last-minute and you don't have much time, but I was wondering if we could have lunch today. I have an important question to ask you about Maggy, and I'd like to do it face to face and not over the phone."

Just then, Mr. Middlefield's call-waiting alert sounded in his ear. "Hang on a second, Luke. My wife is calling, and I better take this one. She's been checking in with me all day about the details of this trip we're taking."

"Sure," said Luke, not even getting out one word before he was put on hold.

Two minutes later, Mr. Middlefield was back. "Hey, Luke, thanks for waiting. I'm sorry, but I can't have lunch today, and I don't have time to talk right now either. Our flight leaves in four hours and I don't want to be late, so I have to go. Let's talk in two or three weeks. Tell your mom and stepdad happy holidays from all of us."

And then there was silence. A no-more-talking-on-the-phone, slap-in-the-face type of silence. Mr. Middlefield hadn't even waited for Luke to answer him, or even to say goodbye, before hanging up. Luke took a few minutes to compose himself, and then he called Maggy to wish her a Merry Christmas and to offer wishes for no broken bones while skiing. But to Luke's surprise, it went directly to her voicemail.

"Hi everyone, and happy holidays from Maggy! In agreement with my whole family, I won't, actually none of us will, have our phones turned on for the next two weeks. No school or work calls to interrupt our family time this year. Leave a message if you'd like. I'll get back to you in two weeks!"

Three days later, Luke was at Ricardo's home for the Christmas Eve holiday, where he was finally getting a chance to get to know his two new stepsisters and their families.

With excitement in her voice and a face filled with joy, Luke's mom came up about an hour into the evening and said, "I have three grandchildren, Luke! Three! Isn't it wonderful? You're an uncle, and I'm finally a grandma!"

Right after the words came out of her mouth, she realized her mistake.

"I'm sorry, honey. I wasn't thinking of you and Maggy when I said that. I should have known better. I'm so sorry."

"I know you didn't mean anything by it. I just can't understand why she won't call me. I can see why they would want to have family time for themselves. I get it. But I thought Mr. Middlefield thought of me as a . . . well . . . as a son. He treated me like just any other guy on the phone the other day. He made me feel pretty bad, Mom, and I can't figure out why he would do that. And why won't Maggy call me, or at the very least send me a text? What have I done to make her not want to even talk to me?"

At the same time, at a ski condo in Aspen, Colorado, the Middlefield family was eating a catered Christmas Eve dinner, and Luke was the topic of conversation.

"I don't get it, Dad! By the way Luke has been acting and talking, I was sure he was going to ask for your permission to marry me. And I thought that proposal would be made sometime over the holidays. And just so you know, if he asks, I'm going to say yes! But all of a sudden, we're taking a last-minute family vacation for two weeks. And you also asked us to turn our cell phones off during the trip. Didn't he call you before we left? Didn't he say anything? Maybe I don't know him as well as I think I do."

To her father's relief, Maggy continued with her rant, which gave him the opportunity to not answer her question directly. He was walking that fine line between the truth and a lie. "And with all our cell phones turned off, how are we supposed to talk with each other? It's fun going on these vacations, but Dad, you're being way too secretive. Even I can see that. What's this all about?"

"Elizabeth, would you like to take this one?"

Elizabeth and Maggy were sitting next to each other on a large leather couch. Her mom slid a little closer to Maggy and put her arm around Maggy's shoulders as she began to share her concerns.

"Maggy, part of the issue we are beginning to have with Luke relates to those conversations you told me you were having with his mom. And it's not just one or two conversations: you have had many of these talks over the last couple of months. It's about their religion and the stances they take on social issues. Don't misunderstand what I'm saying, because I believe that we're all Christians. But they seem to be taking their beliefs to a whole different level. They are way too serious and vocal about their beliefs, almost fanatical. Your dad and I didn't mind that you were going to church with him once in a while, but those conversations with his mother you told me about are getting a little extreme. We don't want you to be brainwashed by their church the way they seem to have been. And we aren't the only ones who are concerned. There are several friends of mine at the country club, ladies who I trust and confide in, who are also concerned about these so-called Christian people and the influence they're having on this country."

Maggy's father then added, "Maggy, we have always taught you and Markus to be tolerant of all people and their lifestyle choices—as long as those choices are legal, of course. But do you have any idea how many home sales we would have lost if we held to the same beliefs that Luke and his mom have? And what would have happened from a legal perspective if we had voiced those opinions to potential clients?"

"But, Dad," said Markus, who was sitting on the sidelines of this conversation until he heard his dad make blatantly false assumptions. "You always told me how much you appreciated Luke's ethics and morals on the job, and how you wished you had more employees that lived up to those same standards. And where do you think he was taught those standards? From the Bible that's taught at his church, that's where. I'm with Maggy. What's changed, Dad? What's going on? Luke's my best friend, so why are you trying to stop him from becoming my brother-in-law?"

After hearing Markus's emotional plea, Elizabeth gave Matthew one of her conciliatory looks, indicating that he might as well tell the kids what was about to happen.

"Matthew," said Elizabeth, "you might as well tell them. They're going to hear it in the news somewhere, either here or back home."

"Did something bad happen, Dad? Are you okay?"

Back at Ricardo's home, Luke was getting up off the floor after a convincing loss in a wrestling match with one of his new nephews.

"Looks like you're the winner, buddy. I think it's time to challenge your dad again. Give me five, little man!"

Luke held out his hand in congratulations, and his little nephew wound up his arm and slapped Luke's hand as hard as he could. Luke received a look of thanks from his dad for giving him even this small respite from his son's never-ending tank of energy.

"Don't these kids ever run out of juice?" Luke asked Ricardo, who was hiding just out of sight of his sugar-glutted grandson.

"Not till about eight o'clock tonight," said Ricardo. "Your mom, however, sure is having a great time with them tonight. I think they love having another grandma in their lives. Watching her with the kids brings a joy to me that I can't explain, Luke. And to see my girls interact with a woman that I hope will be a mother figure in their lives as we all get older, well, that gives me even more joy."

Ricardo, seeing an opportunity to talk with Luke about a topic Rebecca had asked him to bring up, said, "Luke, if you would allow me to change the topic of conversation, I can tell that you're putting on a good face for everyone tonight. So tell me, what's bothering you most about Maggy?"

"Wow, when you want to get down to it, you get down to it. Is this how you handle all your clients?"

"No, Luke, it's not. This is how I try to get my new stepson to open up. I can tell that not being able to talk with Maggy is tearing you up, isn't it?"

"You're either very insightful, or I'm not hiding my disappointment very well."

"It also doesn't hurt to have your mother whispering in my ear about her son. She sent me over here to talk with you about Maggy. Do you feel like a cup of coffee in my new coffee-and-conversation room?"

"You and Mom have one of those rooms too? That's cool, Ricardo."

"Don't give me too much credit, Luke," said Ricardo with a sound of defeat in his voice. "I used to call it my study, but your mom has changed its name. She told me it was for the best, so who am I to argue with her?"

"Yep, sounds like Mom. And speaking of my mother, your wife, I know I'm a little late in saying something, but you know that at the Cruz household we have a no-return policy when it comes to marriage, don't you? You're in for some changes, Ricardo, but I'm guessing that you knew that already. And I can see that you're going to handle them all just fine."

A few minutes later they both had a cup of coffee in their hands and were sitting in the newly designated coffee-and-conversation room. Ricardo started out by asking a direct question related to the last talk Luke had had with Maggy's dad.

"If the intent of your request for lunch with Mr. Middlefield couldn't have been misunderstood, and yet he blew off your request for a private conversation about his daughter, what is your heart telling you will happen when you talk with Maggy next?"

Luke just sat there, gripping his warm mug, afraid to say out loud what he was thinking in his heart.

"I'm not sure what to think, Ricardo, but something must have happened recently that has made him question my worthiness to marry his daughter. I really don't know what that thing might be, but what I do know is that he's going to have two weeks to talk to Maggy and influence her in whatever direction he wants her to go. Maggy loves her dad, and she'll listen to him. Something inside me is telling me to prepare for the worst."

Ricardo was in the middle of a sip of coffee, so it took him a second to ask, "What makes you say that?"

Luke answered that question in a somewhat matter-of-fact and defeated tone, knowing that Maggy's dad would always trump him when it came to Maggy's love and loyalty.

"Markus told me the day before you married Mom that his dad is not the man everyone thinks he is. But keeping us apart for some mysterious reason doesn't seem to be the Matthew Middlefield I know . . . unless I don't know the real Matthew Middlefield."

"Well, then, keeping all this in mind, I have only one more question, Luke: in your heart, do you absolutely believe that Maggy has been set aside for you by our God that we both believe in?"

"Absolutely, Ricardo. Without reservation."

"Then my counsel to you is to be patient and wait no matter what your next conversation with Maggy might bring. Now, how about we go back to the living room with everyone else? Your mom and I have quite a story to tell and an announcement to make."

After getting everyone's attention, an exceptional feat considering there were five children under the age of ten in the room, Ricardo began to speak with more than a little excitement and emotion in his voice. "Now that everyone has had some time to play with, try on, or eat their sweet gifts, Rebecca, your new stepmom, and I would like to tell everyone more about our time at my hometown in Colombia during our honeymoon."

Ricardo began telling this story by describing his emotions at seeing the house he spent the first five years of his life growing up in, though he barely remembered it at all. He attributed this inability to recall any memories to the 50 years of remodeling and updating the old house had received, as had the houses around it. When he had finished sharing his limited memories of these first five years, he then told everyone about his distant relatives that did not make it to the wedding. Once he had finished talking about old houses and long-lost relatives, he glanced toward Rebecca, who gave him an encouraging look that said, *This is the time. Tell your story and make our announcement.* After taking a deep breath and looking at everyone gathered in his home that evening, people who wouldn't have been born without Ricardo living the life he had been given, he began to lovingly tell his family a story of his early life and of God's providence; it was a more powerful story than any of them could have imagined.

"Let's start this conversation with my sister, Rita, whom you all met at our wedding. It turns out she gave me a most exceptional gift without even realizing it. She had simply told me about the orphanage that took care of me for one year and then found me a home to grow up in. What I had never realized was that this feeling—the feeling of a need for closure concerning why I had to go through this heartache of abandonment—had been there from the day I was brought briefly to this new home of mine. This surprise adventure began once we made it to my hometown in Colombia.

"You all need to understand that this unexpected gift from my big sister was a gift from her heart. It has already been almost three years since we first contacted each other. What I didn't know until our honeymoon in Colombia was that it took her almost a month's worth of phone calls in order to speak directly with the director of that orphanage. By the end of that conversation, she had successfully arranged with the orphanage to meet with me if I ever came back to Colombia. By the time Rita had made that decision and set up a meeting with the directors, she had been told about the wedding, so she decided to save this news as a wedding gift. The directors were excited to meet me, and they wanted to hear my story about what had happened to me 'after the orphanage.' Unknown to Rebecca and me, that was the main reason for her pleading with us that we spend our honeymoon in Colombia."

After sharing this surprising news, Ricardo went silent as he took a moment to look at his family and thank God for the blessing that was surrounding him. His girls could see their father's eyes begin to moisten, and because of these overwhelming emotions running through his heart, his throat choked up, rendering him speechless for a minute. In that moment, he sent a silent prayer of thanks to God for blessing him with the gift of such an amazing family. Finally gaining the use of his voice again, he continued with his story.

"Sorry about that, everyone. I got a little choked up for a minute thinking of the past, but I'm okay." Ricardo quickly took one more look around the room, and after landing on Rebecca for a long moment, he continued telling his story. "After spending several days with the staff in that orphanage, we discovered that each one of them had hearts of gold for every little one that came into and then went out of their orphanage. And I was included in that list of little ones, only 50 years earlier. The directors of this orphanage were excited to hear the story of one of their 'little angels' coming back after 50 years of being out in the 'big world.'"

The head director had told them that it was rare for one of their 'placed' orphan children to come back. But to have one show up on their doorstep after 50 years had *never* happened. Ricardo continued telling this most recent story, a story in which he would no longer be passing through doors alone but would have Rebecca at his side.

"After we spent some additional days at the orphanage, and with much prayer, Rebecca and I have made a decision." And then he went silent.

By this time, Ricardo had built up such anticipation in everyone that he heard nothing but cries of, "Come on, Dad. Just tell us what you're going to do! Just spill the beans, Dad!"

And spill the beans he did. "It may seem to be something more than we can achieve, but Rebecca and I have decided to start a small non-profit adoption agency that we hope will be able to partner with other international agencies. We're going to call it 'After the Orphanage.'"

Everyone there clapped for joy. It appeared that Ricardo and Rebecca had just filled the remainder of their lives with a reason to get up every morning.

"We don't know where this idea will lead us, but we can at least start doing something. We also know we can't help every little one find a loving home like I did, but we can help some of them. Think about it, kids. Like I said a minute ago, none of you, except those who married into the family, would be here if I had never been adopted by your grandparents. That thought truly saddens me. But you *are* here, and that thought fills my heart with joy. So there you have it! Our next new adventure in life!

Back in Aspen, Matthew drew in a long breath, knowing what he had to say. He began to speak to Markus and Maggy about some very serious issues, issues that couldn't be ignored any longer. And there was that small voice inside him, telling him exactly what he needed to say and how he needed to say it.

"You both are involved in the construction company and have met most of our clients over the past three years. We have built homes for some very important and influential people during this time, and for many years before. Many of them are self-employed, others are CEOs and executives in some of the largest companies in the state, and most of them have become our friends. Not once have we judged them for any personal proclivities they may have. Actually, Maggy, it was you attending the business college that put everything in motion that I'm about to explain to you."

"I didn't do anything wrong, Dad," said Maggy, hoping that nothing she did at college had caused something bad to happen to her dad. "All I ever did was go to classes and study sessions with some of the other kids."

"And did you meet a young man named Peter VanderMor in one of those study sessions?"

"Yeah, I know Peter," she answered slowly, still not understanding what that had to do with what was going on with her family. "What about it?"

"Well, you must have made some kind of impression on him, because he went home one day after school and told his dad all about you. The two of them then did a little checking up on you through social media and found out more about you, including who your parents are, our occupation, and, in particular, where we live."

"Ugh, he sounds like a creep! And so does his dad!" exclaimed Maggy, visibly shuddering.

"On the contrary, my cautious and beautiful daughter. Peter's dad is a nationally known political mover and shaker. It seems that the district we live in is in need of representation; the current representative got himself into a little trouble and has lost public support. George VanderMor called me more than two months ago to introduce himself to me and your mom. It turns out that he has taken a liking to me, our family, our business, and my stance on all the current political issues. Having the social network that we have is a real benefit as well. He has asked me if I would like to run for the national House of Representatives seat in our district this coming November. That's why we took this vacation—so that we could talk about everything as a family and how this decision will affect all of us. I really would like everyone's opinion about whether I should or shouldn't go into politics. We need to make that decision together. So, there you have it. Our next new adventure in life." Matthew ended this announcement with a self-satisfied smile on his face, casting a sideways glance toward Elizabeth, who also seemed to have warmed up to the idea of being a politician's wife.

"That's pretty cool, Dad. You're going to be a bigwig," said Markus. "But who's going to run the company if you get elected?"

"That will be a big part of the conversation this week. Your mother will be the acting CEO for the time being, but my hope is that you would one day run the company. But first we need to put a solid five-year transition plan in place."

Markus almost visually puffed out his chest while eating another fork full of turkey dressing. He started considering what changes he might institute at the office now that he was on track to run the company. Maggy, on the other hand, was not pleased with this plan at all.

"And what about me, Dad? I have more natural business instincts than Markus will ever have—you said it yourself. You're putting Markus ahead of me just because he's a man, and you know it! And what would this 'George guy' and your future constituents think about your position on that social issue?"

Matthew didn't answer her question right away. He was wondering if this is what he should expect from those he did not agree with in the political world when it comes to issues he believed in. Then Markus, seeing an opening in the conversation, joined in saying, "I can't argue with Maggy's point, Dad, and I don't think you can either, because she's right about that. Maggy is a real business shark, and . . . well . . . I'm not. I don't mind the work, but I'm not a paperwork type of guy."

It was Maggy's turn to voice yet another hypocritical thought, the kind of thought produced by seeing her father over the years say one thing and do another. "And if I'm not going to run this company one day, then why am I going to business college and Markus isn't?"

"Good point and good question, Maggy. It appears that we have more to talk about this week than I anticipated. Or, we will just have to have two presidents in our office—one CFO and one CEO."

It was at that point Matthew heard the voice in his head say, *Good, Matthew. That was a perfect setup. It's time to tell your daughter what she needs to hear, and make sure she's on our side. Don't worry, it'll turn out just fine. Now do it!*

Matthew knew what the next topic of their conversation would be, and he was more than okay with saying what had to be said. "Worrying about who is going to be the CEO of our company if I get elected isn't important right now. What *is* important for you right now, Maggy, is Luke Cruz. We need to talk about him now, which was the second reason we took this vacation. Your mother and I have been talking and we think that if you don't cut him loose, he will negatively affect your future."

Maggy wasn't able to respond to her father's assertion concerning Luke or his desire for her to throw Luke away at this point in their relationship. She was frozen there, looking at him in disbelief. Where did this hard turn in the conversation come from anyway? First, they were talking about going to business school, then about going into politics, then running Middlefield Homes, and now he was insinuating how bad Luke was. A man she thought her family liked and approved of. A man she had intended to marry.

"Now, he is a nice boy, but his beliefs do not run parallel to those you were raised with, beliefs that built this company into what it is today. They are also not the beliefs that I will be expressing while running for office. Now, if he had proposed to you and you had said yes, it may have taken a year or two, but these issues would have eventually come up at some point in your marriage. And then the trouble would have started. I'm only suggesting that you slow down a bit, think all these issues through, and maybe even consider dating some other guys. After all, Luke is the only guy you've ever dated, and who knows what other nice young men are waiting to meet you out there."

Matthew lovingly rubbed his daughter's back, her face void of emotion as she was taking in everything he had said. She wondered if she had truly missed anything about Luke that would have revealed to her a different man than the one she thought she knew.

Before revealing his true intentions for his daughter's future, Matthew turned the conversation around and went back to the young man she had told him about from her study group. "Take Peter VanderMor as an example. He will be graduating this spring with a Political Science degree, and he seems to be a nice guy. I know for a fact his father would be in favor of you two spending some time with each other, and honestly, Maggy, so would I."

Maggy sat on the oversized lounging couch in their rented condominium, stunned at what she heard her father suggesting. *Why is Dad saying these things? Does he know something about Luke that I don't know? I don't believe he would purposely give me bad advice. I need to talk more with him.*

Coming out of her private thoughts, she heard her father say, "You and Luke have been dating since you were 16. I was okay with that when I first recognized his exceptional grasp of construction, believing you two could be a real force in new-home building in our city, but when his social positions became known to me and your mother, I couldn't just stand by and let you be corrupted by those beliefs. We've raised you to be accepting of people for who they are and for their different beliefs; we didn't teach you to judge them as being inferior people because of the choices they have made in their lives. Luke and his mother seem to want everyone to be like them and believe what they believe, and that just isn't right." Matthew held both her hands in his and looked her directly in the eyes. "Now, Maggy, we've been on this earth a little longer than you have, so you'll just have to trust your old dad and mom on this one."

Maggy sat there, thinking about what her father was saying and what he was asking her to give up. After enough time had passed, Matthew went on making his case against Luke and against them as a couple. Then he talked about the difficulties they would endure as spouses. Elizabeth also shared her concerns about this possible marriage in between Matthew's thoughts.

"Maggy, as your father, I have to ask you an extremely important question: are you really sure in the depths of your heart that Luke is the guy for you?" Maggy said nothing. She just sat there contemplating this life-changing decision.

Later that evening, sitting in front of a wood-burning fireplace, Markus and Maggy quietly listened to the sounds of crackling firewood, neither of them saying anything for the longest time. They no longer wanted what they thought they had wanted when they were younger. Everything was changing, and it was changing quickly. They needed to be alone, to talk about the events of the afternoon, away from the influence of their parents.

"Well, Maggy, what do you think about the bombshells Dad dropped on us during dinner?" asked Markus as he began to eat another piece of cherry pie.

How can he be eating at a time like this? thought Maggy, as she watched her brother methodically work his way through the piece of pie, eating the filling first and then his favorite part, the crust, which had sugar and pie filling on it.

Maggy didn't know how Markus did it, but it seemed that through the years he never lost his appetite, no matter what the difficulties the day may have brought. There were even occasional times she thought she heard him singing to himself in his room after a difficult day at school or work. No matter what was happening around him, he was always able to sing or eat his way to a happy disposition. Perhaps these were simple coping mechanisms that made Markus who he was.

"I don't know, Markus. I just don't know what to think. Dad has never given me bad advice before, so why would he say something like this and purposely mislead me, unless there was some truth to it? And why hasn't Luke even attempted to ask Dad for his blessing to marry me? We've been together long enough, and I have been giving him hints for months that it would be okay to propose. He even made comments that made me think it was going to be sometime before the end of the year."

Thinking about that question while washing down another bite of pie with a glass of milk, Markus said, "I don't know, Maggy, but it seems to me that we're only hearing half the story. What I do know is that Dad is a pretty smooth talker and a really good salesman, so he'll make a great politician. And the one thing we can both agree on is that the only thing Dad loves more than money, is power. Being elected to Congress would be like letting a kid run loose in a candy shop. I think he'll do whatever it takes to make that happen, including talking you into dropping Luke. I also don't care how plausible or eloquent his arguments might sound; I refuse to believe them. I'm not walking away from Luke. I've seen Luke at school and at parties; I've seen how he treats his mom; I've seen how he led us guys on the baseball diamond and on jobsites; I have also watched how he treats you, Maggy. The guy has always treated you like a queen. He told me once that he would treat you as though Dad and Mom were on every date you guys were on. Now that's cool—a little odd, but still cool. And if having his social positions has made Luke into the man that he is, then I want to be more like him. Even if you decide not to marry him, he's still going to be my brother for life. So get used to the idea of seeing him around until you're an old woman. You'll be reminded of what you missed out on every time you see him."

Maggy spent the next week talking with her dad and mom and reflecting on what she wanted out of life. The scenic backdrop of this lodge in Aspen, as well as being free from her cell phone, was extremely beneficial in giving her the quiet time she needed to answer some important questions.

Luke was finally able to get ahold of Maggy when she returned home with her family the previous evening. Their conversation on the phone was pretty short, and Luke didn't quite know how to interpret it. They agreed to get together at Luke's house Sunday evening to talk about everything that had taken place over the last two weeks. Luke had just finished brushing his teeth when he heard the back door close.

"Maggy!" exclaimed Luke as he came running down the staircase, bounding up to her to give his girl a kiss and a long hug. Immediately Luke knew something was wrong, because she hadn't given him a Maggy-hug or a Maggy-kiss in return. After giving him a weird, uncomfortable hug, she stepped back away from him and leaned on the kitchen island instead of leaning into his shoulder and resting her head on his chest, as he was expecting.

"Maggy, what's up? What was that? That wasn't the kind of hug I usually get from you. As a matter of fact, it feels like you've just given me the cold shoulder. And it's been two weeks since we've seen each other. That's not normal. Come on, Maggy. What's going on?" Luke probed with a sense of anxiety and dread in his stomach.

She looked at the floor, then started twisting her hair in her left index finger as a tell that she was getting nervous. Then, as if on a mission, she looked up directly at Luke and said, "Calm down, Luke. I just walked in the door! Give me a minute and I'll tell you everything. Now, because of how long we have known each other, I feel obligated to tell you that I had a lot of time to talk with my dad and mom these last two weeks, and I found out some things about myself and about you that need to be addressed."

And with those words, a bolt of fear shot threw his heart.

"And what would these things be?"

Luke was now leaning on the opposite side of the kitchen island from Maggy, somewhat agitated because he couldn't believe what he was hearing or where he feared this conversation was heading.

"One thing we talked about on our vacation was the moral stances your church is taking on cultural changes taking place in America today. Your mom and I have been talking about these topics when we were both here at your house. I told my mom about these conversations, and she is very concerned about what you guys believe and what your church teaches. My dad heard us talking and didn't like what he heard either. And the more we talked about these social issues, and the more I had time to think about them, the more I don't like what your mom was saying either. And if you really believe the things your mom was trying to persuade me to believe, well, we're going to have some problems."

"What kind of problems are you talking about, Maggy? You never had issues with my mom's conversations or our moral stances before this vacation of yours. What exactly did your dad talk to you about? What's *really* going on?"

"I guess when it comes down to it, I can't believe that we both call ourselves Americans, and yet we see social issues so differently."

"And I guess I can't believe that we both call ourselves Christians, and yet we follow the teachings of Jesus so differently."

Luke didn't want to fight with Maggy, but she had just attacked his beliefs, even if subtly. These beliefs —beliefs that he thought she had as well—were given to him and all true Christians from Jesus himself. It was at this point that the words of his grandpa's last letter concerning Maggy came rushing back into his mind.

"I can't talk about this anymore, Luke. I just came over to ask if we could take some time away from each other so that we can both really decide if we belong together as a couple."

"What? You want to take a break? After being together for over three years?"

"I'm sorry, Luke, but I just can't talk about this anymore. I've got to go. I'll call you."

As Maggy turned away from Luke, walking out the back screen door and letting it slap shut, the oven bell rang out. Luke had spent several days over the Christmas holiday at Ricardo's house learning how to make his grandmother's hot tamales for Maggy. They were ready to come out of the oven just as Maggy was walking out of the house; she didn't even give a backward glance or say goodbye. It appeared Luke would be eating tamales alone for the next several meals.

The following Monday morning, Luke found Markus on their jobsite with three other guys framing up the walls to the first floor of another beast of a house. After attaching the hose of his air hammer to the compressor, and in between the noise of 16-penny nails being injected into the wood studs of the walls, Luke asked Markus, "What happened on your ski trip? Maggy wasn't at my place last night for more than five minutes before telling me that we have some pretty big issues. She basically broke up with me. I've always seen you as a brother, Markus, so tell me honestly: what's going on with Maggy? Why are there suddenly breakup issues today that we didn't seem to have before?"

Markus was lifting his air hammer up to the top of a ten-foot wall while standing on an eight-foot step ladder. "Hold the wall plumb, Luke, so I can nail it in place."

After driving three nails into the wall, he stepped down from the ladder and said, "It's not Maggy as much as it is my mom and dad, and I'm almost certain it has to do with his new political aspirations."

Luke almost dropped the plumb line he was holding when he heard that news, wondering what Matthew's political desires had to do with him, and with his relationship with Maggy. "He's got what?" he finally asked Markus.

"Yeah, I know, political aspirations—who would have guessed? Although, it really doesn't surprise me. Aren't most people in Congress pretty conceited and full of themselves? Because if it's true, I think my dad would fit right in."

Luke was confused as to where Matthew's political ambitions were coming from and why these ambitions would affect him and Maggy so directly. Matthew had always seemed happy and content with his construction business, so what happened that would make him change everything in his life so dramatically and so quickly?

Luke and two other guys lifted the next 20-foot section of wall so that Markus could nail it into place. Markus hadn't answered Luke's question on purpose. He had opted to wait for the other three carpenters to go to the lumber pile and bring up more studs for the next wall. When they were out of earshot, Markus said, "Hey, Luke, can we talk about this at lunchtime? I don't think my dad wants me yelling out his future plans at one of his jobsites for everyone to hear."

"Sure. No problem, Markus."

————————————

Three hours later they were sitting in the cab of Markus's truck eating their lunch. After swallowing a rather large mouthful of doughnut, Markus asked, "So what was that last question you asked that I didn't answer?"

Perfect timing, Markus, thought Luke, having taken another bite of his tamale while waiting for Markus to swallow his doughnut. Just about the time Luke was going to ask his question, he saw Markus lifting the final piece of doughnut toward his mouth. Luke reached over, grabbed Markus's arm, and said, "Sorry, dude, but both of us have to stop eating at the same time so we can talk. You said something about your dad giving politics a try. What's up with that? I've never heard him talk about politics before, and why does it have to affect me and Maggy? How long has he been thinking about making this change in careers?"

Markus didn't answer right away. He was digging around in his lunchbox for something else to eat. Finding nothing, he glanced in Luke's lunchbox and asked, "Are you going to eat your last tamale?

"No, Markus, I'm not. You can have it. Just answer my question."

"Don't get snappy, dude. Just relax. I'll answer your question right after I take a sample bite of your tamale." After being satisfied with the taste, texture, and flavor of Luke's lunch, he said, "This is a really good tasting tamale. Where'd you buy it?"

"I didn't buy it, dude, I made it. Now will you answer my question! My life is about to fall apart, and all you can do is eat," Luke said with both amusement and annoyance.

Markus, realizing he had allowed food to get in the way of their conversation, said, "Sorry, dude, I should have realized how all this is making you feel." Markus took a moment to wipe his mouth and set down the tamale before focusing on his friend.

"Here's what I know. It sounds like my dad has been considering a run for the last two months. He has some new political friend who seems to be important in the political world, and he's asked Dad to run for the House of Representative seat that is opening up this November in our district. And it's not too hard to see how it's already changing him. He wants to look squeaky clean to the public. And I guess your religious beliefs aren't what the party is looking for, which means your relationship with Maggy had to be dealt with."

Luke had just taken a drink of his soda, and after hearing what Markus said, he almost spit it out of his mouth and onto the windshield. After swallowing, he said, "You've gotta be kidding me" loud enough to make some of the guys on their crew turn their heads toward the truck. "I had to be *dealt with*? What does that even mean?"

Luke was quiet for a while as he processed not only what Markus said but also the reality of how his relationship with the Middlefield family had changed so drastically, and in such a short time. Luke quickly glanced sideways at Markus who was watching his reaction.

"So where do you stand in all this, Markus? Are we still friends?"

Markus looked out the front windshield, took in a big breath, and held it a second before letting it out. He then turned towards

Luke and looked him directly in the eye before boldly stating, "Dad can't make me think any differently about you, and he can't push me around quite as easily as he does Maggy. I love my family, but that doesn't mean I like them. I've accepted that we have different views and values in life. Luke, you have to believe me when I say that I have always looked up to you. No one can manipulate me into believing there is something wrong with the way you see the world. Not even my own dad."

"Thanks, Markus. I appreciate that." Luke was settling down now after hearing that at least one Middlefield family member still saw him as the good man he tried to be. "But, Markus, I still don't get it. How can your dad and mom, and even Maggy, change so quickly about how they feel about me? And it's over one small opportunity that isn't even a sure thing. I've always thought that your dad saw me as a son, not just something to be dealt with."

Markus took a drink of his coffee and then brought up an old story that had never been fully told. "Luke, do you remember the day before your mom's wedding when I told you that my dad and mom weren't really the good people they portray themselves to be?"

"Yeah, I remember. I just figured that, like most people, they put up as good a front as possible in public. I didn't think they intentionally tried to deceive anyone. I still thought of them as basically good people."

After setting his thermos on the dash and letting out a long sigh, Markus decided it was time to open the door to his parents' private lives so that Luke could peek in. After all, he was almost family. "Once I start telling you about the real Matthew and Elizabeth, you'll start to understand who they truly are and why they treat you so badly."

"Come on, man, I feel like you're exaggerating. Nobody can really be a Dr. Jeckyll and Mr. Hyde in real life, can they?"

"Yeah, Luke, they can. The real Matthew and Elizabeth Middlefield live behind a closed and locked door, a door that is rarely, if ever, open to the public. And I'm guessing that's because they're afraid of how people would react if they saw the real Matthew and Elizabeth. But I can't blame you for not knowing that, because the more I pay attention to their actions, the more I see that they are masters of deceit, manipulation, and cover-up. After observing them for so long, I'm only just now in this last year starting to put together the pieces of their story myself. The stories I've heard through the years about their childhood and about their high school and college years are beginning to show me how they have purposefully become the people they are today. And the people they have become are the ones making the choices you can't understand."

Luke sat there in Markus's truck, finding it hard to accept the realization that the two people he thought he would one day call Dad and Mom weren't the people they portrayed themselves to be. "What kind of stories are we talking about, Markus?" Now Luke may have flippantly asked this question of his friend, but as he thought about the kind of answer he might receive, it made him question if he really wanted to know the full truth.

A minute ago, Markus and Luke were so loud inside Markus's truck that the other carpenters were wondering if something was wrong. But now it was so quiet that it made them wonder the same thing. And then Markus began: "Luke, what I'm about to tell you may freak you out a little, because it sure freaks me out when I think about it. But you asked, so I'm going to answer. Here's just one example of what I'm talking about. Six or seven months ago, I was walking past my parents' bedroom and I heard them talking. The double doors were closed, so their voices were muffled. I was still walking down the hall, headed to the kitchen, but I hesitated when I heard my dad's voice get a little animated. That's when I heard it, Luke. I heard another man's voice. Which is not a big deal, since they're always having people over to the house. But, dude, never in their bedroom. It was really weird. And to make it even more strange, the voice was low and deep—it almost sounded evil. It was really creepy. All I wanted to do was get out of there. I started getting shivers up and down my spine as I listened to the three of them talking, still being too afraid to move away from outside their bedroom door for fear I'd get caught listening in.

The three of them kept talking for several minutes, and when it got a little noisy in the room, I saw my opportunity and bolted down the staircase. I went to the kitchen and had a glass of water, trying to calm down. What was even more creepy was ten minutes later when my dad and mom came downstairs, *and there was no one with them.* I asked my dad if there was someone in the house, because I thought I heard someone else talking upstairs. He just blew me off and told me it was probably the news anchor on the television in their room. He reminded me how he talks back to the television screen because those news commentators say such stupid things. It was weird, Luke, really weird. I know I heard a third voice, Luke, and no one can make me think any different."

Luke wasn't able to respond right away, but when he could, he asked, "Are you suggesting, Markus, what I think you're suggesting about your dad?"

Markus looked back into Luke's stare and said, "I'm not sure exactly what I'm suggesting, Luke. I'm only telling you about what I heard from the two people you have looked up to for years. You probably wouldn't have looked up to them if you had heard what I heard. But let's get off this strange encounter and talk about my mother."

"Okay, dude, but I can see we'll be revisiting this topic."

"Well, the first thing you should know is that my mom absolutely despises weak-minded people, especially men. They are pathetic excuses of the male gender in her mind, and she wants absolutely nothing to do with them. Her words, not mine." He added this last part while holding up his hands, since Luke was giving him a weird look. "She's also pretty quick to pass judgment on a man's character with very little evidence to back up her opinion. In her mind, once she has labeled you, there's no escaping that label."

At hearing that about Elizabeth, Luke interrupted Markus. "That's a pretty serious accusation to make about your mom. How do you know this stuff about her?"

"From the bits and pieces I've heard her say through the years. That's how, man. It turns out that her dad, my grandpa, is the main reason for this mindset. I found out that he was the manager at a local grocery store in the small town she grew up in. The way my mom describes him is: he was a quiet, reserved, friendly man who loved his job and loved serving the people of their town. She apparently hated him for being like that.

"I've never met my grandparents, Luke, but they sound like good people to me. From what I've heard, I would've loved to have spent time with them and gotten to know them. As far as I know, they're still alive, but we're not allowed to contact either of them. From what my mom said, it sounds like she hates them simply because they didn't make much money—which is dumb!"

Luke was confused and disturbed at the thought that someone could hate someone else simply because of their income.

Markus continued, not noticing the frown on Luke's face. "They weren't even poor. Not that it matters. It sounded like his job paid pretty well, but I guess not well enough to satisfy my mother. Her parents didn't believe in wasting money by buying name brand things or trendy clothes. She blamed her father for not caring about her family and not being ambitious enough to get a high-paying job so that they could have nicer things. She acts like it was humiliating. I mean, it sounds like she had loving parents and lived comfortably, and yet it wasn't enough for her." Markus flung his arms out as he got more heated about this topic.

"Well, she sure is making up for it now," Luke quietly mumbled as he thought of all the over-the-top, extremely nice things the Middlefield family owned. They had several of the latest models of high-end cars; their house was full of the newest technology; and Luke couldn't even pronounce half the clothing brands they wore.

Markus hadn't stopped speaking while Luke was reflecting. "I guess her mom had to get a job at a bakery to help pay some of the bills. My mom claimed that this financial stress on her mom affected her health. In my mom's eyes, my grandpa should've been the one to take responsibility for those financial matters, not her mother. She still blames him for her mom's bad health."

Luke was still sitting, not moving and not responding to anything Markus was saying. He hadn't expected to hear these types of stories about Elizabeth and, honestly, he didn't know how to react or what to say. It made him wonder what other stories Markus had about his dad.

Their lunch break was coming to an end, so Luke asked, "Is there much more to tell, Markus? Our lunch break is just about over."

"Yeah, there is. Let me finish telling you about my mom, and after work I'll tell you more about my dear old dad."

Luke said okay and then waited for the story to begin again.

"My mom is actually a pretty smart person, Luke. She's just doesn't have very good people skills. She actually received a full-ride scholarship to college, and that's how she ended up meeting my dad. As soon as she graduated from high school, she packed up her things, left for college, and never looked back. I don't think my mom has contacted my grandparents once since then, which is just sad."

"Wow, Markus. I had no idea. Does your mom hate all men, or just the ones she thinks are weak?" Luke asked, wondering what labels Elizabeth had placed on him.

"Just those she feels are weak and don't deserve to be called 'real men.' Of course, she's the one who gets to decide what the definition of weakness is."

One short water break and four hours later, they were sitting on the floor of the small mansion they had been framing for the last three weeks. Their legs were hanging over the back edge of the house as they admired the lake this home was being built next to. Everyone had left the jobsite now, so Markus could speak freely.

"All right, Markus, you've got me curious, and I've been waiting all afternoon to ask. What's your dad's story?"

Before continuing on about his parents' past, Markus became serious and turned toward Luke with a somber look on his face. "I've been thinking about what I've told you already and what I'm going to tell you now, Luke. You have to promise me that you won't tell anyone. My parents can't find out that you know all this stuff." Markus couldn't even imagine what his parents might do if they found out what he was telling Luke, especially now that his dad was running for office.

Luke looked at Markus in surprise and genuinely asked, "Dude, how can you even ask a question like that?"

"Because I know what I'm about to tell you, and you don't." Markus's response made Luke's back shiver. *Just how bad is it,* Luke wondered.

"Don't worry. We're brothers and we've always had each other's back," Luke assured his closest friend with a serious tone. "You know I won't say a thing."

Markus took a quick moment to gulp down some water from his one-gallon thermos. "First of all, you know from your own experience dealing with my dad that he does not have the character of a weak man. He has a very distinct and strong personality, which is probably why my mom and dad started dating. But what he is, and I have seen this for myself firsthand, is a master manipulator. It's as though he can read people's minds or, at the very least, has someone giving him information he can use against other people. I don't know what made him like this, but I do think he actually enjoys manipulating people. He had to have learned this as a kid, because it just comes naturally to him." Markus stopped again and restated to Luke: "Remember, don't repeat any of what I'm going to tell you to anyone."

"Markus," said Luke with some irritation at this second request, "quit being so melodramatic. Whatever you're going to tell me can't be all that bad, can it? It's not like he killed someone."

"No, I guess not," Markus said with a defeated sound in his voice. "This next bit of information I found out by pure accident. Two years ago, I was walking from the kitchen back to my bedroom one night, and I happened to walk by the living room where my parents were talking. They didn't know I was there, but my dad sounded pretty upset. I heard him say, 'That big mouth brother of mine can't keep his mouth shut. One of these days, Danny is going to say the wrong thing and I won't be able to fix it!'"

My mom then said, "Well, it's not like he's really your brother. You guys simply grew up in the same foster home. If something happens, just cut him off." I didn't know what they were talking about, and I didn't stick around to find out."

"Wow, Markus, that must have been a shock to you, finding out that your dad was in the foster care system."

"Yeah, you could say that. It was more shocking to hear him speak of his past, since he never talks about it. I just always assumed he didn't get along with his family and that's why he never mentioned them. I didn't even know he had any siblings. If the only parental influence he had was the foster system, that would explain why he's so cold and manipulative."

Luke had to interrupt Markus after hearing this part of Matthew's story. "What a terrible childhood he must've had! I can't even imagine what it must've been like growing up in the system. No wonder he turned out the way he did. Maybe we should be cutting your dad some slack after all."

"I know what you're saying, Luke, and this next part will make you feel even worse for what he went through. He was thrown out of our social system, and the house he grew up in, when he turned 18."

As Markus continued telling Luke about his father's story, Luke briefly thought to himself, *Am I feeling sorry for Matthew right now? The man who caused me and his daughter to break up? Wow, this is getting way too weird.* He tuned back in to listen to Markus's story.

"I did some research the following week into the foster care system in our state. I know I should check it out more, but my initial thoughts are that it's kind of a messed-up system."

"Come on, Markus, that program has been around for decades and has helped tens of thousands of kids, and no one is complaining about it. But after checking into this national program for just a few days, you have questions about how it's run? There has got to be something good about the work that this program and its people are doing."

"I don't know what to tell you, Luke, but I learned a lot of disturbing facts. The biggest thing I found out was that in most foster care households that care for kids full-time, there were typically between four and eight kids in a house."

At hearing that statistic, Luke was taken aback, for though he had always wished for siblings, eight kids in one house could be overwhelming to everyone living there.

"I've done a lot of digging and research, and everything I've read has made these foster homes sound horrible. Think about it, Luke. These kids have a mom and dad that aren't really their parents, and the two reasons you're in the house are, first, because your birth parents either didn't want you, or they died; second, because the state is paying them to babysit you for the next 10 to 18 years. And it's even more sad, because apparently you can age out of the foster system when you turn 18. That means the government no longer pays for your care and you are practically kicked out of the house so that another kid can replace you. Dude, can you even imagine? I wonder how many foster siblings my dad has . . ." Markus trailed off with that last thought.

Luke looked blankly at the lake and said, "Wow, that's messed up. That explains a lot about your dad, though. Kind of makes you wonder why he hid this part of his past."

Markus, having also turned his gaze to the lake, went on with another part of the story. "Another weird thing I've noticed lately with my dad is this sort of weird ability to read a person's character within a few minutes of meeting them."

"Well, that doesn't sound too strange to me. He's just gifted at reading people's character," Luke replied. He had worked with Matthew long enough to know that he was good at reading people.

"But that's the thing, Luke. He's almost *too* good. I don't know how he is able to manipulate conversations, but somehow people tell him things they don't mean to, or they end up agreeing to the things *he* wants. Plus, he randomly knows all sorts of secrets about people he's just met! I know I sound crazy, but something about it just feels off to me."

Again, Luke was amazed at what his best friend was revealing to him, because now that Markus mentioned Matthew's calculating character, he was recalling some conversations that he had had with Matthew in the past. Luke could now clearly see what Matthew was doing.

Markus began to share still another gift that his dad had been born with, a gift he had refined through the years.

"When my dad aged out of the system, he was able to get college scholarships, which is how he met my mom. Both of them truly match each other, huh?" Markus said with a deprecating sigh. "Did you know he played football in college? It's why he's so hung up on always winning. Doesn't matter if it's a game of golf, a new work contract, or even personal relationships. He's always told Maggy and me to make sure we surround ourselves with people who can benefit our future. 'Always be a winner, no matter what it takes,' is his motto."

Luke could see that Markus had shared it all, and there was no more to say about his parents. But looking at Markus, Luke thought he saw a mixture of both sadness and relief on his face, as if saying all this stuff out loud was almost therapeutic. Luke leaned back with a sigh, still processing everything Markus had shared.

"I can't believe you've been keeping all this to yourself for all these years, Markus. How do you feel now that you've got this off your chest? Because you sure look better."

"As a matter of fact," said Markus with a big, cleansing sigh, "I do feel better. Thanks for listening to me and letting me dump all this on you. I didn't realize there would be so much."

"Sure, no problem, Markus. I'm glad to help out. But I only have one more thing to say about these insights into how your parents have become the people they are today. And knowing more about them does help me understand the Maggy breakup a little more. But it doesn't fix it. My big question is, Can I do anything to fix the issues with Maggy and your folks?"

"I don't know what to tell you, Luke, except that if you're on my parents' blacklist, don't be too optimistic about getting off it . . . or getting back with Maggy. They have a really big influence on her. As much as I love both of you, this honestly might be for the best. Sorry, bro."

As they finished their conversation, they both agreed to not let these personal issues with Matthew and Elizabeth affect their friendship or their work. If Matthew had issues with Luke, then he'd have to talk to Luke and address him face to face. For the time being, he was going to wait and see what happened before he decided what to do next.

Two weeks later, the first of many of these opportunities arose when Luke and Markus were asked to come into the main office. Matthew wanted them to participate in several subcontractor interviews, something that was not taught at the Construction Management course. For Maggy's sake, and to avoid any uncomfortable interactions in the office, Matthew made sure that she was out running errands when Luke showed up. No matter what Matthew thought about Luke's social opinions, he knew Luke was on his way to becoming a top-rate builder in their city, and he didn't want to lose him to a competitor.

"Hey, Dad, what are these interviews about anyway?"

Markus was standing in the doorway to his father's office leaning on the door jamb when he asked this question; Luke was standing just behind him and off to the side. An irritated look grew on Matthew's face as he looked up at Markus.

While giving Markus this look, he slapped a handful of files onto his desk rather loudly and said, "Markus, how many times do I have to tell you that I'm 'Dad' at home and 'Matthew' at work? You need to be more professional at work if you want to be respected as you grow in the leadership role I have planned for you. Can't you see that, Markus?"

"Okay. Sorry, Dad."

Luke couldn't tell if Markus had been intentionally disrespectful to his dad for a second time, or if he really didn't know what he had done. Either way, and in spite of what Markus had told him about not getting off his dad's blacklist, he thought it was a good time to step in. He was hoping this would be a good opportunity to start getting back on the good side of Matthew.

"I hear that congratulations are in order for you and your run for office, Matthew. It sounds like a great opportunity for you. But how will running for public office affect your ability to run your business? Are you allowed to keep ownership of the company and stay involved in daily operations while running for Congress?"

Matthew gave Markus a look that said, *Why can't you act more like Luke?*

"That's a very insightful question, and the short answer is, I can't be involved in this business much longer. That's why I'm having you and Markus in these meetings. It's because of political laws not allowing elected officials to own or be partners in a private business. They want to avoid any potential conflicts of interest in coming legislation that may arise. So, in saying that, ownership of the company will be transferred 100% into Elizabeth's name next week. We have a good team in the office and on the jobsites, and we have good salespeople in the field. But what I need is new subcontractors to be interviewed by people who understand the construction process. That's why I requested for both of you to sit in and learn. And Luke, like I told you a few months ago, there are many things that your Construction Management course will not teach you that you will need to learn on the job—these interviews being one of them."

Luke saw an opening to extend another olive branch. "Well, Matthew, I for one would like to thank you for giving me another growth opportunity in the construction business. I'm looking forward to learning more about the process of hiring and maintaining a good pool of subcontractors."

Matthew just gave Luke a look that told him, *Don't even try to play my game with me, young man,* and then he continued to give them instructions.

"It would be best if both of you would listen and take notes during today's meeting. I, along with the older and more seasoned construction managers, will conduct these interviews."

"What exactly do you want us to learn through this process, Matthew?" asked Luke, just a little irritated at having Matthew crush the olive branch he had just extended.

"You will learn that to work for Middlefield Custom Homes, every subcontractor will be required to hold all invoices until closing. They will also be required to have enough qualified tradesmen on site every day in order to keep our homes on schedule. And we will be given priority access in scheduling their personnel to complete our service work. We conduct these interviews on a regular basis to keep a list of every potential trade partner three names deep. It is good for them to know that they can make a good living working for Middlefield Homes, but at the same time, if they don't play by our rules, they can easily be replaced."

Luke didn't appreciate Matthew's low regard for the men and women that worked for him on his jobsites. So, deciding to stand up for all the tradesmen working for Middlefield Homes, Luke stepped in front of Markus and further into Matthew's office, and after clearing his throat, he replied, "Isn't that a little harsh?" Luke was thinking about the request he made of Matthew more than a month ago concerning Maggy, and how he had been blown off. Had Matthew handled him like a hired contractor, someone to be discarded at his convenience once he was no longer useful?

It was a strange feeling to Matthew, and even stranger to the voice within him, but neither of them could get a read on what Luke was thinking. It was as if there was a wall, a hedge of protection around Luke that wouldn't allow them to read him in any way. So they went back to the basics. "Listen up, Luke. You need to learn something, and learn it real fast. You have to be tough on those who work for you in order to be successful. Otherwise, they'll take advantage of you every time they have an opportunity."

Again, Luke wasn't about to allow that kind of attitude toward the people he worked with every day to go unchallenged.

"Is that how you honestly see your subcontractors, Matthew? And are those the difficult decisions you told me a few months ago to be ready to make? Are these guys merely tools to be used until they wear out or break and then get replaced without a second thought? It sounds to me like you have a pretty poor definition of the phrase 'building partners.' You know, the ones who are responsible for building your homes. And keeping that in mind, just how do you define success?" asked Luke.

Markus stood there silent, almost stunned that Luke would dare challenge his dad so directly. At the same time, Markus wished he had been the one to have finally stood up to his father. Matthew, on the other hand, seeing a challenge being thrown down at his feet by this young and inexperienced boy who was questioning how he ran his company, responded without hesitation.

"By making money and by being profitable. That's how I define success, and if I need to replace an employee, a contractor, or even a construction manager along the way to achieve my goals, so be it! Now, do you have a problem with my definition of success? And don't forget who has years of experience running a very successful company." Matthew stared at Luke, challenging the young man to further question his authority and how he ran his business.

Luke hesitated, realizing he was walking into murky waters with the man he called boss.

"No sir, I don't have a problem with your definition. I just needed additional clarification on how you stood on this social issue. So let me restate your position, if I may. You determine success by the amount of money you make from the work performed by those 'tools' you call your building partners. And the length of those relationships with your partners is irrelevant, because it's not about people and friendships. It's about the profit margin. It's about the money. And when the tool is no longer working up to your standards, you don't help to repair it. You simply replace it. Does that sound about right? I don't want to be too forward Matthew, but are you teaching these social ethics and morals to your family as well?" Luke asked this final question while maintaining direct eye contact with Matthew. He refused to back down.

Luke didn't receive a response to those questions, only the slightest hint of a smirk of admiration for having the guts to ask them in the first place. This was followed by a gruff command from Matthew to go to the conference room and wait there.

Time on the jobsite and at home was creeping by painfully slow without Maggy by his side. Luke's Construction Management course, which he used to see as something that took time away from him and Maggy, was now a welcome distraction from his issues with the Middlefield family. Concentrating on his studies and keeping up with household duties made the next two months pass by more quickly than he first thought they would. The prize he looked forward to was his grandpa's next letter. Before Luke knew it, the end of February had arrived, and the next day would be March 1. Luke had been patiently waiting for three months for this day to come, so he decided to treat himself and stay up till midnight for this next letter. He needed more than coffee to pick him up and get him through the next three months. He needed a visit from his grandpa. And just like that, his computer screen blinked, and there it was—his next letter. All it took was three cups of coffee, vacuuming the entire house, and doing all the dishes to get him there.

What do you have for me this time, Grandpa? thought Luke as he made his way to the LL button. *I hope it's going to be an encouragement and not a downer. I don't know if I can handle anything heavy today.*

As soon as those words were formed in his mind, he knew they were wrong.

"I'm sorry, Grandpa. That wasn't fair of me to think that. I have enjoyed your first three letters, even though they were difficult for me to hear. I'm sure this one will have as much wise counsel as the others had for me."

At the very moment he finished speaking to his faithful grandpa, he touched the LL button and heard, "Hi, buddy, this is letter number four, with a whole lot more to come! I hope they've been helpful and timely for you. To start with, Luke, I'd like to tell you that my prayer for you at this time in your life is that you would have contentment in all your circumstances. In the last few days, I have felt very much prompted to pray that you would remain strong in facing disappointment and change in your life. I don't know what kind of disappointment or changes you may be experiencing, or how deep into your heart they will go, or already have gone, but here are a couple of Proverbs and other verses to consider. Apparently the biblical authors felt compelled to write about these things.

Let not your heart envy sinners,
     but continue in the fear of the LORD all the day.
     (Proverbs 23:17)

As in water face reflects face,
    so the heart of man reflects the man. (Proverbs 27:19)

Count it all joy, my brothers, when you meet trials of various kinds, for you know that the testing of your faith produces steadfastness. And let steadfastness have its full effect, that you may be perfect and complete, lacking in nothing. (James 1:2-4)

"Luke, according to my calculations, you are almost 19 years old. At this age, life becomes exciting, heartbreaking, dramatic, and tiring, all at the same time. Life will change quite often for everyone in their late teens and into most of their 20s. The main causes of these changes are occupation, school, dating, marriage, children, family, and friends. In some of these changing circumstances, you will have control over the direction of the path you will be walking. With others, you're going to feel like a passenger in a car with no driver—out of control and completely helpless. You, however, have the most gracious advantage life has to offer, and that's Christ. When you see changes coming, pray to him and ask for his wisdom and guidance. Luke, what I am encouraging you to do is to talk to him, and try doing the talking out loud. It's amazing how different a prayer feels when spoken out loud rather than in silence. Then spend time with him. Read the letters in his Word that he has given to us for counsel and guidance. After all, they are the original and best Legacy Letters ever written. These changes are coming, and I'm advising you to be ready for them and to actually *expect* them.

"During the years to come, you will be disappointed by those whom you love, and also gratefully amazed and encouraged by those whom you barely know. Luke, you love the game of baseball. Think of life as that sport: one minute you're losing, the next minute you're winning. Longtime teammates or friends are standing next to you today, and tomorrow they're gone. You may also find a new friend the same way, someone who is unexpectedly brought into your life. I could go on with more analogies, but I think you get the point I'm trying to make."

Luke paused the letter for several minutes, thinking about what his grandpa had just said and what those words meant to him in light of the recent breakup with Maggy. "That was some pretty timely insight, Grandpa," Luke quietly said to himself. He then pressed the start button again and his grandpa began to speak.

"I have just a couple of personal thoughts before I finish up this letter. Here are some changes I went through in my life. The first one is the house you basically grew up in. It was the fourth place your grandma and I lived in, so we had address changes. The job you always heard me tell stories about, well, that was actually the fifth job I had. But once I started it, I knew that I had found a permanent home and that my job changes had come to an end. And about your grandma: she was the third girl I dated, and I was her fourth boyfriend. She was the first one I courted and then married, so there were no more dating disappointments. I also had very kind and honest people in my life . . . along with liars and dishonest cheats. Just as the Proverbs said—the ones I shared with you—once you are able to discern and really know a man's heart, then you will really know the man. People haven't changed at all since the book of Proverbs was written around 3,000 years ago, so I believe we can trust in the counsel of this book."

"I think you're right, Grandpa. It looks like I need to find a way to really get to know the hearts of the people who are in my life," said Luke to himself.

"I gotta go now, Luke. My last words of counsel for this letter are to go to Jesus with everything, bending your knees in prayer to him. Then go to fellow believers for additional prayer, support, and counsel. I love you, Luke. See you in three months."

Chapter 5

Bless the Lord

It was Sunday morning and Luke was eating a slice of cold, leftover pizza sitting at his kitchen table. *Leftovers! What would I eat for breakfast without food from the previous evening?* he thought to himself. This type of meal had become his standard breakfast option since his mom got married and moved out of the house. Drinking a cup of hot coffee with whatever was left over from the day before was standard fare for breakfast. He wouldn't admit it, but it was just plain easier to throw something in the microwave than to prepare a breakfast for one and dirty more dishes. Now Luke had become a pretty good cook over the last two years his grandpa was alive, but truth be told, it simply wasn't much fun cooking for one.

As Luke sipped his coffee, he thought about what Markus had told him the previous evening. Neither one of them had much of a social life, or so it appeared that way to Luke. It made sense for them to hang out more often during the last couple of months than they had in the previous couple of years. And no matter how hard Markus tried to hide it, Luke could clearly see that this was about to change too.

Is this what it's going to be like without Maggy? thought Luke. *Guys are okay to hang out with, but I would prefer to be with Maggy.*

The previous evening they had thrown the football back and forth for a while, until that got old. After that, they moved on to playing catch with Luke's frisbee, until it got too dark to see it flying just inches from their faces. After putting the football and frisbee in the garage, Markus asked Luke, "Hey, Luke, have you ever thought about putting a horseshoe pit in your back yard? I've played horseshoes lots of times, and it's a lot of fun. I asked my dad a few years ago about putting one in our back yard, but I was turned down flat. He said that game was for a different class of people, 'a class the Middlefields don't belong to.' So what do you think? Do you want to do it?"

Luke stood in his garage for a moment and then said, "So what class of people do you think I am?"

Markus smiled right away and said, "My class of people, Luke. You're my class of people."

"Okay, we can talk about it while we eat the pizza we ordered, because it looks like it just arrived." After paying and tipping the delivery man, Luke said to him, "See you next week, Franky." To which Franky responded, "Do you want the same order, Luke?"

"No, I don't think so, dude. Let's make it a number three, thin crust."

"Okay, Mr. Luke, you got it. Have a nice evening."

They decided to take their box of hot deep-dish pizza and a couple of sodas to the back yard and sit down at the table on the patio to eat. Markus gave Luke a fun-loving jab by asking him how long he'd been on a first name basis with the pizza delivery guy.

After swallowing that first bite of deep-dish, all-meat pizza, Luke just slumped his shoulders and said, "Pretty much since Maggy broke up with me. Thanks for asking, man. You sure know how to pick a guy up."

"Sorry, Luke, I didn't mean to bring you down." Markus hesitated before talking again, and then said, "And since you brought up the topic of dating, there's something I need to tell you."

Luke gave Markus a quick and pointed look and then said, "I don't care who she is or what she looks like, I don't feel like going on any blind dates with you and whoever you're dating this week. I think I'll just stay an unattached bachelor for a while. It's emotionally safer for me right now, if that's okay with you."

It was then that Markus burst Luke's little bubble. "This has nothing to do with *your* dating life, man. It's about me! I wanted to tell you that I'm seriously dating Cindy Wellington, and I'm loving every minute we're together."

Luke smiled at his old friend, feeling genuinely happy for him. "When were you going to tell me about you and Cindy being a serious couple?" asked Luke as he slapped Markus on the arm, knocking half his pizza out of his mouth in the process.

After retrieving his slice of pizza, Markus meekly said, "I was going to wait for as long as possible, because I didn't want you thinking we wouldn't be hanging out anymore because of her. Anyway, I figured you had a pretty good idea since you were the one who pointed out the implications of a home-cooked meal prepared by your girlfriend and her mother."

"That was a pretty astute observation, wasn't it? I'd actually forgotten about that conversation. Thanks, Markus. It's good to know I'm not totally lost when it comes to women," Luke said with a smirk.

"Now there's the Luke Cruz I grew up with! Since you know about Cindy and me, I have to admit that I'm in a rut, sort of a dating slump, and I need some help, dude. What I need is your help in creating fun and memorable dates with Cindy. And they can't involve meeting my parents."

Luke dropped his head and shook it back and forth silently. He wondered why everything in their lives always seemed to circle back to Matthew and Elizabeth Middlefield.

Thinking for a moment before answering, Luke finally said, "Okay, sure. I'll help any way I can, Markus. But aren't your parents going to want to meet her at some point?"

Hearing Luke agree to help in any way he could put a beam of light in Markus's eyes, a beam that hadn't been there for almost two weeks. Which was about how long he had been in need of dating advice.

"That's not a problem, Luke. They're never interested in who I'm dating," Markus said with a shrug. He was used to his parents' indifference, and actually glad about it in this case. It just meant he didn't have to expose Cindy to his family, which was fine by him. "Now, the first thing you need to do is tell me the kind of dates you have already been on and whether they were successful. Then tell me the kind of dates you think she would like to go on."

Markus stared at Luke, dumbfounded at his question. "Are you kidding me? That's what I just asked you to help me with. Come on, man, give me some ideas. You and Maggy went on tons of dates. Just tell me about some of them. I'm not going to copy exactly what you guys did, but it will give me something to start with."

Luke struggled past the Maggy reference, knowing Markus hadn't anticipated the memories he had just brought to life in Luke's mind.

"Oh my goodness, Markus," said Luke with a teasing smile on his face, "I totally see what's happening here. This girl has really got you all flustered! You must like her a lot if you're going through all this work to create memorable dates. And I can't believe how much you don't trust your parents enough to introduce her to them."

"Yeah, yeah, I know, Luke. It sounds a little immature, but I really can't let them get anywhere close to her. I'm afraid they'll ruin everything for us. Ever since our ski vacation last winter, and that talk we had about my parents' inner character, I've been watching my dad's actions even more closely. It's only been five months since my dad decided to run for Congress, and in those five months it's become very clear to me that he can be a real jerk to the people who get in the way of whatever he wants."

Luke jumped on that statement and said, "You've got no argument on that point from me!"

"But what I can't figure out is why it's so hard for him to see how hurtful the things he says are to me, and to others who get in his way. But my dad is my dad, and I doubt he's going to see that character flaw in himself or be willing to make some changes. What I do know is that he won't like me dating someone who works for a competitor, and I can guarantee you that would be his only reason." Markus hesitated, thinking about what he had finally spoken out loud, and then he began again.

"Why is that, Luke? What's wrong with my dad? There's more than enough construction work for everyone in this town. Why does he think he should be building every new home? He couldn't do it even if he wanted to. And why am I so afraid of what he'll do to me? Why can't he be like other dads and just be happy for me? Why can't he see that I may have found the girl I want to marry and spend the rest of my life with? Who she might be working for or what her last name is shouldn't make any difference."

Luke had silently allowed Markus to get everything off his chest. After he had expressed these long-hidden thoughts, it was Luke's turn to speak about Matthew Middlefield.

"So, what you are saying is that Cindy may be the love of your life, but you don't want her becoming a target and the person that has to be 'dealt with' by Matthew Middlefield?" said Luke, striking at the heart of the issue.

"I'm sorry, Luke. I knew you would go right to Maggy when I asked you for help. I don't blame you, and that's another reason why I didn't tell you about Cindy right away. I just don't know what to do."

Luke was starting to feel bad, as this evening was becoming more about Markus's dad than about Cindy, but he felt he needed to give Markus some advice.

"You do realize that you don't have to let your dad push you around, don't you? Your life is *your* life, not his."

"Of course I know that, but what would I do for a job? Where would I live? You don't get it, Luke. It's easier to just hide it from him," said Markus.

It was hard for Luke to see his longtime friend in such inner turmoil; it was like he was imprisoned by his own father. But what could Luke say to help him get past this seemingly insurmountable obstacle he called "Dad"?

"Markus, you know that he's going to find out sooner or later, and when he does, what are you going to do?"

With his typical sarcasm, Markus said, "I'm going to hope that he gets elected to the House of Representatives and that he will be gone most of the year to Washington, D.C. And if that doesn't work, there's always an extra bedroom at your place, right?"

Luke was still startled by the thoughts of the previous evening when his cell phone began ringing. It was his mom. He was thankful to have someone to talk with this morning. Of course, he wouldn't tell her that he was already a little on the lonely side of life today.

"Hi, Mom! It's kind of early to be calling, isn't it? Is something wrong?"

"No, nothing's wrong, and it's never too early or too late to call my boy. I still worry about you living by yourself in your grandpa's house. I know you feel comfortable there, but I'll always worry about you, at least a little. It's a mother's prerogative, you know. So I'll keep calling you whenever I feel the need—do you have a problem with that?"

"Okay, okay, okay, Mom. So, tell me how I can help you today."

Without even hesitating, she shot off a very direct question: "How have you been eating on the days I don't come over? And what did you have for breakfast this morning?"

Luke knew he had to think fast and get creative with his answer in order to keep his mother from worrying about him. "I'm eating just fine, Mom, and I'm not wasting any food either. I always make sure that there's not any food left over that needs to be thrown away. I'm also getting the layout of our local grocery store memorized. I really don't like crisscrossing all over the store for just a couple of items. Is that all you wanted to know?"

"Actually, no, it's not. There is one more thing."

Luke said nothing but just waited for the next big question he might have to tap dance around in order to keep his mother from worrying. And then she asked.

"Ricardo and I wanted to know if you would like to go out for dinner after church today. Our treat. And you can help me out by picking the restaurant."

"You know something, Mom, now that I think about it, I was wrong. You should call more often."

It was another Sunday service in which Luke was having a hard time staying focused on what the pastor was teaching. His mind just kept wandering. Without realizing how much time had passed, or what their pastor had spoken about as an encouragement for the week to come, Luke found himself standing up with everyone else to sing the last song of the service. As Luke began to sing this song, the words of this old hymn, and the story behind the words, spoke directly to his soul.

> When peace like a river attendeth my way,
> > When sorrows like sea billows roll;
> > Whatever my lot, Thou has taught me to say,
> > It is well, it is well with my soul.

Luke considered the words he had sung and found himself having to pray a prayer of confession to ask for forgiveness from his Jesus.

"Dear Jesus," Luke silently prayed to the Creator of all, as everyone else continued to sing. "I have not said 'it is well with my soul' whenever I think about Matthew Middlefield or about Maggy. Please forgive me. Help me to trust you and to find my purpose in life, especially when it comes to thinking about Maggy. Amen."

Half an hour later, as they all sat down to eat, Rebecca said, "I would have guessed that brisket barbecue was going to be your choice, and I would have been right."

"Mom, you can stop pretending that you want to talk about the kind of food I prefer to eat. You can't hide whatever you want to tell me, because I can see that twinkle in your eyes. What do you have cooked up now? And does Ricardo know about it?"

Luke was right about his mom, and she was so excited at this invitation that she jumped right in.

"Okay, since you asked," said Rebecca coyly. "To start with, the first thing you need to know is that I've been looking for something to do with my God-given gifts and talents. I'm bored, Luke. I can only clean the house so many times every week. I need to be challenged in my life. I have to have a purpose, a reason to get out of bed every morning. And to answer your original question, not only does Ricardo know about it, but it was *his* idea. He wants me to come work at one of his offices, and I'm going to be what the mental health industry calls a 'life coach!'" She didn't even stop talking to make sure Luke knew what a life coach was. "We were talking a few weeks ago about several of his clients who had no more need for therapy, yet they could still benefit from having a life coach."

Ricardo jumped in when Rebecca took a long breath. "Your mom would be great, Luke, and with everything that she has gone through in her life, she can be a tremendous help to a lot of people."

"That sounds really exciting, but I'm not quite sure what a life coach is."

"You have no idea how many times I have heard that statement," said Ricardo, looking at the blank expression on Luke's face.

"To define what a life coach is, you first have to know that a life coach is *not* a therapist. You see, Luke, a therapist helps a person identify and fix things that are emotionally broken due to their past. Once they have made those repairs, the hope is that the hardest work is over. But quite often, the person will still need help moving forward in life. They'll have to get past small obstacles that could become big problems if not addressed properly. So they still need some help, and this type of help can come from a life coach. Seen through the prism of renewed mental health, navigating the present and future events of their life can be made easier with that life coach at their side."

Luke had a blank look of confusion as he continued to eat his brisket. He didn't understand what Ricardo had just said.

"I can see you still don't get it. Let me try a different way." Ricardo went silent for a few minutes. He was quiet for so long that Luke was beginning to think he had forgotten to answer his question. Luke's mother, on the other hand, continued to eat and enjoy her meal, having become accustomed to Ricardo's long pauses as he considered the best way to help someone understand what he was trying to say. Which, in Luke's case, meant grasping the kind of job his mother was about to take on.

"Okay, Luke, I think I have a good way to describe for you what a life coach is. I want you to imagine your truck breaking down, and in this analogy your truck is your life, and you need to bring it into the shop for repairs, with the shop being your therapist's office. The mechanic, aka, the therapist, begins to help you understand the reason for the breakdown. It could have been because of something you previously hit, ran over, ignored on your dashboard, or neglected. But whatever the case, because you ignored these things, the truck had a mechanical, or we might say *emotional*, breakdown. But not to worry: it can be repaired. Now, once the repairs have been completed, the mechanic's, or therapist's, job is all but over. The mechanic should then recommend that a friend, who would be a life coach, meet with you on a regular basis in your newly repaired state of mental health. This is done in order to help you recognize and navigate around those life-changing potholes you may have otherwise run into once again, forcing you back to the mechanic's shop for more repairs. This life coach will ride along with you until you know what triggers to look for in your life. You know, the things that cause you to make those poor choices. He, or she, will help you learn how to make better decisions, the kinds of decisions that will ultimately help you avoid damaging yourself again."

Luke was starting to understand what Ricardo was explaining to him. When Ricardo took some time to eat his meal, Luke took over the conversation and restated what he thought Ricardo had said.

"Okay, now I get it. Mom is the backseat driver, and she doesn't need a degree to do this job— just a lot of life experiences and permission from the client."

"Well, that's kind of what I was driving at, Luke, and if you really want to know more about the specifics of this job, we can talk about it later. Suffice it to say, your mom will be a great life coach. Now what do you both say we put away the work-talk and discuss some of our upcoming family events while enjoying this wonderful meal."

Luke did have one question to ask: "What about the adoption agency? Are you two still working on that idea?"

"Yes, we are, Luke, but I'm finding out that starting a 501(c)(3) non-profit is a lot harder than I realized. Until we get that set up, your mom can work as a life coach."

An hour later, the three of them had finished their dinner and were making their way to the entrance of the restaurant. As they were about to walk out the door, with Luke's hands clutching everyone's boxes of leftovers, he heard his name from a familiar voice over the noise of the restaurant. He turned around to see Juan Oleeva walking toward him. When Juan had gotten close enough, they shook hands and exchanged typical greetings, after which Luke hesitantly agreed to meet Juan in the parking lot in five minutes. Ricardo and his mom were waiting just outside the restaurant for Luke to emerge. His mom said curiously, "That young man looked like a boy you used to hang around with in high school. Who was it, sweetie?"

"He was, Mom. That was Juan Oleeva. I haven't seen him since we graduated. He was also eating with his mom and dad when he saw us get up to leave. He's never been one to be shy or subtle. He's going to meet me out here in a couple minutes to do some catching up."

Ricardo, having the look of a very proud father, stepped into their conversation, putting his hand on Luke's shoulder and then lovingly rubbing his back. "Did you hear that, Rebecca? Did you hear what Luke just said?" asked Ricardo with a look of pride on his face.

"Of course I heard him, Ricardo. I heard every word he said." But knowing she had missed something important—which was evident from the look on his face—she asked, "Okay, Ricardo, what's going on? What did I miss?"

Luke, also not sure what Ricardo was referring to, asked, "Yeah, what did I say, Ricardo? I must have missed it too."

Ricardo, still sporting a large and proud smile, said, "Luke just said that his friend was eating dinner with his mom and dad *too*, which implies that Luke was eating dinner with *his* mom and dad. Thank you, Luke. Without even realizing it, you just told me where I stand in your heart."

Luke, in a moment of honest reflection, responded, "You know, Ricardo, I didn't even realize it myself until just now, but you're right. You are becoming more of a dad to me, not just my mom's husband. And I didn't even know it myself until you heard me say it just now."

There was an awkward silence for about three seconds as they both just stood there looking at each other. "Well," said Rebecca, "don't just stand there like a couple of guys. It's hug time! It's father-son hug time," she said as her eyes began to well up.

A few minutes later, Juan was walking up to Luke as Luke was waving goodbye to his mom and Ricardo. "Hey, Luke! What a surprise to see you inside the restaurant. I recognized your mom with you, but who was the guy?"

"That was my dad."

"Your dad? I thought your dad died 10 or 15 years ago?" said Juan, visibly confused.

"Sorry, Juan, I should have said stepdad. My mom got married again last September."

"That's pretty cool, Luke. Is he a nice guy?" asked Juan, genuinely curious.

"Yeah, Juan, he is. He's actually a pretty great guy. My mom chose well."

"And what about you, Luke? Are you and Maggy Middlefield still together?"

Luke had to work hard not to show his true emotions. He simply said, "No, Juan, we aren't anymore. It just didn't work out."

"That's too bad. I always thought you two could have made it together. What about her brother, Markus? Have you guys kept in touch, or did the Maggy breakup cause a problem?"

"As a matter of fact, we work together as carpenters every day at his dad's construction company. Mr. Middlefield is also sending us through construction management school, and we just finished the first year of a two-year program. Mr. Middlefield is also training me on how to use some really advanced design-and-build software for the construction industry. I've been working on designs for homes that have living spaces for three generations of the same family living together. It's a special project to me because I grew up that way, and I love every memory of that time and of that house."

"So you're a carpenter? That's pretty cool, Luke. Pretty cool."

"Okay, Juan, now that you've caught up a little on my last year, how about telling me something about yours."

Juan didn't hesitate in telling Luke about what he was doing in life, but it almost sounded rehearsed and emotionally detached.

"Sure, Luke. Let's see. I'm not married. I just started dating a girl about a month ago. I still live at home, and I'm in the food business. I also operate a food truck downtown in the business district. Okay, we're caught up."

"Come on, Juan, it can't be that simple. Let me ask a few questions. You have a semi-steady girlfriend in your life, and it sounds like you have a steady job in the food business. People have to eat every day, right? So your job must be pretty stable? And I'm guessing that you never get a day off because of lack of work, do you?"

"Just Sundays. Otherwise, I have to ask for a day off."

"And no other life changes for you since graduation?"

"Nope, everything is pretty much the same," Juan said with little interest in talking further about his life, or lack thereof, since high school.

Luke hesitated for just a second after hearing the answer to that last question. In his heart, he was trying to quickly decide if he wanted to spend any more time with Juan. After all, he did just say that nothing had changed with him since high school, and that was a little concerning to him.

But in the blink of an eye, Luke decided to find out more about Juan's life. "So how'd you get into this business anyway?"

"My dad got me the job, and he's the one who trained me in the business."

"You work with your dad in a food truck? That's pretty cool, Juan."

"That's not completely accurate, Luke. I don't actually work directly with him anymore. He works in the office and I work in my own food truck."

"What's the name of the company?"

"Pronto Food."

Luke was trying to bring up a visual of a Pronto Food truck in his mind, but he was having a hard time seeing it. "I don't get downtown much, but I think I've seen one or two of their trucks. How long have you and your dad worked for Pronto Food?"

"I worked there part-time all the way through high school, and then full-time for the last year. But my dad has worked there his whole life."

"His whole life, eh? Does he know the owner pretty well?"

"Come on, Luke, knock it off." By this time Juan was getting tired of volleying dry humor back and forth. "My dad and mom are the owners, Luke. They own every one of those food trucks you see driving around the city." Juan was still amazed at what appeared to be Luke's genuine lack of knowledge of his family's occupation. "You mean to tell me that in all the years we hung out in high school, you really didn't know that?"

"I'm sorry, Juan. I guess I really didn't know. There were probably signs through the years that your dad owned it, but it never clicked in my head. So how many of those food trucks has your dad put on the road through the years while I wasn't paying attention?"

"He's having our tenth one built right now. We also have one refrigerated truck that delivers supplies during the day in case the other trucks start to run low."

They talked for another 20 minutes until Juan heard his dad call for him. "I gotta go, Luke. Let's set something up to talk again, and let's make sure Markus is there too. Call me. My cell number is still the same from high school."

"Okay, will do. It was great catching up! Talk to you later."

Seeing his mom's car parked in the driveway, Luke wondered what new recipe from Ricardo's grandmother they would be eating tonight. He hoped he hadn't thrown off the timing for dinner, as he had worked a little longer than usual and forgotten to call. As he walked into the kitchen, his attention was more on where he would set the things down he was carrying than on what he was about to hear.

Calling out rather loudly, he went about emptying the trash from his lunchbox. "Hey, Mom, sorry for being late. But when you have the best son in the world, he's worth the wait!"

"I wouldn't know anything about that, Luke," said an unfamiliar voice. "I only have daughters."

Hearing that strange voice answering almost made him drop his lunch cooler on the floor. His mom was standing right next to Mrs. Warez as they entered the kitchen and saw the shocked look on Luke's face.

"I'm sorry, honey. I should have told you that Lynette would be at the house with me this afternoon for a couple of hours. But, wow, I haven't seen you that surprised since you were a little boy. It was almost worth not warning you to see that cute look on your face. You saw that cute look didn't you, Lynette?"

"Oh yeah, I saw it, Rebecca. And you're right, it was pretty cute."

"Mom, I'm not a little boy. Rather than cute, I'd say handsome, . . . or dashing," Luke said with a smile as the two mothers laughed. "You do realize, Mom, that there will be payback now, don't you?"

"Oh, Luke, just finish cleaning out your cooler and get ready for a special supper. This is another recipe from Ricardo's grandma. It'll be ready in about 15 minutes."

Luke was thinking quickly about what to say to these two women. After all, he didn't want to look like the child from years ago that his mother was describing.

"Well, with two moms cooking, it'll be twice as good!" Luke said enthusiastically. He was clearly attempting to shift the focus off of himself and onto the food and those who were preparing it.

"Oh no, Luke. I'm just here as an observer. Your mom has talked up this recipe at church so many times that when she told me what she was making for dinner, I invited myself over by asking if I could watch it being prepared. I know it was a little bold on my part, but since I was already being bold, I also asked if I might have just a nibble of the finished dish. Our original plan for the day was not to get a cooking lesson but to go shopping. Not that we needed to buy any-thing. We just needed to catch up while we walked around the mall.

But as you can see, I ended up in your kitchen. I won't be a bother to you all much longer, though. My daughter will be here in a few minutes to pick me up."

Hearing that a second visitor would soon be arriving, Luke, who had a growing propensity for spontaneously inviting company over for a meal, thought to himself, *It would be nice to have two more people at the house for dinner, and it would also make the evening less quiet.* So he said to Lynnette, "Mrs. Warez, it's supper time, and unless your husband is expecting you home tonight, you and your daughter should stay and have more than a nibble of this wonderful meal. Would you consider changing your plans and staying for dinner with us? And I'm sure you made more than enough for everyone, Mom. You always do."

Rebecca turned toward Lynnette and asked with a mischievous tone in her voice, the two of them already knowing the answer to her question, "It's up to you, Lynette. Would you like to stay, or did you have something special planned with Lydia tonight?"

Lynette, mustering her well-honed acting skills from high school drama class, said, "Just a mother-daughter evening out to eat, but I guess it would be fun to dine here tonight. Thank you, Luke. I accept. That was a very sweet invitation."

He started walking toward the staircase that led to the bedrooms, and as he was walking away he said, "We're glad to have you and your daughter for dinner, but I'd better go get cleaned up and changed before she gets here. I wouldn't want to embarrass my mom by looking too sloppy."

As Luke ran up the staircase, his mom looked at Lynette and said, "It's just too easy sometimes, isn't it, Lynette?"

About the time the front doorbell was ringing at the Cruz residence, Matthew Middlefield was rehearsing his lines one last time. He was at the West Winds Studios with his family making another political commercial that was part of a series. Each commercial built on the previous one, introducing Matthew and his political positions for the sake of his new constituents.

"Mr. Middlefield," said Jeffrey, the Studio Production Manager, "are you ready for us to begin recording?"

"Yes, Jeffrey, I am. Where would you like me to stand?"

After being directed to the place he was to be recorded from, he looked at Elizabeth, gave her that million-dollar, salesman smile, then turned toward the camera and began to speak.

"My fellow District 7 residents, most of you know me as Matthew Middlefield, the builder of homes. But now I would like you to get to know me as Matthew Middlefield, the builder of a safe and growing metropolis for you to live in. But I can only do that if you elect me congressman of District 7 in this upcoming election. These past several months, it has truly been my pleasure getting to know all of you who have attended my town hall meetings. For those of you who have not had the opportunity to participate and speak with me personally, let me briefly share with you the promise I made to all those in attendance. I promised them, and I now promise you, that I will take as much time as it requires to truly understand the needs of our district and the people living in it. I will then, with great fervor, present those needs to my fellow congressmen and women in order to obtain our fair share of federal tax dollars for our district. This money will ensure that our district remains the beautiful and desirable vacation and living destination of families from around the country that it has always been. I also promise to work for you as tenaciously in Congress as I have in private business. Now, one last thing I would like to do before the coming election and before finishing today. I thought it only fitting, since so many of you have allowed me to get to know you and your families, that you all should meet mine. Come on, guys. Can you step over here and stand with me?"

Taking their cue from Matthew, the three of them came into view and took their place standing next to him as he introduced each of them to all the viewers.

"This is my wife of 30 years, Elizabeth . . . my daughter, Maggy . . . and my son, Markus."

And with that cue, they all said together, "We're the Middlefield family, and we approve this message."

Luke was talking with Mrs. Warez about what kind of house he was building that week when the front doorbell rang. "That's probably

Lydia. I'll go let her in," said Lynette. "Rebecca, can you wait for me while I get the door?"

Lynette had said her lines perfectly, because the next voice she heard was Luke's. He was unaware that his line was predetermined and right on cue, almost like one of those unscripted reality television shows. "Oh no you won't, Mrs. Warez," said Luke. "You stay here and finish your cooking lesson. I'll get the door and let Lydia in."

"Introduce yourself to her Luke," said his mother. "It's been several years since you two first met."

"I've met Lydia before? Huh, I don't remember that," said Luke as he left the kitchen.

The two moms smiled at each other as Lynette said, "You're right, Rebecca, it's just too easy. But do you think they know what we're doing to them?"

"Of course not, Lynette, they're still just kids. They don't have a clue. And by the time they do have a clue, it'll be too late."

Luke went to the front door and upon opening it saw a very pretty Latina wearing skinny blue jeans, a white blouse, a baseball cap with a ponytail coming out the back, and black flats on her feet. After recovering from his deer in the headlights moment, he thought to himself, *How could I have forgotten meeting a girl like this?* Then he thought about Markus's comment a while back about girls with ponytails. Luke went on to introduce himself. After a few minutes, he promptly returned to the kitchen with Lydia at his side, both of them talking about friends they had in common.

When Lydia saw her mom, she said, "Are you ready to go, Mom? It looks like Luke and his mom are getting ready to eat."

"Oh, didn't Luke tell you? We have a change of plans. Luke has invited us to stay for dinner. We will be dining here tonight. Won't that be fun? I don't ever get enough time to talk with Rebecca at church, so I accepted Luke's gracious invitation to stay and eat with them. I hope you and Luke can find something to talk about after dinner while Rebecca and I are catching up and cleaning up."

Lydia was surprised but thankful for the invitation. "Sounds fun, Mom," she said before turning her beaming smile towards Luke and Rebecca.

"Thank you, Luke. Thank you, Mrs. Cruz. Oh, I'm sorry! It's Mrs. Sanchez now—you got remarried last fall while I was at school, and I just forgot. I'm so sorry."

"Don't worry about it, honey. And don't tell Ricardo, but I occasionally catch myself signing my name as Rebecca Cruz."

And with that, they all laughed and then carried the plates, glasses, utensils, and food to the dining room table. "Luke," said Rebecca, as they all sat down, "since we are all followers of Jesus here tonight, would you mind praying for our time this evening?"

"Yes, I would love to, Mom." Everyone took a moment to bow their heads and close their eyes before Luke continued. "Dear Father of all, I pray that you would allow your Spirit to be here with us tonight, and to fill us all in a way that will be undeniable. Help us to know that you love us and care for us every minute of every day, even though we don't always acknowledge you. Amen."

After Luke's amen, the three ladies followed with a unified amen of their own.

"So, what recipe of Ricardo's grandma are we eating tonight?" asked Luke as he held out his plate for his mom to fill up.

"It's called Hispanic Shepherd's Pie," said Rebecca. "And it sure looks delicious!"

They all talked, laughed, told old stories, and ate. It was a wonderful meal. After the meal was over, the two conniving moms said they would talk while doing the dishes—a shrewd move on their part. It left Luke and Lydia alone to get to know each other better.

Seeing it was a pleasant evening, they decided to talk on the front porch of the house, out of earshot of their mothers. As they sat down on the deck chairs, Lydia apologetically looked at Luke and said, "So, how long did it take you to figure out that this whole evening was a setup for us to meet?"

"Oh, good, I'm so glad I wasn't the only one thinking that. Well, I got my first clue when your mom was working just a little too hard to get me to answer the door when you arrived. Getting us out here to talk while they do all the dishes was also pretty obvious. What a couple of manipulative mothers we have. They must be feeling pretty good about themselves right about now, don't you think?" They both laughed.

"Yeah, you're right, Luke. I figured it out when my mom said we would be eating here tonight instead of going out. It was the way she said it, just like her saying they would take care of the dishes."

"You're right," said Luke, "there was something not quite genuine in how they said that, almost like it was a rehearsed line they were waiting to deliver. Plus, they kept giving each other looks, which I knew meant they were up to something."

"Well, since we're out here anyway, and I'm pretty sure our moms will be washing the dishes exceptionally slow tonight, what would you like to know about me?" asked Lydia with a girlish giggle.

"What I would like to know about you is if you would gain as much pleasure as I would if we both walked into that kitchen holding hands and announced our engagement to those two matchmakers." Luke said this with a mischievous sound in his voice, much like his mother's, already imagining just how excited the two moms would be.

"Do you think they're planning our wedding already? I love chocolate cake—I hope that's part of the wedding plans!" Lydia exclaimed as they both laughed again.

Hearing this laughter way out in the kitchen, the two matchmaking moms smiled at each other, with Rebecca saying triumphantly, "Did you hear them laughing, Lynette? They're having a great time out there. It's working!"

Back out on the front porch, Luke was asking Lydia some questions. "Well, you're right, Lydia. Since we're out here anyway, why don't you tell me something about yourself."

"What would you like to know about your future wife, Mr. Cruz?"

"Tell me about your job, your hobbies, any sports you like. That should be a good conversation starter."

"Those are all easy questions. I just finished college and passed my CPA test, so I'll start my new job in two weeks. I'm good with numbers, I love to draw with pencil and ink, mostly portraits and old buildings, and I love playing table games. Favorite sport would be baseball, and in my case, underhand fast-pitch softball. I was a pitcher for three years running at my high school. My coach clocked my fast ball at one of my last games at 72 miles per hour. Not bad for a girl, right?"

Luke sat there in amazement. He couldn't believe what Lydia had just told him about herself. An evening that had started out as an unrequested setup by their two conniving moms had just become more than a simple blind date. Then it was Luke's turn to tell Lydia about himself and his personal interests. At hearing what Luke enjoyed, it was Lydia who was now pleasantly surprised. It turned out to be a most memorable evening for everyone.

Two days later, it was Friday afternoon. It was almost the end of the workday as Luke walked into the Middlefield office. He had several signed change orders from clients and subcontractors to give to the accountant. Luke saw Maggy turning off her cell and took the opportunity to step into her office and say hi.

"Hi, Maggy. Do you have time to talk?" Her head jerked up, being startled at hearing his voice.

"My goodness, Luke! How long have you been standing there? And what are you doing at the office?"

"I do occasionally have to come into the office, Maggy. I had to drop off some paperwork to Susan in Accounting. What's the matter? It sounds like you don't want to talk with me."

"Actually, not really. My dad told me if I spent any amount of time with you that you would brainwash me with your religious beliefs. He said you had a kind of 'persuasive Jesus-talk' that he didn't like. My dad said that he doesn't want to offend anyone, so he never brings Jesus up in his conversations with his peers."

What Maggy didn't realize was that Luke was no longer trying to win her back. He only wanted to catch up a little and find out how she was doing.

"Maggy, I think we both know who is persuading who."

Just then, another voice entered the office and interrupted their conversation. "Hi, Maggy," said Peter VanderMor. "Are you ready to go?"

"Excuse me, you're interrupting our conversation," Luke said, not impressed with the guy who looked like he could be an All-American, pretty boy model.

"Not that it's any of your business, but I'm Maggy's boyfriend, and I'm here to pick her up for dinner."

At hearing the news of Maggy having a boyfriend, Luke visibly froze, not knowing what to say. "Luke, I'm going now," said Maggy in a short and abrupt manner. She pushed past him out of her office and toward Peter. "I've got nothing left to say to you."

As the two of them walked away from her office, the rest of the office staff was keeping one eye (and one ear) on their work and the other on the drama that was unfolding in front of them. They all had grown to like and appreciate Luke over these last few years, and they couldn't believe how he was being treated by Maggy or her parents. Their growing dislike of Maggy's new boyfriend was justified when they heard Peter saying with overflowing hubris, "Gosh, Maggy, that's Luke? From the way you talked about him, I thought he would be better looking . . . and bigger! Oh well, just means we both upgraded."

Luke just stood there in stunned amazement, watching the two of them walk out of the building. He thought to himself, *Boyfriend? Maggy has a new boyfriend? I guess I know what she's been up to lately.* He then heard another voice speaking to him. It was Maggy's mother. Having seen Luke going into Maggy's office, she had positioned herself just around the corner, far enough away to not be seen but close enough to hear every word of their brief conversation.

"Luke, it would be best if you just accepted that Maggy no longer wants anything to do with you or your religious beliefs. What you need to be concerned with is doing your job and doing it well. If you're able to do that, your job is secure. If not, well, I guess it will be you and I that will be having that talk you so desperately desire."

Mrs. Middlefield didn't wait for a response but simply spun on her heel, turning her back toward Luke, and walked out of the office, leaving him standing there alone.

"He's a political ghost, and that's exactly what we need for this race," said George VanderMor to the board on their Zoom meeting. "Since they first met through a study group at college, my son and his daughter have become fast friends. Through that relationship, I have been able to gain a tremendous amount of trust in the eyes of Matthew Middlefield."

The chairman of this board, whose main purpose was to search out new political talent, then said, "Are you asking us to give you permission to perform a complete search and background check on

Matthew Middlefield, including his immediate family, their friends, and the extended family, two generations deep?"

George looked directly at the chairman and said, "Yes, that's exactly what I'm asking for. I believe this man has the potential to be more than just a ten-term congressman. His political views line up perfectly with the party. He has that movie star look in his face, and he has a smile that makes you feel like you're his best friend. His natural instincts in working a crowd are amazing. It's as though he knows what you're going to say before you say it, and he has the perfect response for you every time. I think he can go all the way to the big chair! And if we nurture him properly for a while, we could own the White House for another eight years. The timing and the candidate are perfect! If the party is going to back him, we need a deep dive into his background, just like everyone else we support."

The chairman took a minute and talked over George's request with the rest of the board. After completing this discussion with the others, he turned his attention back to George. "You have always had an uncanny ability to find new talent, so we're approving your request, George. But it also sounds like you're holding a tiger by the tale with Matthew Middlefield. Therefore, we feel it necessary to put our best man on this investigation. You've never used this man before, George. He's a little odd but very good at what he does. We will let Special Agent Williams know that you will be contacting him. Keep us updated with your progress so we can determine how much money we should put into the new congressman's campaign coffers."

Before any final words could be said, the Zoom meeting was terminated.

———————————

Two days later, after consolidating everything he had on Matthew Middlefield, the other members of his family, and anyone else who had any kind of dealings with him, George was on the phone waiting for his call to be answered by the man who would give Matthew the "all-clear" to begin his political journey. It seemed to be an eternity before the call was answered. But then it came.

"Hello, Agent Williams here."

"Agent Williams, this is George VanderMor. We have a mutual friend who should have already contacted you about this call, and I trust he has given you the necessary introductions for me. This long-time friend has recommended that I use your services for a job that needs to be taken care of in a particularly professional, thorough, and discreet manner."

There was no hesitation on the other end, for Agent Williams had been asked to this dance many times in his career. "Yes, I've been informed you would be needing my services. I assume that you have a pen and paper, so write down the address I'm going to give you."

George wrote down the address and then asked, "What's at this address, and what do you want me to do with it?"

"As far as you're concerned, this address is meaningless to you. As soon as you mail everything you have on Matthew Middlefield to that address, destroy the note. This is a one-use mailing address. Now, tell me exactly what information you're going to need me to dig up."

George thought about that question briefly and then went on for a few minutes, telling the agent the same old things he always hears from a new client. But that wasn't what Agent Williams was asking for, and he let George know it.

"That's not what I was expecting to hear. With a little effort you could find all that information yourself. Now, what you have to understand is that the services I offer are at a whole different level. What you have to decide, Mr. VanderMor, is if you are willing to work with a man who will do whatever it takes to find what you want. Apparently my special talents of investigation weren't well articulated to you. What I am most proficient at is finding dirt on people who have worked very hard to make that dirt disappear. Or, it may be they simply have no dirt to find. But from my experience, *everyone* has something they don't want brought to the light of day, and I do mean everyone. Now what do you really want to know about Matthew Middlefield?"

George was a little taken aback by this type of candor, but after thinking about the question for a minute, he got off his moral high horse and admitted to himself that what this man was offering was exactly what he was looking for.

"Everything. I want to know everything about him. I want to know about his two children. I want to know about his wife, who is estranged from her parents—find out what that's all about. Matthew himself is a product of Social Services; he was dropped off at foster care when he was two years old and never picked up again. Now there's a mystery ready to be solved. So, in summary, I want you to turn over every rock in his life and see what slithers out. We don't want a single political opponent to find any information about him that we don't already know about. That's about it, Agent Williams. Now, what kind of a time frame can I expect?"

Again, the agent replied with almost no emotion: "The tools I'll be using to conduct this investigation have to be used in such a way as not to attract attention. The United States government is a stickler about these things. Give me three to six months, then you will hear from me again."

Two weeks later, Luke was sitting in his grandpa's favorite chair eating supper. His laptop was open on the coffee table in front of him, and he had been staring at the subject bar for almost an hour, trying to decide what he should do. In the last year, Luke kept finding himself in a conundrum when it came to his grandpa's Legacy Letters. Should he open the letter the day it arrived, or should he wait a day? Would he like what his grandfather had to say, or would he feel a sense of regret after hearing something he would rather not have known?

He had grown so excited—and needy—that he was beginning to lose sleep the day or two prior to the arrival of a letter.

"Grandpa, I really don't know if I want to open this letter. I'm afraid of what you're going to tell me about yourself through a personal story, or through Bible stories, and I'll have to change some part of my life again. Not that I don't need to make some changes, of course.

"Well, here goes. What else do I have to lose, except more sleep?" Luke went through the list of questions and finally pushed the LL button.

"Hi there, Luke. You know something, every time I say hi to you, only a few days or a week has gone by for me. But for you, it's been another three months. I see you in the house and talk with you every day. But when I make these recordings, I have to talk to you as though it's been years. It's hard to keep the time periods straight in my head. For instance, remember that baseball game where you hit a triple, a double, and a single? That just happened last Friday for me, but for you it was two or three years ago . . . depending, of course, on when I went home to our Jesus. It kind of messes with you, doesn't it?"

Luke hit the pause button and thought about that game. "I forgot all about that day, Grandpa. Thanks for reminding me. That is a really special memory." Luke then touched the play button again.

"Before I continue on, listen to the verses that follow at least a couple times. I am going to keep this letter short today, but the point I want to make will hopefully stay with you for a lifetime. If you can accomplish the admonitions of the author of these verses, you will do well in representing Christ in every difficult situation you find yourself in.

> . . . we rejoice in our sufferings, knowing that suffering produc-
> es endurance, and endurance produces character, and character
> produces hope, and hope does not put us to shame, because God's
> love has been poured into our hearts through the Holy Spirit who
> has been given to us. (Romans 5:3–5)

> The LORD gave, and the LORD has taken away; blessed be the
> name of the LORD. (Job 1:21)"

After he had finished reading these verses, Luke could see his grandpa's eyes close and his lips moving. He was praying before he began to speak again.

When he had finished his personal prayer time, Gus began sharing his thoughts again. "In my last letter, I spoke to you about the disappointments and changes you will face in the years to come. What I should have spent more time encouraging you with is the reality that things and people may be taken out of your life, but our God is so loving and gracious to his people that he will always make sure we are emotionally and spiritually cared for. So, Luke, be just as ready to bless the Lord when he takes people or things out of your life as you are when he puts someone or something into it. You need to learn this kind of patience at an early age. Don't wait to be an old man like your grandpa to develop this kind of understanding and awareness. You must also learn to do more listening than talking in all your conversations with people. You'll be surprised at how much you can learn that way. At the same time, be as gracious as possible to everyone that you interact with on a daily basis. Grace means giving to someone something good that they didn't work for or deserve. Remember, as Jesus has been gracious to us, we must also be gracious to others. I gotta go, buddy. Love you. See you soon."

"I love you too, Grandpa."

Luke sat for several minutes, pondering what his grandfather had said. Reaching into his pocket, he pulled out a piece of paper his mother had given him three weeks earlier. There was a name and phone number written on it; all he had to do was decide if he was ready to take a chance again. He stared at the name, flipped it around in his fingers several times, and then stared at it again. Finally, he picked up his phone and made the call. After six rings, a voice said, "Hello?"

Hearing her greeting, Luke said in a soft, and almost apologetic, voice, "Hi, Lydia. This is Luke . . . Luke Cruz."

The next thing he heard was, "What took you so long? And just so you know, I didn't answer right away because I was deciding if I was going to answer at all! But since you *did* call, why are you calling me three weeks after we had such a good time at your house?"

Luke felt terrible that he had taken so long to call her, but in that moment of guilt, he realized something very important. "Hey, Lydia, can I ask you a question?"

With a quick response, and with a desire to make Luke squirm just a little more, she said, "Of course you can. I'm assuming that's why you called in the first place."

Luke cautiously asked, "When you answered your phone, you didn't say hello. You let it ring six times before deciding to answer my call, right?"

"Yes, Luke, that's what I said. I was honestly deciding whether I was going to answer your call because you took so long to call me. I do have my pride to consider, you know."

Hearing this answer, Luke cautiously asked a second question: "So, Lydia, just out of curiosity, how did you know it was me calling?"

Luke heard nothing but silence after asking that question, and then he said, "I'm assuming your silence is telling me that you had my cell number in your contact list for as long as I had yours. Otherwise, you wouldn't have known it was me who was calling. So, if I may pose your original question back to you, why didn't *you* call *me* when you first got my phone number, Lydia?"

The next thing Luke heard was the sweetest and most congenial sounding voice he had ever heard in his life. "Luke, honey, do you suppose we could start this call over from the beginning and not worry about who called or didn't call? I suppose it doesn't really matter how long it took."

Chapter 6

Encouragement

Past

"Do I have to go, Mom? I don't know anyone there," said a six-year-old Luke who was sitting on a small, three-legged pine stool in a corner of his room. He was slightly covered up by his dresser, and if he crouched down while on the chair and sat quietly without moving, you wouldn't even know he was there. Which was exactly what he wanted to do at that very moment.

Continuing to plead his case, his mother came into his new room and sat on his bed across from him and listened. "I want to go back to our old house," pleaded Luke. "I already know most of the other kids in our neighborhood, and I'd be going to school with them right now."

Meanwhile, at another house not too far away, a similar but different conversation was taking place. "Dad, how come you and Mom aren't going to take us to school? Everybody else's parents take them. Why can't you and Mom?"

"Well, Markus," said Matthew as he sinched up his silk tie, speaking with more than a little arrogance, "the Middlefield family is no ordinary family, and because we have worked hard to achieve that status, we are simply too busy to be driving you and your sister around. That's why we are having someone from the school office come to our home and pick you up."

"But, Dad, can't you go to work after you drop us off? I don't care if our family is different."

Matthew couldn't believe what he was hearing. He would have to spend more time with this boy of his and teach him what the world is all about. He didn't say it out loud, but he knew Markus's heart was too soft to be successful in this world. On the other hand, Markus had a twin sister who was growing up to be just like her father, with all the unyielding and tenacious attributes needed to make it in a business environment that operates based on the survival of the fittest.

Rebecca's heart was breaking for her little man, not sure how to explain to him why he would have to add all his old friends to his list of losses, losses that had started with his dad and grandmother. Walking slowly into Luke's bedroom, Gus saw Rebecca kneeling in front of Luke and at a loss for words.

Looking down at his daughter and gently putting his hand on her shoulder, he said, "Rebecca, let me take care of this one. I think I know what Luke needs to hear."

Rebecca stood up, allowing Gus to sit down across from Luke. She made her way to the door and leaned on the frame as she let out a sigh of desperation. She wasn't sure how to encourage Luke at that critical moment. Gus looked at his grandson, who was broken but didn't have a tear in his eyes. It appeared to Gus that Luke had done enough crying over this past month, and he simply had no more tears to give. Rebecca, on the other hand, had plenty of tears left and headed for the hall bathroom to get a hand towel to wipe her face with.

"Luke, can I tell you something very special about the elementary school we want you to go to?"

Luke lifted his head off his arm and said, "I guess so, Grandpa, but only if it's special. What is it?"

"Do you remember Mom's friend, Miss Jane? She's the one who visits once a year, and Mom visits her once a year too. They talk on the phone all the time."

"Yeah, Grandpa. I know Miss Jane. She's a nice lady."

There was the opening Gus was looking for: "Well, what you don't know is that your mom went to this same school when she was a little girl, and it was at this school that she met her very first lifelong friend, Jane. And I'm sitting here right now to tell you that if your mom could find a lifelong friend at this school, you can do the same thing."

Luke looked at his grandpa for a long time, and only the spinning wheels of a six-year-old's mind could have come up with the question Luke asked next.

"Grandpa?"

"Yes, Luke, what is it?"

"I'm just wondering, if my best friend is at this school, why were Mom and Dad going to put me in that other school? If they had done that, I never would have met my best friend that I haven't met yet."

It was there and then that Gus knew this grandson of his was going to be one special boy, and that he would grow up into one special man.

"Dad," said Maggy in a cute, high-pitched, squeaky voice. Walking to her father, with her arms full of manilla folders, she said, "I have all the papers from your desk that you said we needed for enrolling. Do you want to look at them, or should I hold onto them and give them to the person who is going to pick us up?"

"That's my girl. And to answer your question, here's a small brief-case for you to carry them in until the office person at the school asks for them. And Maggy," said Matthew with a little concern in his voice.

"Yes, Dad, what is it?"

"Would you keep your eyes on Markus for a week or two at school? Make sure he only plays with the good boys."

An hour later, they were all in a public elementary school where the noise level was approaching uncontrollable. An hour after that, the parents were gone, having given their precious children one last hug and kiss before releasing them into the care of these educators.

Just before lunch, the class Luke had been assigned to was outside playing on the school's teeter-totter and monkey bars. There was a boy close to where Luke was playing, but he was just watching. Luke thought this was a little odd, but then he thought about what his grandpa had told him. This might be the best friend he hadn't met yet.

"Hi, my name is Luke. What's yours?"

The other boy looked at his sister, who was playing on the swings, and then looked back at Luke and said, "My name is Markus. I'm not different like my family is."

Luke answered back, "I don't care what your family is like. Do you want to be my friend?"

Present

Metal was flying all around them, and Luke couldn't do a thing about it. *Why did I agree to this as a first date?* Luke thought to himself. Lydia was easily able to control her flying metal, while Luke looked like he was throwing bricks at a floating party balloon. At this point in the game, he was just glad that no one who knew him was there to watch. And there it was. It happened again. Lydia swung her arm back and then forward with just the right amount of force, letting go of her projectile at just the right moment. She could see that it had the perfect arc, the perfect speed, and the perfect rotation as it flew through the air. A moment later, all they heard was a solid *clink* coming from the metal stake she had been aiming at. Luke couldn't believe it. *She did it again. She got another ringer. How does she do that?* Turning toward Luke, and not feeling the need to let a guy win a game just because he's a guy, she said triumphantly, "Okay, Mr. Athlete, beat that one!"

Luke stepped up with more grit on his face than he had shown in his previous ten attempts. After clinking his two horseshoes together for good luck, he was determined to duplicate the same motion he saw from Lydia mere moments ago. But he failed again. His horseshoe was neither high enough nor fast enough, nor was it rotating properly. He didn't achieve the coveted 'clink' of victory. What he *did* hear was the sound of defeat as his horseshoe once again made a terrible thumping noise in the sand. It was at least a foot to the right of the stake, and a foot short. He knew he had lost again.

After picking up her horseshoes from the stake box, Lydia said to Luke, "When I suggested that we could go to the park and play a few games of horseshoes for our first date, I thought you would have figured out that a girl who was a pitcher in fast-pitch softball might be pretty good at throwing horseshoes."

Luke was quiet as he picked up his two metal shoes, even as Lydia was teasing him about his poor performance. "Come on, Luke, you're not upset because a girl beat you in horseshoes, are you? You do know that you can't be the best at every sport you play, don't you?"

"Actually, Lydia, no, I'm not upset. I can lose a game to anyone and be okay with it, because if they're better than me, then they're better. But I do have a question for you."

"Sure, what is it?"

"Now, understand that this is just out of curiosity. But are you just as good at bowling, skee ball, and bean bag toss as you are at softball and horseshoes?" Luke asked this question with an indiscernible expression on his face.

She thought for a minute and then said, "I guess I never thought about those games before, but, yeah, I guess I am. Why do you ask?"

Luke paused and then said, "So, you're saying that any sport you can play in an underhanded way, you're pretty good at and will have a better than fair chance at winning. Does that sound about right?"

Missing the sarcasm in his question and wanting to play it safe on their first date, Lydia answered him honestly: "Yup, that sounds about right. I love to play underhanded games." Lydia froze for a moment as Luke burst out laughing. Thinking about what she just said, Lydia felt her face getting warm and knew she was blushing. However, she was not so flustered that she couldn't get in Luke's face. "Hold it right there, Luke. Wait a minute, because I don't believe I heard what I think I heard. I want to hear you say that one more time, Luke."

Luke said "okay" with a teasing smile and then proceeded to ask her his question very slowly so she could understand what he was saying. At the end of his repeated question, he added, "And in case you didn't hear me, I said I would like to go on another date with you. That is, if you don't mind being seen with a guy that is less underhanded than you are. Did I say that slow enough for you?"

Lydia stood there, watching and listening to Luke clink his horseshoes together as he waited with a boyish grin on his face. Apparently, he was just as willing to dish out a good tease as he was to receive one. She decided right then that she liked this guy. And if he didn't mind taking a chance with her, she wouldn't mind taking one with him. Lydia didn't hesitate in answering Luke's rather direct question: "Sure, I'd like that, Luke. Did you have anything special in mind?"

Still sporting a boyish grin, he said, "I was thinking about trying my hand at bowling. Would you be up for another underhanded sport?" His grin grew as he waited for her response.

She narrowed her eyes as she got in a competitive mood, and then she said, "Only if you're in the mood for another loss."

If anybody happened to pass by this couple as they made their way through the rest of the park, they might have overheard the young woman offer to help install a horseshoe pit in the young man's back yard.

While he waited for Markus to arrive, Luke was rocking on an old chair that his grandfather had purchased years ago. Through the years, Grandpa Gus had brushed on layer after layer of exterior varnish on these chairs. This allowed them to keep their shiny, smooth surface while at the same time protecting them from the outdoor elements. And now it would be Luke's responsibility to continue this family tradition. The four rockers had been placed on the front porch years ago, and they had always been comfortable chairs. They had that unmistakable character, and they made that creaking sound that only comes with use and age. Facing toward the street, the rocking chairs were positioned perfectly. You could catch the eye of anyone walking by, call out a greeting, and give them a wave. And if it was late enough, you could enjoy a beautiful sunset since, as this side of the house faced west. Another benefit to this porch perch was the clear view of every vehicle passing by.

Luke was waiting for his two childhood friends to arrive for dinner, but one vehicle was a bit late in arriving. He had expected Markus to arrive more than an hour ago, and he began to wonder if something had happened to him. After checking the time on his phone, and seeing how late it was getting, Luke became concerned.

Nope, Luke thought to himself, *there's nothing wrong with the clock on my phone, and I haven't missed any text messages or calls. Still, I'm going to go with the old adage that "no news is good news."*

Luke had just finished this thought when he saw Markus's truck coming down the street. Markus slowly turned into the driveway and parked next to Luke's truck. He turned off his engine, slid out of the front seat, and started walking to the front porch where Luke was waiting. He had a noticeable saunter to his walk, which made Luke wonder what had happened. When Markus was halfway to the porch, Luke asked in a very curious tone, "Where'd you go, Markus? I thought you were right behind me when we left the jobsite. After taking two quick turns to get on the highway, I looked in my rear-view mirror and you were gone."

"Yeah, sorry about that, dude. And sorry I didn't tell you, but at the last minute, I decided to go home to change out of my work clothes. I see you did the same thing. What I didn't anticipate was what I found when I got home, which was something you don't have to worry about. I realized, after seeing two additional cars in the driveway, that my dad was having a meeting with George and Petey-boy VanderMor."

Markus made that last statement with extreme sarcasm. "I sat in my truck for a while, trying to decide if I should go in or not. I didn't feel like having an argument with my dad or mom if they happened to see me and ask questions about where I was going or who I was hanging out with tonight. So I decided to sneak in and avoid my dad's home office and the VanderMors. My mom was easy to avoid because she was hovering around the first floor close to the office, in case they needed anything. It was easy to sneak up the steps at the back of the house. Maggy was in her room listening to music and getting changed for a date. I assume she had set it up with Petey-boy after his meeting, so I decided to leave my truck on the street and come in the house through the garage service door. I went through the kitchen and up the back staircase to my room. I almost felt like a burglar. It was actually pretty exhilarating!" Markus said with a big smile before continuing.

"When I finally made it to my room, I took a very quiet shower, changed my clothes, and snuck out the same way I got in. It was a ridiculous waste of time. If I had known changing my clothes was going to be that difficult, I would never have gone home to begin with. But here I am—looking good and smelling fresh."

Markus had been walking across the front yard this whole time, talking loudly and showing using wild arm motions to demonstrate all the cat burglar moves he had to make. He wanted Luke to visualize this stealthy mission. It wasn't until he stepped onto the front porch and walked over to sit down next to Luke that he took in a deep breath and stopped talking. Luke had wanted to explain to Markus about the coming evening's events, but he wasn't fast enough, as Markus started in again.

"So, about our old buddy, Juan. Has he changed much, or is he the same Juan we both know from high school?"

Luke didn't answer right away, almost expecting to be cut off again by his exuberant friend. In that brief moment of hesitation, he was deciding if he should ask any questions about Markus's clothes-changing adventure, or if he should listen to the wisdom speaking in his mind and just let it go. He opted to listen to wisdom and move on with the new topic of conversation; he figured it would just be easier.

"I guess that's what tonight is about, Markus. We'll know in a couple of hours whether our old buddy has changed or if he is the same Juan we all saw at the graduation ceremony."

"Yeah, I get it, Luke. It shouldn't take long to find out, and I really do hope he's changed. But when is he going to show? Or am I the only one getting hungry?" At this remark, Markus's stomach growled.

"Dude, you just got here. Relax and be patient. I'm guessing he'll be here around 5:30. He's coming straight from downtown where he works with his food truck, so he might hit some traffic and be a few minutes later than that."

Luke noticed that when he mentioned Juan arriving in his food truck, Markus's eyes sort of glazed over and a look of confusion covered his face. It was then that Luke realized that Markus didn't have a clue what was going to happen tonight. He took in a deep breath and asked him, "Markus, you do know what we're doing tonight?"

Markus looked at Luke with a truly blank expression on his face and then softly mumbled, "Nope, not really. Yesterday all you said was that I should come over to your house for dinner, and you said Juan would be there to eat with us. I just did what I was told to do, man, so here I am."

Luke rolled his eyes at his friend. "Well, Markus, here's the plan for tonight. When Juan arrives in his food truck, he'll have the ingredients for supper. All we have to do is prepare it ourselves, bake it, and then eat it. It'll be fun."

After hearing those plans, Markus's look of confusion turned to one of a bewildered—and pampered—young boy. He barely knew how to use a toaster and microwave, let alone prepare a meal that was edible. The look of fright on Markus's face was priceless.

"You mean I have to help make the food we're going to eat?"

Luke could see the wheels slowly turning in Markus's brain, and as slow as they were, at least they were moving. "I don't know how you do it, Luke. You maintain this house, you cook, you clean, and I guess you're okay with living all by yourself. I don't think I could do it, bro."

Luke knew that his longtime friend could and would make it on his own someday, although he may be eating a lot of peanut butter sandwiches, Pop Tarts, and mac and cheese. "First of all, Markus, I don't do it all alone, and having a 50-hour-a-week job also fills up a lot of my time. My mom stops by three times a week to help me clean the house, and she prepares dinner for me on those days too. And believe it or not, when Ricardo isn't meeting with a client in the evening, he comes over with my mom to teach me how to cook. As a matter of fact, I'm going to prepare tamales for dinner tonight that he taught me how to make last winter. You know the ones I'm talking about—you grabbed one out of my lunchbox about a month ago and ate it pretty fast."

"You're making those tonight? That sounds great, Luke. That was a really good tamale!"

"Forget about the tamales for a minute, Markus. I want to talk to you about your cooking skills, or, should I say, *lack* of skills. I know your parents have a full-time cook in the house, and I bet if you asked her to give you some cooking lessons, she would do it. And I bet both of you would have a good time too."

Deep down, and unknown to Luke, Markus saw this encouragement to learn how to cook as more of a challenge or a dare, like a bet that Luke assumed he couldn't win.

Luke went on, honestly attempting to encourage Markus. "Cooking is fun, Markus. You just have to try it to know what I'm talking about."

Markus sat and thought for a while before saying, "But if I marry a girl that loves to cook, wouldn't all those cooking lessons have been a waste of time?"

Luke just sat and stared at his best friend, not believing what he had just heard come out of his mouth.

"Markus, I can't believe you just said that!" Thinking about the best way to help him understand why learning to cook is a good idea for everyone, he decided to follow Markus's reasoning. "Markus, about this imaginary wife you referenced, what if she gets sick? Who's going to cook for her and for you, and what if she gets sick and you have children—who's going to cook for them?"

Markus was deep in thought at this very plausible scenario, so in his reflective silence, Luke continued to talk.

"Now, I'll admit to you that up until eight months ago, Maggy made it easier for me to live on my own, as she did her share of the cooking. But what you have to understand is that she didn't do all of it. As a matter of fact, some of our most enjoyable dates were when we would cook together. I loved those times. And now that I think about it, that would be a good idea for several dates for you and Cindy. The only thing I don't know is where you can do all that cooking."

Hearing Luke bring up some of the good times with his sister, Markus felt compelled to say, "Since you brought it up, dude, and I hope you don't mind me saying, but I'm still just as confused as you are about the whole Maggy thing. I'm not sure what made my dad and mom turn against you the way they did, or why Maggy did the same thing. It was strange, dude, *real* strange. And what was even more strange was that while all that drama was taking place, he was telling her to go ahead and date a guy he had known for less than a month. I don't know what it is, but there has got to be more to this story than your religious beliefs."

In Ricardo-like fashion, Luke slowly ran his fingers through his hair while leaning way back on his rocker. He was taking a moment to consider his words before he responded to Markus's thoughts.

"You know something, Markus, I'm past the whole Maggy-drama. She made her choice. And in the process, she made it real clear several months ago that she wanted nothing to do with me. It was at that very moment that I realized I never really knew her. I don't know why I never saw it before. I'm starting to think it all worked out for the best, and now that I think about it, it would have been just as easy for your dad to have said yes rather than no to my request to meet up with him to ask his permission to propose to Maggy. But he blew me off, and here we are. Think about it, Markus: if your dad hadn't treated me so poorly and ignored my request, I never would have met Lydia, and I would be engaged or married to Maggy right now."

Markus immediately straightened up in his chair and looked at Luke in stunned amazement. "You mean to tell me that you asked my dad for his permission to propose to Maggy, and he said no?"

"Pretty much. Like I said, I called him and asked him to have lunch with me because I had an important question I wanted to ask him concerning Maggy. I told him I wanted to speak with him face to face about it. Believe me, he knew what that request was for. *Every* dad knows what that call is about when he gets it. Before he could give me an answer, your mom was calling in and she interrupted our conversation. He flipped over to her call so fast I barely heard him ask me to hold on. When he got back to me two minutes later, it took him about five seconds to say no to lunch. He just blew me off. That was the same day you guys turned your phones off and left for Aspen for two weeks. And, surprise, surprise, after having those two weeks of alone time with your parents, the first thing she does when she gets home is break up with me."

This time it was Markus's turn to lean way back in his rocker. After letting out a long sigh, he said, "Wow, I can't believe we were that close to becoming brothers, bro! Does Maggy know about that conversation with my dad?"

"Not unless he said something to her. I'm guessing he never did, and probably never will. But like I said, Markus, it's in the past and it's over."

Luke had no sooner gotten those words out of his mouth when this normally subdued and quiet neighborhood was awakened by an obnoxious-sounding horn that was attached to a long, motorized shoebox on wheels. The name "Pronto Foods" was written on the side of it. And there he was, their old friend, Juan. He still had a flare for making an entrance. He was headed toward Luke's driveway and had decided to pull past it while slowing down. It was masterful watching him maneuver this 30-foot-long food truck. He had turned it hard to the left and into the other lane. This swung the back end of the truck to the right and toward Luke's driveway; then, after coming to a complete stop, Markus put the engine in reverse and adeptly backed into the driveway. Luke and Markus never would have believed a truck that size could make such graceful moves. It was like watching a hippo dance the Minute Waltz. After Juan had come to a complete stop and turned off the engine to his mobile restaurant, the guys could see how impressive this maneuver was. Not only would the cooking and serving side of this monster food truck be facing Luke's front yard, but the truck's position would also make it easier to leave later that evening when it was darker outside. It appeared that Juan had a knack for thinking ahead.

———————————————

While Luke and Markus walked over to Juan's restaurant on wheels, excited to greet their old friend, Elizabeth Middlefield was walking into Matthew's home office with drinks on a tray for these three new friends. She had poured two brandies and a bourbon, and she sat the tray on Matthew's desk.

"You boys looked like you needed a little pick-me-up before dinner. I hope I got everyone's drink order correct."

They were all appreciative and reached for their drink of choice. After the tray had been emptied of its contents, Elizabeth looked at Matthew and asked, "If it's okay with you all, could I speak with Matthew in the hallway for just a minute before you get too deep into your meeting?"

"Sure, Liz. Excuse me, George, Peter. I'll be back in a moment."

Matthew stepped into the hallway and closed the door to the office behind him before saying, "Liz, I know that look. What is it, honey?" Elizabeth wasted no time and got right to the point.

"Matthew, I'm getting a little nervous about all this political talk, and I don't know where it may or may not lead us. Like I told you when George first contacted you a few months ago, I'm fine with exploring the possibility of running for public office, but don't forget, Matthew, none of this political stuff was part of the plan when we agreed to get married. You know what I want for my life, and I know what you want for yours, and none of our past plans included you becoming a politician. I don't want to do anything that will get in the way of the goals we set for ourselves. Now, I'm not saying that I'm against you running for office. What I *am* saying is that I'm okay with committing to one election at a time and seeing where it goes. But I want you to remember that we're a partnership, a team. Don't agree to anything until we've had a chance to talk it over. We've worked too hard to get where we are today, and we can't be taking any foolish or unnecessary chances and risk losing everything. I refuse to give up our lifestyle!"

"Don't worry, Liz, I'm not stupid," Matthew responded in a placating voice.

"No, you're not, but you *are* impulsive, and you know what I'm talking about. Just make sure we talk before agreeing to anything." Elizabeth took a moment to regain her composure before switching topics: "Now, what would you like the cook to make for supper?"

While that conversation was taking place out in the hall, a second one was quietly taking place on the other side of those office doors.

"Peter, slide your chair over here, and be quick about it. I need to talk with you."

Peter gave his dad a look that said, *You're kidding—you want to talk now?* But instead of voicing his thoughts, he hid his true feelings and replied in a calm voice, "Sure, Dad, what is it?" He was sliding his chair, as requested, closer to his father while he was speaking to him.

George's inner thoughts were more along the lines of, *This son of mine just graduated from university and he better start taking life more seriously. If he doesn't, we could be in a lot of trouble!* Then, with unmistakable resolve in his voice, he said, "Peter, why didn't you answer my call last night, or the three times I tried to get ahold of you this afternoon right before this meeting? I had some very important topics I needed to talk over with you concerning Matthew."

Again, what Peter thought to himself and what Peter said out loud to his father were two different things. He couldn't believe the way his dad was trying to control his life. He didn't see the need to talk to him two, three, and even four times a day; it felt oppressive. And all because he told him about a pretty girl he met in a study group at school whose father built multi-million-dollar homes. But instead, he said, "I'm sorry, Dad, it won't happen again." Peter was attempting to sound genuinely concerned about his father's needs, but he fell a little short in his presentation. "So, what did you want to talk with me about?"

Don't think that you're getting off that easy, thought George to himself. Not willing to let his growing frustration with his son get in the way of the bigger picture, he went on to explain, "We'll have a longer talk later, but for now I'll have to make this brief." He hesitated a minute, checking to be sure Matthew wasn't coming back into the office, while also thinking about his three other children, all grown and responsible adults. They all followed his lead and his advice, and they were now working for the government. They had great jobs that carried huge responsibilities, significant influence, and incomes to match. *Why is Peter so difficult?*

George came back to the present and said, "Peter, I need to make sure you understand the gravity of your position and how your role in all these current political maneuverings is critical for your future success. I also want you to know that I have hired a private consultant to conduct more research on Matthew's past. This consultant is a real pitbull, so I have no worries that he's going to find out everything about him. Now, one big negative we'll have to contend with in digging into Matthew's past is the fact that we'll be working so closely with him that we may get swept up in his investigation. We need to be aware that he may find out things about us we would rather keep hidden, so be careful what you do and who you do it with. I just hope you haven't done anything in your past that we may have to clean up. Now, once we learn the finer details of Matthew's past, we can decide how we might use that information to our advantage. For now, you've got to understand that we're here today to solidify with him that you are the best candidate to help him run his state congressional office. You will, of course, have my personal oversight and guidance.

Feeling a bit overwhelmed with all this information, Peter stretched before leaning closer to his dad.

"You need to continue to stay very close to Maggy Middlefield. Staying close to her will allow you unlimited access to Matthew, not only on a professional level but also on a personal one. You will also have to covertly keep track of what Matthew says and does in those private times when he believes no one is watching. Peter, I can't stress this enough, but you need to do all this without tipping your hand as to our motives. That could create an unreconcilable and destructive situation. In the game of politics, Peter, one never knows when elected mustangs need to be roped and forced into a corral so that they can see who is actually in charge. That's why it's critical to have some sensitive information at our disposal when the time is right. So, make sure you take lots of notes on what takes place behind the curtain when he thinks no one is paying attention. Matthew Middlefield is much more arrogant than a normal politician, so it shouldn't take long for us to build a book of activity that he won't want to be made public. We need all this information to keep him in check as he gains more popularity and power. This will be the key to your future, keeping control of Matthew Middlefield."

And with that last statement, they heard the door of the office begin to open and saw Matthew walking back in. What they didn't notice was the look on Matthew's face when his "spirit friend" rejoined him, for *it* had opted to stay in the office while Matthew was out in the hall with Liz.

Back at Luke's place, after Juan had skillfully parked his kitchen on wheels close to the back patio of the house, he spun to the right, got out of the driver's seat, then disappeared into the bowels of this mobile box. The next thing Luke and Markus saw were the sides of the truck flying up and exposing the food preparation areas. After disappearing inside the truck for a moment, Juan reappeared from the back of the truck, facing toward the guys on the front porch. Markus was the first one off the deck, and he walked over to give Juan a handshake and a chest bump.

"I can't believe it's been over a year since I've seen you, dude!"

"I can't believe it either," said Juan as he reached out his hand. "And you're looking pretty buff, man. Being a carpenter must give you quite a workout."

"Well, I do go home tired every day, that's for sure. But what about you, Juan? Besides looking as slim as the day we graduated from high school, Luke hasn't told me much of what you've been up to—so spill it. What have you been doing for the last couple of years?"

"You're looking at it, Markus. I've been learning the fast food business from my dad via food trucks. He keeps telling me that one day it'll all be mine—like I want that kind of responsibility! Wait a minute, you do know my dad owns the Pronto Food company, don't you?" He gave Luke a look while he asked that question.

"He does? I didn't know that. But out of curiosity, and since we're talking about our dads, did you know my dad builds homes for a living? And he wants me to run the company someday—like I want that kind of responsibility!"

"Real funny, Markus. And, yes, I know your dad builds homes. The whole city knows it. I'd have to be living in a hole under a rock not to know it." Luke and Markus could see that Juan was getting a little heated over this jabbing, so after one more statement from Juan, they decided to let him off the hook.

"Am I the only one of us who is paying attention to what is happening around him?"

There was a long moment of silence after Juan asked that last question, and then Luke and Markus exploded into laughter.

"Sorry, Juan, I didn't mean to mess with you like that," said Markus. "For years I've known that your dad owned Pronto Food. I've actually had quite a few meals at the side of your dad's trucks, and they were great. I always thought I might run into you but never did. And just so you know, dude, while we were waiting for you to arrive, it was Luke's idea that if you asked that question, I was supposed to play dumb and see how you reacted. We were just messing with you—sorry, man."

Juan, looking at his two old friends, relaxed the irritated expression on his face and replaced it with a mischievous one.

"You're pretty good at playing dumb, Markus. Are you sure it was only an act?"

Luke interrupted, "Okay, you two, let's call it quits on this conversation. I'll tell you guys what: if Juan shows me how to use the oven and where all the food is stored, I'll make supper while we all do some more catching up. How does homemade enchiladas and hot tamales sound? It comes from my stepgrandma's cookbook of secret recipes."

Markus stopped messing with Juan when he heard Luke offer to cook. He then blurted out, "I still can't believe I'm the only one here that can't cook!"

"You can't cook? Well then, I've got an idea for you, Markus."

"Yeah, and what would that be?"

"Why don't you have your daddy build you a house with a gourmet kitchen in it so Luke and I can come over and teach you how to use it."

"Are you kidding? I can only help *build* them. I can't afford to *buy* one!"

The business meeting and supper were over now, and George was driving away, leaving Peter alone with Maggy by his car. Everything was going according to plan. From the inside of the house, Matthew and Elizabeth were looking out of a large picture window at this beautiful young couple, both of them completely unaware of what Peter VanderMor was about to bring into their lives. Deciding to let them have their privacy, they walked back further into their home and relaxed as Elizabeth made another stop at the wet bar.

"Here's another drink, Matthew. Now why don't we go to that big, fancy office of yours and talk about what you men just agreed to. I do hope you told George that we discuss life-changing decisions as a family before making them."

"Of course I did, Liz. He actually commented to me about how refreshing it was to hear that. He also said that that type of attitude solidified his choice to back me in his future political plans."

"Future political plans? We're already running for the House of Representatives, so I'm assuming that 'future plans' went beyond that?"

"Yes, and when George talks about the future, he is really talking about the future."

"Well, lay it out for me and then we'll decide together what our future will be."

Matthew quietly sighed before explaining the plans that he and George had agreed to a couple of hours earlier. Matthew was a little miffed that Elizabeth thought he was unable to make a well-informed decision for the both of them without her approval.

"Take it easy, Liz. There's no need to get worked up. I'll tell you everything we talked about, and even a few things we didn't. My friend heard George telling Peter some things while we were in the hall outside the office. And I know you'll agree with everything I agreed to."

Liz sat there, sipping her glass of wine rather aggressively, and then said, "Well . . . what are you waiting for? What did you and George talk about? What did you agree to? And what did your friend tell you?"

Matthew took in another long breath and then let out a sigh. *I've got to get my beautiful wife enrolled in a course on people management skills if she's going to be any help to me on the campaign trail.* He continued, "The first step is happening right now, and the race we are in appears to be in the bag. We're up by ten points and we haven't even started campaigning. The second step is a second term in the House. Then, the next step after that is a big one: if everything falls into place, the party leadership wants me to run for governor."

Elizabeth was shocked into a moment of silence as she processed this revelation. "Did you just say 'for governor'? You're not kidding, are you? I never expected that to be part of this meeting. Now *that's* planning for the future."

Elizabeth was almost giddy, having already forgotten about Matthew's friend. She began thinking about the possibilities for her as the first lady of their state. This might just be better than being married to a luxury home builder. She gleefully thought about the power that would be at their fingertips and the national recognition they would enjoy.

"I think I'm going to get along just fine with the party leadership, and I've heard the governor's mansion is quite spectacular! Tell me, exactly what makes them think this could happen? And why us?"

Matthew could see right away that Elizabeth was now on board with this new career change, so he continued by telling her about the final step in their plans.

"The first two terms in the House are merely for public exposure— for face and name recognition here in the state. The party leadership isn't concerned about me coming up with any novel legislation on my own while I'm in Congress. They'll take care of that for me. My main job will be to make as many power-wielding friends as possible while I'm in D.C. for those four years."

"I don't understand, Matthew. Why would you need to make friends in D.C. if they want you to be governor of a state?"

Matthew paused for a second before he gave Elizabeth a bright smile that spoke of greater things to come for their family. "Because at the end of my first term as governor, they want me to throw my hat in the ring for President of the United States. I'll need as many friends as possible in D.C. if I'm going to have a successful campaign."

Back at Luke's house, with the preparation of their meal now complete, Markus, Juan, and Luke were sitting down on the back patio table enjoying the dinner they had prepared for themselves. Juan was the first to compliment Luke.

"I've been making tamales for over four years with a Pronto Foods recipe, and I've been eating them my whole life, but I've never had any that are this good," Juan exclaimed. "What's your secret? What ingredients are you using?"

Luke didn't hesitate in answering that complimentary and inquisitive question: "Sorry, dude, but those secret ingredients are several spices I got from Ricardo, and they're stored in the kitchen. I never asked if I could share that information or the spices. And that recipe is certainly not mine to share either. It belongs to Ricardo, not me."

"I get it, Luke, but I would still like for my dad to taste them. Are there any left over for me to bring home?"

"Only if we stop the eating machine over there," Luke responded while gesturing toward Markus, who had just grabbed another tamale.

"What?" said Markus unapologetically. He was enjoying the tamales more than the conversation Luke and Juan were having. "Hey man, I can't help it if they're good! So that's a compliment to you and your dad's grandmother. And I worked hard today, so I'm extra hungry!"

A half hour later, after they had finished eating, Juan was cleaning up the food truck when Luke got a text from Lydia. He answered her text message without saying anything to the guys and then slid his phone back into his pocket.

"Come on, Luke," said Markus as he threw a wadded-up napkin at him. "I know you guys haven't been dating all that long, but what did she want? I know it was Lydia—I saw that smile on your face when you saw the text." Markus said this with a teasing twinkle in his eyes.

"It's not a big deal, Markus. Lydia is coming over tomorrow and she was asking if it was okay for her to invite another couple from church that I haven't met before. You know something, this is a new experience for me. When I was dating Maggy for all those years, it was just her and me hanging out together and no one else . . . well, except for you and whoever you were dating that week. Maggy never took the initiative to introduce me to her friends, probably because I already knew all of them. But Lydia wants me to meet all her friends, and in the process, I'll have the chance to meet the type of people she hangs out with. I feel like I'm getting to really know her on a deeper level than I was able to with Maggy.

"That makes sense to me, Luke. You can tell a lot about a person by the people they hang out with. It sounds like you guys are going to have fun," said Juan.

"But this friend-meeting thing also frightens me," Luke admitted in a serious voice.

"Why is that?" they both asked at the same time, confused as to why meeting Lydia's friends would be scary.

"If I'm going to meet her friends, she might want to meet mine. And if meeting my friends tells her a lot about who I am, I may be in some trouble. Don't you see my dilemma? I would be obligated to introduce her to you two jokers."

"That's it, Luke! Just for that, I'm not going to eat any more of your tamales. Juan can have the rest to give to his dad. If I'm the kind of friend that you're embarrassed to introduce to your new girlfriend, you might as well tell her that I don't like your cooking either."

Luke knew Markus better than Markus realized, and he knew exactly how to see through the smoke and mirrors of his bravado.

"So what you're telling me is, the next time we get together for dinner you won't be eating Grandma Maria's 'Hispanic Shepherd's Pie' that I'll be preparing?"

Markus stopped dead in his tracks. In the blink of an eye, he had forgotten about not eating any more of Luke's cooking. With a boyish look on his face, he said, "What's that? I've never heard of that kind of pie before. Is it any good?"

"I guess you'll never find out, will you?" Luke teased.

At that moment, Markus mustered all his strength, trying not to laugh. With a completely straight face, leaving only the slightest flicker of truth in his eyes to indicate he was teasing, he said, "Okay, fine! You made your point. When you introduce me to Lydia, I'll behave. Just don't cut me out of any future dinner gatherings we have together."

Luke smiled at hearing Markus's submission and started walking to the food truck to help Juan clean up.

"Wait a second, Luke," said Markus, surprised at his own flash of brilliance. "I just had the most awesome idea!"

"Oh no," said Luke, attempting to feign true fear in his voice, "I see trouble coming down the road, and it's a food-eating machine."

"No, really. All kidding aside, I have a great idea. Since we're talking about meeting new people and eating new kinds of food, why don't we all have dinner together next Friday? But this time, let's include our girlfriends."

"I like that idea, and I'd be up for meeting your girlfriends," said Juan as he walked back to his food truck and continued to put things in order.

Switching gears for a moment, Luke asked Juan, "Do you need help cleaning up in there? Can I throw out any garbage or recycling?"

"Thanks, Luke, but everything is good in here. We take care of all trash and recycling back at the warehouse. What do you say about dinner next week? We can all try your shepherd's pie together, including Markus."

Giving up on his attempt to see if there were any empty longneck bottles in Juan's truck, Luke said, "That actually sounds like a lot of fun. Let me verify with Lydia that it works for her too and I'll get back to you guys and confirm."

"What's this checking in with Lydia and then confirming stuff? Why can't we call it a plan and then let each other know if our girls can't make it?" suggested Markus, believing he had just become brilliant for the second time in one night.

Luke turned toward Markus, hardly able to believe what he had just heard. "Are you serious, Markus? When you're in a relationship, don't you agree that your girlfriend's opinion should matter just as much as your own, especially when it comes to obligating both of you to do something? That means you need to consider her opinion, and she should consider yours. Not to be mean, Markus, but you sound a little like your dad in expecting Cindy to go along with whatever you say."

Markus stood there, silently considering what Luke had said. He realized that he had disrespected Cindy by ignoring her desires for next Friday. He didn't like what he had just learned about himself.

"Look at that, Luke," said Juan with a rather large smile on his face. "For once, Markus doesn't have a comeback."

"I'm not trying to play the 'got you' game with either of you guys, but my grandpa taught me some things about how I should treat the women in my life, especially the one I am dating or courting."

"Courting?" Markus said while laughing. He had just come out of his deep-thought mode. "How many decades ago did your grandpa give you that kind of advice?"

"He actually gave it to me just last year."

Markus said, "That's impossible. There's no way he could have done that, Luke. I was at the funeral almost two years ago—we were standing there together and both of us saw him being buried."

Though he didn't intend to ignore what Markus was saying, Luke didn't answer him immediately. He looked over to where Juan was cleaning up and noticed him throwing away a couple of empty long-neck bottles. This kind of bottle typically had only one type of beverage in it, and Pronto Foods didn't sell that kind of refreshment. Still worried at what he had just seen and what it might mean, he asked Markus to take a seat on the front porch. Luke wanted to clarify some things about the recent counsel he had received from his grandfather. Juan would be sitting to his left, and Markus to his right. He had a story to tell them and a digitally recorded message he wanted to show them.

As Juan sat down, Luke began this story by asking, "Have either of you ever heard of a service called Legacy Letters?"

They both shook their heads and said at the same time, "Nope, never heard of it." Luke took the next 15 minutes to explain what the service was and how it worked. He then told them what his grandpa was doing for him through his recorded letters. Finally, he told them that Grandpa Gus had taught him about the differences between noticing, dating, courting, engaging, and then finally marrying that one special girl. When he had finished, they were amazed. "

"Wow, I've never heard any of this stuff before, not even from my dad," said Markus, who had been silently considering what Luke had told them about girls and marriage. Unknown to his friends sitting on this porch, Markus was furthest down the relationship road, well on his way to marriage.

"That's actually some pretty solid advice, Luke." But deep in his heart, Markus knew that he was like thousands of other guys his age, having received absolutely no advice or counsel from his father on this topic. Not wanting to sound too needy but wanting to hear more from Luke's grandpa, Markus asked, "Did your grandpa have anything else to tell you?"

"Oh yeah, there's a lot more. And my hope is that you are ready to hear it," said Luke before continuing to tell the guys what his grandpa was doing for him. "What you guys have to understand, and you may not believe what I'm about to tell you, is that all this wisdom that my grandpa is teaching me is not his own. It's coming from the Bible, and it's being filtered to me through his own life experiences."

Markus and Juan had never heard of such a service, nor did they know that Luke's grandpa was somehow using the Bible to help him make these letters. They were sitting on their rockers, wondering if their own fathers would ever consider leaving them letters like this; they also wondered what kind of books their fathers would use for inspiration. Seeing the looks on their faces, Luke asked them, "Do you guys feel like watching a letter or two from my grandpa right now?"

Luke had asked that question as the sun was setting and a cool, fresh breeze drifted across his front lawn and over his porch. It was a beautiful sight to enjoy with his friends, and the three of them would also be enjoying beautiful words of wisdom if they wanted to hear them.

"Sure," they both said together. The three of them settled into the porch chairs, rocking and creaking, ready to hear more about what Gus had to say.

"Why don't we start out by listening to the letter from my Grandpa Gus that I just told you about, and then we'll see where it goes from there."

Markus, looking at the clock on his phone, said to Luke, "Dude, I didn't realize how late it was getting, but I can't stay much longer. I have an appointment tomorrow morning I can't miss, and I need to prepare for it a little more. Sorry, guys."

"No worries, Markus," said Luke as he set down his phone with the Legacy Letters logo. "What's so important that you're willing to leave early on a Friday night and get up early on a Saturday morning for?"

Markus had a look of embarrassment on his face. "It's nothing, Luke. I've been having these meetings on and off for two years; it's nothing special. Sorry I brought it up."

"Come on, dude, you can't leave us hanging like that. Now you *really* have to tell us what you're doing."

"Nope, I can't tell you guys, but if it makes you feel any better, my family doesn't know what I'm doing either. Tell you what, though, I'll let you know what I'm doing in a month or two if everything goes according to plan. But don't ask any more about it, or I'll change my mind. Now, show Juan and me what's on your phone before I have to go."

Even though Matthew made it sound as if his entrance into the political world would be a lock, Elizabeth was still unsure as to what the future might have in store for them or how secure a life in politics would be. After all, they had no experience in this arena, and their only connection to the party was George VanderMor. It was this inexperience that left her feeling unsettled and needing to know more about where they were headed.

"Matthew," said Elizabeth slowly, still trying to wrap her head around how their life could drastically change in such a short amount of time, "are you sure that George has the kind of influence needed to make all this possible? We are talking about potentially putting our company and our lives on a political chopping block for a man we really don't know. And what if you lose this election? Or, even worse, what happens to us if you win this first election but lose the second or third election on down the road? What then?"

Matthew responded quickly and with confidence. He was glad to have the opportunity to clarify things. "First of all, Liz, you keep forgetting about the voice that guides me from within. He agrees with George about making this move into politics. He told me it will be very, very good for us. Can you remember even one time when my inner friend has ever misdirected us in any way?"

Elizabeth considered Matthew's question and his words of encouragement as he continued speaking. She had noticed over the years that he had started bringing up his inner friend a lot more. She had always thought it was one of his quirks, a way of addressing his conscience, but now she wasn't so sure.

"Secondly, Liz, I've probably done more checking up on him than he's done on me. Based on how this first step in our new journey is going, along with the stable of politicians that are in office because of him, I'd say yes. He absolutely *does* know what he's doing, and as for a possible loss in the future, that's a good question. I'll ask him about that at our next meeting." Matthew stated these last several words looking Elizabeth directly in the eyes so she could see that he truly meant what he was saying.

Elizabeth certainly trusted Matthew, but she was still learning to trust George. That would be a matter of time. She wasn't as impulsive in some matters as Matthew was, so she had yet another question that might help her gain more confidence in George VanderMor's political opinions, insights, and abilities.

"But what made him choose you over all the other candidates he had to choose from? Why you, Matthew? Why did he choose *you*?"

Matthew didn't answer quite so quickly this time, mainly because he had thought the very same thing when George first asked him to run for office. Still, he didn't faulter in his response.

"From what he told me, it was our blue-collar, rags-to-riches story and our solid family life. We have a perfect marriage, two kids, and the city knows us. We have a great reputation with all our clients. They love my face—my winning smile and the way I give a speech. I look good on television: apparently the gray hairs I have never liked on my temples give me a fatherly and trustworthy look. I also look good on a poster and any other political flyer they want to plaster my face on. We are basically the quintessential American family living the American dream."

After hearing Matthew's excitement over what he truly believed would soon come to fruition, Elizabeth mustered all the faith she could in his decision to change the course of their lives. "Well then, Matthew, if you're up for all the changes and disruptions this will cause in our lives, so am I! I'm going to trust you with this decision, so don't disappoint me. But next time, I expect to be part of these meetings. Politics isn't just a man's world anymore. Now, what did George say our next move would be?"

Matthew could see in Elizabeth's eyes that she was now on board with him. She may not be leading the "Matthew Middlefield for Congress" train quite yet, but she was definitely on board.

"I have to keep shaking hands, smiling, and charming the people, and then I've got to get ready to give the first of many victory speeches. I've been successful at reading people so far, haven't I? How can I lose?"

"I still can't believe this is happening. And what about our income? Will we be okay financially? You do know you can no longer be on the company payroll while you're running for office, and certainly not when you get elected. At least, that's what I've heard. So how will this impact us financially? Because can't spend all our money on a political risk only to end up with nothing in the end."

Matthew was finishing off his drink and getting more relaxed when Elizabeth brought up the money question. He knew she had been raised in a poor household and had no tolerance for that type of lifestyle again, so he reassured her by saying, "No worries there, Liz. House members make a pretty good salary, and George made it very clear that if we play ball with the party leadership during the years of our public service, we will retire with more money than we could ever spend. In the meantime, just because I can't take my old salary and bonuses doesn't mean you can't. I already have a plan for our finances, and it will end up benefitting your reputation as a leading woman in the business world. Also, don't forget about our savings account."

Tonight was Lydia's turn to sit with Luke on the front porch of his house. The two of them were rocking and talking, reminiscing about the first time they had sat there together. This was the same place where they were set up by their mothers for a blind date a little over two months ago. And as far as Luke was concerned, it was the best motherly interference in his life that could have happened to him. Tonight, though, would be different. He would be meeting up with a married couple, but not as a single guy. He and Lydia were now a couple. The couple, friends of Lydia, had been invited over to meet Luke and to have some coffee, conversation, and dessert.

After getting comfortable, Luke started their rocking chair talk-time by asking, "Have you known Alan and Mary Reid long?"

"Not long, just since I graduated from college and started attending our church again this past Spring. I'm actually surprised you haven't met them before now. You all have been attending the same church for years."

Luke dropped his head in embarrassment, looking down at the shiny, gray-painted deck floor and not at Lydia's chocolate brown eyes. He knew it was time to fess up to another character flaw of his. He had done this a few times now since he started dating Lydia, and he was wondering if it would stop. It wasn't a bad occurrence, just a recurring one.

"Yeah, that would probably be my fault. I've been pretty focused on my own life with all its drama, especially with Maggy and her dad—which, by the way, thanks for listening to me vent about that. And let's not forget about my precarious job, and a future that I thought I had more control over than I actually have. Most girls would have walked away by now from a guy that doesn't have his future all figured out and secure. Are you sure you want to spend time with a guy like me?"

Lydia looked at Luke with an almost irritated expression on her face, thinking to herself, *If he's fishing for any "girlfriend sympathy" from me, he might want to think again.* "I'm a big girl now, Luke, and I think I know the kind of guy I like and am willing to take a chance on. And I like the kind of guy you are. Anyway, the job a person has does not define who that person is, at least it doesn't for me. After all, jobs come and go, but my hope would be that the character and soul of the person working the job would stay the same. What I'm trying to tell you, Luke, is that I'd rather trust in the person and not in their profession. I'm willing to take a chance with you, if you're willing to take one with me. And don't think you have the market cornered on personal baggage from the past. Everyone has a little of some kind—be it a handbag or a steamer trunk—and that includes me."

"You sure do have a way of getting right to the point, Lydia. I have to say, if we're really going to be spending more time with each other and doing something I don't do well, opening up emotionally, then there is another confession I need to make."

Lydia looked at Luke and teasingly said, "Another confession, eh? I love a good confession. Okay, Luke, let's hear it. What do you have for me? I hope it's juicy."

"Don't make fun of me, Lydia. I'm trying to be serious here. My grandfather encouraged me last month to make more friends, so that's what I'm doing tonight, and I'm doing it with you."

Lydia immediately felt bad and put on a more serious face. "Okay, I'm sorry, Luke. I didn't mean to make fun of what you wanted to tell me. Go ahead . . . what is it?" She said this as she reached out her hand toward his, holding it softly for two or three seconds and then giving it a loving squeeze. She then let go of his hand while looking him in the eyes.

Lydia listened to Luke's confession and realized that things he believed to be nearly unforgivable were actually pretty minor. But in the process of listening, she was finding out something wonderful about him: he had a very soft heart. And that was lucky for Luke, because that's the kind of guy she had been trying to find for the last three years. Coming out of her own thoughts, she continued to listen to Luke speak.

"My church-attending habits have a little to be desired. My problem is that I have a tendency to show up on Sunday mornings without giving or receiving care. You know, the social side of church. And I don't put much effort into making new friends. I have to admit to you that I pretty much just show up and listen to what the pastor encourages me to do in the coming week, and then I leave. Honestly, Lydia, I was satisfied with the friends I already had and didn't see the need for more. To become a real friend to another person takes time, and apparently I wasn't willing to make that effort."

Luke was quiet for a moment, as a personal revelation was coming into focus.

"You know something? The more I think about it, I have to admit that I don't have any Christ-following friends. I am a true follower of Jesus, but I don't have any like-minded friends to show for this belief. The people I am closest to are either from high school or work. Of course, they all call themselves Christians, or religious to some extent, but without judging them, it seems to me that their actions show me they are not true followers of Jesus. However, based on a conversation I had last night with two of these longtime friends, I'm hoping that's about to change."

Lydia sat there totally taken off guard by Luke's frank sincerity. *This isn't a boy I'm dating—he's a man in a boy's body, a man who is searching after God, though I don't think he even knows it. I think I'll hang onto this one,* thought Lydia to herself, not taking her eyes off him the whole time he was confessing.

"And speaking of these two friends," said Luke shyly, "I have to ask you something before I forget."

Not wanting to break the spell they both seemed to be under at that moment, she softly said, "Sure, Luke, what is it?" She crossed her left leg over her right leg, getting more comfortable as she leaned back a bit more in her chair. She proceeded to bounce her foot up and down lightly as Luke continued speaking.

"Well, you can say no if you want to, but they wanted to know if we would like to get together with them and their girlfriends here at the house next Friday for supper, which I would be preparing."

Lydia smiled rather coyly at Luke and then said, "You say these friends of yours are bringing their girlfriends here to have dinner with us, huh? Why, Luke Cruz, is this your way of asking me to be your steady girl?"

Luke was momentarily at a loss for words after hearing Lydia's interpretation of his question. But not wanting to be verbally worked over quite so easily by this beautiful young woman, he responded by saying, "I mean, if you're busy that night, I suppose I could get someone else to be my girl for the evening."

Knowing in her heart that if this verbal bantering was allowed to continue, no one would win this game of words—and feelings could be damaged in an unintended but irreversible way—Lydia said, "Sure, Luke, I'd love to meet your friends and their girlfriends. That sounds like a fun evening. It'll be like a triple-date night instead of a double-date night! Now, what do you say we add two new friends to your growing list—starting tonight?"

Looking out to the street in front of the house, Luke relaxed after hearing Lydia agree to come to dinner next Friday.

"I'd say yes to making two more friends. But can you tell me a little about Alan and Mary before they arrive? Maybe things like, how you met them, why does a single girl hang out with a married couple, or is there an old boyfriend still attending the small group that I should know about? You know, things like that." Luke was trying to be subtle about asking if Lydia had any guys still lingering around that might have feelings for her.

"Well, aren't we the inquisitive one tonight. Why don't I just give you the short answer. First, there are no old boyfriends." At this statement, Lydia could see Luke perk up a bit before she quickly backtracked. "Well, let me reword that statement. I have had *several* boyfriends, but they are all in the past and long gone, both emotionally and geographically." Luke lifted his right eyebrow in astonishment at Lydia's emphasis on just how many guys she may have dated that are, *thankfully*, no longer around.

Lydia knew it was time to change the topic of conversation when she saw this eyebrow dance, so she began to talk about the couple that was coming over.

"Luke, I'm sure Alan and Mary will invite you over to their house to join our Bible study. It's not a large group of people, about ten in all, that meet outside the church. Getting together like this gives us a chance to know each other much deeper than we could by talking after a church service for only a few minutes. Alan and Mary lead our group through different topics of study, which helps us grow closer to Jesus and each other. We sing, we share personal stories, we laugh and cry together, and most of all, we pray for each other. I'm already getting pretty tight with a couple of the ladies in our group. I love having people in my life that I can share private thoughts with or call for advice, people who will help me and not hurt me."

"That sounds like a special group of people," said Luke with an almost envious and embarrassed inflection in his voice. "I've known about the small groups at church and have been asked to join a couple through the years, but I never accepted those invitations. I was always too busy, at least that was my excuse. Thanks for setting this up tonight so I could meet Alan and Mary."

They talked for another 20 minutes or so before Lydia saw Alan's car coming down the street. Lydia was the first to stand, with Luke only a second behind her, as they both waved them into the driveway.

A few days later, another Legacy Letter decision had to be made. Luke decided to listen to his grandpa's letter right after work the next day. He would then go to his new small group meeting for the rest of the evening. He had to admit to himself that having Lydia in his life was making it easier to wait to hear his grandpa's words of wisdom. Monday night came and went, as did the Tuesday workday. Luke was home now with supper set out in front of him; it was leftovers from what his mom had prepared the night before. It was time to open another letter.

Again, after answering all the questions, Luke tapped on the Legacy Letter button.

"Hi, buddy. I'm back. I know you can't answer me, but I have to ask you a question. Are you getting tired of me calling you 'buddy' every time I start one of these letters?"

Luke answered with a soft and loving, "Not at all, Grandpa. I actually look forward to hearing you say it."

"I started calling you 'buddy' about the time you learned how to say 'Grandpa,' and I never stopped. I remember going over to your dad and mom's house when you were just a little guy. Your grandma would go inside to talk with your mom and I could always find you and your dad playing catch with a wiffleball or baseball in the back yard. I would walk out the side door of the house and yell out, 'Hey! How's my little buddy doing?' You'd look my way and, without fail, you would yell 'Grandpa! Grandpa!' as you ran toward my open arms. Your dad would just look at me and say, with a smile on his face, 'C'mon, Dad, how am I supposed to get Luke ready to play ball with the other kids if you keep interrupting our practices?'"

"You have to understand that your dad had been the high school varsity baseball coach for eight years by that time and was preparing his son to play on the team, even if it was ten years away. Now, of course, your dad knew you pretty well and had told me more than once that he could see a lot of potential for success in you. But what he had discovered in your personality was a type of contentment to play alone, or with just one other person, rather than needing to be part of a large group of kids. He had a knack for accurately reading people's personalities, and he was right about yours, Luke. And that's what I want to encourage you to start doing more of. I have to agree with your dad and tell you something about yourself that I never told you when I was still with you and your mom. Luke, you have 'lone wolf' and 'small pack' tendencies. You need to push yourself into larger social settings, especially those settings that involve other believers in Jesus. God designed us to be social, not solitary. And by 'social' I mean more than one person at a time. You can do this, Luke. You probably don't see this in yourself, but you also have leadership qualities in your personality. I know you'll love all your new friends once you start developing more of those relationships. A good way to start being a good leader is to keep in mind that it's not much different than being the captain of your baseball team. Here are a couple of verses to keep in mind as you make future social decisions:

For where two or more are gathered in my name, there am I among them. (Matthew 18:18)

And let us consider how to stir up one another to love and good works, not neglecting to meet together, as is the habit of some, but encouraging one another, and all the more as you see the Day drawing near. (Hebrews 10:24–25)

"Luke, there is another very important consideration to keep in mind while you are getting to know other people. It will be a comfort to you, of course, to have good, Christ-following friends in your life that you can go to for advice. But don't count yourself out of the equation. You are going to make a wonderful friend for someone else to go to when they might need some counsel. Now, in the eyes of the world, you are still relatively young, but in these years you have lived so far, because of the experiences you have lived through, God has given you much wisdom at a very young age, so don't be afraid to share it. Once again, Luke, I have come to the end of my advice for you. My hope is that these letters are a help to you, as well as timely in their arrival. Bye, buddy. Love you."

"They are more timely and helpful than you could imagine, Grandpa. Love you too."

Chapter 7

Trust

Lydia stood on the opposite side of the island counter, watching as Luke lowered a pizza-sized piece of thinly rolled-out dough onto the bottom and then up the side of a large crockery-style cooking pot. After pressing the dough in place, brushing melted butter onto the sides, and cutting the excess from the rim, he poured in all the pre-mixed ingredients for this evening's shepherd's pie.

"That's a pretty big pot, Luke. Are you sure your mom knew how big it was when she gave you the recipe?"

"Yep, I told her I was going to double the recipe, and Ricardo agreed with me that it would fit in the pot and cook evenly."

Lydia stood there watching Luke prepare this meal, having no clue or opinion about any part of its preparation. In her formative years, she had spent more time playing sports than learning how to cook. Now she was silently hoping that Luke wouldn't ask her opinion about the preparation of this meal. But there it was, the question that would plunge the first dagger of disappointment into the heart of their budding relationship.

"You agree with those directions, don't you, Lydia?" It was a simple question, not meant to hurt or expose her lack of cooking skills; he was just making conversation. He asked that question as he slid the oversized pot into the preheated oven. Then he closed the door and set the timer. Lydia didn't respond to Luke's question, but he didn't notice. He just continued rambling on about the coming evening. "In 45 minutes, provided everyone arrives on time, we should be sitting at the table and eating."

Luke was never very good at filtering the thoughts that formed in his mind before they came out of his mouth. It wasn't surprising, then, when Lydia noticed that he was glancing at the dessert she had brought for dinner. It was easy to see that he was acting a little funny, and when Lydia caught him looking at it a third time, she finally asked, "Okay, Luke, I'm getting to know you pretty well, and by the way you're fidgeting right now, I know something is bothering you. What's the problem?"

Luke had only a second to decide if he should say what was really on his mind or simply answer her question in a more vague way. As he continued wiping down the counter tops and putting dirty cooking utensils in the sink, Luke knew he'd better say something, and say it fast. His time was running out. He finally decided that honesty was the best policy. Maybe not always the brightest course of action, but still the best. Turning away from the sink and toward Lydia, he said, almost apologetically, "Well, since you brought it up, I was wondering about the pies you brought over tonight for dessert. I noticed the sticker on the cover. It's store-bought, isn't it?"

"Yes, it is," said Lydia, answering her unsuspecting boyfriend's question. Her hands were firmly planted on her hips as she waited for a 'stupid guy statement' to come out of Luke's mouth. Luke knew he was in trouble when she assumed this position, because it was a stance he was all too familiar with from his childhood. *This must be a female* DNA *thing,* he thought to himself. So what's your point, chef Luke?" Lydia was still waiting for an answer to her question, and she had to prepare herself: if this conversation were a pie, it would be filled with stupid.

Like most guys, Luke was totally unaware of the minefield he had just stepped into. Lydia, on the other hand, couldn't believe what she knew was about to come out of his mouth.

I wonder, she thought, *how often in one lifetime a man's brain locks up and freezes while his mouth keeps on talking? Do all men think that just because you're a woman, you automatically know how to cook and bake?*

Luke continued speaking, not even taking the time to look at Lydia's face and body language. If he had, he would have immediately reassessed the situation and not said what was about to come out of his mouth. "Couldn't your mom have helped you make these pies at home? I bet you two could have made wonderful apple pies—much better than store-bought pies."

"Luke, I'm a working woman!" Lydia's hands flew off her hips and up into the air. "I'm not Julia Childs!" At this point, Lydia placed her hands back on her hips for a second time before fully turning to face her oblivious boyfriend who had gone back to a safer course of action, namely, washing his cooking utensils. "I work eight to nine hours a day, five days a week, and sometimes on Saturdays, just like you. And just you wait for tax season to come around in a few months. You'll be lucky if I show up with hot soup from a vending machine, let alone a homemade meal. Now it's *your* turn to answer a question for me."

Luke stopped cleaning up and looked at his now irritated and inquisitive girlfriend. Only then, after seeing the expression on her face, did he realize that what he had said was going to cost him some boyfriend points. *Yeah, that probably wasn't the wisest thing I've ever said.*

"What's with the home-cooking questions anyway? I mean, who really cares whether you buy all your own ingredients and prepare your meal at home or just purchase a meal that's already prepared?"

"Well," said Luke, avoiding her chocolate brown eyes and trying to think quickly on his feet, which he was miserably failing at. For it was only at that moment that the cloud of stupid had begun to clear from his mind, and he realized he had stuffed his foot into his mouth. "I guess I was just wondering if you had any desire to become as good a cook as your mom or my mom."

"What did you just say?" Lydia exclaimed as Luke bit into another slice of the stupid shoe pie.

As soon as those words came out of his mouth, he knew he had just made room to wedge a second foot right next to the first one.

"*Desire?*" said Lydia.

Luke winced when he heard the tone in Lydia's voice, wishing he could take back the last two minutes. "That's a pretty intense word wrapped up in a pretty direct question. And why would I *desire* to ascend to the heights of 'mom-cooking status' anyway? Why on earth would you think it would be a smart move to compare me with not only my mother, but *yours* as well?" Lydia paused to cross her arms, and then she leaned against the counter to stare at Luke. "What are you talking about, and exactly what are you asking me? Are you trying to imply something here?"

Luke knew what *he* meant by that question, and honestly, he didn't believe Lydia would pick up on what he had insinuated. For a second time, he couldn't have been more wrong. He realized, again, that this girlfriend of his was more attentive to their conversations than he was.

"Well, like you said, you never know when you might be called on to cook for people that you love—day after day, for extended amounts of time." Luke had just opened his mouth a third time, and now both of his feet were firmly lodged in this throat.

"Luke," she said once again, this time getting a little more direct with her questioning. "Just what or who are we talking about? And just how big, or small, are these people who might need my love—and need to be fed every day?"

The words had no sooner left Lydia's mouth when they heard Markus and Cindy walking in the back door and into the kitchen. Luke had just dodged a bullet, if only temporarily, and it was one he himself had placed in the chamber.

"Hey guys," said Markus as he walked through the door, holding it open for Cindy. "We stopped at the store and picked up some snacks to nibble on. I hope that's alright."

Lydia, who had not been introduced to Luke's friends yet, saw an opening to make a point to Luke. With more than just a little sarcasm, she said, "So you brought store-bought snacks—how thoughtful! But have you ever considered making homemade snacks and bringing them to a dinner party? I bet they would taste better than store-bought ones. Go ahead and ask Luke. I bet he'll agree with me." Lydia's smile was a little too sweet as she made it a point to stare in Luke's direction.

Markus just said, "Huh? What? Is that a real thing, Luke? People actually do that sort of thing? I mean, kudos to them, but that just seems like a lot of work. Personally, I buy snacks that are already made, because I don't know how to cook."

Luke knew where this conversation was going, so he jumped in and quickly changed its direction. "Hey, that's great, Markus. Thanks for picking up those snacks. Let's just set them on the island counter for now while we do introductions for the girls. This is Lydia, my girlfriend, and this is my best friend, Markus, and his girlfriend, Cindy. They have been dating a little more than a year now."

Luke got the look from Lydia, and they weren't even married, as he smoothly transitioned from one conversation to the next. It was the look that said, "This isn't over yet, Mr. Luke Cruz." Lydia turned her head toward Luke's friends, smiled warmly, and shook hands with them. About the time those greetings had finished, they all heard a second car pull into the driveway. Juan had arrived. They all walked out the door and greeted Juan and his girlfriend. Juan stepped out of his 1968 Dodge Charger, and when everyone saw the chrome and root beer brown, metallic custom paint job, they knew where a fair amount of his income was going.

"Hey, everybody! Looks like we're all here, so let me do some introducing for all of us. To the two girls I haven't met yet, my name is Juan and this is my girlfriend, Juanita, but everyone calls her Nita."

Luke and Markus took turns introducing themselves and their girlfriends to Juan and Nita. When this initial greeting had finished, Luke said, "Why don't we head for the back of the house where the patio furniture is and get to know each other a little better. If my memory is correct, the shepherd's pie should be finished cooking in about 30 minutes, and then we can eat."

While they walked to the back patio, Luke suggested to the girls that they get seated under the shade of the table umbrella. He and Markus made a quick detour into the kitchen for serving bowls. "Markus, let's get those big plastic bowls from the pantry and pour your snacks into them. Then we can bring them out to the patio for everyone."

Having walked far enough away from the girls that they couldn't hear what he was going to say, Markus apologized to Luke. "Hey, Luke, sorry for not bringing homemade snacks. Do you think everyone will still like these store-bought ones?"

Luke smiled and said, "Don't worry about it, Markus. Lydia was just making a joke at my expense."

Juan, not having been present to know what they were talking about, did hear what they were going to do with the snacks. He followed them into the kitchen carrying a grocery bag that he had taken out of the back seat of his car. "Luke," said Juan as he held up a medium-sized plastic shopping bag, "Nita and I stopped by the grocery store and bought some grapes, strawberries, and clementines to add to the meal tonight. I hope everyone likes fruit."

Juan took in a quick breath as he stepped into the kitchen behind Markus. He started talking again before Luke even had a chance to answer his first question.

"Luke, that smells really good! It's going to be wonderful eating homemade food for a change. You wouldn't believe all the fast food I eat every day because of my job. It's that fast food that gives me cravings for healthy food, and fruit is at the top of that list. I hope what we brought goes well with your shepherd's pie."

Luke jumped into the conversation and answered as fast as he could before Juan had time to breathe again. "Are you kidding? That's a great idea. Let's get some more bowls for the fruit and see which snack food disappears first."

"Well, girls," said Lydia, as they all sat down around the patio table, "I know we just met, but I have to admit to you both that I'm not much of a cook. So when Luke said he was doing all the food preparation tonight, I was totally on board with this dinner party. I'm also okay with letting the guys serve us, if you're okay with it too." Seeing a look of agreement on both of their faces, Lydia went on to say, "So what do you all think? How about we enjoy the moment and wait to be served out here on the patio by our boyfriends?"

Luke and the guys came out of the house a minute later with their arms full of snack bowls and several soft drink options. They found the girls in the midst of a rather well-informed discussion about politics.

"Wow, this is quite a conversation you all are having. Not that I don't love that you guys are getting along and chatting, but I was hoping we would take this evening slow and easy while we get to know each other better and make some new friends. Then we can ease into deeper conversations if the evening goes in that direction. I was hoping we wouldn't talk about politics or other heavy topics right off the bat. So, what do you say? Should we keep it casual and light to start with?"

Luke apparently had some more 'getting to know Lydia time' ahead of him, because she wasn't about to waste the evening talking about trivial topics.

With just the right amount of sarcasm, she responded, "While you boys were in the kitchen talking about important stuff, like some local professional athlete's opinion on underarm deodorant, we girls thought, what better way to get to know each than to talk about the most taboo dinner party topics. Topics like: our political views, religion, the moral and ethical condition of the country, and, finally, the best topic of all—money. Sounds fun, doesn't it?" Lydia said this with a hint of sass in her voice.

Luke often found himself playing catch-up when it came to Lydia's social desires; she certainly made every event they attended together a lot more fun. Luke was dating a girl who wasn't the least bashful in expressing her opinions.

"I don't know about fun, but that does sound like the girl I've been dating for almost three months," said Luke. "Always getting right down to what's most important at the moment!"

Lydia, after considering everyone's opinions, and not wanting to be pushy, did have a thought as to how they might have an opportunity to talk about all these topics. "Actually, I've changed my mind, since Luke does make a good point. In order to work up to the heavier conversations, how about we all take turns telling each other how we met our boyfriend or girlfriend. Does that sound like a good icebreaker and a fun way to get to know each other?"

Cindy and Nita said they were ready and willing to start the evening off with the heavy topics by talking politics, but they also said slow and easy worked for them too. It was hard to decide what to do. Before Lydia made the slow and easy option for starting their evening available, Nita had brought up the fact that it appeared there was a connection to a political celebrity with them tonight.

Knowing who this celebrity was, Markus gave Cindy a look that said he didn't want to talk about his family at all. But it appeared that she did, because it was the only way the other girls would know who his father was.

"I'm with Luke," said Markus. "What's happening to our dinner party?" As everyone's eyes turned toward Markus, he continued to make his case. "I thought we were going to eat some amazing shepherd's pie, tell some jokes, have a few laughs, and throw the frisbee around. Or maybe play a few games of horseshoes in the pit that Luke and I made a few weeks back. But you all seem to want to go deep to get to know each other. Cindy," Markus said softly, turning his attention from the group to her, "do you really want to spend the evening talking about my father and politics?"

"Yes, I do. It would be nice to have some deeper conversations, and you haven't shared anything about your family. It would be nice to know a little more than what the media shares about you and your family," Cindy said gently but insistently. She was tired of waiting and ready to learn something about his father; she also wanted to get to know the friends closest to Markus.

"You're not afraid of letting people get to know who you really are, are you? I bet Luke would be pleasantly surprised by some of your beliefs, stances, and opinions. Markus, let your guard down. These are friends of yours, even Lydia and Nita who you just met tonight. Let them know the Markus I have grown to know so well over this last year. And let me learn more about you as well."

After Luke had been gently kicked in the shin by Lydia, he piped into the conversation. "I've got an idea: why don't we wait to have our political conversation in the house over dinner? In the meantime, we can start talking about how we met out here on the patio while we eat some snacks. What do you all say?"

"I say the couple who has been together the longest should go first," Lydia chimed in.

It only took a minute for them to find out who would go first, second, and last.

"Cindy, Markus, looks like you're up first. Which one of the two of you will be telling us how you met?" Lydia asked inquisitively.

It only took a moment for Markus to say, "Why don't I tell you all how we met, and Cindy can correct any of my mistakes." He looked at Cindy for approval before beginning.

"Go ahead, Markus. Tell it the way you remember it and I'll correct whatever you get wrong." Cindy gave him a sweet smile and her approval to tell their story.

"Alright then . . . it all started when Luke and I walked in the classroom where we had our training to become certified construction managers. When we got there, Luke found us a couple seats. He was excited for class, but I was only there to keep my dad off my back. I remember walking towards our seats and seeing this beautiful brunette sitting on the other side of the room. We happened to make eye contact while I was walking, and it felt like we were locked in on each other. And that was it: I knew she was the girl for me. As they say, the rest is history."

After hearing this recounting of their meeting, Luke said, "How come I don't remember any of this?"

"Because you were too busy paying attention in class, you didn't notice anything else. You were there to get a builder's certificate, but I wasn't," Markus said with a good-hearted laugh. "Did I miss anything, Cindy?"

"Yeah, just a few things, but let's let Juan and Nita tell their story and I'll fill in what you missed later."

"Nita," said Juan, "why don't you tell our story and I'll fill in if needed."

"You know something, I've never told anyone how we met, except my dad and mom. This should be fun. I hope I don't forget anything."

"You'll do great, Nita. And like I said, I'll jump in and help when you need me to."

"Well, first of all, you all should know that I'm an elementary school teacher. The day Juan and I met, I was downtown with my fifth-grade class taking a field trip for Social Studies. While we walked up and down the city sidewalks, I would point out all the social activities and businesses that made a city work. We also talked about how hard it would be for the city if some of the things we all mentioned and took for granted weren't there, like places to eat. And I'm sure you have already guessed what restaurant on wheels we were walking past at that very moment. Well, all the kids wanted to buy their lunches that day at Juan's place. I thought it was a great idea, so we all lined up to order our meals. What I learned about Juan that day is that he is not a shy or quiet person. He has quite the flare for the dramatic, which he displayed when it was my turn to order lunch." She looked over at Juan and gave him a loving smile.

Juan cut in for a quick second and said, "This is the fun part, everyone . . . I'm just saying." Juan had the look on his face of a mischievous little boy.

Nita gave him quite a big eye-roll and then continued, "As I was about to say . . . when it was my turn to order, Juan must have looked at my hands and seen no jewelry on my fingers. He must have felt pretty confident at that moment, because he proceeded to get the attention of my entire sixth-grade class.

"Hey kids, I have a question for you about your teacher. Are you ready for it?"

Nita made sure to lower her voice in an attempt to imitate Juan's. "Of course, they all said yes. He asked if I was the best teacher at the school, and then he asked if I was married." As cheesy as it was, it still made Nita blush to remember how they first met.

"My class said no very loudly, and because there were other people around watching, I remember being super embarrassed. I had no idea what he was up to with all the questions. Then he asked my class, "If your teacher agrees, should I take her out on a date?" Nita looked over at Juan, who was grinning ear to ear, thinking about how smooth he was with that pick-up line. Nita had a pretty good idea what was going through his mind as they all sat there listening to her story, and she couldn't help rolling her eyes at his bravado. She also couldn't hide a little grin as she recounted the events of that day.

"Of course, since these kids were nearly middle schoolers, everyone screamed and yelled. And so did several other loyal patrons of Juan's food truck who had been standing in line the whole time. They all yelled with my students, 'Yes! Yes! Yes!' After my face had turned sufficiently red and everyone had settled down, Juan asked me out on a date, and I said yes. There, I'm done with my story. All additional questions should be directed to Juan."

"Nita, that was a great story, but can I ask just one question before Luke and Lydia take their turn?"

"Sure, Cindy, what is it?"

"I'm curious: where did you two go on that first date?"

Nita had a growing smile on her face, while Juan's was disappearing. "I wanted to go horseback riding, but this time we should let Juan tell the story of that date. I'll do the filling in."

After Juan had finished his version of their first date story and the laughing had stopped, Lydia said, "I love this. Isn't this a great way to get to know each other? And now it's our turn. I think Luke should tell our story."

"Okay, I can do that . . . but it's going to be a short one."

"Just start the story, Luke, and I'll do all the filling in."

"Well, in short, our moms set us up to meet each other at this very house, and we ate the very meal we're having this evening. And it worked out for us. That's about it, right, Lydia?"

Lydia couldn't believe the way Luke was downplaying their story. Narrowing her eyes at him, she decided that if he wasn't going to elaborate, she would. "Actually, Luke, I think you missed a few things. I never told you, but my mom told me the day after we met how easy it was to get you to invite her and me to stay for dinner that evening. And when I rang the doorbell, they worked it so that he would answer the door instead of one of them. We all talked over dinner that evening and then Luke and I were given the option to talk some more on the front porch while our moms slowly washed the dishes. But the most interesting part of how we met was our first date. It took Luke three weeks after that first meal to call me and ask me out. Even though he was a little slow, I do agree, Luke, it did work out for us."

"I can't believe it, man. It only took Nita and me three days to go out on our first date."

"And it only took me three *hours* to ask Cindy out on our first date. And that's because I had to wait for the class to finish so I could talk to her."

Cindy glanced at Luke before turning to address Lydia. "Can I ask one question about that first date of yours?"

Lydia smiled just as big as Nita had smiled when Cindy asked her that same question.

"Do you want to know what we did on our first date?"

"I sure do!"

Luke's head drooped down as Lydia said, "We played horseshoes at Lakeside Park. I'll let you direct all fill-in questions to Luke."

They were having so much fun that it seemed as though only a few minutes had passed when they heard the oven bell ringing. They all got up and grabbed the snack bowls, each having some food left in it, that is, except for the grape and cutie bowls, which were totally empty. It appeared Juan wasn't the only one who had a hankering for fruit that evening. Carrying the bowls back to the kitchen, they exchanged them for silverware and dinnerware. They then headed for the dining room, where Luke was setting the large crockery pot of shepherd's pie on a large trivet in the middle of the table. As they all sat down, Lydia first told Luke they would be talking about that new horseshoe pit in the back yard sometime tonight. However, before asking about the horseshoe pit, she asked him if he would pray before the meal tonight.

Luke agreed, even as he thought about how he typically didn't pray out loud to Jesus at meals when there were non-Christians with him. But this time was different. Lydia was right in asking him to pray.

Luke knew in his heart that thankfulness to Jesus for everything in life should never be hidden, apologized for, or concealed from others.

Luke announced, "Okay, guys. I'm going to pray to the Creator of everything and everyone tonight before we eat."

Luke was surprised to see everyone bowing their heads when he said this.

"Dear Jesus, Creator of all and supplier of all we need and all we have. I ask you to give each one of us extra grace for everything that will be talked about tonight through the power of your Holy Spirit. Let this house be a special dwelling place of love and understanding tonight . . . for your glory and honor. Amen."

Again, to Luke's surprise, everyone said "amen" at the end of his prayer.

After everyone had been served and had started eating, Nita asked, "I don't get it, Luke. This is a pretty big house and you live here alone. This may be a nosy question, but how can you afford to live here? Paying all the bills by yourself on a carpenter's salary? They must pay you guys pretty good over there at Middlefield Homes."

Luke smiled at her question, supposing he might think the same thing if he didn't know what he knew.

"Carpenters make pretty good money, but not as much as you think. Although, it is easier to pay all the bills than you might realize. You could do it too if you were in my circumstances."

"No, I definitely couldn't, Luke. Come on, how do you do it?"

By this time, everyone but Markus wanted to know the answer. "Markus, would you like to tell everyone my secret?"

Markus quickly swallowed the food in his mouth before answering. "Sure, like Luke said, it's simple. The short answer is that he doesn't own the house. When his mom got remarried and moved out, she asked him if he wanted to live here or at his new stepdad's house. He chose to live here. It was actually his grandpa's house. From what Luke has told me, Grandpa Gus paid it off years ago, so there's no monthly house payment to make. All his mom asked him to do is keep it maintained and pay the electric, gas, and water bills. Pretty sweet deal, isn't it?"

Everyone was silent, thinking about what it would be like not to have a mortgage or rent payment.

In that moment of silence, Cindy remembered what Luke had said about talking politics. They began to share their core beliefs and opinions on political, religious, moral, and financial issues. They could all tell that there would be plenty of laughs tonight over what someone said or thought, but all agreed to pass no judgement on each other for personal beliefs.

Juan, who had not really stopped eating, broke the silence by bringing up a totally new topic of conversation. "Luke, this shepherd's pie is better than those tamales we ate last week!"

Markus quickly piped in, "It sure is, Luke. Also, tell your stepdad thanks for sharing both of those recipes with you."

Juan raised his eyebrow at Markus for cutting him off mid-sentence. Looking a bit sheepish, Markus gestured for Juan to continue.

"Anyway, I don't know if you saw last Friday, but I was able to hide two of those tamales from the eating machine over there to take home." At hearing there were two more tamales he could have eaten, he sat there frozen with his mouth hanging open.

"The next morning, after heating them up, I had my dad try one of them to get his opinion as to whether or not he thought they might sell at our food trucks. He ate his first tamale and, before saying anything about its flavor and quality, asked if he could sample a second one to verify his thoughts, only this time he asked me to put a little sour cream and salsa on it. He had barely finished swallowing his last bite when he asked me to have you ask your stepdad if he would like to meet up to talk about buying the recipe. He may want to buy this one too!"

"Hey, guys," said Lydia, interrupting the conversation, "and I'm not trying to be rude, Juan, but before we change topics and move past our political conversation, don't you think it would be good to hear what Markus thinks about his dad running for office? I saw you with your whole family in a television commercial a few days ago, and I assumed you knew and agreed with all your father's positions. So I didn't think you would mind sharing a little about his position on some of the hot topics of the day."

Markus's demeanor went from hopeful to downcast. He thought everyone would forget the political conversation when Juan brought up such a unique topic of interest. "I'm not trying to be pushy, Markus, and you don't have to share your thoughts if you don't want to, or if you're not allowed to. But election day isn't very far away, and it would be good to know our potential elected officials better. You do have personal insights the rest of us don't have, except perhaps for Luke."

After Lydia had finished her rather long-winded question, Markus turned towards Cindy. "Well, Cindy," he said with a tone of warning, "Lydia just opened up a big can of worms with that question. You did ask me more than an hour ago to open up to everyone here tonight, so what could be a better topic to talk about than my dad? But before I go any further, I'd like to ask everyone a big favor."

They all agreed to his request, though they were curious about the favor Markus wanted from them. Markus hesitated for just a moment before looking towards Cindy again. "Can we all agree—and have a high level of trust in each other—that whatever is said within this circle of new friends in the Cruz house stays in the Cruz house?"

Everyone wholeheartedly and immediately agreed to his request, even as they silently wondered what would cause him to say such a thing. Some even had second thoughts about whether they would be able to keep the trust Markus had requested of them.

"Thanks, everyone. Well, here goes. I'll just make it simple and get straight to the point. I don't trust my dad." Everyone there, except for Luke, was stunned at hearing this revelation. Markus, seeing the astonished looks on everyone's faces, went on to explain his statement in more detail.

"I have been watching my father closely for the last year, and I have seen some concerning patterns. If others were aware of these patterns, it would give my dad's opponent a landslide victory. As I took more time over this past year to consider his actions from a life-long perspective, I started remembering events at home and at work that prove to me that this pattern of behavior has been a part of his character for a long time. No wonder I don't like it at home; there's just something in my spirit that won't allow me to be around my dad for any length of time. And it's not just my dad—it's my mom too. There is something offensive about how she treats people, so I try not to hang around her very long. Both of my parents are unsettling and something in my heart tells me that I need to put distance between them and me."

Markus took a moment to glance around the room to see every-one's reaction. Most of them had a serious look on their face as they digested what Markus was telling them.

"When I think about my dad, I just wish he wasn't the kind of per-son . . . the kind of father he is. I just want a father who I can trust to be consistent with his words, his actions, and especially his reactions. I just want a father who loves me for who I am, one who I can truly trust to guide me through life. I'm not getting any of that from him. So, in my opinion, if I can't trust him with simple family matters, how can I trust him with local, state, and national matters?"

With that raw moment of honesty, Markus had unintentionally opened up the evening to more personal confessions from all six of them on a wide range of topics. Juan talked about his dad and how he always put the opportunity to make money before everything else. Luke talked about how it affected him to not have his dad around when he was growing up. The girls all shared about their relationship with their father and how that relationship had contributed to the person they had become, as well as the type of man they were attract-ed to. Four hours later, after much talking, laughing, and even some crying—and a lot of store-bought pie—they decided to call it an eve-ning. As they all brought the dinnerware to the kitchen, Luke stopped and shared one more revelation.

"You know what I just realized, guys?"

"No, what?" Lydia asked as everyone paused what they were doing.

"At the beginning of dinner, I prayed to Jesus that he would give each one of us extra grace tonight through the power of his Holy Spir-it. I also asked him to let this house be a special dwelling place of love and understanding tonight, for his glory and honor. I can't speak for the rest of you, but I have never experienced an evening like this in my life. The only answer that will explain to me how this could hap-pen is that the Holy Spirit of God was here with us tonight, and he is still here. And because of what I'm sensing among us, I'd like to share something with you and then ask you guys a question. I've never done this before, so if you would give me some grace that would be great."

One month later, Luke, Markus, and Cindy were finishing one of the last Construction Management courses in their program. They were all excited, knowing it wouldn't be long before they would graduate and put their new skills to work. As they were talking to the other students after class, Mr. Arlyn approached Luke and asked to speak with him away from the others.

"What is it, Mr. Arlyn?" Luke was curious about why a private conversation was needed. He followed Mr. Arlyn toward the front of the classroom as his instructor gathered his classroom materials.

"Luke, do you remember me telling you that if you continued to show an advanced understanding of home construction and design, I would introduce you to some important and influential people in the construction business?"

"As a matter of fact, I do remember that conversation. Why, has something happened I should know about?"

"Actually, something did happen. I know I didn't speak with you before doing what I did, so I apologize for not checking with you first."

Luke didn't hesitate in calming his teacher's nerves. "Don't worry about it, Mr. Arlyn. I'm sure you had the best intentions for me. So, what did you do?"

"Well, what I did was to take a few impromptu opportunities to show several of your designs to the city's planning committee, along with two well-known land developers, and I'll have you know that they are all very impressed with what they saw."

"Wow! That's amazing, Mr. Arlyn. I had fun drawing up those designs, but I honestly didn't think they were that good. So what does all this mean?"

Mr. Arlyn was again taken aback by this young man's God-given talents and his humble spirit. Other builders and designers would have already asked about money several times by now. *How refreshing this young man is,* he thought to himself. Coming out of his thoughts, he answered Luke's question: "It means they would like to interview you for a possible slot as a new generation home builder. By agreeing to participate in what they would be offering you, you would be introduced to the general public as an independent builder in a brand new, single-family-home subdivision that would be ready for homes in two years."

"That's amazing! But I don't get why they would be interested in me. Aren't I a little too young and inexperienced to be given this kind of offer?"

"Actually, Luke, you're not, and that's just the point. They are always looking for the next innovator in home building, regardless of age, and they think you may be that person. You need to understand that no one is trying to lure you away from Middlefield Homes, but at the same time, you may have to make some very difficult decisions in the coming months pertaining to who you will be working for and giving your allegiance to. Because one of the biggest requirements for getting into this kind of development is that you must be able to build one of your new designs within code and under your own name." Luke suddenly drifted back to last year and the talk he and Matthew Middlefield had concerning this exact situation. He wondered if Matthew knew at the time that this kind of offer was going to be made to him. He figured that that talk was Matthew's way of keeping him at Middlefield Homes and away from competition. He remained in his own thoughts for another moment, wondering if this was what Matthew had experienced when he had to make a similar decision to leave Hanson Homes 25 years earlier.

"They're really excited about your multi-generational home designs, Luke, with all the baby boomers retiring and this latest generation living at home longer than every other generation before them. You may have inadvertently stumbled on the perfect home design at the perfect time in North American culture and history."

Luke was getting visibly excited after hearing that both the city planners and several land developers liked his ideas. He knew in his heart that designing and building a home like that is one thing, but to have the opportunity to explain why he is so passionate about this idea would be a dream come true.

Luke came back down to earth when he heard Mr. Arlyn talking again. "I don't know if you knew this or not, but your current employer, Matthew Middlefield, was the most recent innovator in town . . . until now, that is."

"No, I didn't know that, Mr. Arlyn," said Luke as he continued to listen.

"Everyone who wanted a new home built and had the money to build it wanted Middlefield Homes as their contractor and designer. Isn't that amazing? And here you are working for him."

"Yeah, that's amazing, Mr. Arlyn. You have no idea how that makes me feel."

These days, however, he has to work harder at being innovative, because the other builders have walked through enough of his model homes. After looking at his designs, they would simply steal his new ideas. It's hard to stop that from happening and still stay at the top in this industry, but if Matthew Middlefield could do it, I have every confidence you can too."

As much as Luke didn't agree with Matthew Middlefield's views and manner of treating people, he had to agree that the man was talented when it came to construction and remodel designing.

"Now, don't forget, Luke, that one of the city planners' requirements is that you have built at least one new home that you designed under your own company name. And they would have to inspect that house before they would award you a place in the new subdivision. You have two years to make that happen."

Here they were, one year later, and the day of the national elections had arrived. With all the votes being counted, Matthew Middlefield had easily defeated his opponent. It appeared that he was going to Washington. Luke had been invited to his parents' home for dinner the same evening as the election. After casting his vote, he drove to the house and ate dinner. Later, after helping clean up, he settled into a comfortable chair and watched the news with Ricardo. Luke wasn't sure if he should be happy that Matthew would be spending most of the year out of town in Washington, D.C., or if he should be more concerned that Matthew would be close to so much national and international power.

Having had enough political food for one evening, and at Ricardo's request, Luke got out of his chair and made his way into the coffee-and-conversation room. He was sitting in a soft leather recliner while waiting for a cup of coffee to be delivered when his phone rang. Seeing that it was Markus on the other end, Luke knew that his friend likely needed to talk with him after seeing the election results come in. He had to answer the call.

"Hey, Markus," said Luke with a jovial sound to his voice. Not waiting for Markus to say hello, Luke asked, "How is your family and the congressman-elect doing?"

Markus didn't respond to that question right away, but he was thinking to himself, *I can't believe my dad has done it again.* Markus had two reasons for calling Luke this evening and he needed to talk with him about both of them. By the time he had decided to make that call, he had been aimlessly wandering around his parents' home for almost 30 minutes. He was replaying everything in his mind he had seen and heard in the last hour. He was so worked up over the events from earlier in the evening that he didn't even remember Luke answering his call. Having most of the lights off in the house gave it a gloomy and depressing feel as he walked from room to room talking to Luke. The ambiance in the house matched the way he felt inside his heart.

"I'm home alone, Luke. I couldn't stand to be around him anymore today. Everyone, including Maggy and Peter VanderMor, is at another victory and thank-you dinner party tonight. I guess it's required to pat the little guys on the head once in a while and thank them for all their hard work in getting you elected." Luke could hear a bit of disdain for his father in his friend's last statement.

"Isn't that a little cynical, Markus? I know your dad thinks pretty highly of himself, but he wouldn't have that kind of opinion of the people who had just worked so hard to help him get elected, would he?"

Markus had just walked into their family room when Luke asked that question. He was looking squarely at a picture of his dad and mom hanging on the wall. "Luke, I don't think you understand. That was a direct quote—from his lips to my ears. He said those words not more than one hour ago before leaving the house. You haven't been around him much this past year, but the idea of the kind of power and influence that he is going to have is really changing him. It's almost scary to look him in the eye when he's not putting on a face for the public."

Luke was getting concerned about Markus and didn't want him saying something volatile to his dad that he wouldn't be able to take back. He thought it might be a good idea for Markus to spend some time with Luke's family at Ricardo's house, and maybe even sleep at his home tonight.

"What are you going to do tonight? Do you want to come over to Ricardo's house and spend the evening with us?"

"Thanks, Luke, but I'm going to pick Cindy up in half an hour and spend the rest of the evening at Alan and Mary's home. I'm so thankful that you invited Cindy and me to join your small group from church. It's been especially good for me that I have you and Alan and the other guys from the small group to talk with and to lean on for some solid advice. Just keep praying for me, Luke, especially for the day I tell my parents where I have started going on Sunday mornings and Tuesday evenings."

Luke could see that Markus not telling his dad about important decisions being made in his life was beginning to become a habit, a habit that one day would be exposed.

"You mean to tell me that they don't know anything about your new faith?"

"Nope, but I read through the book of John a couple times this past week. I need to ask Alan some questions about what I read so he can help me explain more clearly to my parents why I believe what I now believe."

"Okay, Markus, I'd better let you go so you can pick Cindy up on time."

Markus rushed to interrupt Luke's goodbye before he was able to hang up so he could talk about the second reason for calling. "Wait a minute, Luke—don't hang up!"

Luke stopped before hitting the button to hang up and said, "Yeah, okay, Markus. I'm here. What else do you have?"

"Oh, good. Thanks for not hanging up. You need to know that unloading my feelings about my dad wasn't the only reason I called you."

"Then what is it, brother? What's up?"

"It's pretty exciting news, Luke. And you're the first person I wanted to tell."

Markus went silent at this point, and Luke wasn't sure if he was building up enough courage to tell him what the news was or whether he wanted him to guess what it might be. He finally blurted out, "Come on, man, don't keep me waiting. What's the good news?"

Markus hesitated for another moment, but he couldn't keep it inside any longer.

"I wanted to tell you I just received permission from Cindy's dad to ask her to marry me. I needed to tell someone, and you were the first person I thought of."

"What! Oh, man, I can't believe you're taking the big step! Congratulations, Markus. That's fantastic news. And Cindy is such a sweet girl too. You are one very blessed guy, Markus. So, when are you going to ask her?"

Markus had just turned on the gas fireplace in the family room and sat down in a comfortable chair when he started describing his proposal plan to Luke.

"I know it's almost seven weeks away, but I'm going to be spending Christmas at her house this year, so I thought, what better time and place to tell everyone how much I love her? And there's one more thing, Luke."

"What would that be, Markus?"

The past 15 years of his friendship with Luke flashed through Markus's mind as he asked his question. "I was wondering if you would consider being my best man."

Luke was so caught off guard by this request that he choked up and couldn't talk right away, fearing he would break down into tears of joy. He was actually quiet for so long that Markus asked, "Luke, are you still there? Are you okay? Did you hear what I asked you?"

Luke had composed himself by this time and was finally able to speak. "Ah, Markus, you knew the answer to that question before you asked it. Of course I will!"

They talked for a few more minutes before Markus had to go, but they agreed to talk the next day about all the coming decisions Markus would have to make. After hanging up, Luke quietly sat in his recliner thinking about the changes taking place in Markus's life. He also contemplated how much his own life had changed over the last two years. Ricardo then came in with a coffee mug in each hand. As he gave one to Luke, he said, "The coffee may not be as hot as you typically like it, Luke, but I noticed you talking on the phone. I thought I should give you some privacy to finish your conversation, so I waited in the hall for you to hang up. Is everything okay? I only ask because you have a somber look on your face."

"Yeah, everything is good, Ricardo. It's actually fantastic. I was just talking with Markus, and he called to tell me that he is going to ask Cindy to marry him on Christmas Eve. He just received permission from Cindy's dad. Markus is really excited about being married to Cindy and starting a family, but I'm sad for him at the same time."

Taking a sip of his coffee and trying to figure out why Luke was reacting like this to such good news, Ricardo asked, "What makes you say that, Luke? You should be totally excited for Markus, shouldn't you?"

"I know I should, Dad. I know. But instead of sharing the news of the biggest event in his life with his parents, he called me first. He didn't share it with his dad or his mom or Maggy. He was with them just a few minutes before he called me, but he didn't tell them. He's about to start a whole new life with a whole new family, and he's doing it without support from the family he grew up with. It's sad."

"You're not wrong to notice that brokenness in his family. I've seen it thousands of times in my counseling practice. But from what you told me and your mom, Markus and Cindy now have the Father of all to lean on, along with a community full of other believers."

"And don't forget about Juan and Nita. That was such a special night. There is no doubt in my heart that God sent his Spirit to us that evening to see two of our lifelong friends and their girlfriends truly accept Jesus into their heart and soul. I knew they had been called, and I mean truly called. It was nothing anyone did or said that night. The only thing Lydia and I did was tell them the story of Jesus and the things he did and said while he was physically on this earth. Right there in the kitchen of our house, with tears in all of our eyes, we all prayed to Jesus. And, wow, did he ever listen and answer those prayers!"

It was the end of November, and Luke was driving to the office for a meeting he had scheduled with Elizabeth Middlefield earlier in the week. Now that Matthew was spending most of his time in Washington, D.C., Elizabeth was taking care of the day-to-day operations. It appeared to everyone who was watching that she was good at her job and would treat everyone fairly. Matthew only hoped that part of doing a good job would be following through with a verbal promise made to everyone at Middlefield Homes at the beginning of the year. Luke had a very important topic to discuss that affected every employee in the company. When he entered the building, every eye was watching him and some were texting. Luke began making his way to Matthew's old office, which was now Elizabeth's new office. He knocked on the door and leaned in to say, "Hello, Elizabeth. Jennifer wasn't at her desk, so I just popped in. Would now work to have the meeting I called about earlier in the week?"

Elizabeth looked up from the screen on her laptop and said, "Good morning, Luke. Yes, of course, come on in. Would you shut the door before you sit down? I've set aside 15 minutes for whatever you are here to discuss. I have to tell you, Luke, you were a little too cryptic for my taste when you asked for this meeting. I don't like meetings that start out that way. From what I gathered, it has something to do with money, which is a difficult topic for most people to talk about. Not me, of course, but most people do find it hard to talk about money. Go ahead, tell me what's on your mind."

While she was talking, Luke had made his way to one of the three plush cherrywood office chairs and sat down. Years ago, Matthew had his entire office custom trimmed-out with this rare cherry wood; it had paneled wainscoting and a coffered ceiling. Luke remembered many pleasant conversations with Matthew in this office the first two summers he worked for him, but times had certainly changed.

"Thank you, Elizabeth. As you know, Matthew had a big meeting here at the office last January to let everyone know he was running for Congress. In that meeting, he asked all of us if we were willing to help him with his campaign by simply picking up any slack as a result of him not being here. He said that by helping him to not worry about Middlefield Homes, they would allow him to fully focus on his campaign. He also said that if all went well with the business, he would remember everyone at Christmas with a gift of his own."

"Alright then, Luke," said Elizabeth with unveiled sarcasm. "Thank you for having such a good memory, but what's your point? What is it exactly that you want from me?"

"Elizabeth, I've been asked by people in the office—in the sales centers and in the field—to see if the gift Matthew was referring to last January was going to be a year-end profit-sharing check. They are asking as a result of all the extra effort they put into Middlefield

Homes throughout this past year—on Matthew's behalf and at his personal request."

"I don't understand, Luke. Why didn't these loyal employees of mine go to Markus rather than you? He is, after all, the next Middle-field in line to take over the company."

Luke sat there, quite amazed at Elizabeth's question. Was she really unaware of the position that that would put Markus in, or was that the kind of leverage she wanted over all the employees all along? Not being able to discern her motives, he took a deep breath and then explained why he was asked to take on this responsibility.

"Probably because there could be a conflict of interest, and they don't want to put Markus in a difficult position. It would be like Markus asking himself to make that decision. Elizabeth, he has to work direct-ly with these people every day, profit-sharing or no profit-sharing, and that's why they asked me to meet with you. But that's not the point. The year is almost over, and everyone has worked hard the entire year for the Middlefield family and the company. They're just excited about the promise Matthew made."

"Well, thank you for the company history lesson, Luke, but I have a couple questions of my own. This extra work you say everyone put in this past year—did they get paid for that extra work they performed?"

Luke hesitated for a minute and then said, "Yes, of course they did. But the few dollars they were paid is nothing compared to the revenue and profit margin they helped generate. The employees who are salaried worked extra hours every week because of the additional workload, and they did it to help create that revenue for Matthew and for you. But they didn't get paid extra on their payroll checks."

"That's right, Luke, they *chose* to be salaried. Working extra hours for no additional compensation when needed is just part of their agreement."

Luke couldn't believe what he was hearing from Elizabeth, or what he was about to hear.

"And I'm sorry to disappoint everyone, but there won't be any profit-sharing this year. See, wasn't that easy? Like I said, I have no problem talking about money."

"I don't understand, Elizabeth," said Luke, ignoring her sarcasm. "We sold eight more homes this year than the previous year—that's an 11% increase in sales, and we didn't hire any new staff to process all the paperwork and on-site management needed to build those homes. Everyone wanted to do their part in helping Matthew by working harder, and they were happy to do it. And now they are excited to hear how you and Matthew will show your appreciation for this long year of hard work, but apparently you don't have the ability to see this additional effort on their part as worthy of any kind of a financial 'thank you' on your part."

Not even acknowledging, or caring, what Luke had just said, Elizabeth slowly and intentionally looked at her watch and thought to herself, *Luke's 15 minutes are just about up. I've got to get him out of here if I'm going to be on time for my hair appointment.*

Luke restated his case as to why there could be profit-sharing checks, and then he waited for Elizabeth to respond differently.

"Again, Luke, I'm sorry, but the numbers don't lie. There just isn't any room for profit-sharing."

"But, Elizabeth, by the end of the year, we will have closed 62 homes at an average price of $2 million each. That's almost $124 million in annual sales, and with an 8% profit after expenses, that's just under $10 million in profits. I don't see how there can't be even a little to share with your employees."

Hearing Luke quote that last bit of private business information was too much for her to handle. Elizabeth said quite abruptly, "Okay, Luke, that's it! I don't know who has been giving you all this private financial information, and I certainly don't need you telling me how to interpret it or how to spend whatever profits we may or may not possess. But I've given you my answer. This meeting is over. Perhaps next time these employees of mine should consider having Markus come to me instead of you. I can guarantee you the result of that meeting would be much different than this one. You can let everybody know they should stop worrying about a nonexistent profit-sharing check and be happy they still have a job. And as for you, stop pushing your luck with me, Luke, or you won't have a job either. As I just said, this meeting is over. I am a very busy woman. You can leave now."

Luke felt totally defeated as he left Elizabeth's office. More importantly, he felt that he had let everyone in the company down. They had been depending on him to remind Elizabeth about their loyalty and work this past year, and their hope for profit-sharing as a result. He began second-guessing their decision to have him rather than

Markus meet with Elizabeth; even the two of them together might have been a better strategy. As he made his way to the entry doors, some of the office employees looked at Luke with curious and hopeful eyes, silently asking how the meeting went. He could only shake his head no as he lowered it and walked out the door. The office staff who had received this silent message immediately got on their phones and started texting the rest of the employees. Luke hadn't even reached his truck before his phone rang. It was Markus.

"Hey, Markus, what's up?" said Luke with a soft and defeated voice.

"Here's what's up: from the multiple texts I have been receiving in the last two minutes, and from the sound of your voice, it appears the meeting with my mom didn't go so well."

As Markus talked, Luke continued slowly walking to his truck, kicking an occasional rock with just a little more gusto than was needed, and at the same time, working hard not to imagine that Elizabeth was that rock. He was going over the meeting in his mind, wondering if he could have handled it differently.

"It doesn't make sense, Markus. There should be more than enough money in the bank to send out profit-sharing checks, at least small ones. Hey, I just had a thought: do you think it's possible that the company obligated itself to purchasing building sites in some new housing developments? Maybe that's where the money is going."

Markus let out an audible sigh of irritation after hearing Luke try to defend his mother's decision. "Luke, you're way too gracious. When will you consider the thought that my parents are just plain greedy? If they lose a few employees along the way, they'll simply hire new ones and train them to do the job, just like they've done in all the previous years. What these new employees don't realize is that they are, in the eyes of my dad and mom, temporary and completely expendable. My parents will simply use them until they find a reason to fire them, or until they are subjected to such poor working conditions that they simply quit. We know who is creating that terrible work environment. It's always for money."

Luke went on defending the idea that if this request had been handled differently, bonuses would have been given to everyone. "But your mom told me point-blank that if you had come to that meeting instead of me, she would have given out profit-sharing checks."

"Oh, Luke, are you still that ignorant of my parents' true character? In case you don't know, greed's brother is deceit. My mother was lying to you. It's no more complicated than that."

"Then I have a direct question for you to answer: how can you live with parents like that? I'm asking because, even though you grew up in their home, I don't believe that's your character, and I can't believe you would want to live with people who are like that, regardless of who they are."

"I can't live with them, Luke. That's why I'm getting out of their house as soon as it's best for me. One thing I don't want to do is ask you if I can move into your home. I'll wait until Cindy and I are married and then we can move into an apartment together. I have no idea what my parents might do to you out of spite if they knew you were helping me. And believe me when I say that they *would* do something to you. Luke, there may be a big change coming in my life. I know I say it all the time and put no action behind my words, but I'm honestly getting to the point that I want to get out of the new-home construction industry altogether. I'm not sure what I would do, but I'm relying on Jesus and praying to him for that answer and for his direction in my life."

Being distracted from what had just occurred in Elizabeth's office, Luke was surprised at Markus's maturity in handling difficult situations.

"That's amazing, Markus. When did you come to that decision?"

"Last Tuesday at our small group meeting. After everyone left, Cindy and I stayed afterward for another 30 minutes and talked with Alan and Mary about what I should do. His two thoughts of counsel were to pray and take it slow."

Luke liked that advice from Alan, but he followed it up with a warning.

"I'll tell you what, Markus: your dad and mom won't like that decision, but I sure do. I'm going to be praying for you starting today—that you'll know what our Jesus wants you to do with your life. By the way, it's been a while since I asked you this question, but have you told your parents that you are a true follower of Jesus, the Christ?"

"No, Luke, I haven't. That time is coming—I can see that for sure. But before I have that conversation with my father and mother, I want to learn more about my Father in heaven. I can't tell you how my life has changed since I found out who Jesus really is."

"Markus, I feel as though I'm watching you mature right in front of my eyes. I'm not sure what God has planned for your life, but I can see you running toward it with your arms opened wide. I'm so excited to see what the future has in store for you."

"Luke, do you have one more minute to hear something I have been working on? After you hear it, I'll make a whole bunch of calls to the people in the company and, as nicely as I can, tell them who they are really working for."

"Well, thanks, Markus. What do you want me to hear?"

"I'd like to sing a song we sang at church last week. I just finished memorizing the words and they speak directly to my life."

Luke was completely caught off guard at this revelation. He lit up with surprise and anticipation at the opportunity to hear how well Markus could sing. After his disastrous meeting with Elizabeth, this was exactly what he needed.

"I didn't know you could sing, Markus. Why haven't I heard about this before? And when did you first know you had this talent?"

"I guess I was born with it. It's in my DNA. But I've been relegated to being a shower singer at home. I think I have a pretty good voice, but my dad and mom said it wasn't a manly trait. They wouldn't let me take lessons or join any school choirs or musicals; but ever since I turned 18, I've been taking voice lessons. Remember when you, Juan, and me were at your house for dinner a few months ago and I said I was doing something I couldn't tell you about? Well, I was taking voice lessons, and my teacher said I'm pretty good too."

"Okay, so that was the big secret. Pretty cool, dude. Now that you have me sufficiently curious, let me hear you sing."

"Alright, here goes . . . and just so you know, I'll be singing acapella.

Luke was still sitting in his truck in the office parking lot when he connected his cell phone to his truck's speakers for better sound. He had just made the connection as Markus began to sing. It was absolutely beautiful. Markus's strong tenor voice floated through the speakers, and the slight rasp at the end of his notes gave his voice a type of depth that spoke directly to the heart. As the words of this song came out of Markus and through the speakers, the tears began to flow from Luke's eyes. These words told the story of Markus's life right up to that moment. Luke had been given the ultimate privilege of explaining to Markus who Jesus was, and of seeing an angelic look of understanding form on Markus's face when he answered the call of Jesus. And then came Markus's pure and strong voice:

When I think about the Lord,
How he saved me, how he raised me,
How he filled me with the Holy Ghost, how he healed me to
    the uttermost.
When I think about the Lord, how he picked me up and turned
    me around,
How he placed my feet on solid ground ...

It makes me wanna shout!
Hallelujah, thank you, Jesus!
Lord, you're worthy,
Of all the glory, and all the honor,
    And all the praise.

Unknown to Luke, Elizabeth had walked out the front door of their office building shortly after he had left. Not realizing that Elizabeth was now watching him, he continued listening to Markus's singing. His eyes were closed and he was silently worshiping Jesus through the words of this song. She looked at Luke crying in his truck and thought to herself, *What a weak and pathetic boy. I despise that kind of person. He didn't get a profit-sharing check, so he goes to his truck and cries. I'm so glad we listened to Matthew's inner voice and urged Maggy to break up with him. Now I see him for what he is—just a weak and pathetic little boy! When I tell Matthew this story, he'll know we were right about him.*

The next day was a much-needed Saturday day off. It also happened to be a Legacy Letter day. Luke once again went through the ritual of signing in, and then he heard that familiar voice.

"Hi, buddy! This is a letter that I'm going to jump right into; no easing in today. Although, I do have to share an observation with you about your mom. She spent most of yesterday with Ricardo Sanchez, and today she is in a particularly sweet and happy mood as a result. Maybe I should be sending her a letter as well. I still say there's a wedding in the future for the two of them."

"Right again, Grandpa."

"Okay, I got that thought out before I forgot it. Now back to your letter. I'm going to take a guess that you're 19 or 20 now and that you can still be easily impressed by pretty, shiny, or expensive things. I say that because, while I was enjoying your mother's good mood, I also noticed you were in a good mood when you left with Maggy in a rebuilt Ford Mustang GTO. An expensive toy given to a young girl by her loving but hovering father. Luke, you may not like what I am about to say, but I hope you are not married to Maggy at this point in your life. You need to consider more of my counsel on life and marriage before making that commitment."

"Nope, not married to Maggy, and never will be."

"On the topic of relationships and marriage, I'd like to ask some refresher questions from a previous letter I sent you. If we are still talking about Maggy, did you follow my advice and learn more about her home life? How her parents treat her, how they treat Markus, and even each other? And what about at work? How are they treating their customers, their suppliers, and their employees? Going back to the Mustang, how do they spend money? Do they spend it lavishly on themselves and sparingly on others, or are they a generous family? On the other side, how are they making their money? Are they honest in their business dealings? Do they hold on to it loosely, or with an iron grip?"

"I'm starting to see what you are getting at, Grandpa. I had forgotten all about that Mustang of Maggy's."

"I realize I just asked you quite a few questions: some will be easy to answer, while others will be more difficult. For the easy ones, you can probably ask a direct question to the person who needs to respond to you. For others, you will have to learn to be more observant of the small money matters in life. Here are a few examples of what I'm talking about. When you are out to dinner with Maggy, does she tip the wait staff well? Does she tip at all? Does she freely and happily put money into the Salvation Army kettle as she walks by? Is she generous in paying for things for her friends? Does she keep track of the times others pay for her and then complain under her breath if they don't return the favor? Does she have to have the best of whatever it is she is buying, and does she feel the need to let everyone know about it? Who is she learning these traits from? A girl typically follows her mother's lead, so find out how her mother values money. This will tell you much about both Maggy and her mother. Here are a couple of verses to consider and meditate on, Luke, while you are finding these answers.

> For where your treasure is, there your heart will be also. (Matthew 6:21)

> Do not withhold good from those to whom it is due,
>   when it is in your power to do it. (Proverbs 3:27)

"Luke, I know it appears that this letter is mainly about Maggy and her potential predisposition to money, but I am also asking you not to ignore your own tendency to desire money. You will soon discover that these desires show themselves more quickly when you have more money. Yes, money and materialistic desires can be learned from parents, but we all have to fight those desires. Some more than others. Now don't hear what I'm *not* saying: there isn't anything wrong or sinful in having nice things or a big house or an extremely large bank account. But what can be sinful, if not kept in check, is your heart's desire. You should continually ask yourself what you desire more, the material things of the world or our Jesus. Over the next three months, Luke, consider yourself and how you might answer those same questions I just mentioned. One way you can easily show yourself how money might be mastering you is by keeping track of every dollar you spend over these next 90 days. Take note of what you spend money on and how often you purchase the same things. At the end of those three months, you may be saddened or encouraged by what you find out about yourself. Master those money desires before they master you. Just as I encouraged you in the previous letter, master money at an early age, for you never know what God may give you to manage in the years to come. See you in three months . . . and say hi to your mom for me. Love you, buddy."

Chapter 8

Do Not Plan Evil Against Your Neighbor

"Thanks for letting me know, Juan. I'll tell my dad. See you in a few minutes. Bye."

Luke hung up his phone and said to Ricardo, "Hey dad, you don't need to look out the front picture window for Juan and his father for about ten minutes. I guess they were so deep in conversation about this meeting that they drove right past the exit ramp to your house. It'll take them another ten minutes to turn around and get back to the right exit."

Hearing it would be a few more minutes before they would arrive, Ricardo sat down and started flipping through his grandmother's handwritten cookbook again. In his mind, he was wondering if there could be other recipes good enough for Pronto Foods.

"I'm going to take that as a good sign, Luke. And since we have a few more minutes before they arrive, can we take those minutes and use them to talk about the type of man Mr. Oleeva is? I'd like to know as much about the man I may be doing business with as possible."

Luke had never thought about Mr. Oleeva as anything other than Juan's dad, so he hesitated a little before answering.

"Honestly, Dad," said Luke in a soft-spoken voice, trying to pull up any memories of Michael that would best answer Ricardo's question,

"I really don't know much about him as a person. Whenever we would go to Juan's house to hang out, his dad was never home. He was always at work. And from a business perspective, I know nothing about him. I also don't know any of his employees or what they think of him. Juan told me a few weeks ago that they have very little turnover with their staff because everyone who works for him loves their job. But, like I said, Dad, he was always working or doing something that was job-related. Maybe that's what has made his business so successful."

Ricardo jumped into the conversation and said, "It sounds like he loves his job and is working hard to take care of his family. I like that in a man."

"Yeah, but it seemed to be more than that to me. I got the feeling that he was a workaholic and that loved his job just a little too much. And like Markus's dad, he really wasn't around much for Juan when he was growing up."

Thinking about what he had just said about Juan's upbringing, Luke remarked to Ricardo, "You know something, Dad, hearing myself say those words makes me wonder if Juan is headed down the same path."

"Really? And exactly what is it that Juan is doing that makes you think that?" asked Ricardo, curious to find out the criteria Luke was using to make that determination.

"Most of the time when I call him, I get his voicemail. And the times I do leave a message, it takes a day or two for him to get back to me, which is irritating and impolite. It makes me wonder, what's so important in his life that it's causing him to take such a long time to call me back?" Luke stopped talking for a minute and then said, "Do you think this is Juan's way of spending time with his dad, or maybe even showing his dad that he's just like him?"

Ricardo chuckled at hearing Luke's thoughts, and then he heard another voice.

"Look who's calling the kettle black. Aren't you the one who is okay with working Saturdays and Sundays? It makes me wonder if you're trying to impress Matthew Middlefield, at least a little?" said Rebecca with a motherly smirk on her face. She had just walked into the living room and heard most of Luke's rant about Juan.

"Although, I must say, you are very good at promptly returning missed phone calls and text messages."

"It's not the same, Mom . . . and when did you join in this conversation anyway?"

"I jumped in about the time you appeared to be in need of a life coach, but in this instance, I'll be happy playing the part of your mother. I don't understand how you could even ask me that question; at your age, you should know better than that! I can't believe you could forget so quickly the rules of the household—after all those years of living with me! It appears that living on your own for only a few months has already made you forget about a mother's prerogative when it comes to household conversations. If words of any kind are spoken out loud in the house, and the mom hears those words, the mom has the option to engage or ignore that conversation as it pleases her. And since I'm the mom in this house, I'm exercising my option to engage."

Luke looked at Ricardo for support, but Ricardo was staying out of this one. He threw his arms up in a type of defensive posture and said, "You've lived with her longer than I have—you should know the rules."

Rebecca, after taking a much-needed breath, went on to say, "Let's get back to the conversation I just opted to engage in. It *is* the same, Luke. Overworking is overworking, no matter what your reason is. And don't think I'm only talking to Luke, because that goes for you too, Mr. Sanchez. Working too many hours every week can be bad for your family, and for your physical and emotional health. Be careful not to blindly slide into that kind of personal work pattern."

Luke just mumbled, "Huh? What just happened to the talk we were having, Dad?"

"Don't feel bad, Luke," said Ricardo. "I got the same directive from your mother soon after we were married, but in my case, it was a *wife's* prerogative to engage or to ignore words spoken by the husband. When she told me about that prerogative, she did it with such a beautiful smile on her face while softly holding my hands. I saw no benefit in arguing the point."

Rebecca had just begun to open her mouth to give her two boys more insight into her household rules of engagement, when Ricardo and Luke were saved by the bell, that is, the front doorbell. The Oleevas had arrived, and they brought with them an opportunity to have a conversation in which the guys were more acquainted with the rules.

Ricardo stepped past Rebecca and opened the door, welcoming Juan and his father into the house with a large, warm smile. Juan's father held out his hand to Ricardo as he introduced himself: "Thank you so much for having us to your home for this meeting. I'm Michael, and I believe you know my son, Juan."

Ricardo shook Michael's hand while saying, "I have heard a lot about him, but this is actually the first time I have met him. Nice to meet you, Juan."

Ricardo put out his hand and shook Juan's.

"It's good to meet you too, Mr. Sanchez."

Rebecca was allowing the men an opportunity to get acquainted. When she heard the slightest pause in the greeting ritual, she pounced. "Hello, everyone, and welcome to our home! Michael, my name is Rebecca. I'm Luke's mother and Ricardo's wife," she said as she stood in the entrance to the kitchen. At hearing her "in charge" voice, something that transcended families and cultures, all four of these men turned their heads toward her and waited. They had all been programmed through the years to respond accordingly, and they knew how to react to a woman's "in charge" voice.

"What do you boys say we start this meeting here in the kitchen and eat some freshly baked hot tamales for a mid-morning snack?"

Without saying anything, the four men looked at each other and then at Rebecca. They were foolishly wondering, *Who is going to be in charge of today's meeting?* As the light of understanding began to glow within each of them, they all performed the "yes mam shuffle"—without saying a word—as they took their seats at the kitchen table. An hour later, after eating several tamales, Michael said to Ricardo, "So it was your stepgrandmother who taught you how to cook this fantastic food?"

"That's right, and no matter how hard Grandma Maria tried to teach my stepsisters to cook, they just couldn't master that next level of cooking skill. Now don't misunderstand what I'm saying: her kids and husband didn't starve. They just couldn't treat the palettes of their families to fine dining. I suppose it was also my desire to please my grandmother for paying so much attention to me while I learned how to cook. It didn't take long for me to occupy a special place in her heart, and as a result, I became Grandma's favorite. We cooked together all the time, and when it became apparent that I had the cooking gene, she decided to leave her handwritten cookbook to me for safe keeping and for the sake of the next generation of the Sanchez family."

By the time they had finished talking about the origins of the family cookbook, they had left the kitchen and made their way to the living room where the talk became more serious.

"Just how many recipes are in that cookbook of your grandma's?" asked Michael, who was already thinking about more than just that one recipe.

"You know, I've never counted, but I'm sure there are at least 100 or more."

Michael, sensing that the time had come to talk business, got right to the point.

"If you'd like, Ricardo, can we talk about the possible purchase of the tamale recipe? Perhaps after that we can discuss some of the other recipes in your grandmother's cookbook?"

Ricardo was still amazed that he was about to sell an old family recipe for real money.

"We sure can, Michael. I'll let you start since I don't know how these negotiations work."

Michael sat forward in his chair and took a moment to look at each person in the room, attempting to read their faces. "Alright, then. First, I would like to say that Juan has a discerning pallet for food, and he was dead-on in his opinion of this tamale recipe. Without attending that chance dinner he was invited to at Luke's home, this meeting would not be happening. So, putting aside how we all got here today, the first big question for you to answer, Ricardo, is this: would you be willing to sell me this tamale recipe?"

It was at that moment that the reality of what he was about to do hit him. Should he or shouldn't he sell this family treasure? What would his grandma say about this?

Michael recognized the hesitation on Ricardo's face, something he had seen before on the faces of other cooks who had sold him their recipes in the past. He knew he had to say something, and say it quickly. In order not to lose the opportunity to purchase this recipe—and potentially many more in the future—he said, "Ricardo, I want you to understand that your grandmother will be helping us feed thousands of customers because of her recipe. That begins after we make a deal, train our cooks how to prepare these tamales, and then offer them at all of our food trucks."

Ricardo said nothing. He just sat there, quietly considering everything he heard up to this point. Michael saw that Ricardo was thinking over what was being requested, so he continued speaking while hoping that he wasn't overselling his desire to purchase this recipe.

"Now, there are two different directions we can take in terms of payment. We can either agree to a one-time, flat purchase price, or we can do a per-tamale payout based on gross monthly sales for a specified length of time."

Before answering that question, Ricardo said one more time, "I'm still amazed that companies in your industry are willing to pay good money for a simple recipe."

To which Michael quickly responded, "Says the man with the million-dollar recipe!"

"What!" Ricardo exclaimed with shock and amazement on his face and in his voice. "You mean to tell me that you'd be willing to give me a million dollars for something my grandma wrote down over 70 years ago in a handwritten cookbook?"

At that revelation, the jaws of Juan, Luke, Rebecca, and Ricardo dropped.

"No, not a million. . . but I would be willing to give you $20,000."

"You have to be kidding me—that's still a lot of money! Just how much margin is there in the food business anyway?"

"If you do it right, you can't even imagine. But if you do it wrong, you could lose everything."

Juan sat there, quietly thinking about what his father had inadvertently revealed to him about their business and family finances. Knowing Pronto Foods was a well-run business, and based on what his father had said, there was no reason for his dad to be working so many late hours and weekends. *I wonder what dad is doing?*

Upon hearing that revelation, Ricardo fluttered through his grandmother's cookbook with his thumb, then laid it on the table and said, "If I told you that this tamale recipe is near the bottom 10% of the best-tasting dishes in Grandma's cookbook, what would you say?"

"I'd say we need to set up another meeting, only this time at my commercial kitchen. I would also say we should talk about getting patents for the best recipes."

"They can do that?"

"Yes, they can, and yes, they do."

At hearing all this talk about patents and large amounts of potential income, Ricardo needed to take a breath. "Michael, I'm wondering if we might pause this conversation for a few minutes, or even a few days."

Ricardo then looked at Rebecca and said, "In order for us to make this decision, and perhaps others as well, Rebecca and I would like to talk with you about the reason we agreed to this meeting in the first place."

Michael leaned back in his chair, seeing a look of confusion on Ricardo's face. Not wanting to lose this opportunity to purchase such a recipe, he toned down the sales pitch and the excitement in his voice. "I'm sorry for digging so quickly into the business side of the food business, Ricardo. I'm just so excited about this meeting and passionate about food that sometimes I walk over people in conversations without even realizing it. I'm sorry, Ricardo. I apologize for moving so quickly. Please, go ahead . . . what did you want to tell me?"

Seeing Michael back away from the business side of this meeting, Ricardo relaxed. Leaning back in his chair, he gave Rebecca a quick look and then began to tell Michael about their dream.

"Remember the story I told you in the kitchen about my childhood and how I came to this country? I never want to forget that I was freely and lovingly adopted into my new family. Keeping that in mind, we don't want to sell Grandma's recipes solely for the money. Over the last several days, Rebecca and I have been talking about this meeting, knowing there would eventually be talk about money. And depending on the amount of money, we were hoping that a dream that has recently been planted in my heart might be funded through the sale of Grandma's recipes."

"And what might that dream be?" asked Michael, who was slightly curious about what was enticing Ricardo to sell some of these family recipes.

"Well, first of all, Rebecca and I are already in the process of creating a non-profit adoption agency. Our goal is to raise money to help couples who are wanting to adopt a child but are having difficulty raising the required funds. Our goal would be to fill in that financial gap. Whatever money can be generated from selling Grandma's recipes would go directly to this non-profit. Our goal is to get as much money as we can raise so that we can help as many families adopt as many children as possible."

By the time Ricardo had finished telling Michael what he was passionate about, Michael was no longer sitting back in his chair. Leaning forward again, he was now the one doing the listening.

"I love the idea, and I'm really starting to like you and Rebecca too. What a great way to give back to society."

They talked for another hour before setting a time to meet at Michael's commercial kitchen where Ricardo and Michael would spend the day cooking. Everyone was getting ready for the meeting to end when Luke received a call from Markus.

"Excuse me, everyone," said Luke as he walked toward the coffee-and-conversation room. "I have to take this call."

After closing the door and sitting on one of Ricardo's soft brown leather chairs, he said, "Markus, what's up?"

"Hey, I'm just wondering how you guys are doing with your meeting. Are you almost finished?"

"Yep, we're just wrapping it up. I think it went well. They're setting up a second meeting right now. Why? Is there something you need?"

Luke heard that awkward moment of silence and knew it was once again about Markus's dad.

"Yeah, I need to talk with someone about Cindy. I can't talk about her with my dad and mom, so I'm calling you, brother. Do you have plans for the rest of the afternoon, or can we get together for a couple of hours?"

"For you, Markus, I always have time. Where do you want to meet?"

"How about if I stop off at the Chicken Hut and buy us two number threes for lunch? We can eat at your house before I tell you what I need to talk about."

"I like the sound of your plan. Can we meet in one hour? Will that give you enough time to pick up the food and be at my place?"

"That'll be perfect."

Just then, Luke's phone buzzed again. It was Lydia. "Markus, I gotta answer the other line. Lydia is calling. I'll see you in an hour. Oh, hey, can you make my number three a medium spicy?"

"I sure can, Luke. Say hi to Lydia for me. Bye."

After switching to the other line, Luke said, "Lydia, what a nice surprise! What's happening in my girl's life on this beautiful Saturday?"

"Wow, somebody is certainly in a chipper mood. The meeting with Juan's dad must be going well."

Lydia was right: it had been quite a while since Luke felt as though life was hitting on all eight cylinders, and it felt great.

"Yes, I am in a good mood. And, yes, I am just finishing up a great meeting with Ricardo and Juan's dad. I'll tell you about it later. Markus is buying me lunch. He needs to talk to me about Cindy, and since he definitely can't talk to his parents about her, we're going to talk at my house."

"That's why I'm calling you, Luke. I just finished setting up a time to meet with Cindy. She wants to get together this afternoon and talk with me about Markus's parents before she talks with Markus about them. I wanted to get your advice on how I should handle this."

Since the dinner party at Luke's house, Lydia and Cindy had become fast friends. Lydia saw this request to be a listening ear for Cindy as a real honor. On the other hand, there wasn't the same kind of growth in friendship with Nita; something seemed to be bothering her and, whatever it was, it was making it difficult for everyone.

"Did you know in all the time that Markus and Cindy have been dating, she hasn't met his dad or his mom, not even one time? I don't know what you think of that, but to me, that seems pretty strange."

"I know you and Cindy don't know his parents the way I do, but that reality shouldn't surprise either one of you based on what Markus told us about his dad when we had our triple date."

"Well, she still wants to get together and talk, so I'm going to meet with her this afternoon. Do you have any words of wisdom for me?"

Luke had an inspiration for these two meetings and immediately shared it with Lydia.

"I'm not sure what Markus wants to talk about, and it sounds like you're not really sure why Cindy needs a listening ear either. Keeping that in mind, let's not give any advice to either of them. We'll tell them we need to think and pray about how we might best counsel them, which is true. What do you think about getting together later this evening and comparing notes for both talks? That way, we won't give out conflicting advice as the days go by."

"As long as I don't have to give up on this conversation, I'm in."

"Okay, I'll call you later this afternoon. I've gotta run and see how this meeting I set up has finished. Bye, Lydia."

The meeting had gone from "just about over" to "going strong again" by the time Luke returned. He got caught up as quickly as possible and then excused himself and left to meet Markus.

Special Agent Williams casually entered a downtown Java Hut where he patiently stood in line behind three other customers. If you didn't know him, you would have thought he was a mid-level executive picking up a coffee on his way into work. It wasn't long before he was standing in front of a young and perky barista who said, "Good morning, and what can I get you this morning?" She said this while producing a genuine smile of interest. He smiled back and ordered a small caramel espresso while thinking to himself, *It's too bad that people as sweet as this young girl will one day soon be taken advantage of by this cruel world.*

After paying cash for his drink, he walked to the pre-arranged meeting place where George VanderMor was impatiently waiting and sat down. George had strategically chosen to sit at the most secluded table in the coffee shop for this rendezvous. Being seen was an odd thing to worry about since George had never seen Special Agent Williams before today. He had been waiting for this meeting for over six months and was irritated at having to wait for an additional hour for Agent Williams to arrive. What George didn't know was that Special Agent Williams was, in fact, early to this meeting. He had been waiting and watching to see who was coming and going from the coffee shop, as well as who might be sitting in their car for a suspicious length of time. He waited until he felt confident that it was safe to enter. Precautions like this had given him such a long life in his chosen occupation.

"I don't like being made to wait, Agent Williams. My time is valuable too, so if you would keep that in mind for our future meetings, I would appreciate it."

Completely ignoring George's request, Special Agent Williams responded rather matter-of-factly by saying, "As you can see, I have ordered a small coffee. When it is empty, this meeting is over."

George sat there, irritated that his request for punctuality had been completely ignored. Worse yet, he had been given a kind of ultimatum, making him somewhat fearful of the kind of man he had gotten mixed up with. After taking the first sip of his coffee, Agent Williams began his verbal report. "Here's what I have discovered about the Middlefield family to this point." After taking another sip of his coffee, he said, "Markus and Maggy Middlefield seem to be perfectly average young adults. No problems with the law, not even a parking ticket. Elizabeth Middlefield, it seems, left for college after high school and never went home again. I'll have to dig deeper to find out what that story is. Her parents are typical blue-collar, middle-class people, but with one big surprise." Agent Williams took a photograph he had pulled from his briefcase and slid it in front of George. George looked at it and said, "I don't get it. What's so special about a picture of Elizabeth Middlefield?" To which Agent Williams responded, "Nothing, except that the woman in this photo is not Elizabeth Middlefield." He then slid a document in front of George.

All that George could say was, "Who would have known?"

Taking another drink of his coffee, Agent Williams continued, "Matthew, by all appearances, seems to be exactly who we think he is. But there is something wrong with his foster care record that I can't quite put my finger on. The big question in this investigation, Mr. VanderMor, is where did Matthew Middlefield come from? And who was his mother? Who was it that dropped him at the door of the foster care home, and why was he never allowed to be adopted out of that system? There's something different about this particular foster care home. It's different from every other foster home I have ever investigated, probably because the house and the foster parents aren't listed anywhere in the foster care records in the U.S. It's strange, very strange. To find the answer to this mystery will take more time. Because, as I stated when we first met, the foster care agency and its records are more tricky to access than adult records. I may also need to have a face-to-face conversation with his foster parents to get the information you are looking for. Other than that, they are the perfect American family."

After taking the last drink of his coffee, Agent Williams stood up and said, "I'll contact you when I obtain that information. You can keep the photograph and the document I gave you."

Picking up his empty coffee cup before turning to walk away, he crushed it and slid it into his coat pocket before promptly leaving the coffee shop.

The spices on their chicken meals were as delicious as ever and the small talk was enjoyable, but it was time to get down to the important business they had come together to discuss.

"Lunch is over now, Markus. Are you ready to tell me what you wanted to talk about?"

Markus didn't need a second invitation to talk about what was bothering him. He dove right into the conversation. Luke was standing next to him when he received this last batch of irritating news.

"It's my dad—it's *always* my dad. He's coming home next week for the congressional Christmas recess. He sent me a text. Not a personal phone call, but a text. I'll bet one of his aids actually sent it. I am expected to be at the family dinner on Christmas day. That was the first time since going off to D.C. last fall that he has contacted me. What kind of a father treats his children like that? You know my plan was to propose to Cindy on Christmas Eve and then spend the next couple of days with her entire family, not mine. I love Cindy and I'm looking forward to spending this first Christmas with her family. Luke, I don't know how to say it any other way, but I've had enough of the phony Middlefield Christmases. At this point in my life, I don't really care if I ever spend another Christmas with them or not."

Luke had sat with Markus and heard him talk about his dad enough to know that it was best to let him get everything off his chest before giving any advice. So he quietly sat and listened.

"What was really going to be exciting for me over these next two holidays was getting to know Cindy's dad better. After I received permission to marry his daughter, he told me that he was especially looking forward to getting to know me better as well. My dad, on the other hand, well, you know him, the man I call 'Dad.' The executive home builder. Mr. Congressman. The absentee father. Whatever you want to call him, he has never shown any interest in wanting to really get to know me like Mr. Wellington does. It makes me wonder why my parents had kids to begin with. Think about it, Luke: how many rides home from a ball game did my dad ever give you? The answer is *zero*, and that's the same number of times he and I played catch in the backyard . . . and the same number of my baseball games that he watched throughout high school. And now he wants to take this Christmas holiday away from me? It's not going to happen, Luke. It's just not going to happen."

Meanwhile, at Lydia's house, Cindy was asking some questions of her own about Markus.

"Lydia, you've heard that Markus is supposed to come over to my house for Christmas Eve this year, haven't you?"

"Yes, I have. That's a pretty big step in a relationship. Are you ready?"

"With my sweet Markus, yes, I am. But Markus isn't the problem. It's his family. He's told me a lot about his dad, mom, and sister, and I'm not sure if I have what Markus has. I don't know if I can push back on their demands for control over our lives. Do I even want them in my life? Will Markus still love me if I am his only family? Am I enough for him?"

"Cindy, if you are asking for my counsel, I'll give it to you. But understand one important thing: whatever you finally decide to do or say concerning his family, it has got to be *your* decision and not mine."

Lydia could see on Cindy's face that she was thinking over that last statement, so she paused before saying more.

"First of all, from the way he looks at you, the way he treats you, and the way he talks with you, yes, in my opinion, as a single girl, I believe he would be very happy if you were his entire family. Secondly, I believe Markus has found a true Father through faith in Jesus Christ, and he is now in need of a good and loving earthly father. Though your dad is not yet a follower of Jesus, he is a good and loving man, and because of that, I believe your dad can be that father to him. Take him into your family, Cindy, and don't worry about his family. Give your worries, and your father, to Jesus. Jesus has more control over your life than Matthew Middlefield ever will."

Markus had been gone for several hours when Lydia arrived for their Saturday evening date. Luke was almost finished vacuuming the living room floor when she walked in the side door. In her hands were two cobb salads she had purchased from a grocery store on her way over to Luke's house. Lydia stood there for a moment with her mouth hanging open in disbelief as she watched Luke wrap up the electric cord.

"You know something, Luke, I have to make a confession to you."

Luke was taken a little off guard by that statement. After all, to this point in their relationship, he had always been the one confessing something. He smiled and said, "So this time it's *your* turn to confess. That's pretty cool, Lydia. And what would that confession be?" he asked as he put the vacuum back into the hall closet.

"I always thought it was your mom who kept the house clean. I didn't think you even knew where the vacuum was, let alone how to use it."

"That's it? *That's* your confession? I can see that we're going to have to work on the kinds of things you feel you need to confess. And I suppose we could also talk more about your attitude toward men and their domestic, or lack of domestic, abilities. But I think Markus and Cindy deserve better than having to hear us go back and forth over who keeps a cleaner house. I believe we both know the answer to that question already."

Knowing she had lost this debate before it got started, Lydia opted to set out the food on the dining room table.

As they were eating, Lydia began sharing what Cindy had told her about Markus's family and the potential struggles she may be facing. When she finished, it was Luke's turn to share, and the first thing he did was say to Lydia, "You gave Cindy some counsel, didn't you? I can see it in your face. I thought we decided to talk first and then counsel. What happened?"

Lydia answered this pointed question by saying, "It was all girl stuff, Luke. I made the decision that you couldn't have given any good advice because of the 'girl stuff' factor anyway. So I gave her some counsel, and it worked out fine. Don't worry about it, Luke."

Without taking a breath, and to avoid taking questions, she asked, "So how did everything work out with Markus?"

Luke let his beautiful girlfriend get away with no additional questions. Instead, he opted to tell her about Matthew's Christmas demands. Then he told her the really good news.

Markus had given Luke permission to tell Lydia about his proposal plans. "You mean to tell me that Markus is going to propose to Cindy next week? Oh, Luke, how exciting! And how romantic."

Lydia's mind went directly from romantic to tragic when she remembered what Luke had just told her about Matthew's demand.

"But what about having to show up at his parents' house on Christmas Eve? How's he going to take care of that problem?"

A somewhat sinister smile formed on Luke's face. "Well, Lydia, I took a page out of your counseling playbook and gave Markus some advice."

Lydia's mouth dropped open: "Well, aren't we just two peas in a pod." Sitting back in her chair, she chewed her salad and waited to hear what Luke had advised Markus to do.

"I also took a page out of Matthew's playbook on how to skillfully rebut a demand to be somewhere with someone you don't like because of a previous engagement you can't get out of. I advised Markus to send his dad a return text message telling him that there has been a scheduling conflict and that he would be unable to attend that evening's event."

"But that sounds like something Matthew would say to Markus."

"That's exactly the point! His dad should have nothing to complain about; he has used that same line on hundreds of people in the past and will probably use it hundreds of times in the future. We're just turning the tables on him. I'm guessing he's not going to like it one bit."

While Luke was sharing the good news of the coming marriage proposal from Markus, Matthew and Elizabeth Middlefield were walking through their largest model home, inspecting its preparedness. In their opinion, the preparations for their Christmas party were completely unsatisfactory. Apparently the subcontractors who prepared this model home for their party didn't care who this party was for. Their closest personal friends, their growing political family, their most generous donors, and, of course, their family would see this wreck of a model home, which would reflect on Matthew as a legislator. Everything had to be perfect, down to the finest detail. Matthew's future political career depended on every event going smoothly. In the middle of making notes for needed repairs, they received a text message from Markus.

"Elizabeth, I can't believe what I'm reading! Get over here and look at the text message I just received from your son. He can't do this to me! This party is too important for my future—he has to be here!"

Elizabeth took Matthew's phone and read the text. "You're right, Matthew. He shouldn't be doing this to us . . . but it sure looks like he's going to try."

Elizabeth leaned over toward Matthew, who was still fixated on the text message, and gave him a comforting hug to try to calm him down. "Until we have an opportunity to speak with Markus personally, let's stay focused on preparing for the party."

Matthew knew Elizabeth was right. He needed to stay focused on the work at hand and on the people he could control. An hour later, their list had been completed and his first call after receiving that troubling text from Markus would be to his unsuspecting painter. If Markus wouldn't listen to his demands, he would be happy to make some unrealistic ones of someone else and, at the same time, take his anger out on them. John Peterson, his painter, was one of Matthew's longest-standing contractors. He was also one of the kindest and most loved of all his tradesmen. All of John's painting employees had at least one or two stories of how John had personally helped them out of some difficulty in their life. Unlike most other employers, he didn't mind getting to know his workers personally. In short, John had done nothing deserving of what was about to happen; he had simply answered a call from the new congressman, which set into motion a series of events that almost ruined Matthew's new career before it even got started.

"Hello, John? This is Matthew Middlefield calling."

This unexpected call would be nothing like what John thought it might be.

"Hi, Matthew. Good to hear from you, and congratulations on your victory. Is there anything I can do for you?"

This innocent offer was merely a colloquialism, not meant to be taken literally, but that wasn't going to stop Matthew. He lit into John like fire into kindling. "I'll tell you what you can do for me—you can get a crew of painters down to the big model tonight and get it touched up for a party I'm giving. It looks terrible."

John was caught completely off guard by such an attack, and he responded defensively. "But, Matthew, I completed those touch-ups yesterday with two of my best painters. I inspected the entire house myself at Elizabeth's request. It looks great, Matthew. Really, it looks great."

"Well, I guess we have a difference of opinion on what looks great and what looks like shabby craftsmanship. Elizabeth and I are in the model right now, and it looks like *crap!* We have a list for you to work from, so if you're not down here tonight fixing what I see as sloppy work, I'll get another painter to do the work. Then I'm going to back charge you for the work, plus our management fee."

"Matthew, it's Saturday evening and I have my whole family over to the house. I need to spend some time with my wife."

"John, does it sound like I'm kidding around? I don't care who's at your home or why they're there. Either get down here and fix this mess or you can start looking for another builder to work for!"

John was silent as he looked at his frail wife, not knowing what to do. He knew he couldn't afford to lose a contractor this time of year. "Matthew, when is this party of yours planned for?"

Matthew couldn't believe what he was hearing. It sounded like John was about to negotiate with him as to when he could perform these repairs. "That's irrelevant to you, but our party is one week from today, and there are too many repairs to put off this work any longer."

Now John was truly confused, looking at everyone who had come to his home to visit with his wife. Looking at his watch, he asked, "If it's not for a week, Matthew, how about we get to the model early to-morrow morning and attend to your concerns?"

It was at this point that Matthew erupted: "So you don't think I know how to schedule work now? Is that what you're telling me, John? I've got six other lazy subcontractors that have to come in after you, so *no*, you can't come in tomorrow! Get down here tonight, or you know what's going to happen!"

"But, Matthew," pleaded John as he continued to watch his wife thank everyone for coming over, "you have always scheduled us to come in after the other trades have finished their work so that we can fix any damages."

"Matthew's friendly voice that lived in his soul told him to calm down. "John, I don't think you understand. Make the repairs tonight, or you're fired. Is that clear enough for you?"

One week later, Luke was at Ricardo's home for a second Christmas; Lydia was with her family; Juan was at Nita's home; the Middlefields were throwing a political party; and Markus was knocking on the door of Cindy Wellington's house. Two hours later, he was still being introduced to the rather large extended family by Cindy and her mom. Out of nowhere, Cindy's dad stood up and loudly requested that everyone quiet down. He then took the opportunity to slightly embarrass Markus by asking if there was anyone in the room who had not had a chance to meet Cindy's "young man," implying that Markus belonged to Cindy. To her father's surprise, not a single voice was heard. Cindy had done a great job with all her introductions that evening.

Satisfied that everyone knew who Markus was, Cindy's dad gave him the floor, at which point Markus said to Mr. Wellington, "Thanks, Dad." Mr. Wellington surprisingly replied, "You're welcome."

At hearing what Markus had just said, not only did all the relatives have confused looks on their faces, but Cindy immediately leaned into her mother, anxiously grabbing her arm and quietly whispering in her ear, "Do you have any idea what's going on, Mom? Did Markus just say what I think he just said?" To which Cindy received a blank stare. Her mother was equally confused, saying, "I don't know, honey, I don't know. Your dad hasn't told me anything."

Just a minute ago, the room had gotten quiet when Mr. Wellington asked for the floor. Now you could hear a pin drop. It was as if everyone was thinking, *Did Markus just say what I think he just said?* Ignoring the confused look plastered on everyone's face, Markus turned away from Cindy's dad and looked directly at Cindy, who was now holding even more tightly to her mother's arm. All the other family members were equally as surprised as Cindy was.

"Cindy," said Markus, "six weeks ago I asked your dad a question, to which he answered yes. Now I really need to ask you the same question, and I'm hoping to hear the same answer."

She stood there with tears running down her trembling cheeks as her mother wrapped her arm around Cindy's shoulders. Markus turned and took one step toward the family Christmas tree and then reached into its middle. He removed one small, shiny ornament off one of its branches. It had been there in plain sight for two weeks, and yet no one but Markus and Cindy's dad saw it. It was surrounded by other family ornaments, some old, some new, some blue, some made by hand, and some store-bought. As Markus held the diamond ring in his hand, he turned to Cindy and said, "Cindy, the first thing I want to tell you is that I love you. And I have had that love for you in my heart from almost the first time I saw you. Every moment I have spent with you since then, that love has continued to grow. I hung this expression of that love on this tree for your entire family to see. But now, instead of hiding this expression of love in these branches, I would love to show your family and the world how much I love you by asking one very important question.

"Cindy, would you make my life complete and marry me?"

Cindy left her mother's embrace and entered Markus's as she said, "You know I will, Markus! Yes, I'll marry you!"

At the same time Cindy was saying yes and the entire extended family was exploding into cheers of congratulations, Cindy's dad was reading the lips of his wife.

"How come you didn't tell me?" One marriage was just beginning, and another was about to experience a bit of fun-loving turbulence.

Markus spent Christmas Eve and the next two days at the Wellington's; the evenings were spent at Luke's house sleeping in the guest room.

"Thanks for letting me stay at your place these last couple of days, Luke. It made it much easier to visit with Cindy and her whole family, and I didn't have to answer 101 questions from my parents. I'm sure I'll get enough questions in about an hour when I get home."

"No problem, Markus. Are you leaving for home right now?"

"Yeah, I think so. I might as well get the wrath of Matthew Middlefield out of the way and get on with my life. You know something, Luke, I'm almost 21 years old and I'm engaged to get married this spring—and I'm *still* afraid of my dad. I'm praying to our Heavenly Father that all this fear will soon end. I'm wondering, "Would you pray with me before I go home? I'm getting a feeling that my life with Cindy won't be the only thing I'll be sharing with my parents. I don't mind that they will know about me and Cindy. It's their desire to manipulate me, and now possibly Cindy, for their benefit that bothers me most.

"Let's do it right now, Markus."

The two of them spent about 20 minutes in prayer before Luke asked Jesus to give Markus the right words to speak to his parents, and to help him speak those words in love.

After Luke had given Markus a brother-hug before he left for home, he gave Ricardo a call.

"Hi, Dad, this is Luke."

"Luke, you have no idea how hearing you call me 'Dad' makes me feel. I know it's been almost 15 years since you've had someone to call 'Dad,' so I have to say it again, Luke: thank you for letting me be that person."

While Ricardo was sharing those thoughts with Luke, he was reminded of the first time he called his own adoptive father 'Dad.' Like Luke, he hadn't even realized what he had done. He called out that name so honestly and effortlessly in the moment. It was then that he knew he had a father for life, even as he hoped Luke was realizing that he too had a father for life.

"I have to admit, the word 'dad' doesn't roll smoothly off my tongue quite yet, but it is getting easier. And I do enjoy having you as the one I call 'Dad.' But the reason I called is to see if we are still meeting at Mr. Oleeva's kitchen to show him some more recipes."

Ricardo answered that question with more than a little excitement, for the meeting he had with Michael a few weeks back had energized him in his desire to help couples adopt children even more. It seemed as if this dream would, in fact, become a reality.

"Yes, we are still meeting today. The meeting time is 11:00 a.m. We thought we could combine cooking with lunch and have more time to make some of the meals that might sell at the food trucks."

It was a pleasant sound hearing the excitement in Ricardo's voice, and Luke was looking forward to helping in any way he could.

"You do have the address to their kitchen, don't you?"

"I sure do, Dad. I'll see you and Mom after I pick up Lydia. It shouldn't be more than an hour or so.

"Okay, Luke. By the way, I'm really starting to like Michael. I believe he will be a man I can put much trust and faith in."

Back at the Middlefield home, Markus had pulled into his parents' garage and pushed the button to close the overhead door. He had no sooner walked in the back entrance when he heard his father call out, "Markus, is that you? Are you finally home?"

At hearing that question, Markus dropped his head, shook it slightly, and said to himself, "And so it begins."

"Yes, Dad, it's me."

Matthew soon found Markus in the kitchen with the refrigerator door open.

"Oh, so you can't make it home for my first Christmas party but you *can* come home and dig through my refrigerator for something to eat."

"Come on, Dad. I answered every one of your text messages that you sent me. I just didn't answer them the way you wanted me to answer them. I'm an adult, Dad. I can come and go as I please, unless you're planning on kicking me out of the house."

Markus could see the growing irritation on his father's face. He assumed his father wasn't used to being told no.

"Yes, I can see that. Apparently you'd rather spend the holidays at the Wellington home than ours."

Markus snapped his head around from looking in the refrigerator and said rather loudly, "How did you know I was at the Wellington home, Dad? Were you having me followed?"

Not answering Markus's question directly, Matthew said, "I'm a sitting member of the House of Representatives, and because of that position, there are options open to me for investigative purposes that are not available to the general public. I also know a whole lot more than their names. For example, Jonathan Wellington and his wife, Laurie, have been married for 27 years and have two sons and two daughters. Jonathan writes software code for the Apple Corporation. He may not know it, but he is in line for a promotion in four months. Laurie works as an RN three times a week at the hospital down the street from where they live. Would you like me to go on?"

Markus was visibly showing his anger at his father's invasion of the Wellington's privacy. It almost seemed that his father took pleasure in showing Markus how easy it would be to always know what he was doing, where he was doing it, and who he was with. This is exactly what Markus was worried about.

"How did you learn all that information? What kind of stuff are you into?"

By this time, Elizabeth had walked into the kitchen. Seeing Markus, she took her turn at showing her displeasure by taking a verbal swipe at him. "Markus, why couldn't you have come to at least one party we were hosting? There were some very important people we wanted to introduce you to. I don't think you understand how these people could have helped *you* in *your* future, and you have no idea how embarrassing it was for us to make excuses for you all night as to why you weren't there."

Markus didn't want to disrespect his mother, but he still felt compelled to ask her one question, a question that would show her that he knew she was trying to manipulate him. "Okay, Mom, name three people who were at your party that specifically asked for me because they wanted to help me in some unknown career."

His mother opened her mouth as though she had three names on the ready, but then she stopped and thought about his question again. Having no names to share, she said, "I can't remember their names, Markus. But that's not the point. You should have been there to support your father."

"Mom, Dad, I don't care about meeting politically connected people. What I want you to tell me, Dad, is how you knew where I was and how you obtained all that personal information about my girlfriend and her parents."

"Girlfriend? You have a girlfriend? I guess that explains why you just spent three days at her house and not ours. At least you slept at Luke's house. Thanks for all the honesty, Markus."

"You know where I slept too? Sorry, Dad, but you're not going to work this conversation to your benefit. Now, if you would be honest with me and explain how you got all this information, that would go a long way in resolving this argument."

"I'm not at liberty to discuss that information, Markus. National security reasons, you know."

Matthew smirked, believing he had put Markus in his place, which was under his thumb, exactly where he wanted him. But Markus wasn't having any of what his dad was giving out.

"Oh, but you *are* at liberty to use the government to invade my privacy?"

"Markus, you have to understand that as the years go by, I will be moving into positions of great power and authority. I will soon be responsible for making decisions that will affect millions of people."

Matthew had assumed a posture of authority, as though he was speaking to a room full of his staffers. It almost appeared to Markus that he had puffed out his chest as he continued to speak about what he fully expected to happen at some point in the near future.

"What you don't understand yet, Markus, is that some people are born to lead while others desire a strong leader to follow, and one day soon, I'm going to be one of those leaders. And the more information I have about everyone I could possibly come in contact with, the better I can decide how to deal with them, or others like them, be they friend or foe. Because of these well-informed decisions, I will become a better leader."

"No, Dad. The way I see it is, some people decide they want to be a manipulator of others for power and personal gain. Therefore, they run for public office. And these other people you're referring to as simple "followers" are the ones you are manipulating—they just don't know it. And if you've used whatever secret government system you had access to in order to track me like a dog, well, that is unbelievable. Dad, you haven't even been a congressman for two months and you're doing this kind of covert stuff already. It makes me wonder what you'll be doing in two years . . . or 20 years . . . or even when you're out of office. No thanks, Dad. I'll take care of myself . . . if that's okay with you, that is."

Just then, a fourth voice entered the conversation.

"Come on, you guys," said Maggy as she walked in the kitchen while running her fingers threw her bed-head hair, untangling the snarls from the evening's sleep. "It's Saturday morning. With all this loud talking, it's pretty hard for a girl to sleep in. What are you all arguing about this time?"

"Maggy, did you know that Markus had a girlfriend?"

"Sure, doesn't everyone know? How long has it been, Markus? It must be almost two years by now, right?" said Maggy very matter of fact.

"Two years, Markus? You've been dating the same girl for two years and didn't tell us? And Maggy, you've known about this and didn't tell us? Why haven't you said anything until now?"

"Like I said, Dad," said Markus with an accusatory sound in his voice, "you're too busy manipulating everyone in your life. You don't even know what's happening in your own home, and I didn't want that to happen to Cindy."

Maggy, seeing an opening in the conversation and wanting to keep her father informed about what was going to happen in their home, blurted out, "Since we're on the topic of knowing what we are all doing with our lives, I have an exciting announcement to make."

Markus, Matthew, and Elizabeth all stopped talking and turned toward Maggy.

"At the end of the month, I'm going to be moving in with Peter. He asked me on Christmas Eve at the party, and I said yes!"

"That's wonderful, honey," said Matthew and Elizabeth. Elizabeth came over and gave Maggy a hug of congratulations. "See what you missed out on, Markus, all because you didn't want to come to our holiday party."

"Sorry, Dad. Sorry, Mom. I was a little busy that evening myself."

"Busy doing what?" asked his dad, indignant at Markus for insinuating there would be anything more important happening that evening than attending their party.

"You mean to tell me you don't know something about me? Well, here it is: I asked Cindy Wellington to marry me on Christmas Eve . . . and she said *yes*!"

It was now Matthew and Elizabeth's turn to be visibly upset at hearing this life-changing news.

"Oh my gosh, Markus!" said his father, taking a more aggressive stance after hearing this terrible news. "Are you serious? Are you sure that she's the right girl for you and the Middlefield family?"

Markus couldn't believe what he had just heard. He looked at his parents in amazement in light of the contrast between their reaction to Maggy's announcement and their reaction to his.

After Matthew had returned to Washington, D.C., and the new year had arrived, everyone's work schedule went back to normal. Luke was hoping to immerse himself in his work, wanting to build some homes for a while with no distractions or drama to put up with.

His hope, however, was short-lived when he saw the owners of the three largest subcontractors used by Middlefield homes walking straight toward him. He knew that whatever had brought these three men together wouldn't be good for Middlefield Homes. Trying to prepare for whatever they were about to say would be fruitless, so he decided to let them speak first. After all, they had been the ones to track him down.

"Hey, Luke," said John Peterson, the owner of Precision Painting, "do you have a couple of minutes to talk with us?"

Standing there next to John was Charlie Gunderson, the framing contractor, and Gordy Radando, the sheetrock and taping contractor.

"Of course I do. You guys are the backbone of construction. Without you guys, we couldn't build a single home. What's up? How can I help you?"

"We'd like to start by asking that you not share with anyone what we are about to tell you."

These three men had never approached Luke like this before, so his initial thought was that whatever they wanted to talk about was either going to be very good or very bad.

"Sure. As long as it's not illegal, it shouldn't be a problem. What do you all want to talk about?"

The three men chuckled to themselves as John continued. "No, Luke, it's not illegal. Nothing like that. But what we *would* like to tell you is something about yourself. Of course, it's obvious that you are more than 30 years younger than any one of us, and we have been watching how you interact with and conduct yourself around your fellow employees and the subcontractors. In our eyes, you have grown to be a man of your word and a man we can trust, unlike the owner of Middlefield Homes."

Luke was struck by their frank honesty. He couldn't argue with their opinion of Matthew Middlefield, so he continued to listen.

"We can also see that one day soon you are going to become a gifted builder with your own construction company. The three of us standing here today want nothing to do with becoming a general contractor." The other two men emphasized what John had said by saying, "You got that right!" John continued, "We love our individual trades and will never change that part of our business, but we have all been in construction long enough to know what kind of general contractor we *do* and do *not* want to work for."

Still not quite sure what these men were implying or where this conversation was going, Luke did have enough sense to look around the jobsite to see who might be watching them. To his relief, no one was paying them any attention, so he asked, "I don't understand. Just what exactly are you all telling me?"

"All of us are tired of working for the Middlefield family . . . well, except for Markus. He's nothing like his old man."

Again, Luke couldn't argue with these conclusions, so he kept listening.

"We wanted to let you know that we have all decided to start interviewing with other builders in order to replace the Middlefield Homes work that we will soon be turning down. And it's not only the three of us who don't want to work here any longer. In the next several months, you can expect there to be a complete change in the faces you are used to seeing on the jobsites. We wanted to give you a heads-up for when we start turning down work so that it won't affect your schedule. What we're suggesting is that you get your replacement trades up to speed so your customers won't suffer. Otherwise, this decision will affect the whole company, and we don't want anyone working in your office to be hurt financially in any way. There's one thing, however, that we will not compromise on. Please understand, if we are searched out and asked by those replacement trades why we are leaving Middlefield Homes, we'll tell them. But we won't be searching them out in order to hurt you all."

"But, guys, why now? You've been working here for years. What happened? Matthew isn't even working here, and he doesn't own one share of Middlefield Homes stock. It's all in Elizabeth's name."

"Maybe someone should tell that to Matthew," said John with no little disdain in his voice for that man. "But to get you up to speed, Luke, I'll tell you what happened. Two weeks ago, I was having a family party at my home on a Saturday night when I got a call from the old man. You know, the man who is legally not supposed to have anything to do with Middlefield Homes. And then there was his wife, squawking like a crazy woman nonstop in the background. The call was about the poor condition they claimed that I had left their big model in. Come on, Luke, when was the last time you saw any of their model homes in poor show condition? They were both demanding that I go immediately to the big model home and touch it up again. I told him I had the whole family over to my home and what I was doing that evening, but he didn't care. He just threatened me and hung up the phone."

"That does sound a little harsh, and definitely like something Matthew would do, but is it worth quitting over?"

"Luke, you don't understand. The old man didn't care, but that was a party for my wife before she started chemotherapy the next day. I can't work for a man like that anymore. *My* family comes first, not his. And I sure won't be voting for him again at the next election. The other guys have had similar run-ins over the years and have decided with me that they have had enough of Matthew and Elizabeth Middlefield. One last thing, Luke. On a more personal note, we have all agreed that when you too have had enough of the Middlefield family and decide to start your own construction company—and believe me when I say, we have been around long enough to know who has the talent to succeed and who to stay away from—you, Mr. Cruz, will be a great general contractor. If you need our services, you can count on us."

Toward the end of February, after getting back to Luke's place following an early movie, Luke and Lydia were sitting on the front porch
of his grandpa's house holding hands as they rocked in unison. Luke
said, "Right now, Lydia, sitting here with you is perfect. After all the
drama with the Middlefield family, not to mention everything that
has happened at the Middlefield business these last three months, it's
nice to have a carefree Luke and Lydia evening."

They continued rocking, still holding hands, saying nothing while
they enjoyed the cool, fresh air and the star-filled sky that evening.
It had been Luke's idea to ask their mothers to his grandpa's home
to prepare another meal using a recipe from Grandma Maria's cookbook. Everyone, including Lydia, enjoyed these evenings of cooking
together. Mr. Oleeva was already selling several hundred tamales a
day, and he was excited to see what other meals could be purchased by
his loyal customer. New meals were being prepared and taste-tested
all the time.

Still holding onto Luke's hand, Lydia added to what he had just
said while gently speaking in rhythm with the rockers. "You're right,
Luke. It *is* a perfect evening. I can't imagine how it could get any better, except for eating that meal our mothers are making for us."

"Yeah, you're right, Lydia. It would have to be a pretty life-changing
event to make this evening better than it is right now." Then, smiling
as she considered how their Jesus was taking care of everyone in their
lives—in spite of the occasional speed bumps and the unexpected turbulence that had come their way—she said, "Look at your dad and
mom. They sure do love each other, and everything is going so well
with their adoption agency. Pronto Foods is doing great, and it appears that Markus and Cindy are handling Dad and Mom Middlefield
as well as can be expected."

"You're right, Lydia, but one more event must take place for my
heart to be at peace. I need to tell you a few things."

Lydia's first thought was, *Oh good, another confession. I wonder how
trivial this one is going to be?*

Luke turned his rocker toward Lydia and held her left hand even
more tightly. "First of all, Lydia, I have got to admit: you have effortlessly and unintentionally changed me for the better. I don't really

believe that you understand how you have affected me over these last nine months. You have helped me to grow into the man I am today, and you've helped me to understand what that means for us as a couple. You have also gently encouraged me to be a better leader of my friends for God's honor; introducing me to Alan, Mary, and the small group from church was a big part of that. Most of all, I have grown dependent on just having you in my life. When a day goes by that I don't see your smiling face or hear your sweet, sweet voice, I start feeling sad."

It was at that last statement that she held his hand more firmly than he was holding hers. With the Lydia-type conviction Luke had grown so accustomed and attached to, she looked directly in his eyes and said, "You stop right there, Mr. Luke Cruz. You'd better not be messing with me if this conversation is going where I think it's going. Don't you dare trifle with me or my emotions!"

"And there's the girl I have fallen in love with! Always getting right to the point. Lydia, we sat in these chairs nine months ago on the night our conniving mothers set us up on a blind date, a date that neither of us knew was taking place. Do you remember what I asked you if you were willing to do as a way to get back at our moms?"

Through a now haltering and cracking voice, Lydia began to recount that evening's events.

"Yeah, Luke, I remember. You asked me if I would hold your hand and walk back into the kitchen and announce our engagement to them."

As Lydia was telling the story of that evening nine months ago, Luke was taking a ring from his shirt pocket with his free hand. He held it out to Lydia between his thumb and index finger.

"The first time we had this conversation, I didn't have this ring or the love I now have for you in my heart. But tonight I have both. Lydia, will you accept this ring as a symbol of my absolute love for you and my lifelong commitment to stand at your side until death alone separates us? Lydia, will you be my one and only . . . will you marry me?"

Lydia was crying now, and Luke also had tears running down his cheeks.

"Yes, Luke, yes!" she said as she stood up in excitement. "I'll marry you forever!"

After placing the ring on her finger and then receiving a rather long and passionate kiss for all the attentive neighbors to see, Luke said, "Now what do you say we go and share the good news with our moms?"

"Yeah, let's do it! But before we go in, I've got a quick question."

"Sure, what is it?"

"Did anyone else know that you were going to propose to me tonight?"

"Yep, there were just a couple people. Your dad, of course, was the first to know. I asked his permission to marry you. Then there was Markus and Cindy, Juan and Juanita, and Ricardo. As a matter of fact, our dads are right over there, just down the street sitting in my dad's car. They witnessed the whole proposal."

While directing Lydia's attention to the silent car, Luke waved. The car started its engine and then flicked its headlights on and off as though it were winking at the two of them.

"Lukas Cruz!" said Lydia as she slapped him on his arm. "You had this set up all along. And my dad saw me give you that kiss!"

"Of course I had it set up, and don't forget, my dad saw the kiss too. Now, except for that unexpectedly passionate kiss, which was a pleasant surprise, everything went according to plan. Like me, I don't think our dads will ever forget that kiss either. Now, let's go tell our match-making mothers. They have no idea what just happened out here."

When the dads saw Luke and Lydia walk into the house, they knew that was their signal to come in as well. After parking the car in the driveway, they walked into the kitchen just in time to be slightly stunned by hearing all three women screaming with joy at the news. After everyone had calmed down, the two moms looked at each other and said in unison, "It's just too easy."

Three days later, Luke was still flying high, so high that he forgot it was time for a Legacy Letter. But there it was, staring at him from his laptop screen.

"I guess I'll be seeing you later this afternoon, Grandpa. Sorry about forgetting about your letter, but it's been a pretty exciting couple of days here at the Cruz house.

That day's work went by fast, not because of what was waiting for Luke on his laptop but because of the continued words of congratulations from the guys on all the jobsites. Luke was home now, coffee in hand and sitting in grandpa's recliner.

"Here we are again, Grandpa. I wonder what words of insight you have for me today?" And with that, he touched the Legacy Letter button on the screen.

"Hi, Luke. This is letter number eight and you're almost 20 years old. Time is sure flying by, isn't it?"

Yes, it is Grandpa. Yes, it is.

"Today I'm going to tell you a story that I have never told anyone, not even your grandmother. I am actually very ashamed of this time in my life. The reason I feel compelled to tell you this story is because last night I absolutely believe that our Jesus gave me a reminder dream of this event. I believe this dream was sent to me in order to humble me and remind me that it is only through the free gift of forgiveness from our Jesus that I can look forward to being with him very shortly. Even at my ripe old age, I still have much to learn. At the same time, I'm hoping to teach you God-given wisdom through the revealing of my sinful actions.

Luke touched the pause button and said, "Oh boy, Grandpa, this must be one of those letters that will disappoint me. But I guess if you're willing to tell me whatever shameful thing you did in your past, I promise to start opening up more to others in my life, particularly to those who love me as much as I love you."

He then touched the start button.

"I think you already know that I enlisted in the Army right out of high school. A friend of mine went with me to the recruiting office to enlist. The Korean War was over at that time, but conflicts were flaring up constantly all around the world; it was the Cold War era. At that time, it was either enlist or be drafted. We chose to enlist. One other thing we promised each other after signing away our lives was to meet back at that recruiting office two years later, when our hitches were up, and kick each other in the backside for being stupid enough to enlist instead of waiting for our draft notice to be delivered.

"Well, we both made it through our two-year hitch, and we did meet to kick each other on our backsides. But the story I am going to tell you took place between these two events. After my basic training had been completed, I found that I didn't mind the military life. There was discipline, order, and military law everywhere. This was different than my home life and high school, which were both out of control, with little or no consequences of any kind for those borderline illegal activities I was participating in. It was then that I decided to make the military my career. But to my disappointment, so did a few of the other guys in our company. What that meant to me was competition for rising to a higher position of authority and power. Yes, Luke, power. Be careful when someone offers you too much power of any kind. It'll change you.

"What they didn't know is that I had an advantage that the other guys didn't have. You see, Luke, I found out earlier in my life that I was able to make friends very easily, and I was gifted with the personality of someone who is always the life of the party. I was willing and ready to use these gifts for my own personal advantage. So, in order to attain those promotions, I began to sabotage my fellow military brothers and their attempts to gain those same promotions. It was almost too easy to manipulate people to get what I wanted. My deceitful efforts were beginning to bear fruit when I saw one man transfer out of our unit and another man named Ralph Reid leave the military completely when his hitch was up. Well, Luke, it turned out that my superiors were well aware of my activities. They told me that if I didn't leave the military when my time was up, I would be dishonorably discharged. They said that the army didn't need men like me in its ranks. Men like me—what did that mean? At the age of 20, what kind of a man had I become? I had to take a long look at myself and decide what kind of a man I really wanted to be, and what kind of a man I wanted to be known as.

"Of course, I left the military, personally disgraced for what I had done and for leaving such a negative stain on my name. I am telling you this story in order that you might learn at a young age that the road to success in life is not by damaging another person's character through dishonesty and deceit. Success is gained over time through hard work, integrity, honesty, and always treating those around you fairly and justly. Here are a couple of simple and to-the-point verses that will help make my point.

> Do not plan evil against your neighbor,
>> who dwells trustingly beside you.
> Do not contend with a man for no reason,
>> when he has done you no harm. (Proverbs 3:29–30)

"I'm going to leave this letter right there for you to dwell on, Luke. It's also okay with me if you want to play this letter for Ricardo and then have a good big brother to little brother talk, or a father-son type talk, whichever seems best. I never found out what happened to those other two guys, but I always wanted to ask for their forgiveness for what I had done to them. I did, however, confess this sin to Jesus and ask him for forgiveness. It's time for me to go now. Bye, Luke. See you in three months."

Chapter 9

Paths Taken

Everyone was talking among themselves when a final knock was heard on Alan's front door. After hearing the knock, Luke opened the door for Lydia to walk in first. It was always the same on Tuesday evenings: knock and then enter. Everyone in attendance was there for their weekly small group gathering and Bible study. There was no need for a formal greeting ceremony.

"Hi, y'all. Sorry we're a little late. Have we missed anything?" asked Luke as they made their way into the living room to some empty seats, which, regretfully, were not next to each other. Luke thought someone might give up their seat so that he could sit next to his girl, but there was no such offer made by anyone. But as far as Lydia was concerned, it was no big deal. She was sitting by two of her better friends and had news to share.

As Luke made his way to a chair, Allen answered his question: "No, we've just been small-talking. Now that everyone has arrived, we can get started."

Alan refreshed everyone's memory about last week's study, and then he briefly described what would be discussed tonight. Lydia was sitting where Cindy and Nita were, which meant Luke would be sitting with Markus. After taking his seat, Luke looked around the room. Not seeing Juan, he leaned toward Markus and whispered, "Hey, where's Juan? I don't see him."

Markus then leaned back toward Luke and whispered, "In a minute, Luke."

Unable to keep quiet any longer, Lydia showed the girls her left hand, to which she received muffled squeals of excitement, along with smiles and hugs. Alan missed this exchange between the girls. Oblivious to this exciting news, he continued on by saying, "Why don't I open this gathering in prayer to our Jesus."

Hearing he was about to pray, everyone lowered their heads in respect and honor to the One to whom they would all be speaking to.

"Dear Jesus, the Creator of all that there is, the Sustainer of all that there is, and the One who provides for our needs when needs arise. We all, with unity of heart, ask that your Spirit would be strong in his presence with us tonight. We also ask for your healing hand to be on Juan . . . heal him of his injuries, we pray. Amen."

As soon as the prayer had finished, a surprised Luke asked with concern, "What happened to Juan? Nobody called to tell me he was hurt. How bad is it?"

Everyone looked at Nita to fill Luke in as to what had happened to Juan. She was the one who told everyone about him when she first arrived, so it only made sense for her to do it again. She repeated to Luke the information she had been given by Juan.

"It's nothing big, Luke. I'd say probably more embarrassing than medically serious."

"Juan called me a couple hours ago and told me he wouldn't be picking me up or making it to small group tonight. And that's when he told me what happened. Apparently, he had an accident on a friend's mini-bike. Juan said it was an older scooter that was not maintained very well. He admitted to me that he was driving too fast for the type of figure eights he was doing. Due to the poor maintenance, the speed he was driving, and the loose gravel he was driving on, his brakes locked up. He went into an uncontrolled skid and was thrown off the bike, dislocating his shoulder."

Luke sat there in front of everyone, trying not to show anger toward Juan. The rest of the group wouldn't understand, except for Markus and Nita. But he was almost steaming at what he had just heard, thinking to himself, *Here we go again*. Then he spoke out loud to the group: "Will Juan ever grow up and stop doing stupid things like this? He's not a kid anymore. I can call him out on this so-called accident because, besides Markus, I've known him the longest."

Everyone sitting there got the distinct feeling that Luke knew something they didn't. Luke then looked directly at Nita with an expression on his face that said, *Don't worry, Nita. I know exactly what happened to him.* Then, speaking to the group again, Luke said, "It's nothing to worry about, guys. He's been doing stuff like this since high school."

Alan, being concerned for Juan, asked Nita, "Is there anything any of us can do for Juan to help him get through this?" Before anyone else could offer to help, Luke jumped back in and said, "You know what, Nita, I don't think he'll be going to work tomorrow. I'll take off work early and stop by his house and tell him that everyone is praying for a quick recovery. I'll be able to get an update on how he's doing, and then I'll get that information to everyone here. If I know Juan, I'll bet he's feeling terrible about what happened and about not being here with us tonight."

Alan, seeing that this crisis was being taken care of, took this moment to see if there were any other major events taking place in anyone else's life. Lydia couldn't hold it in any longer. As she lifted her left hand into the air for everyone to see, she turned the backside of her hand out and shouted, "Luke and I are engaged!"

Everyone cheered and congratulated them. After the room had quieted down, Alan asked again, "Does anyone else have something to share before we move on?"

As he asked this question, he glanced around the room and noticed David and Sue Talcott. They were sitting in this room filled with boisterous people, yet they weren't engaging with anyone in the excitement of the coming wedding. Rather, they were quietly sitting next to each other holding hands. The Talcotts had always been the most soft-spoken couple in the study group. They were in their late 20s and definitely out of their comfort zone around outspoken and gregarious people. But even for them, this was an abnormally reserved reaction in light of the evening's disclosure. David and Sue had been attending this small group meeting more than they had the church because of a new house they had purchased over a year ago. Driving to church almost an hour each way was impractical. But coming to Alan and Mary's house was a short drive from their new house, and because they loved this small group of people so much, they continued attending.

When Alan saw a slight look of sadness on their faces, he said, "Hey David, is there anything on your heart tonight you'd like to share with everyone?"

The room got quiet as they saw David looking at Susan, his face becoming flushed at the prospect of sharing his problem. He was going to need all the support she could give him in order to tell everyone what had happened. He held her hand tightly as he struggled to get out the words that were stuck in his throat. With great difficulty, he began to speak.

"Susan and I are thinking of moving again because of a job offer I may be accepting."

"David," said Alan, a little confused at hearing this news, "how come you never told us about this? You have to admit, that's a pretty big life event to keep to yourself. Tell us about this new job . . . where it is . . . and why all the secrecy and emotion."

Susan looked at her husband and said with trembling in her voice, "Tell them, David. Just tell them."

"Okay, honey, okay. I'll tell them. Just give me a minute."

Everyone in the room sat in silence, and like most people in a setting like this, they began to think the worst, even as they prayed for the best. As they waited for David to begin, his long pause was making all their imaginations run wild. Then he began to speak, slowly at first, and with a shaky voice. But it wasn't long before he was letting it all out.

Well, first of all, the reason for my being so emotional and a little secretive tonight is not because of this decision to accept, or not accept, this new job. It's a completely different matter.

"David," said Alan with a fatherly tone in his voice—after all, he was old enough to be everyone's father—"you know you can trust all of us. We love you both and we're here to help, no matter what that might mean."

David was still holding tightly to Susan's hand and was looking around the room at their friends. He said shamefully, "To be totally honest with all of you, I'm running away from my current working conditions, and the reason is embarrassing. I know it shouldn't happen to a grown man, but I'm being bullied . . . I'm being bullied at work. I've decided that it would be easier to leave my current place of employment than to stay and continue to work under these conditions."

Hearing what was happening to David, almost everyone there had thoughts of retaliation and payback for how this gentle man was being treated.

"This isn't junior high, and I'm not in the seventh grade anymore, yet here I am being bullied again, just like back then. But this time I'm being bullied as a grown man, and I'm reacting like a 13-year-old, still running away. It's embarrassing."

"That's terrible, David," said Alan. He was irritated at the thought of those men bullying such a nice guy like David. "What happened? How did all this start? Can you go to Human Resources about this situation?"

"In short, Alan, I've tried all that. And believe it or not, because this situation is related to my religious orientation, HR actually warned me to stop trying to proselytize my fellow workers. Otherwise, I may lose my job."

The entire small group groaned loudly in disgust. "This response by HR is apparently consistent with their proselytizing policy," said David. "No matter the religion a person might belong to." Alan asked David again how this bullying had started, wondering to himself if there was a way to help.

"It all began very innocently over a lunch break when a couple of co-workers asked about my religious beliefs. I thought about how I should answer their question, and after saying a short prayer, I decided to answer directly. Because of the answer I gave, they have become relentless in harassing me. Like I said, it all started over a lunch break six months ago and I'm at the point of just wanting to run away from it all. I, we, need prayer and counsel from you all. I want to ask everyone for forgiveness for not asking for your prayers and counsel sooner."

After David had shared for several more minutes, Alan said, "First of all, let's all pledge to pray for understanding for both of them. Secondly, does anyone have a word of counsel for them right now?"

At the moment of that request, an older man, a visitor to the group, responded by saying, "It would be a privilege for me to pray to Jesus for you both. I would also like to offer to spend time counseling you through this difficult and embarrassing time in your lives. But I have to be honest with you and with everyone here tonight. I'm no saint in making this offer to David and Susan. The reason I am able and willing to help is because I went through a very similar time in my life, though it wasn't because of my faith in Christ that I was bullied. It was out of pure hatred from another man that I was bullied as an adult. So I completely understand what you're feeling and experiencing right now."

Alan followed up this newcomer's offer by saying, "Everyone, I guess this is as good a time as any to introduce our visitor to you. This is Rick, my father."

After Rick had been welcomed by everyone in the group, Alan said to him, "Dad, how come you never told me you were bullied so severely by someone in your past?"

"It's not something you broadcast to the general public, because it portrays you as a weak and feckless man. As David and Sue know very well, it's a very personal, private, and emotional event in your life. I don't think you all realize that what he just told you took a lot of courage—just the opposite of feckless. There must be something very special about this small group that would make them willing to share that kind of heartache with you. After all, it only took me hearing David's story, and a little more than 50 years of living with this hidden embarrassment, before I felt like I could share my own bullying story.

"David," said Rick, in a wise, grandfatherly way, "how about the four of us spend some time together these next few days? I can see that our stories are the same *and* different at the same time. Still, in my opinion, there won't be any need to be changing jobs or moving. You already have six months of standing up for our Jesus at your current job, so I would encourage you to not waste this investment by walking away from your mission field."

The next day, having taken off work a couple hours early, Luke drove to the house of Juan's parents to see how he was recuperating from his accident. After arriving at the house and ringing the doorbell twice, he waited several minutes for someone to answer the door. Then he saw Juan's mom through the glass coming to let him in. Luke could see that she had been crying, but she was able to hold it together long enough to say, "Oh, Luke, I'm so glad to see you. I wasn't sure if any of Juan's friends—and I mean his *real* friends, not those other so-called beer-drinking buddies of his—would come by and check up on him."

Luke stood there, looking at the collateral damage Juan's choices had caused. He wanted so much to reach out and give her a hug, but he wasn't sure how appropriate it would be. He just said quietly, "Where is he, Mrs. Oleeva? I'd like to talk with him."

"He's out back by the swimming pool. He won't talk to me, but maybe he'll talk to a friend like you."

"Was it another one of *those* accidents?" asked Luke.

Juan's mom stood there a moment and then leaned on the spine of the door, her shoulders drooping and her head down with a look of desperation on her face.

"Of course it was, Luke, and he was doing so good." She hesitated, trying to decide how much she should share about their family secrets. "There are more accidents around this house than I care to share with you right now, Luke. I don't know if I can take many more of them, and I'm not sure what to do with Juan. I know he has a serious drinking problem, but his father thinks it's just a phase and refuses to talk with him about it. Michael claims that Juan will grow out of it, just like he did, and that he will learn to handle his drinking habits on his own. Juan, of course, is listening to his father and also claims he has it under control. But anyone who spends any amount of time with him knows the truth. Poor, sweet Nita. She's not stupid. She can see what's going on but is still hanging in there. But for how long, I don't know. She must see something in Juan the rest of us can't see."

The look on her face was heartbreaking. She had two men in her life and both of them were trying to make this problem go away by ignoring it. Luke said a short prayer in his mind, asking Jesus to give Juan the courage to publicly face his problem. Then he said to Juan's mom, "You said he was out by the pool, Mrs. Oleeva?"

"Yeah, he's probably sitting in one of the deck chairs feeling sorry for himself."

"Okay, thanks. I'll go talk with him."

When Luke walked out the back patio door, he saw Juan standing at the edge of the pool with a skimmer in his right hand and his left arm in a sling. He was unsuccessfully trying to clean some leaves from the surface of the water. As Luke walked over to where Juan was standing, he said, "You know, dude, it's a lot easier to do that job with two good arms."

Juan didn't look up at his friend, knowing Luke was just trying to lighten the somber mood of the house. He went directly to the reason Luke had stopped by. "Mom told you what really happened, didn't she?" Juan continued to stare down at the pool water, not wanting to look into Luke's eyes.

Luke stood there silently, not knowing what to say. Finally, he decided truth was what Juan needed: "She didn't have to tell me a thing, Juan. As soon as I heard the story and saw Nita's face at small group last night, I knew what caused this accident, dude. I knew. And Nita knows too."

Still staring at the pool water, Juan reflected back several years and then asked, "Do you remember that pool party we had here with the whole baseball team the summer before our junior year in high school?" Juan had just dropped the skimmer, which, like his life, was floating around aimlessly with no direction or purpose. He had a blank look on his face.

"Yeah, I remember. Why do you ask?"

"Cause that's when it started. That's when all the drinking, deceit, and disappointment in myself started. A couple of the guys brought some six-packs they had taken from their parents' home bars and brought them to the party. It wasn't part of my plan to have any beer there . . . it just happened. But we all had some that day, and I loved it, Luke. I loved that taste of beer."

"Yeah, Juan, I do remember that day. Maggy and Markus were at my side when you made a monster belly flop for everyone there, and after climbing out of the pool, you finished the beer you asked me to hold for you."

"You know what's funny, Luke? Right now, standing here right in front of you, I couldn't care if I ever had another drink in my whole life. I feel like I have power and control over my decision of whether or not to have a drink. But that desire, that need, comes out of nowhere. I don't know what it is, Luke. It's like a switch is flipped in my brain telling me that it's time to have a beer, and I can't turn the switch off. And it's not just 1, 2, or 3 beers; it's 10, 12, or 15. I love the taste of it and the feeling I get from it, and I don't want to stop. I usually *don't* stop until I do something stupid or pass out."

Juan was looking directly at Luke when Luke asked, "You mean something like dislocating your collar bone?"

"Yeah, something like that."

Momentarily looking at the cement surface surrounding the pool, Luke was deciding if he would be making a confession of his own to Juan. Realizing it was time, he said, "I have to be truthful with you, Juan: it wasn't just living life that caused us to drift apart after high school. It was all your drinking that made me walk away from our friendship. I was even a little hesitant in agreeing to get together again when we ran into each other at the restaurant last year. I want to, no, I actually *need* to, apologize for not sticking with you and helping you through all this. I was wrong, Juan. I was wrong. But it's different now, and you can count on me this time. I won't be walking away from you. That is, if you want my help. If you're willing to put in the work and you really want to kick this addiction, I'll help you get through this."

Juan stood there, completely still, considering what Luke had just said and thinking about the last several years of his life. After a full minute of reflection, he said, "Don't let it bother you, Luke. I lost a lot of friends over the last four years. Honestly, until now, I never really wanted to stop, even if that meant losing another friend."

I'm so tired of it all, Luke. Why is it that everyone else is able to have one or two drinks and just stop, but I can't? I see the tears in my mom's eyes, and I'm tired of making my dad lie for me at work. And Nita . . . I'm starting to drag that beautiful girl down, but I know she won't let that happen to her. She'll leave me first, and I wouldn't blame her. Luke, I need help. I need to stop. I *want* to stop."

These two old friends just stood there, not knowing what to say or who to turn to for help. That's when Juan said, "I was thinking about your stepdad this morning. Do you think he knows someone I can talk to so I can get some help?"

"If you're really asking, I know he'll help you, Juan. But you have to make the decision to ask for help on your own—no one can do that for you. And with our Jesus at your side, just know that he is the only friend that will never walk away from you."

By this time, Juan was beginning to visibly shake at the realization that he may actually have a chance to beat this addiction.

"Juan, I think the first thing you can do to get started with your recovery is to walk back into your house and tell your mom what you have decided to do. And I'll be standing there right next to you."

Luke is right, thought Juan to himself. *It's time to get some help. It's time to face my demons.*

As Juan started walking toward the house, he stopped in front of Luke. In a moment of unveiled emotion, wanting to tell no more lies or be the creator of continual deceit, Juan looked directly into Luke's eyes, reached out his arms, and grasped him. He hugged Luke as he buried his head into his shoulder and sobbed uncontrollably. He knew he was at the end of his rope. He could no longer control the drinking on his own, and he couldn't keep lying in order to cover it up. Luke returned this hug with one of his own, wrapping both his arms around Juan's shoulders as he shed tears of his own. But these were tears of thankfulness to Jesus.

Unknown to these two friends, a third set of eyes from inside the house had joined them. Juan's mother was weeping as she participated in this celebration. They were all getting their Juan back. Luke also took that opportunity to pray to Jesus out loud, asking for Juan's addiction to be completely and utterly broken.

The graduation ceremony was simple and short, over in less than 30 minutes, which was exactly why Luke told his mother she didn't need to attend. Luke, Markus, and Cindy, along with the rest of the class, received diplomas of completion along with their builder's license. Along the way, they had made friends with others in the class, and these friends represented six other custom builders within their city. Luke saw these friendships as opportunities to become a better builder and, eventually, a better contractor.

"Mr. Cruz," said Mr. Arlyn, "can I expect to see a construction company with your name on it coming into our market soon? Our main city's population and all its suburbs have grown by eight percent in the last two years, and we will be needing a few more good contractors to build them homes. And don't forget: as long as you meet the entrance requirements, you still have an invitation to be a builder in the new subdivision we talked about last year. Those lots will be ready to build on in one year, so you had better decide if you're going to be an employee or an employer."

"That's certainly a lot to take in, Mr. Arlyn, but I still feel like I'm too young to take on that kind of responsibility. To be perfectly honest, I'm afraid of failing and disappointing everyone."

"That's why I invited Mr. Thomas Seeverson to the graduation ceremony today." Mr. Arlyn waved to the back of the room and called for Mr. Seeverson to come up and meet Luke.

"Luke Cruz, I would like to introduce Mr. Thomas Seeverson to you. He is one of the largest land developers in the western half of North America. He is also, at my request, one of the men who agreed to watch your progress in this class very closely."

Luke extended his hand and said, "It's good to meet you, Mr. Seeverson."

As he shook Mr. Seeverson's hand, Luke was wondering where this new friendship might lead. Mr. Seeverson was a large, muscular man with sandy brown hair, at least six feet four inches tall, and for being in his late 60s, he had a grip like a vice. As they continued to get acquainted, Luke discovered that he played football all the way through college. Apparently he was a dominating force on the field, and he carried that tenacity with him into the business world.

After several more minutes of talking, Luke, not wanting to monopolize his time, said once more, "It's been wonderful meeting you, Mr. Seeverson, but I'd better let you go so you have time to visit with the others in the room."

"Don't worry about the others, Mr. Cruz. The reason I came here today was to meet you, not them. And I'm glad to have finally met the young man that has Hank Arlyn and Matthew Middlefield so excited about the next generation of home builders."

At hearing that statement, Luke had to work hard to cover up what he thought was a look of astonishment. He was already aware that Mr. Arlyn was impressed with his coursework and design plans, but hearing that Matthew Middlefield was quietly impressed with his design skills was a complete shock to him. He was equally taken off guard by the fact that Mr. Seeverson was also aware of Matthew's opinion of him.

"Mr. Middlefield," said Luke with a noticeable quiver in his voice, "is excited about me? What is he excited about?"

"He's excited about your innovative home designs, of course. I've been keeping an eye on your design progress since Mr. Arlyn first showed them to me almost two years ago. I have also spoken to Matthew several times over the last two years about your exceptional progress, and I encouraged him to give you more time on the CAD software in his office. I made this suggestion so that you might be helped in developing what I see as exceptional, God-given talent. Matthew also indicated that he would allow you to design one of his next model homes, so I'm looking forward to seeing a completed Cruz model home soon, be it with Middlefield Homes or your own company."

Luke was surprised again by Mr. Seeverson's last statement. "Well, thank you, Mr. Seeverson. I'll keep working on more designs for your new development. You wouldn't happen to have a business card, would you?"

"I sure do, Luke, but let's do one more exchange. I'd like to have my picture taken with you so I can prove to everyone that I knew you before you became a big shot. And where's Markus Middlefield? I understand he took this course and graduated with you. I'd like to have him in the photograph as well, if that's okay with you?"

Luke immediately began looking around the room for Markus as he continued to talk. "Of course it's okay, as long as I can get a picture of my own standing with the man who is going to give me my start."

"You've got a deal, Mr. Cruz. Now go find Markus Middlefield and let's get these memory pictures taken!"

After finding Markus, they both exchanged contact information and took the photos on their phones. Mr. Seeverson put on a smile that looked just like the salesman smile Matthew Middlefield always used when closing a deal. Luke wondered to himself whether that smile was typical of all salespeople, or if these two men shared a "big smile gene" in their DNA. After the photos had been taken, Mr. Seeverson said his goodbyes and left for another appointment.

When Markus saw that Mr. Seeverson had left and Luke was finally alone, he walked over to where Luke was getting a cup of punch and said, "Luke, you don't really have any idea who you were just talking to and taking pictures with, do you?"

"Sure I do. That was Thomas Seeverson. See, I have his card right here. You saw him give it to me, remember?"

Still believing that Luke had no clue as to the kind of influence or money that Thomas Seeverson possessed, Markus said, "That guy and my dad have known each other for years. He's the man who decides which builders are allowed to build their homes in his housing developments and which ones aren't. Basically, he decides who's going to make a lot of money and who's just going to get by. I know for a fact that my dad has made millions off deals they have put together through the years. So why was he talking to you and Mr. Arlyn? How did you get that kind of introduction?"

"It's not a big deal, Markus. He told Mr. Arlyn that he liked some of my home designs and wanted to meet me. But is it okay if we talk about this later? It's getting late and I've gotta run right now and see how Juan is doing at his first AA meeting. I promised him I would go through this rehabilitation process with him, and I won't be deserting Juan like I did two years ago."

Markus stood there for a slight moment before saying, "Okay, no problem, bro. But I just had a thought about our brother Juan."

"What kind of a thought would that be?"

"Do you think he would mind if I came along to support him as well?"

"What a wonderful offer, Markus! I don't believe he would mind at all. Now, let's go see our brother."

A week later, Luke was driving to church on Saturday morning. Lydia had recently joined the choir and had asked him to pick her up from practice. She had a better than fair singing voice and was looking for a place to use this talent, so she joined the church choir and was loving it. On that Saturday morning, Lydia got a ride to church from one of the other girls in the choir because she and Luke were going to watch another MLB game that afternoon.

Luke didn't know how she kept all the statistics straight in her mind, but she had a superior memory when it came to baseball analytics. She loved to follow statistics like a professional analyst. As a result, Luke spoke very carefully when he started quoting baseball stats of any kind. The fear of being corrected by his girlfriend was acceptable to him; he had gotten used to it. But what Luke had purposely failed to do for his friends was to inform them about her exceptional giftedness in this area. The way this sweet girl would gently correct their mistakes would, without fail, make him smile and laugh. Of course, it didn't do much for the confidence of the guys who tried to go toe-to-toe with her in quoting baseball statistics. No matter how much they thought they knew, they didn't know more than she did. But it did make for good entertainment when they tried.

Walking into the main worship center, with the choir still singing, Luke was pleasantly surprised to see Markus singing with them. He sat down in one of the chairs in the last row of the sanctuary, and, closing his eyes, focused on the words of the songs, allowing their message to fill his heart.

Lydia always claimed to possess a simple choir voice, nothing special. She said she wasn't a soloist but that she could sing on key. But then Luke heard another voice, different from all the others, a voice strong and pure. He continued to listen and finally zeroed in on it. It was that raspy sound that gave it away. He couldn't believe it—it was Markus he was hearing! *His voice lessons must really be helping,* thought Luke, *because he was much better today than what I heard in my truck several months ago.* It was then that the choir director motioned for the others to begin singing more softly while Markus opened his mouth and began to sing a solo. There it was again. You couldn't help but listen to him sing the words of that love song to Jesus . . .

> I come to the garden alone,
> While the dew is still on the roses;
> And the voice I hear falling on my ear,
> The Son of God discloses.
>
> And He walks with me, and He talks with me,
> And He tells me I am His own,
> And the joy we share as we tarry there,
> None other has ever known.

Luke wasn't sure if it was his voice, the meaning of the words to the song, the accompanying music, or a combination of all three, but when Markus raised the last note to heaven, half the choir continued to sing quietly in the background while the other half sat quietly in awe at what they were hearing. After Markus had finished singing the last few words, the entire choir turned toward him and began asking questions about his voice. He tried, in a most humble way, to explain that he didn't know where that voice had come from; he was just as surprised as they were. Seeing that it would be almost impossible to continue with their practice, the choir director decided to end that morning's rehearsal and dismiss the group.

After saying goodbye to several of the other choir members, Markus made his way down to where Luke and Lydia were talking. Luke said, "I'm going to guess that those must have been quite the personal concerts in your shower as you were growing up. Did your parents just ignore what they heard? Unbelievable, just plain unbelievable, Markus. You have a fantastic voice!"

Markus honestly thought nothing about the way he sang. "Ah, come on, Luke. All I did was turn up the volume on the stereo in my room and sing along with the music when I took a shower. My parents could never tell the difference between my singing and the singing coming from the radio. It worked out perfectly—I could get some singing practice in while showering. As far as this choir practice is concerned, I just turned up the volume again. Maggy saw what I was doing and did the same thing. I bet you never heard her sing either. She's quite good too. Anyway, I haven't really sung anything for the last couple of years until I sang that song that meant so much to me over the phone for you. That is, except for the audition I had with the choir director. He heard me sing earlier this week. That's why I was singing that solo. After hearing me sing, he asked me to memorize that song and sing it today to see if it would work for the Sunday morning service."

Luke just shook his head and said, "Well, it certainly sounded to me as though you turned up the volume again, only this time you weren't in the shower. I'll say it again: it was amazing to hear you singing, Markus. I really enjoyed it."

Markus stood there, silently trying to decide if he should share a little more about his singing talent. "Luke, do you remember a few months back when I told you I was taking voice lessons?"

"Yeah, I remember. What about it?"

"Well, I may have a pretty good voice, but without my voice teacher, I'd still be pretty rough around the singing edges. A couple of weeks ago, my voice coach began showing me how to sing from my diaphragm. She said if I could master using my diaphragm, I would get more power and volume from my voice. And it worked. Did you hear that last note I sang? It was crazy, wasn't it? I actually surprised myself at what came out of my mouth."

The choir director came up to Markus and politely interrupted his conversation with Luke. He asked to speak with Markus for a few minutes, and when Markus returned, Luke said, "Is the world tour all planned now?"

"Yeah, real funny, Luke. Can we go outside and talk about something that happened at the office yesterday afternoon?"

As the three of them walked out the front door of the church, Luke could see Markus's demeanor changing with every step he took. Not wanting to wait any longer, Luke said, "You look pretty upset, Markus. What happened?"

Markus was pacing back and forth by their cars. His arms hung down, his fists were clenched, and his jaw muscle was flexing. "You know John, the owner of Precision Painting, right?"

"Yes, he runs a great company. Your dad and mom should count their blessings that they have such a talented and honest man like John working for them. I also know that his wife is fighting cancer, so it's a little harder for him to get to all the jobsites because he has to take her to her treatments. I've been working with a couple of his foremen and everything is working great. Why? Is there something wrong with John?"

Markus bit down hard, flexing his jaw muscles as he tried to control his anger. He knew what Luke's reaction would be, but he needed to tell him anyway. "John is sort of okay, but I'll give you the condensed version of what happened. My mom called me into the main office yesterday just before lunch and then sat me down and told me to wait there. Then she called my dad in Washington, D.C., using video conferencing. She had me sit in a chair next to her so that my dad could see both of us. My dad just jumped into what he wanted to talk about and what was about to happen. There wasn't even a courtesy greeting. He started out by saying, "Markus, it's been almost two years since our Aspen ski trip when you first indicated to me and your mother that you wanted to be president of Middlefield Homes. You have already taken the first step in making that happen by obtaining your builder's license. Today you will be taking your second step in your journey to become president. What is about to happen is going to be the first of many important business lessons you will need to learn. Once you learn them and have made them a part of your character, you are going to have a very good chance of passing this company on to the next generation of Middlefields. Today's lesson is going to be courtesy of John Peterson, our painting contractor.

"That's when a terrible feeling came over me. It quickly became apparent that he was going to use John to teach me how to conduct business the Middlefield way. So whatever John thought he was going to get that day wasn't going to happen. John just didn't know it yet. John was nothing to my dad but a plaything, a pawn. Like you said a while ago, Luke, just a tool to be used until it has no more usefulness. I felt terrible, and I couldn't do anything to stop it. He kept describing in morbid detail what he would be saying to John and how he would respond to John's pleas for help and understanding. My dad was literally smirking the whole time he was speaking. I honestly believe he enjoyed talking about this. I can't believe I'm even going to say this, but I almost get the feeling he's possessed by something. Nobody in their right mind acts like that."

Luke and Lydia stood there, motionless, waiting to hear what happened next. At the same time, they didn't want to hear what Markus was going to tell them.

"Now, just so you know, the reason he was coming to the office was because he had requested to be paid earlier on some work he had completed. My dad just kept talking, already knowing how every aspect of this meeting was going to play out. Then my dad said to me, 'Pay close attention to how I handle this meeting and this subcontractor, Markus. In the future, as you gain more experience, you will be the one handling these meetings, and you have to look out for the interests of Middlefield Homes, not the interests of our contractors.'

"My dad, who was looking me directly in the eye, spoke with a sound in his voice I had never heard before. 'Today, Markus, I am going to crush John Peterson's spirit, and you have the privilege of watching it happen. He will learn to never ask for anything that has not already been agreed to, no matter the circumstances. And you, Markus, have the DNA in your heart and soul to ascend to the same great heights I have attained. Watch and learn so that may soon follow in your father's footsteps.'

"Hearing those words coming from his mouth made me nauseous. Honestly, I almost threw up. I couldn't respond to my dad, and my mom sat there saying nothing, as if what my dad had just said was business as usual. It was at that very moment that I knew it was time to start searching for a different occupation, a vocation that would give meaning to my life. I needed to find something other than construction, and I could no longer be under the influence of this man I call 'Dad.'"

Luke and Lydia could not have imagined what Matthew did next as they continued to listen to Markus's story.

"My dad had just finished this opening statement when the secretary beeped in. My mom answered, "What is it, Jennifer?"

"John with Precision Painting is here for your noon meeting."

She put her secretary on hold and said to my dad, "Are you ready for the meeting? John is here."

To which he said, "Let's get this over with. I've already spent too much time on this matter, and I have other more important meetings to attend."

My mom then took her secretary off hold and said, "Jennifer, send John in please."

"John walked into the office carrying a folder with some paperwork in it. He was wearing his painter pants. You know, Luke, for being in his late 50s, he's in pretty good shape, and he wears his painter pants every day, just in case one of his crews needs a little help. I've seen him work a full day with his younger painters and actually push them to keep up with him. He's a great guy, which made my parent's actions even more disgraceful.

"He sat down on the chair next to me, shook my hand, and said, 'Markus, I didn't know you would be here for this meeting. What a pleasant surprise.'

"I really believe he felt I would be an advocate for him during the meeting. My mom, knowing how the next 15 minutes were about to play out, sweetly asked if he would like a mineral water or a cup of coffee before they got started. John politely said, 'No, thank you,' and the meeting began. My mom informed John that Matthew was on a video call and that he would be conducting the meeting.

"My mom then turned the monitor toward John, and my dad started out the meeting by saying, 'John, I understand that you're here looking for some money. I've taken a look at all the home closings your company is involved with, and we're current on all payouts.

I don't know what you're looking for. Can you help me understand what it is that you want?' John responded by saying, 'I'm sorry, Matthew, didn't Elizabeth tell you that I was looking to be paid on the two model homes we are holding for you? The big model is $45,000 and the smaller one is $38,000.'

"Then my dad said, 'No, John, there's no need to be sorry. Elizabeth did mention that to me. I was just confused because our contract stipulates that you will hold the total cost of painting the model homes for two years, at the end of which time you will complete a final touch-up and then be paid. John, it hasn't been two years, so we can't help you. If I started ignoring all the agreements in the contracts I signed, I'd be out of business. You have to understand that some people believe that contracts are written to be broken, but I adhere to the belief that they are written to maintain order and to remind us of what we all have agreed to do or not do.'

"It was at that moment that John broke down. Looking directly at my dad, he said in a shaky voice, 'I know you've been in Washington, D.C., since your election, and I don't know if you have heard, but my wife is extremely ill. I'm not asking for an early payment for myself. I'm asking for my wife, Matthew. I'm here asking for Karen. The three months of chemotherapy didn't work. Surgery is our last hope, and it has already been scheduled for her. I'm asking for these payouts because the insurance company is requiring some large payments on our deductible. Without these payments, they say they'll postpone the surgery and all future treatments. Matthew, this surgery will save her life. I wouldn't have come to you if it wasn't this important. You have to believe me—it'll save her life, Matthew!'

"I saw John take a clean rag out of his back pocket and wipe the perspiration from his face and the tears from his eyes. 'I'm only six months from the two-year payout. It's for my wife, Matthew. It's for my wife, not for me.'

"I saw John think for a moment, and then he went on to say something that my dad really didn't like. 'Matthew, you know that I've been working for you for 18 years, and I have helped Middlefield Homes get past some difficult financial times. Can't you return these favors and make an exception just this once? I'm sure if you explained the circumstances to everyone in the company, and to the other contractors, they would understand.'

"I was right: I could see in my dad's face that he didn't appreciate John bringing up those previous times that he was the one who had received help. In typical Matthew Middlefield fashion, he ignored what John had said and returned that statement with one of his own, which made John get up and leave. He looked at John with the slightest hint of a smile on his face and said, 'Can't you draw on your line of credit?' The last thing I heard my mom say after John left was, 'What a pathetic man, crying over money.'

"Luke, I honestly think my dad gained a certain amount of pleasure at treating John the way he did. It was almost evil what I saw him do."

Markus hesitated before speaking again, wanting to make sure what he was about to say wouldn't be misunderstood. "I said this a few minutes ago, and I'll say it again: I can't work for my parents, and I certainly don't want to become anything like my dad. After what I saw yesterday, I'm absolutely planning on leaving the construction industry altogether. I just don't know when I'll make that move or what to do with my life."

"Markus, Luke," said Lydia, "that's an incredibly heart-breaking and unbelievable story. It makes me angry just thinking about it. I feel like slapping your mom across her face and punching your dad right in his mouth!"

"Let's cool down, Lydia. Take off the boxing gloves. Violence isn't the answer, and you know that in your heart."

Lydia's response to Luke was swift and to the point: "Who said anything about boxing gloves?"

"Come on, Lydia, you know better than that."

"Yeah, Luke, I know, I know. But isn't there anything you guys can do for John?" Like Markus, Lydia had clenched fists at the ends of her straightened arms.

"Not really," said Luke. "At times like this, all we can do is pray. And I think that's what we should do right now."

The next day after church at the Warez home, Luke, Lydia, and her father were sitting in the living room with laptops humming. They were carefully filling out the required state and federal documents needed to incorporate a business for Luke. Based on the revelations shared by Markus the previous day, it became abundantly clear why John and the others didn't want to work for the Middlefields any longer. Hearing that terrible story made it easier for Luke to take the next step in his working career. He had decided to start down the path of self-employment. Having seen an example of how *not* to treat the people who work for you, he was determined to treat anyone who would work for him, including subcontractors, better than his current employer treated them. Having a soon-to-be wife and a father-in-law who were accountants was a benefit as he took on the task of creating, maintaining, and building a business.

"Okay, Luke," said Mr. Warez, "here's the big question, the answer to which will define you for decades to come."

Luke wasn't expecting such a serious question when he decided to incorporate a construction company. "I have no idea what you're talking about, Mr. Warez, so tell me, what's this big question I need to answer?"

Mr. Warez sat back in his chair, knowing Luke wouldn't have an answer to his question. "Okay, my young business owner, here it is: what do you want to name your company?"

To say that Luke was not ready for that question would be an understatement. He just sat quietly, contemplating both the question and how he would answer.

"I don't know," said Luke with a puzzled look on his face. "I've thought about that question for a little while, but I haven't come up with anything yet."

Mr. Warez had seen that bewildered look before in the eyes of past and current clients. He knew that if he gave Luke some options to consider, he would find a name.

"Well, from my experience, people name their companies after themselves—a family member, a city, a location, or some object that is very special to them. Does that help at all?"

"Actually, Mr. Warez, it does. I don't know why I didn't think of it before. I'd like to call the company Rosewood Custom Homes. Yep, it rolls right off the tongue, don't you think? I love it."

"Rosewood Custom Homes it is," said Mr. Warez. They all sat there watching Mr. Warez fill in the required box with the chosen name. "I'm going to ask you one last time, Luke: are you sure you want to do this? Because once we register your name and the name of the company with the federal and state governments, it's final. Anyone can look up the information on these application forms, including your current employer, Matthew Middlefield. You will also be legally obligated to file tax returns with both entities."

"Yes, I'm sure I want to do this. I'm ready for the challenge of self-employment, Mr. Warez."

"And you, Lydia, are you prepared to guide and direct Luke in all his accounting decisions? Are you willing to put in the work and effort needed to learn the answers to his questions so that you can be 100% confident in all your advice and recommendations?"

"What's going on with all the forever-type questions, Dad? We're not marrying this company, just incorporating it."

Mr. Warez chuckled at his daughter's youthful ignorance. "Oh yes you are! Owning a company is like a marriage . . . like a marriage that births a child that is always growing and changing, causing both irritation and joy. And it won't move out of the house until you file the last tax return and officially shut it down! It will always be there, right next to you; always in your thoughts, sitting next to you on your vacations; attending all your children's activities; it will be with you on all your dates; it will keep you awake at night; and it will always be demanding your time."

"Alright, Dad. I get it, I get it. Yes, I accept those responsibilities."

After spending a couple hours completing all the required paperwork, Lydia asked Luke, "Well, Mr. Business Owner, now that this part of starting your company is finished, what's next?"

Luke, now more relaxed because all the paperwork and filings were complete, leaned back on the soft brown leather couch, reached for Lydia's hand, and said, "First, I'm going to meet with Ricardo's business attorney and ask him what legal matters I should be aware of as I move forward. Then I'm going to meet with Cindy's dad about building me a website. I was also really hoping that you would go with me to these meetings."

All Lydia could think of at that moment was, "I hope the longer he's in business, the better he gets at reading body language, because he sure didn't read me at all."

"I thought you'd never ask. Of course I'll go with you."

Another month had come and gone, and it was time for everyone in their small group to get together at Alan's house again. Unlike most of their previous arrivals, this time Luke and Lydia were on time. Actually, it was Luke who made it a point not to be the last to arrive or the last to hear any breaking news concerning anyone in their group. But to their amazement, though they were only 15 minutes early, Luke and Lydia were the first to knock and enter. It actually worked out great, because they had a chance to talk more with Alan's father, who happened to be there that night. Whenever his father was in town on business, he would always spend a couple days at Alan's home.

"Tell me, Mr. Reid, and I know it's a very broad question, but I like asking it to people who are more seasoned and mature in years. My grandpa taught me to learn from those who are older and wiser than me. The question is this: how have you spent the life God gave you?"

"You're right, Luke. That's about as wide open a question as can be asked of any person. I'll give you a quick answer since the others will be arriving soon and I don't want to take time away from the group or the study."

Mr. Reed thought for a minute, trying to determine where to begin his story. "Yes, okay, I know where I should begin my story. What do you say we start when I became a believer in Jesus? I was a teenager when I first believed the story told to me about Jesus and who he is. The next biggest stage in my life came when high school was over and I joined the military for two years. Next, I got married and started working with companies that were involved in computer technology development. It turned out that I was a computer-coding nerd and didn't know it. Over the last five years, I and three other senior-aged friends started our own little software company. Throughout my entire life, regardless of my successes or failures, I never stopped living for Jesus. It didn't matter what was given to me or taken from me, or what obstacles appeared on the path I was traveling."

It was then that several knocks and voices were heard coming from the entry of the house. Luke looked over to see who had arrived and saw Juan and Nita coming toward him.

"Excuse us, Mr. Reid, but we need to say hi to a very special friend who just walked in."

"You go ahead, Luke. And what do you say we stop the formalities—just call me Rick."

As Luke was turning toward Juan, he replied to Rick, "Okay, I'll do that. I'd like to finish our conversation before you have to leave town again."

Then, turning to Juan, he said, "It's great to see you back here again, but why didn't you tell me you were coming the other day when I saw you? It has been six weeks since you were with us last, and I could have told everyone you were coming. Nita, you seem to be in a good mood tonight. Is it a safe guess that a big part of that excitement is having Juan here with you?"

"Yes, I am, Luke. You can blame me for Juan not telling you he was coming to the group tonight. I didn't want to put any pressure on him if he wasn't ready to see everyone again. You have no idea how much Juan has changed. What no one realizes is that with everything Juan has done to beat this addiction in the last two months, he has given me an even better version of the Juan I first met almost one year ago."

She said this as she held his arm tightly and rested her head on his shoulder.

"Guys," said Juan to Luke and Lydia, "can we do some catching up after the small group is over? I need to talk with Alan before we get started."

"No problem, Juan. You go ahead. It's great to have you back with us."

Juan went over to where Alan was standing and spoke with him privately for a few minutes. Afterwards, he made his way over to where Nita was saving him a seat. Alan, in his typical loud voice, got everyone's attention and asked for silence.

"Hey guys, as I'm sure you all can see, one of our brothers has returned to us after being gone for almost two months."

At that point, everyone welcomed Juan back. After the room quieted down again, Alan continued: "Juan asked me a few minutes ago if he could share with you all what has been happening in his life these last two months. Of course, I told him that is exactly what this small group is all about. Juan, you have the floor."

Juan received a strong, loving look of support from Nita, as all eyes now focused on him. Sitting up and forward in his chair, he folded his hands together and then began to speak. "Thanks, Alan. Well, as everyone can see, I'm back, and it feels wonderful. I'd like to start by saying that I am a sinful and broken man. I also need to confess to you that I have been living a life of lies and deceit in front of you these last six months. I'm Juan Oleeva, but not the Juan Oleeva that you think you know. You wouldn't recognize me if you were to follow me and watch all my daily and nightly activities. I have been living two different lives for years now. In the process, I have lost a lot of really good friends. At the same time, I have gained just as many friends who have been a bad influence. Let me get to the point. First of all, I know this is not an AA meeting, but I need to introduce myself . . . the real me."

Then came a long moment of silence as Juan turned his head to look around the entire living room, briefly stopping to look into the eyes of each person there. With a mixture of humility and confidence, he said, "Hi, my name is Juan, and I'm an alcoholic. With the help of Jesus, and the help of you all, I plan to stay sober for the rest of my life, one day at a time. I came here tonight to confess my sin to you all publicly, to ask you for forgiveness and patience in my desire for sobriety, and to ask you to give me tough but loving counsel when it's needed."

Before he could take a breath and continue, everyone in the room stood, clapping and cheering. They gave Juan words of encouragement and affirmation, and they told him they would be available whenever he needed help. Everyone came over to hug him.

After the room had quieted down and everyone had taken their seats, Juan continued speaking. "I know it's not possible, but I wish my grandpa on my dad's side of the family, who is deceased now, had sent me the kind of letters that Luke is receiving from his grandfather. You see, my Grandpa Vic was also an alcoholic for many years and was able to beat the addiction. It would have been a real gift to hear from him personally as to how he defeated his own alcoholic demons. That's all I wanted to share, guys. Alan, I'd also like to thank you for giving a young drunk some time to get all these sins out in the open tonight."

As soon as Juan had finished, everyone stood up again, clapping for him and giving him more hugs of encouragement. This time, all of them were wiping their eyes dry as they sat back down.

"I've got a quick question for you, Juan," said Alan. "What kind of letters were you referring to when you mentioned Luke and his grandfather?"

Juan looked at Luke and said, "What is that service called again, Luke?"

"It's called Legacy Letters."

"That's what I thought you were going to say."

"Then why'd you ask me?"

"Because I wanted to make sure that the service you were talking about was the same service I was thinking about. I thought it only made sense to clarify my statement before I introduced everyone to the one who was responsible for creating that software to begin with. Dad, you have the floor."

It was Friday, June 1, and Luke had gotten up early to watch his grandpa's most recent Legacy Letter.

"Looks like I'll be listening to your words of wisdom first thing this morning, Grandpa. Like I told you during your last couple of letters, I have a new girlfriend. I love her so much that I had to ask her to marry me—and she said yes! Yep, that's right. I'm getting married soon, Grandpa, and you don't know how much I wish you could be there with me. Anyway, I'll be at Lydia's house this evening for my birthday, so that's why I'll be listening to your letter this morning. One more thing before we get started, and I know you can't really hear me, but I have to say it out loud anyway. A couple of days ago, I met the man who actually created the Legacy Letter software and service. Again, I know you can't hear me, but I just had to say it out loud before starting your next letter."

It was then that he touched the LL button and once again saw his grandpa on the computer screen.

"Hey, Luke, happy 20th birthday! This is a big one. My prayer and hope for you lately has been that you are following the promptings of the Holy Spirit of God, not just with outward action but with an internal desire to honor God. When I was your age, I had no plan or counsel from anyone concerning the decisions in my life. I just did what I thought was good based on my own opinions. I was only looking at what was best for me in the moment. I had not considered the eternal consequences of my actions or thoughts. Of course, I couldn't think like that because I wasn't a true follower of Christ at that time. In life, Luke, some of the paths we begin to walk down are by personal choice. Others we are forced to take due to circumstances beyond our control or understanding. For example, I chose, in my youth and ignorance, to walk down the path of military enlistment. If there was a purpose for this decision, I don't know what it was. On the other hand, I did not choose to leave the path of military service; that decision was forced on me. Later in life, as I matured, I finally recognized it as divine intervention. God had chosen me, and I didn't even know it. He brought about changes in my life that made his calling irresistible. In sharing these thoughts with you, I am counseling you to be very aware of every action you take and every reaction from others in response to your actions. Every word you speak and every decision you make has consequences.

"In finishing this letter, and in thinking back to my time as a young man, fresh out of the military and trying to figure out what to do next, I can honestly say today that God was watching over me even then. I don't recall how it all came together, but events in my life brought me down another path—to the steps of the church. This where I was introduced to Jesus and where I put my trust in him. Looking back at that time, what I once saw as a 'chance' meeting was a gift from Jesus. The gift I'm talking about is the moment I met your grandmother at that same church.

"Here are two proverbs and one psalm to keep in mind as you ponder these things.

> Let your eyes look directly forward,
>   and your gaze be straight before you.
> Ponder the path of your feet;
>   then all your ways will be sure.
> Do not swerve to the right or to the left;
>   turn your foot away from evil. (Proverbs 4:25–27)

> For a man's ways are before the eyes of the LORD,
>   and he ponders all his paths. (Proverbs 5:21)

> Let the words of my mouth and the meditation of my heart

be acceptable in your sight,
O LORD, my rock and my redeemer. (Psalm 19:14)

"I was chosen by God to be part of his family, just as you have been, Luke. And we both freely accepted his calling. With this acceptance comes a responsibility to honor him with every action, word, and thought we have.

"God has graciously kept a loving eye on me for my entire life, correcting and protecting me when needed. Keep in mind one very important distinction as you live your life, Luke: God will make corrections in your life *for your good,* because he loves you, not for his own entertainment. Don't accept any teaching that says differently. Show him honor in everything you do with the life he has given you. It's time for me to go, Luke. See you in a couple of months."

Chapter 10

Set Your Mind on The Spirit

Luke was pouring himself a cup of coffee when his phone rang. It made the sound of a small bell, which told him he had received a text message. It was Markus. "Running a little late . . . be there in 20."

Luke picked up his coffee and walked to his grandpa's recliner. "It'll always be 'your chair,' Grandpa, as long as I'm alive," he whispered quietly to himself as he sat down. In his mind, he could clearly see his grandpa sitting in the chair.

"This is going to be a good morning," thought Luke to himself while taking that first sip of coffee. The girls had decided to spend the day shopping for wedding-related items for Cindy, and they didn't want the guys tagging along.

Luke had no idea what that meant or what they would be buying. He was just glad not to be going along. He would have a day to relax and spend some "guy time" talking with Markus— throwing the football back and forth, playing catch with a baseball, or, even better, throwing some horseshoes. After all, in two weeks Markus would be married, and it would be Luke's turn three months later. Luke had no doubt that Lydia would be challenging him—in her sweet way—when it came to horseshoes.

Waiting for Markus to arrive, Luke's mind wandered back a few weeks to the Tuesday evening when that incredible revelation was made known to him at Alan's home.

Luke remembered how stunned he was to be standing right in front of the man who had created Legacy Letters, a website that had been providing him with so much comfort, guidance, and counsel over the last two years. When he found out who Rick was, he was quite literally rendered speechless at that revelation. It was such a long and awkward pause by Luke that evening that Rick finally asked, "Luke, is there something wrong? Are you okay?"

"Yeah, yeah, Rick. I'm okay. My mind just flashed back four years to when my Grandpa Gus first heard a radio commercial for your service. It only took him a few hours to see the value in it, and the value was primarily for me. It was at that moment he decided to use it to counsel me through life's events in the years following his death."

"One radio commercial in this market four years ago? Wow. Oddly enough, I remember that. It was a one-week advertising commitment on an oldies station for our target audience, the baby boomer generation and their parents. My partners and I had agreed that if we received positive results in this market, and three other target markets, we would roll out Legacy Letters to all of North America. And here we are today."

Still thinking about what Luke had just told him, Rick offered Luke a little business insider information.

"Luke, you probably don't know this, but I never get much of an opportunity to find out how our clients are using our services. Unless, of course, they personally tell us. It's those legal privacy laws, you know. The only information we have access to is the client's name, their contact information, and a limited amount of information about them and the person they're sending the letters to. But I'd like to say thank you for telling me how your grandfather is using our service. What a wonderful idea! I never would have thought of that. I can see that I'll be suggesting a new radio commercial campaign during our next marketing meeting."

"I appreciate those words of kindness about my grandpa. I only wish you could have met him. But seriously, all I have to say to you, Rick, is thank you for listening to the prompting of our Jesus. This is such a wonderful service and gift to me, and I'm guessing to tens of thousands of others who are also using your service. It's such a novel idea that it makes me wonder why no one had thought of it before you. So, just out of curiosity, if you don't mind me asking, how did you do it? How did you come up with the idea to begin with? What was your inspiration?"

Rick hesitated briefly, trying to decide if he should share this personal story. But it didn't take long for him to determine that the business inspiration was pretty well-known among most of his friends; it was certainly well-known to the family that benefited from his first, and rather crude, attempt with this service. So Rick began telling the story.

"It was actually a very sad day that sparked the idea in my mind. I was sitting alone at the bedside of a very old and dear friend who was dying. I had the honor to be with him when, just after midnight, he passed away. I had been helping his family by taking a shift sitting at his side. When the time came, I didn't want him to pass alone. I was the only one in his room when for no apparent reason or medical explanation, he simply woke up, stared directly into my eyes, and said, 'Hi, Rick. How's it going?' It was truly an odd event. He was speaking to me as if that day was no different than the thousands that had preceded it. And then he started talking. He had to have known that he was going to die, because for the next ten minutes, he lucidly and coherently shared some last-minute words of love, encouragement, and instruction he wanted me to pass along to his family members. He died within two minutes of his final words. While the hospital staff was caring for his body, I quickly found some paper and a pen to write down what he had said and to whom he had said it. It was in the middle of writing down these words that I realized that I was helping a now-deceased man speak to those whom he loved. It was at that moment I felt God graciously giving me the idea for this service and this business. That was five years ago."

"Wow, that's amazing, Rick. But now I'm even more perplexed at what you have done. Before you developed the business plan for Legacy Letters, had you ever started any kind of business? Or was this your first attempt at self-employment?" Luke wanted to know how Rick had made it all work.

"No, I never had a desire to own my own company. I was always employed by a large corporation, I and was content with that position. But I knew I couldn't ignore this wonderful and unique gift of an idea. I knew at that very moment that I had to do something, so I called three of my old colleagues, all of whom were retired and completely bored with their lives. They were closing in on 70 years of age and looking for something to do. I told them the story I just shared with you and then pitched my idea for this service. They all jumped on board with me, not really caring if we would be successful or not. They were once again excited to have a reason to get out of bed each morning. What you need to know about getting old, Luke, is that by the time I made those calls to those men, they were all several years into retirement, and they had found out that retirement wasn't what they thought it would be. Each of them told me they were looking for something more fulfilling to do with these so-called golden years. It was pretty simple, Luke. They were bored, and what they needed was meaning in their lives again. This service was going to be that meaning. One of my old buddies commented that you could only play so many rounds of golf before all the courses started to look the same. A second friend was tired of looking for trinkets with a metal detector on the beaches of Florida while wearing a Speedo. Sorry about that visual, Luke."

Luke smiled and said, "Don't worry about it, Rick. Having that visual in my brain will help me to never consider retiring." They both laughed and then Rick continued.

"What helped us succeed in this venture was that we all knew how to code. One of my friends was quite good at marketing, and another was a born salesman. Each one of us brought vital talents besides coding to this small upstart company."

"Wow, what a story. If you hadn't gotten into technology all those years ago, we wouldn't be standing here today."

"Oh no, Luke, my story goes back even further than working for companies like Univac in those early days of technology."

"You mean there's more?"

Rick looked at his son as if to say, *Is it okay? Can I keep on going?* Alan responded by saying, "Go ahead, Dad. I haven't heard all of this story myself, so I'm just as curious as Luke is."

"Okay, then, let's start this story when I was in middle school. I was so curious in those days to learn how mechanical and electrical things worked that I was unintentionally breaking or ruining quite a few of my mother's household appliances. And in those days, they weren't cheap. If my father were still alive, he would tell you that I was great at taking things apart, but not so great at putting them back together again."

"I have many things to thank our God for, but having a father who was a patient and insightful man is right at the top of the list. When my father saw that I had an aptitude for this type of work, he came to the conclusion that I wouldn't stop tinkering with the household appliances. He knew the best way for me to expand my understanding of how electronics worked—without ruining his kitchen appliances!— was to go to garage sales and flea markets. He could purchase used items for pennies and then let me take them apart to discover how they worked. If he were alive today, he would tell you that he had one of two choices when it came to my inquisitive mind: he could either purchase garage sale items for me to tinker with, or he could watch me destroy those same items in our house. He chose the garage sales."

"Boy, Dad, you must have loved it when you saw me end up in computer graphics."

"You have no idea, Alan. Although, I have to admit, the thought of tearing apart an old blender or two with you does make me wonder what might have happened if we had walked that road together."

Luke couldn't get enough of Rick's story. It was like getting a real live Legacy Letter that you could talk with. Rick continued: "But enough of my youthful antics. Let's get back to the story that will answer your question. Several years later, when it came time to graduate from high school, I decided to enlist in the military. They had all the best electronic and mechanical equipment to play with. You know what I'm talking about—big boys and their big toys. That was in 1958. It turned out that the military was not going to be all the fun and good times I dreamed it would be. In particular, there was a guy in our platoon that made my life so miserable that I decided not to re-enlist when my two-year hitch was up. I figured if that was the kind of man I would have to work with for a career, I wanted nothing to do with the military. It turned out, to my surprise, and to my benefit, that if I hadn't left the military, I never would have found my home in software development. So if it hadn't been for that jerk of a man in my platoon, I would have never developed the skills or connections to create Legacy Letters."

At hearing this portion of the story, Luke grew very quiet. He was thinking about another man who had a similar but different story. He continued to listen quietly.

"As the years went by, I began to realize that my path in life was similar to that of Joseph in the Old Testament. It was the actions of someone else that placed me on the path I needed to travel. To paraphrase Joseph's famous saying, "What man intended for evil, God intended for good." That comes into my mind every so often. If I ever ran into that man again, I would hold out my hand and shake his. I would thank him for what he had done *for* me not what he did *to* me."

For a second time, Luke was silent. There were too many similarities for this not to be the same story that his grandfather had recently shared. After composing himself, Luke said, "Is that the end of your story, Rick? Because I have a couple questions about your short time in the military that may add one more chapter to the book of your life."

Rick stood there, amazed that this young man, whom he had met right out of the clear blue, would know anything of his past. "Now it's my turn to be curious. Go ahead—what is it?"

Luke took a deep breath and then started telling his grandfather's story. He had the privilege, for a second time, to have his grandfather's back. "I'm wondering, Rick, would this man who treated you so badly in the military have been Gustav Lipzig?"

In complete shock, Rick just sat there with his mouth hanging open. After a very long and awkward pause, which Luke could absolutely relate to, he mumbled, "Yes. Yes, it was. There aren't many men in this country with a name like that. Why, yes, it was. But how could you have known?"

Oh, Grandpa, thought Luke, *if you hadn't told me that story about a youthful indiscretion . . . and if you hadn't had the courage or the desire to apologize and ask for forgiveness after 50 years, none of this would be happening.*

Luke was awakened from his thoughts by the sound of the back door slamming shut. In a rather loud voice, Markus said, "Hey, Luke, I hope you don't mind but I stopped off at the Doughnut Hut on the way over and bought us some doughnuts."

Luke was coherent now after coming out of his thoughts about Rick Reed. "What kind did you get?" he hollered from the living room.

"Our favorite—old-fashioned glazed cake doughnuts. They're the best!"

Luke took a sip of his coffee and realized that it was full and cold. It was time to warm it up, so he got up and walked into the kitchen where his friend, the delivery man, was placing their sweet treats onto some plates.

You can eat these two doughnuts, can't you? If you can't, I can."

"I appreciate your thoughtfulness, but I can handle two doughnuts, thank you."

"Okay, I was just trying to help a brother out," said Markus as they walked to the coffee-and-conversation room. He had hot coffee in one hand and a plate with two doughnuts in the other.

"Luke, what have you been doing this morning while the girls have been out shopping?"

After slowly chewing and enjoying that first bite of his doughnut and then washing it down with some hot black coffee, he said with a melancholy tone, "I was thinking again about everything Rick told us about his life story and about how Legacy Letters has been such a blessing in my life."

"Yep, that was a pretty jaw-dropping evening. I would say that it was slightly more impactful and life-changing than what happened to John the painter three weeks ago. I can guarantee that nobody would do for my parents what was done for him."

"Yeah, I guess he's also following through with his decision to not work for Middlefield Homes anymore. I'm not even sure if your dad or mom are aware of that situation. It's obvious to all of us out in the field what's happening, because we're seeing less and less of John, or any of his painters, on our jobsites. And now that you mention it, I missed most of the drama your parents created. Tell me the story again so I get it straight, in case I'm asked about it."

Markus stuffed the rest of that first doughnut in his mouth and chased it down with some coffee of his own. It was then that he started telling the story Luke had asked about. "Let me begin, Luke, by saying that it had to be God's timing that one of John's long-time foremen was in the Middlefield office the same day of that terrible meeting. Miguel, a 25-year employee, was the foreman who saw him there that day.

He saw John leaving the building in quite an emotional state. Then he saw me leaving right behind John, also upset and emotional. Miguel followed us out to the parking lot to talk about what had happened, but John was already gone. Miguel caught me before I had a chance to leave, and we talked briefly. I told him everything that had happened and I apologized for how my parents had treated John. It was at that point I told him about Karen. Miguel looked at me and said, 'I knew Karen wasn't feeling well for a while, but he hasn't told any of us that she is fighting cancer. Thanks, Markus, for being so honest with me. And don't worry, I think I have an idea about how we can help John and Karen."

It was at that point in the story that Luke interrupted and said, "Hang on a minute, Markus. I have to get some more coffee."

"Hey, since you're going there, take my mug with you. I need a second cup too," Markus said before taking a bite of his second doughnut.

Luke was back in no time, and after sitting down, he said, "Okay, go ahead. What happened next?"

"Just so you're aware, I heard the Precision Painting part of this story directly from Miguel last week, so it's absolutely reliable. After leaving me in the parking lot, Miguel called their office and explained what had just happened to John at Middlefield Homes. It was at this point that he told John's office manager about Karen and how serious her medical condition was. He also told her his idea about how they might be able to help John and Karen. This happened on a Friday, and the next day, unknown to John, every one of his 58 employees came to his office for a meeting while he was at the hospital with his wife. I don't know what was said at that meeting, because Miguel didn't tell me that part of the story, but what he did tell me was that every one of John's employees agreed to the plan.

"The next Friday following that meeting was payday at Precision Painting. What typically happens on these days is that the foreman picks up the payroll checks from the office and hand-delivers them to the guys working in the field. But on that particular Friday, the checks weren't going to be delivered to the employees at the jobsites. It was going to be a different kind of payday for Precision Painting. Every one of John's employees came to the office at noon and they were given their checks. John didn't understand why all his painters kept showing up at the office and why they wouldn't leave, unless he had done something that made them all want to quit at the same time. Miguel told me that when John saw everyone standing in the main office, holding their payroll checks in their hands and looking toward him, he began to nervously shake. Sweat was dripping off his forehead and he was stumbling to sit down. Between not knowing how he was going to take care of his wife and not knowing why all his employees were at the office, it appeared as if he was going to have a nervous breakdown.

Miguel stepped into John's office and asked him to come out to where everybody was waiting for him. Once they were with everyone in the main office area, he said, "John, there's nothing wrong with all the guys here today. Everything is hopefully going to be very good in about 30 minutes. The reason everyone is here today is because I was in the Middlefield Homes office last Friday and I saw you leaving in quite an emotional state. I followed you out of the office and spoke with Markus Middlefield in the parking lot just after you drove away. It was then that I found out how his parents had treated you. Your wonderful office staff helped me organize an emergency company meeting the next day. Everyone here today met together that following Saturday so that I could explain to them about your wife and about that terrible meeting. I was also able to explain to them a possible solution that would help you pay for Karen's medical bills until you get paid for those model homes in six months."

John was still having a hard time standing, and as he wiped the sweat and tears from his face, he managed to ask in a soft and broken voice, "Everyone here knows about Karen? You know how sick she is?"

"Yes, John," said Miguel, "we all know, and we all want to help, every one of us. Jobsite painters and the office staff too. As you know, today is payday here at Precision Painting, and all of us have been given our payroll checks. What we would like to do is give our checks back to you to hold onto for the next six months. We all want you to use our payroll money to take care of your wife. We can survive for two weeks until our next checks come along, but we're not sure if Karen can. And when Middlefield Homes pays you for those model homes, you can simply use that money to cover these checks. Now that I've explained why we're all here and what we're going to do, it would be my honor to be the first one here to give you my check. I also want to thank you for all you have done for me through the years I have known you, and please tell Karen we'll all be praying for her." Miguel then handed John his check.

One by one, his employees took their turn walking up to John and placing their check into his hand. As the pile of checks continued to grow, many of them reminded him of how he had helped them through some difficulty in the past. Some shook his hand, others gave him a hug, but everyone gave him a check along with words of encouragement. By the time the last envelope had been placed in his hand, John was so overcome with emotion that he could barely get out a choked-up thank you. They all left pretty quickly after that because they had to get back to work and make up for the time they had just taken off.

"What an amazing story," said Luke. "And by the way, have your parents heard about this? I'm guessing with this many people talking about what happened to John at Middlefield Homes, and knowing the story behind what initiated this gift, there will be quite a black mark on the Middlefield reputation, both as a builder and as a newly elected congressman."

"Oh yeah, you have no idea. They know, and they're worried. I mean *really* worried! It was just after lunch on a Friday when those checks were given back, and it didn't take long for the word to start spreading. As soon as John's employees returned to work, they began to tell this story to anyone who wanted to hear it. My dad and mom are almost in panic mode trying to figure out how to reverse public opinion about them. Dad was home this last weekend and I heard him talking to Mr. VanderMor late one evening. I've never heard him apologize so many times in one conversation. I have to say it again, Luke: I really can't stand being around my parents. They lie, they deceive, they manipulate, and they are lovers of money and power. They are everything I don't want to be."

"Well, then, Markus, what are you going to do about it? You can't keep talking like that and put no actions behind your words."

They talked about this for a couple more hours and then switched to talking about how their lives were going to change after marriage. They also talked about their desire to always have a guys' night out, just to do guy stuff. Later that morning, while enjoying some leftover spaghetti pasta salad that Luke's mom had dropped off, Markus said, "Hey, Luke, I just had a great thought."

"Another great thought, eh Markus? And what would that be this time?"

"Do you think Ricardo would spend a few evenings or Saturday afternoons over the next few months explaining what changes we can expect from our girlfriends-turned-wives?"

"You know something, Markus, that is a great idea. We could both use some counsel in that area. Plus, my grandpa told me in one of his letters to spend more time with Ricardo, and having you there with me would make it even more fun."

Through the years, Markus had gained the reputation of being the one who would have an idea every minute. Some worked out great and were a lot of fun, and others, well, not so much. Lately, though, Luke thought Markus's ideas all seemed very inciteful and mature.

"That's a pretty good idea, Markus. I'll ask him when I see him tonight. But we should also be prepared to listen to him talking about boyfriends-turned-husbands." Almost as if on cue, Markus received a text from Cindy.

"Looks like it's time for me to go. That was a text from Cindy. She and Lydia are finished shopping, and I need to meet her and her dad at the apartment complex where we're going to live. Her dad is going to look over the terms of the rental with us so that we don't make any mistakes."

Luke's longtime friend was a boy growing into a man. Luke was amazed at what he was privileged to see taking place in Markus. Markus was maturing right in front of him, which made Luke wonder if others were seeing the same changes that he was seeing. It wouldn't be long before they both had spouses. And who knows how long it might take before there were three—or four or five!—people in their respective families. That will make a guy grow up in a hurry! For now, though, Luke's attention was drawn back to Markus's laments.

"I'm really excited to be part of his family, and he's going to make a great father-in-law." After making that statement, Markus immediately went silent as he thought about his own father. "You know something, Luke, it doesn't matter to me what my dad has done to me through the years. I still wish he was part of my marriage celebration. But he's not, so I'll just have to learn to accept that fact. Markus was again silent for a time before he started talking about everything he had to do before the big day. After we sign the rental agreement, it's off to pre-marriage counseling with Pastor Tim."

Markus was talking so fast that Luke didn't even try to get a word in. He simply sat back in his chair and listened to Markus ramble on. Luke loved seeing his best friend so excited about his life, and about having Cindy to spend it with.

"Luke, it's going to be a busy two weeks coming up, and I'd like to say ahead of time, thanks for all the help and support I know you're going to give me. But right now, I have to jet to go meet Cindy and her dad. I'll call you later." And he was out the door.

———

Later that evening, Luke left his home and drove to his mom and dad's house. It wasn't long before he was pulling into Ricardo's driveway. The front door of the house swung open as Luke's mom and Ricardo came walking toward his grandpa's truck. His mom met him with a very happy and nostalgic smile. "Oh, Luke, how wonderful! You're driving your grandpa's truck—I'm so glad. You should take it out more often. Every time I see you driving it, I almost expect to see Dad pop his head out the window and say hi."

When Rebecca stopped to take a breath, Ricardo slipped in a quick goodbye kiss and said, "We'll be back in three or four hours, sweetie. Love you."

Rebecca replied with an "I love you too" and a warm smile that could only be given by a wife who was in love with her husband. Luke stared at his mom and thought to himself, *Is mom actually looking younger since she got married?* After he had slipped into the truck, he said to Ricardo, "Are you buckled in and ready to go? I've gotta make sure I get you home safe to your beautiful wife."

"Yes sir, I'm in and secure. It's off to Scott's home we go."

As Luke was shifting into reverse, Ricardo called out to Rebecca from his window: "Enjoy your quiet evening, sweetie. I won't be late in getting back."

Rebecca knew Ricardo better than Ricardo knew himself. She knew that when those guys started talking, the time would disappear. He would be home later than he promised. But it gave her comfort to see her two men doing something together.

While driving to Scott Lemieux's home, Luke couldn't help but show his excitement at hearing what Scott thought about his plans. "So, Dad, did you have a chance to speak with Scott this week about the designs I drew up for him?"

"I'm sorry, Luke, but no, I didn't have time to ask about your blueprints. It was a busy week at work, and with all the last-minute information Scott was requesting in order to finalize the incorporation of the adoption agency, the topic of his addition never came up."

Ricardo could see on Luke's face that he was a little nervous and disappointed. Not knowing the type of reaction he would receive before the meeting, Luke put on a good face and said, "That's okay, Dad. We'll be there in five minutes and I'll ask him myself. I'm just a little concerned about how he'll react to my three-generation design concept. On the other hand, I shouldn't worry about anything."

"Why's that, Luke?" asked Ricardo, just a little curious as to why he was no longer worried.

"Correct me if I'm wrong, Dad, but Mr. Lemieux doesn't strike me as the type of man who would waste my time or your time or his if he weren't interested in what I have already sent him."

"No, Luke, he's not. I believe you have read him correctly."

It wasn't long before they arrived and were knocking at the front door of the Lemieux residence. As he waited for someone to come to the door, Luke surveyed the walk up to the entry and the landscaping in the front yard. He noticed how it rolled around the corner of the house and disappeared on its way to the backyard. *In the future*, he thought, *I'll have to pay more attention to the home's landscaping and how it will be affected by these additions.* A moment later, Scott's wife, Mary Ellen, opened the door and greeted them. She was a slender woman in her early 50s with auburn-colored hair and vivid green eyes.

"So this is the gifted young designer Scott has been raving about for the last week. I'm so glad to meet you. And Ricardo, good to see you again."

When Luke heard that Scott considered him to be a gifted designer, he immediately began to relax about the coming meeting.

"It's good to meet you too, Mrs. Lemieux," said Luke as they were directed into the house and then into the room where Scott was waiting for them.

"Ricardo, Luke, thanks so much for coming here to meet us tonight."

While Scott walked over to meet them, an older couple that was also in the room stood up and followed Scott.

"Ricardo, Luke, I'd like to introduce you to the couple who will be occupying this addition you have proposed to build for us. Dad, Mom, or should I say, Don and Kathy, this is the gifted young designer who created the blueprints I showed you earlier this week. And this is his father."

Both of Scott's parents were in their late 70s and had obtained "the crown of white hair" status. Kathy was a trim woman, dressed to perfection; Don was just a little bit on the portly side. Like Luke's grandfather, Don had to use a cane to sturdy himself when he walked. Other than that, both Don and Kathy seemed to be in good health.

"It's nice to meet you, Duke, and you too, Geraldo." said Kathy.

Immediately Don piped in: "Kathy, their names are Luke and Ricardo, not Duke and Geraldo! You took out your hearing aids again, didn't you? Turn your head to the side so I can look in your ear."

"I'll do no such thing!" said Kathy as she stepped away from her loving husband's attempt to see what may or may not have been in her ear. "Donald, you just keep your hands away from my ears. I said their names just fine. You just heard me wrong! And keep your eyes to yourself."

Scott, having played referee for his two aging parents on more than a few occasions, stepped into this dispute and lovingly said, "Mom, Dad's right. I can see you're not wearing your hearing aids." He gently put his arm around her and leaned in close to her ear. "You look just fine with your hearing aids in. They're so small that most people don't even notice them. If they do, they'll think you're wearing ear buds for a fancy smart phone hidden in your purse. Come on, Mom, you'll enjoy the evening much more if you can hear the conversation clearly. Would you put them in for me, Mom?"

"Okay, Scotty, I'll put them in for you. You're so sweet to me, much more than some other man I know," she said as she looked at her husband of almost 60 years.

"What? What did I say?" said Don, defending himself from this unwarranted attack. "I was just trying to help."

Kathy turned and began walking to the powder room in the hall so that she could use the mirror to help her put her hearing aids in. She called for Don to come help her turn the hearing aids on because the arthritis in her hands was acting up again. As Don began to slowly walk to the bathroom, he turned to the three other men and said, "Luke, are you married like the rest of us guys?"

"Not right now, but in three months I will be."

"Then remember this: 'He who turns and walks away, lives to fight another day.'" Don then turned and walked away in the direction of his beloved wife.

Then, with a little smile and some concern, Scott said, "And now you can see why I want my parents living with us."

After Kathy's hearing aids were in, they all settled in to some rather comfortable leather chairs. Mary Ellen rolled a tea cart into the living room with both hot and cold drinks on it. She was a gracious host. Rolling the cart in front of each of them, she allowed everyone to choose the beverage of their liking.

"Luke, the reason I invited my parents here today was for them to tell you a little about themselves, and for you to hear some of their concerns and desires. Also, I wanted them to hear your own story about living in a multi-generational home. I have to tell you, Luke, I have long been a fan of all of us living under one roof, but I never found a builder as passionate and creative about that style of living as I was. Well, until now, that is."

Feeling the positive energy in the room, Luke jumped right into the conversation and asked, "Well, I'll let you all decide: would you like me to start with the personal experiences, or should we talk about the actual design of your future living space?"

"Luke," said Kathy, who had just sat down with her hearing aids in place, "could you first talk about your personal experience of living in a house that had more than two generations in it? I'm excited about the idea, but I am a little concerned about being the second woman in this house. I love Mary Ellen as though she were my own daughter, and I wouldn't make this kind of a move if it meant hurting our relationship."

"Okay, then, let me begin my story back when I was six years old."

One week later, after the wedding rehearsal had finished, Cindy left the church with her sisters, Lydia and Nita, for some last-minute shopping. The purpose of this outing was to do find some things for their apartment. They needed to pick up the kinds of things that are not typically given as wedding gifts, things like toothpaste, hand soap, nose tissues, dish soap, air freshener, and whatever else they might find. It was fun going out with her friends, and it's a safe bet that Markus wouldn't have even thought about these necessary household items until he wanted one and couldn't find it. It only made sense to pick these things up sooner rather than later.

Markus was standing in the common area of the church with Luke, Juan, Alan, and Pastor Tim, when Luke started barking out orders and reminders to everyone there. "Hey guys, don't forget to meet at my place later this afternoon for the bachelor party. We'll leave for the paintball park at three o'clock, shoot paintballs for two hours, and then head back to my house for dinner. Alan, will you remind the guys in the small group about the meeting time?"

"I can do that, Luke."

"Juan, you're going to bring your food truck over to supply dinner, right?"

"It'll be there, Luke, along with my parents and your parents. They're all going to be the cooks tonight. All we have to do is give our opinions on the food they'll be serving us."

"More of Great Grandma's recipes?"

"You got it, Luke. I'm betting that dinner is going to be wonderful. After all, your great grandma hasn't created a bad meal yet. I'm looking forward to whatever is on the menu. Luke, I hope you don't mind, but I gotta run and take care of a few things before the bachelor party. I'll see you all in a couple of hours. And don't forget who's the better shot at paintball!"

After saying goodbye, Luke turned around and walked toward Markus in time to hear Pastor Tim say, "Markus, you're showing wonderful progress in understanding our Christian faith. I've been watching from a distance how you interact with those around you, and I can see that you love to encourage others to keep trusting in the promises of Jesus. You're going to make a great small group leader."

After finishing with Markus, he turned to Luke. "Thanks for inviting me to come play paintball with you guys. I've never really understood it, but for some reason people think that when you become a pastor, you're not allowed to have fun like everyone else. I'd better get going too. I need to look over my sermon notes for tomorrow one more time and then lock everything up before leaving for your house."

Luke looked at Markus and said, "Did I just hear Pastor Tim correctly? Are you going to be a small group leader? How come I didn't know about this?"

"Cool your jets, Luke. Yes, you heard correctly. But the only people who know are Pastor Tim, Alan, their wives, and, of course, Cindy. That's why I've been spending so many evenings at Alan's house. He and Pastor Tim have been preparing me for this next step in my faith, and I'm really excited about it."

"That's wonderful news, Markus," said Luke as he gave Markus a congratulatory hug. "When do you start leading the group?"

"Pretty quickly. Cindy and I will start leading about a month after we get back from our honeymoon."

"Markus, every time I turn around, you amaze me at your relentless devotion to Jesus. You may not believe me, but at times I get a little jealous of your passion to learn more about our God. I feel as though I'm letting him down because I'm not as bold or passionate about my faith as I should be. You know what I'm talking about, don't you?"

"Oh yeah, considering the environment I grew up in, believe me, I know. If I might encourage you, Luke, make your passion grow by spending a little more time with Jesus each day, just like you did when you first met Lydia. Your desire to spend more time with her increased as your knowledge of who she is continued to grow. Do you see it, Luke? The more you got to know her, the more you *wanted* to know. And it didn't take long for you to know it would be forever. It'll be the same with Jesus."

"Markus, I think the heads of your dad and mom would explode if they heard you counseling me like this."

"Yeah, Dad and Mom—what a couple! You *do* know my dad is flying into town tomorrow?"

"Yep, I'm guessing his arrival is connected to the meeting he wants all the subcontractors to attend at 9 a.m. on Monday morning at the River Bluffs development?"

"Yeah, you can bet on it. That whole incident with John the paint-er and his employees has been a media nightmare for my dad. On the other hand, John has been picking up so much work that he's not sure how he's going to get it all done. Apparently, a contractor who has such loyal employees is in high demand. Despite all this negative pub-licity, Mom told me it would go away after Monday morning. A state-ment like that coming from my mom sure makes me wonder what those two have cooked up this time."

Luke, being tired of Markus's parents once again becoming the center of their conversation, tried to change the topic of discussion. "Markus, what do you say we move these next two hours in a more positive direction? My first question is kind of important, or at least you should consider it as being important."

"Okay, Luke, what is it?"

"Do you think your dad will stay for the rest of this week and spend some time with you and Cindy to get to know her better?"

Markus still couldn't believe Luke didn't see his parents for who they were. "Don't you mean, get to know her *at all*?" But then, chang-ing his disposition toward his parents—from complete despair to slight hope—Markus acknowledged that he hoped to get an answer to that question after church the next day. "It's funny, Luke, no matter how many times I get knocked down or become disappointed because of something my dad has done, I still want my parents in my life. So, to that end, I'm really praying that he will stay."

The next day, around one o'clock in the afternoon, Markus walked into his parents' house and found his family, which apparently now included Peter VanderMor, in the dining room finishing their meal. Markus walked in and said, "Hi, everyone. Hi, Dad. It's good to see you back home." There was no response from Matthew, who was read-ing a news release at the table while everyone else ate their food. Look-ing at the large platter of roast beef, vegetables, and dessert the cook had brought to the dining room, he asked, "Is there enough food to feed one more?"

"Markus, don't talk so foolishly," said his mother, who in all her years of living was never quite able to grasp people with a dry sense of humor. Can't you see the empty plate at your place at the table? We knew you would be dragging yourself back home sooner or later. Sit down and eat. You know there's plenty of food for everyone."

"Come on, Mom. I was just trying to keep the mood light. I know there's plenty of food at the Middlefield dinner table."

Walking over to where his plate was, Markus asked Peter, "How's life at the congressman's local office these days? Do you and my dad have the spin all figured out for tomorrow's gathering of subcontractors?"

Peter glanced at Matthew before answering that question, making sure there wasn't anything about the event he should be careful not to reveal. "It's a little challenging, brother, but we're handling it."

For some reason, when Peter called him "brother," Markus snapped. He lost self-control and any filter that might normally keep him from saying certain things.

"Pete, let's get one thing real clear right now: you can call me 'Mark' or 'Markus,' but you can't call me 'brother.' Not until you are legally married to my sister, that is. And Maggy, I still don't understand why you agreed to move in with him."

"Markus, that'll be enough of that talk!" said his mother rather sternly.

Ignoring what his mother had just said, he kept gazing at Peter as he continued talking to Maggy. "Honestly, Maggy, I don't know why you allow him all the benefits of a married man but with none of the legal responsibilities that benefit you."

This time it was Matthew who attempted to stop Markus's verbal assault: "Markus, that's enough! Show some respect at our dinner table!"

But Markus didn't stop.

"I'm also guessing that you both have separate checking and savings accounts, and let's not forget about the credit cards. I'll even wager money that if you told him that if he didn't marry you, he would have to leave, he would leave."

With that last statement, Peter stood up, threw his cloth napkin onto his half-eaten plate of food, and said, "Matthew, I don't have to put up with this abuse, even if he is your son. I'm outta here!"

And with that, Peter was gone.

"My point is proven. I turned the heat up on him just a bit and you saw how he reacted. He didn't say, "C'mon, Maggy, we're leaving. He just left . . . and left you in the process.""

"Tell you what, everyone, for the sake of the family, I'll eat my meal in my room. And in case you all forgot, I'm getting married this coming Saturday. Is anyone coming?" It was dead quiet for what seemed like forever. "I didn't think so."

An hour later, there was a knock on Markus's bedroom door.

"Markus, can I come in?" asked Maggy.

"Sure, come on in, Mags."

When Maggy walked in, she saw Markus packing the rest of his clothes into a duffle bag and one large suitcase. His parents hadn't even noticed that the rest of his things had already been moved to the apartment he would soon be sharing with Cindy.

"First of all, Markus, I'll be attending your wedding. I can't imagine not being there for you on such a special day. And what you said about Peter: I want you to know that I didn't say anything in front of Dad and Mom about him because I'm not up for an argument today."

"That's okay, Mags, I get it. And thanks for coming to my wedding."

"Markus, I can't believe how you stood up to Peter for me the way you did. I've been thinking about that same question the last couple of months."

"What took you so long to start asking? Dad and Mom never should have encouraged you to move in with a guy without a lot of discussion about what could happen to you emotionally or physically. So what's up? What changed?"

"My whole life is about to change, or at least it could. Markus, I haven't even told Mom and Dad the news yet. I'm even having a hard time building up enough courage to tell *you* what's happened to me. I know you love me, Markus, no matter what I've done. I'm just going to say it."

Before Maggy lost her nerve, she said, "I'm pregnant . . . and I've known for almost three months."

"Maggy, wow, that's a life-changer. I can't believe you've been keeping that to yourself all this time! You should have told me sooner. You know I would have helped you with whatever you needed." Markus had stopped packing his bags and he walked over to his sister to give her a hug. Maggy continued speaking, but now more quietly and with a tearful sound to her voice.

"That's why Peter reacted the way he did when you were going on about his lack of legal responsibility to me, and to our baby. He probably thinks I told you about me being pregnant. You were right, Markus. He could have stayed, held my hand, and told Dad and Mom the truth. He could have told them that they were going to be grandparents. But he chose to walk away. His solution to this unplanned pregnancy is to have an abortion, but I'm not sure I feel good about doing that. After all the time we've been together, we've never talked about children. An abortion seems to be his answer to an unplanned child coming into his life and the responsibilities that come with being a father."

Markus stood there for a minute looking at Maggy. She looked as if she were alone on a desert island with nowhere to go and no one to help her. Markus continued to hug his sister and then said something that went straight to her heart: "Maggy, I want you to do something that may help you know what you should do."

Looking up with tear-filled eyes at her older and protective brother, Maggy said, "Sure, Markus. What do you want me to do?"

"I want you to put out of your mind what everyone else might tell you to do about this pregnancy." He waited for a few minutes until a more peaceful look appeared on her face. Then he said, "I want you to tell me from your heart, what is it that *you* want to do with your baby?"

Her voice was more controlled but still quivering. "I want to talk with Luke. Can you make that happen?"

———————————

It was almost 9 a.m. the next morning before Luke was able to find Markus in the crowd of over 200 tradesmen at the big Middlefield model.

"Hey, Markus," said Luke, loud enough so Markus could hear him over the noise. "Have you been here the whole time? I've been looking for you for 30 minutes, but there's so many people here that it's hard to move around."

Markus turned to see Luke making his way toward him and said, "Yep, I've been here the whole time, watching the crowd growing bigger every minute. I'm sure my dad is loving the turnout."

"You got that right, dude. This is a bigger turnout than I ever expected him to get from all his subcontractors—unless they're all here to see what kind of lies he's going to spin today. You don't happen to know what your dad is going to say, do you?"

Markus shook his head, knowing deep inside that he deserved to be totally uninformed. But since his verbal assault on Peter Vander-Mor yesterday afternoon, his dad hadn't spoken a single word to him. And with that silence, Markus could see more clearly now where he stood with his father.

"Nope, I don't have a clue what kind of shiny, spinning ball is going to be presented to everyone today as he turns on the charm. But believe me, with his smile, smooth talk, and ability to spin anything in his favor, we should be treated to quite a show."

Everyone had been directed by the office staff to the stamped concrete patio area in the back where there were several tables of doughnuts, bagels and cream cheese, and coffee. Next to these tables was an elevated deck where Matthew and Elizabeth were standing. Matthew was wearing a blue denim shirt with short sleeves with the Middlefield Homes logo on the left pocket. He also had on blue work jeans and work boots. He was trying to look like one of the guys this morning. Elizabeth, on the other hand, was wearing her typical $500 designer jeans and her $300 white blouse. She didn't care what anyone thought about her. She would dress however she wanted to.

To Markus's surprise, Maggy was also on the deck with them. He wondered to himself, *What's her play here? Why is she standing with Dad and Mom?* Matthew, seeing that the crowd wasn't going to get any larger, raised his hands in the air as a signal, asking everyone to quiet down. When he had everyone's attention, he wasted no time in getting right to the purpose of this gathering.

"Good morning, everybody! Let me start out by saying how wonderful it is to see so many members of the Middlefield Homes family here this morning. I have known many of you for years, and I also see many new faces. It's good to see you all. Today we are here for one very special reason, and that is to recognize one longtime partner—John Peterson, the owner of Precision Painting. John, I know you're out there because I saw you earlier. Would you mind coming up here and joining us?"

Through the years, John had many interactions with Matthew, but none were as difficult as the one he endured one month earlier. As John began to cautiously walk to the steps of the deck, he kept his eyes glued on Matthew, trying to read his facial expression to find out what he might have planned. Matthew saw John hesitate slightly as he made his way to the steps, so he began to clap. He was joined by most of the crowd. When John was a few feet from Matthew, Matthew stopped clapping, indicating to everyone else that they should also stop clapping.

"Just so everyone here knows, John had no idea that he would be asked to come and stand next to me today. Now, the reason we have asked John up here this morning is so that I could make a public apology to him." At hearing this, Markus leaned toward Luke and softly said, "Okay, dude, this is it. Get ready for the big bait and switch."

"I wanted to let all of you know that we made a grave error one month ago during a conference call with John. I was in Washington, D.C., for the call, and several critical talking points that would have changed the outcome of that meeting were not made clear to me. Since then, after looking into John's request further, we are here today to correct that mistake and grant his request. Elizabeth, would you give John the first envelope, please."

Cautiously, John held his hand out toward Elizabeth as she handed him an envelope. Without opening the envelope, John continued watching Matthew guardedly, for Matthew was speaking more to the crowd than to John.

"When you look inside that envelope, John, you'll find two checks. These checks should cover you in full for the work you did on two model homes, the ones you came to us about one month ago."

A large round of applause erupted as Elizabeth handed John the envelope, for everyone had heard the story, including the details about John's wife, the payment request, and the holding of the payroll checks. Matthew continued as he addressed John and the crowd: "And in my hand, I have a personal check written out to you and Karen from Elizabeth and me for $25,000. We know it's not enough to pay all the bills, but you go ahead and spend it however you need to for Karen."

Matthew held that second check out to John as he repeated exactly what his inner spirit was telling him to say, though his inner spirit only said it loud enough for John to hear. "Please take it. It's my way of saying I'm sorry for what I did."

With that, a second and louder round of applause was heard as John accepted the second envelope and shook Matthew's hand at the same time. And at that photo-op moment, Peter VanderMor was positioned at just the right location to take the picture, while another staffer was recording the entire event.

Matthew continued to speak to the crowd as Markus stepped closer to Luke. "He did it again, Luke. He pulled off another win for the Middlefield name."

"What do you mean?"

"It's as plain as day to me. My dad just made a big deal out of giving John a check for work he had already earned. He was just being paid early. That was nothing spectacular. And that personal check they wrote to him—they could have written one for a hundred times that amount and it wouldn't have touched their net worth. Even more insulting is that my dad is using his doughnut theory to buy off the rest of the people here today."

"Doughnut theory? What's the doughnut theory?"

"Whenever my dad wants people to be in a good mood and have positive thoughts about him, he spends a few dollars on doughnuts or pizzas for everyone. He figures it's an inexpensive way to buy off blue-collar loyalty."

Again, Luke couldn't believe what he was hearing about Matthew, and he started thinking about all the pizzas he had personally eaten on Matthew's jobsites, pizzas purchased by Middlefield Homes.

"Look over there," said Markus, pointing toward Peter VanderMor.

"Over where?" asked Luke.

"Over there by the lawn furniture. Peter VanderMor and another man are recording this entire staged event, clapping and cheering and all. This is going to be some inexpensive political advertising for Dad. It only cost him $25,000.

Matthew went on to say several more kind words about John and about everyone attending that morning. He then apologized for having to leave so soon, but "Congress is calling."

Markus stood there, listening to his father and watching the re-action of the people attending that morning. He was also looking at Petey-boy, and the thought that came to mind was that his dad had only one goal in life—to win. And then to win again. His dad had no idea where he had been this past week; he didn't even know that Markus was living in his new apartment where Cindy would soon join him as his wife. His dad didn't ask where Markus was sleeping be-cause, as Matthew had said himself only minutes ago, Congress was calling. And Markus wasn't part of that call.

The Friday night before Markus's wedding, Luke had invited him to spend his last day as a single man at his grandpa's house. Although they had both agreed not to stay up too late, they unintentionally began playing the "remember when" game, reminding each other of long-forgotten stories and events they had experienced together through the years. Seeing that it was getting too late to continue, Markus told Luke that he had to go to bed and get some sleep. He knew that his last night of sleeping alone had come and that it would soon be gone.

Early the next morning, when Luke saw Markus in the kitchen, he asked him, "Markus, are you absolutely ready for today, and all the days to follow?"

Markus didn't miss a beat in answering Luke's question: "I know it's happening today, but I can't believe she chose me to marry. She chose *me*, Luke. Yes, I'm ready! I want to marry her as fast as I can before she changes her mind. Now that I think about it, it's proba-bly good that my parents won't be there. You never know what they might say."

"Do you really mean that about your parents?"

"Kind of, yes, . . . kind of, no. It's strange, Luke. I'm moving into a whole new phase in my life and they apparently don't approve of my marriage or want to be a part of it. Their own personal goals seem to be trumping anything I'm doing."

"What about Maggy and Peter? Will they be attending?"

I'm sure Maggy will be there, but that's it for my family. And speaking of Maggy, there's something we need to talk about."

They continued to get cleaned up, changed, and ready to leave for the church as Markus talked about Maggy. He shared a lot about what was happening in her life, but not everything. Those things were too personal and needed to be shared by Maggy herself.

Luke drove them to church in his grandpa's old Chevy while Markus sang love songs along with the oldies station. He was thinking of Cindy with every mushy lyric he sang, just like his grandpa had done for so many years while thinking of his grandma. When they arrived at the church, Luke dropped off Markus at the front door and left to park the truck.

When Luke came in those same doors a few minutes later, he was told by the wedding coordinator to stay in the foyer with the other groomsmen. Markus, on the other hand, was directed to make his way to the waiting room, which was at the front of the church on the right side of the sanctuary.

Markus walked slowly up the right side of the aisle, astonished at how the church had been transformed into a beautiful garden of flowers, ribbons, and candles. There was even a red carpet unrolled up the length of the center aisle leading to the spot where he would be standing with Cindy in just a few minutes. Markus knew that Cindy and her mother had been making a lot of decisions related to the wedding, but this was amazing. He had no idea they had done all this. It was beautiful!

Markus was now standing in the small waiting room where he was told to remain until he received a nod from Pastor Tim. That was the signal that it was time to come to the front of the sanctuary and wait for his bride to walk down the aisle with her father.

Markus had many emotions running through his spirit as he silently stood there in this small waiting room all alone. He watched the seats fill up through a door that was slightly cracked open. Most of the people who were being seated he recognized, but there were a few he didn't know. Everyone was there to show support for him and for Cindy. He was now nervously waiting for the wedding to start and for his cue to enter the sanctuary. His mind wandered again as he continued to wait. A year ago, he didn't even know this church existed, but today he had friendships here that were stronger than family bonds. And he would need all of them as he and Cindy started their life together.

There it was, in the midst of all the hushed talking, Markus received the nod from Pastor Tim. Once he had made his way to his place, just in front of Pastor Tim, Markus began to wait for his bride to make her appearance. First came the groomsmen and bridesmaids, followed by what seemed like an extremely long minute. And then, there she was, stepping into view at the back of the church holding her father's arm. Markus had never seen such an incredibly beautiful and precious woman in all his life. Then came the wedding march. Everyone stood as Cindy and her father made their way to Markus.

Just before they reached the front of the center aisle, the music became hushed and Pastor Tim asked everyone to sit down. "Cindy, as a gift to you, Markus would like to sing a song just for you. He wants everyone here today to know the place you have in his heart. So if you and your father can stand here for a few more minutes, that would be great."

After being handed a microphone from one of the ushers, Markus held it up to his mouth and said in a lighthearted way, "I've been practicing this song all week at our apartment, and I got no complaints from the neighbors. By the time I've finished this song, I'm hoping you will know, just as our neighbors now know, who holds my heart in her hands."

Markus then glanced at the musicians, and they began to play. As he waited for the musical introduction to finish, Markus looked back at Cindy and silently mouthed the words "I love you." He then began to sing the song he had chosen. Their eyes were locked on each other as the words left his lips and entered her heart; it was as if they were alone in the church with no one around them to break this beautiful spell. Markus began to sing of the love he had for the wife of his youth. He sang of the love he would have for the mother of their children and grandchildren. And, finally, he sang of the love he would have for Cindy when one of them, after a lifetime together, had been called home to be with their Jesus. As Markus finished the long, final note of this love-filled song, with his gaze still on Cindy, he again silently said, "I love you."

Markus finally noticed Cindy's response, which came in the form of tears, but he didn't notice the tears rolling off the cheeks of her mother and her normally stoic father. Every other married couple in the sanctuary had the same reaction. They had all reached for their spouse's hand with tears in their eyes as they listened to the words of this song. Markus then stretched out his hand toward Cindy's, and as she released the grip on her father's arm with one hand, she took Markus's hand with the other.

It wasn't long until the vows had been taken and the new couple was introduced to a room full of witnesses. Markus and Cindy then proceeded to walk back down the aisle toward the entrance of the church. As the groomsmen and bridesmaids were walking down the aisle, Pastor Tim made a quick announcement: "If everyone can remain in their seats, the bride and groom will be right back in. They would like to release each row themselves and personally thank you for being here with them today. A meal will be served behind the church in the wedding garden."

Within a minute, Markus and Cindy were back at the front of the church greeting and releasing everyone with promises to talk more in the wedding garden. Thirty minutes later, Markus turned to the elderly couple in the last row and said to Cindy, "Cindy, if you would please introduce me to the most patient friends you have, I would like to thank them for attending our wedding."

"Markus, I don't know who they are. I thought they were here for you."

They looked at each other for a minute and then looked at the mysterious older couple and said, "We're glad to have you here today celebrating our wedding with us. Could you tell us which one of us is the reason you are here and how you know us?"

"We sure can," said the man. "We're here because of you, Markus. My name is William Summerly, and this is my wife, Kate."

"Summerly . . . Summerly . . ." Markus was starting to remember that name, and his eyes became more hopeful. "That's my mother's maiden name. Would you happen to be related to Elizabeth Summerly in some way?"

"As a matter of fact, we are. It just so happens that your mother is our daughter, and that would make you our grandson."

While Markus was in shock inside the church, Luke was about to get a shock of his own outside in the wedding garden.

"Hi, everyone," said Maggy as she walked up to the table where Luke, Lydia, Ricardo, Rebecca, and several others were eating.

"Lydia, could I borrow Luke for a couple minutes? There's a private matter I would like to speak with him about."

Luke looked at Lydia and received an approving nod.

Excusing himself, Luke stood up and followed Maggy to a more private place in the garden. Lydia did not take her eyes off them for even a moment. After a few minutes of Maggy talking, she began to cry and buried her face into Luke's shoulder. He said something to her, and she shook her head yes. Luke immediately looked over to the table where Lydia was sitting with Rebecca and Ricardo, and he waved for them to join him.

The news that Maggy had shared was quite a life-changer. Luke was relieved when his mom offered to guide Maggy through the next six months of her life. In less than a month, there would be even more changes in Luke's life on account of his marriage to Lydia. As they all sat down and began to eat, Luke thought about how these kinds of unexpected events were made for movies and storybooks, not real life. He couldn't help but wonder what unscripted storyline might come about that would change his life again.

Luke knew it was always three months when it came to waiting for the next Legacy Letter, but because of the current circumstances, it felt like his grandpa's next bit of advice couldn't get here soon enough. All Luke had to do was stay up until midnight, so he put on another pot of jitters and drank his coffee with creamer while he watched reruns of *Hogan's Heroes*. It wasn't long until it was time to change channels and watch another episode of Grandpa Gus's Legacy Letters.

"Hi, buddy. Looks like we've hit a milestone. This is letter number ten. How about we share this achievement by drinking a cup of jitters together? As you can see, I already have mine. Pause this recording if you need to and I'll wait for you to get a cup."

"I'm way ahead of you, Grandpa," said Luke as he took another sip of his wonderful black brew.

While Luke sipped his coffee, Gus continued.

"My goal for you has always been 40 letters, and now I know I'll reach that goal. But it's time for me to share with you how it is that, while fighting cancer, I'll have the strength and time to finish them all. I told you in a previous letter that our God has something special for you to do with the life he has given you. Luke, you have to understand that those were not the words of an overly prideful grandfather concerning his grandson. No, those were the words given to me in a dream from Jesus himself . . . and I'm guessing you're finding that statement a little hard to believe. Luke, think about it for a minute. I'll bet that each one of my previous letters has been so timely in content and counsel that it has always made you wonder how I was able to know what your current counseling needs were. Be assured: it wasn't me. Our God is the God of all time—past, present, and future. Luke, the absolute truth is that I have been receiving dreams from Jesus himself concerning you. I then use my own words and life experiences to explain what the dream is teaching you. Jesus truly has something special for you to do with your life, and it's going to take another seven years to prepare you for that task. So, what do you say we move on to the teaching of this letter? Listen to the following verses several times before finishing this letter. It'll give you more to think about.

> Do not enter the path of the wicked,
>   and do not walk in the way of the evil.
> Avoid it; do not go on it;
>   turn away from it and pass on. (Proverbs 4:14–15)

For those who live according to the flesh set their minds on the things of the flesh, but those who live according to the Spirit set their minds on the things of the Spirit. For to set the mind on the flesh is death, but to set the mind on the Spirit is life and peace. (Romans 8:5–6)

"Now that you've got these verses in your mind, I want you to consider a few things. Luke, the words you just read were given to another man by divine inspiration. They were for him to write down and for us to read. In these words, we are admonished as to how we should live the life that God has given us to live. We are also warned about what to avoid. These words were not intended to be used as a tool by us to condemn or control others. That's not our right. But we can certainly learn by observing others. They give us examples of what to do or what not to do. But we must never pass judgment on them, thinking we are better than they are."

Luke paused the letter and thought about his secret motives for doing the things he was doing. Middlefield Homes, Matthew

Middlefield, and the incorporating of Rosewood Custom Homes immediately came to mind. Luke toggled the pause button again.

"It's your mind, Luke. Where do you have it set? What do you think about in the privacy of your own thoughts when no one else can see your true desires? Luke, continue to be both persistent and consistent in learning more and more about who our Jesus is. And as you do this, you will learn God's desire for your life. By constantly setting your mind on the Spirit, you will be living in the Spirit. It's time to go now, buddy. See you in three months."

"Bye, Grandpa. Thank you for all these letters. I love you."

And a special thank you to all you readers who decided to help make this book a success. The second book, which continues to follow Luke's life and Gus's Legacy Letters, will be available soon. My hope is that everyone reading this first book, as well as the books to follow, would gain not only some reading pleasure but also some encouragement in your own personal life.

Till we meet again,
R.L. Zimmermann

Recipes from Grandma Maria

Enjoy these three recipes from Grandma Maria.

Tamale Recipe

INGREDIENTS

- 4 lbs Maseca
- Tamale leaves (soaked overnight)
- 1 ½ lbs Manteca (lard)
- 6 chicken breasts
- 20 New Mexico dry chiles
- 2 dried chipotle chiles
- 2 dried morita chiles
- 4 dried chile de árbol
- 5 jalapeños
- 7 garlic cloves
- 4 tomatoes
- ½ white onion
- 8 tomatillos
- Cumin
- Salt (to taste)

- 3 tbsp baking powder

INSTRUCTIONS

Step1: Preparation

1. Soak the Tamale Leaves
   - Soak the tamale leaves in water overnight.
2. Cook the Chicken
   - Boil the chicken breasts with 3 garlic cloves, salt, half an onion, and 1 gallon of water.
   - Once the chicken is fully cooked, save the broth and shred the chicken.

Step 2: Chili for the Masa

1. Boil all the chiles (20 New Mexico chiles, 2 chipotle, 2 morita, and 4 chile de árbol) with the tomatoes until the chiles are soft.
2. Blend 8 of the New Mexico chiles with a pinch of cumin and 2 garlic cloves.
3. Strain the mixture and set it aside. This will be used for the masa.

Step 3: Red Salsa

1. Blend the remaining chiles with the tomatoes, a pinch of cumin, and 1 garlic clove.
2. Strain the mixture and cook it in a pan with some oil for about 5 minutes.
3. Add 2–3 cups of water and salt to taste.
4. Let it boil, then add half of the shredded chicken.

Step 4: Green Salsa

1. Boil the jalapeños for 6 minutes, then add the tomatillos and cook until soft (but not too soft).
2. Blend the jalapeños and tomatillos with 1 garlic clove and a pinch of cumin.
3. Cook the mixture in a pan with some oil and add salt to taste.

4. Add the remaining half of the shredded chicken.

Step 5: Masa for Tamales

1. Soften the manteca in the microwave until it's pliable but not liquid.
2. In a large container, mix the Maseca with the strained chili mixture (from the 8 New Mexico chiles). Work the masa and chili with your hands until combined.
3. Add the softened manteca, 3 tablespoons of baking powder, and the chicken broth.
   - Add the broth gradually until the masa is greasy and manageable.
4. Add salt to taste.

Step 6: Assembling the Tamales

1. Take a soaked tamale leaf and spread 2 tablespoons of masa on it.
2. Add your favorite salsa (red or green) with chicken.
3. Wrap the tamale securely. Repeat until all the masa and fillings are used.

Step 7: Cooking the Tamales

1. Arrange the wrapped tamales in a bain-marie (double boiler) or steamer.
2. Cook for 3 to 3 ½ hours or until the masa is fully cooked.

Chiles Rellenos Recipe

INGREDIENTS

1. 6 poblano chiles
2. 8 Roma tomatoes
3. ½ onion (sliced)
4. 1 garlic clove
5. Mozzarella cheese (for filling)

6. All-purpose flour
7. 6 eggs
8. Salt (to taste)
9. Oil (for frying)
10. Knorr Suiza (or chicken bouillon powder, as a salt substitute)

INSTRUCTIONS

Step 1: Prepare the Chiles

1. Roast the poblano chiles until the skin is charred and blistered.
2. Place the roasted chiles in a plastic bag and let them steam to soften (about 10–15 minutes).
3. Peel the skin off the chiles, then carefully clean out the seeds and veins from the inside.
4. Stuff each chile with mozzarella cheese.

Jell-O Peach in Tres Leches Cream

INGREDIENTS

1. 2 packages peach Jell-O (7 grams each)
2. 4 gelatin packets (7 grams each, unflavored)
3. 1 (12 oz) can evaporated milk
4. 1 (14 oz) can condensed milk
5. 1 cup heavy whipping cream
6. 8 oz cream cheese
7. ½ cup water
8. 1 (29 oz) can of peaches
9. Gelatin mold
10. Spray oil

INSTRUCTIONS

Step 1: Prepare the Peach Jell-O

1. Boil 8 cups of water and prepare the 2 packages of peach Jell-O according to the instructions on the package.
2. Pour the Jell-O into a large container and let it set overnight in the refrigerator.
3. Once the Jell-O is fully set, cut it into small square pieces and return it to the fridge.

Step 2: Prepare the Peaches

1. Drain the peaches from the can and cut them into small pieces.
2. Set aside for layering later.

Step 3: Prepare the Mold

1. Lightly spray the gelatin mold with oil to prevent sticking.

Step 4: Prepare the Tres Leches Cream

1. In a small bowl, mix the 4 packets of unflavored gelatin with ½ cup of water. Stir well and let it sit for a few minutes to bloom.
2. Blend the evaporated milk, condensed milk, heavy whipping cream, and cream cheese in a blender until smooth.
3. Microwave the bloomed gelatin for 45 seconds until fully dissolved.
4. Quickly pour the dissolved gelatin into the blender with the milk mixture and blend for 4–5 seconds to combine.
   - NOTE: Work quickly, as the mixture will start to thicken and curdle if left for too long.

Step 5: Assemble the Jell-O Mold

1. In the prepared mold, add a layer of the peach Jell-O squares and some diced peaches.
2. Pour a layer of the tres leches cream over the Jell-O and peaches.

3. Repeat the process, adding more layers of Jell-O, peaches, and cream until the mold is full.
4. Tap the mold gently on the counter to remove air bubbles.

Step 6: Chill and Set

1. Cover the mold and refrigerate for at least 2 hours, or until fully set.

SERVING

1. Once set, carefully unmold the dessert onto a serving plate.
2. Slice and serve chilled.